A.J. SCUDIERE

NightShade

FORENSIC FBI FILES ✦ BOOK 9

THE SHADOW FILES

SABOTAGE

NightShade Forensic FBI Files: Salvage

Copyright © 2020 by AJ Scudiere

FIRST EDITION

1

To the outside world, it appeared that Christina Pines sat at a bar sipping scotch neat and interacting with no one.

In reality, Christina was drinking a Diet Coke that the bartender had poured into a whiskey tumbler for her, even though she had said the words, "Scotch, please." She swirled the dark liquid in the glass occasionally as though it actually were fine, high-proof liquor.

The other thing no one else noticed was that the bartender spoke to her. Every time he went past, he'd let her know whatever he gleaned from the other patrons in the bar.

She'd sent him on little missions. The bartender would ask someone what they'd like to drink and, in the same breath, ask them if they'd seen a man. He'd flash them the picture Christina had handed to him: Dr. Murray Marks. The patrons would check their memories for the tall, lanky man whose dark hair was shot through with strands of silver. And the patrons would say yes or no.

Mostly, they said no.

In fact, all of them, but one. And that was all Christina needed.

Next, she'd parked herself next to the man who said he'd seen Dr. Murray Marks about three days ago. Swirling her Diet Coke in her glass one more time, she leaned in close.

The low buzz permeated her brain as she pushed him a little harder than usual, though she hardly noticed the sensation anymore.

Casually, as though they'd been in conversation for some time, the man said, "Yeah, I saw him. He stopped for gas at the convenience store while I was there."

"What was he driving?" Her tone suggested she was asking about the weather.

"Blue Volvo."

Not his car, Christina thought—at least, not the one they'd known about. She nodded. "What else should I know?"

The man shrugged as though his remaining information was trivial. She didn't care how he felt about it, though—only that he gave it to her. "Anything is helpful."

"He bought granola bars and bottled water, paid for gas, then headed north."

"Which gas station was this?" She pulled a napkin out of the little holder and a pen out of her pocket and slid them over to the man. He answered not with words now, but with a fair enough sketch that she could find the place.

Christina polished off the last of her Diet Coke and mouthed *Thank you,* even though he wouldn't remember it later. None of them would remember any of it. Even if they were questioned by the police, it would all be fuzz. It wasn't worth the effort on her part to replace the lost memory with something else.

The only part of it that had been real was the shot of pink color that ran through her hair.

2

Donovan had ridden in the back of the town car all the way down the rural road and up to his house. He should have been relaxing. The case was over. He had a driver from the airport to his front door. He didn't even have to pay attention to the roads.

But there was nothing to relax about.

Eleri had told him not to contact her. She'd been clear that she needed time and space. But how much time? And how much space? She hadn't given him numbers, and it had already been far too long in his book. But what did he know?

All of this was out of his wheelhouse. If he couldn't sniff something and determine a disease, then it wasn't anything he was comfortable with.

He ignored the twisting in the base of his gut, the one that said Eleri was his first real friend. Who else should he talk to about the fact that his friend needed time and space but the friend who wasn't answering her phone? He'd already broken down and called her.

Just to check, he told himself.

He'd rung through to her voicemail—not a surprise—and left a brief message.

"Ell, I don't have your skills, so I have no idea how you're doing. Please, message me back… something. Any form of contact is acceptable. Let me know you're okay…. Thanks."

It had been only a few short, choppy sentences that he hadn't constructed well, despite the fact that he'd agonized over what to leave on the message for quite some time. He'd shoved the phone back in his pocket, not expecting anything. After all, he hadn't gotten any reply the last three times he'd reached out. Now he felt he was bothering her when she'd specifically asked him not to.

But what if she *wasn't* okay?

The car turned the corner and Donovan could see his house in the distance. The long road was partially shaded by trees. He usually felt so good when he reached this street, and though he was forcing his shoulders down and his muscles to unclench, simply being here felt better.

This was home.

This was a house he owned—the only permanent residence he'd ever had. He'd fixed this place to his own needs with no concern for any landlord. He'd worked on it, knowing he'd stay and enjoy it, not get ripped out in the middle of the night or have to find something new at the end of the semester.

The wide, covered front porch and tan paint job made it look like every other house on the street. Even though they were well-spaced —a selling point for him—he still tried to go unnoticed. He'd come a long way, but not that far. The house was the only thing about him that looked and felt like it belonged.

In the backyard, he'd built the high fence himself. The lot was large enough and private enough that he could use the space in any form he chose, and it opened into a national park, giving him acres and miles and hectares of woods. He could run and stretch his legs, his paws pounding the ground, the smells of nature luring him farther. Even now, he was thinking he might go right in the front door and right out the back.

The car pulled up the long drive, slowly winding its way across the gravel and coming to a stop.

Donovan once again looked at his little house. No cursory glance this time, but a thorough evaluation.

Everything was in place.

Breathing easier, he slowly opened the car door. The driver had already hopped out and gone around to the back to pull out Dono-van's bags. Whether he was trying to be ahead of his fare in a polite and courteous way, or if he was simply trying to get rid of the rider that had taken him so far out into the country, Donovan couldn't tell.

For the effort, he offered a generous tip.

Grabbing his largest bag, he headed up the walk, leaving the other luggage on the drive. No one was around for miles—at least not close enough to steal his suitcase. He would fetch the other pieces once the car was gone—and once he'd done a walkthrough. The large suitcase bumped along behind him, the gravel of the drive uneven. The walk to the front door was only a little smoother, though it was definitely more charming with its matching tan pavers. But it was not an easier place to drag the suitcase.

He knew better than to try, and with a grind of his teeth, he slid the long handle down inside the case and reached for the short leather one, hauling the luggage up by his side.

As he lifted it the last few feet, he reached the top step—and stopped dead.

Despite the breeze, a scent lingered in the air around his front porch. With a sharp turn of his head, Donovan looked to see that the car he'd arrived in had already backed out and was heading down the street, far enough away. Donovan whipped his head from side to side. No neighbors were in view, so he took a chance.

Tipping his head back slightly, he let his nose expand. He was listening, too, but some of what he might have heard was obscured by the slight popping of the bones in his face as they shifted. He felt his lower jaw ache as it dropped and moved forward.

He didn't need any more transformation to open his nasal passages. Sure enough, his initial assessment had been right. He felt the scent bloom in his head.

Bodhi had been here.

In fact, his brother had been here only moments before. Dropping the suitcase with a heavy thud, Donovan whirled around. Bodhi could not have gotten far.

3

C hristina stared at the burner phone in her hand.

To use it or not to use it?

Across the street, she saw an old-fashioned payphone. *I wonder if that still works ...*

The problem was, if someone found the call, they could trace it back to this location.

But would it trace to *her?* And who would even think to look for it?

She could easily cover up the things she knew to cover, but could she cover an idea?

Interesting.

She hadn't grown her skills much in the past decade. She hadn't really needed to; she'd been quite capable before she left high school. She could make people see or believe all kinds of things. Christina had gotten herself the most-sought-after prom date that way. She'd aced all her college interviews. In fact, to this day, she wasn't quite certain that she would have made it into the FBI without her special skills. Once she'd been accepted, she'd made a point to actually earn high marks during her training at Quantico. It was one of the few things she was proud of.

Now, she needed information. It seemed the burner phone was the way to go.

The place didn't look like it had too much going for it. The aging payphone in front was a mark against it. Christina stepped toward the small parking area at the side of the building, where no windows would allow anyone to look out and see her. She tapped the numbers she knew by heart and waited as the phone rang several times.

"Westerfield."

"Pines," she replied.

"Oh, wonderful. We've been waiting to hear from you—" But the last word cut off as she'd intended it to.

She couldn't let him think to hit a button or start tracing the call. She couldn't let him move his fingers and type out messages to himself across his screen... something that he could read later, after she'd wiped her boss's memory.

Moving fast, she took control of the situation.

"If I told you that Marks had followed de Gottardi's family around the country and now it looks like he's beelining for their old compound, what would you say?"

"I'd say I'll send you four more agents."

"No," Christina blurted. "I don't want more agents. I want your Intel."

There was a brief pause, which Christina found odd, but she waited it out. She was still pushing on him, even from across the country. He wasn't going to do anything to help himself remember this call. He spoke again.

"Members of the de Gottardi/Little crew have been moving back to the compound in small numbers. Flyover satellite data is showing a little bit of activity, though not as much as we suspect would match the number of people that we believe are now there."

There's a lot of conjecture in that statement, Christina thought. Then she remembered what she'd seen the last time she was at the compound. "Do we believe they're using the tunnels?"

"It's entirely possible. In fact, it's highly plausible," Westerfield commented, sounding like his usual self. She could hear his fingers drumming on the tabletop. In a moment, that would end as the quarter began walking across the backs of his knuckles. To this day, none of them had figured out if the trick was a physical skill or a mental one.

For a moment, the conversation lagged. Westerfield apparently didn't have anything else to add, since he hadn't been really mentally present for the conversation in the first place. Christina had not expected to find that anything was happening at the de Gottar-di/Little compound. In fact, she'd believed that Marks was headed back there for his own purposes. But now, maybe not.

Another thought crossed her mind.

"Did anyone ever find Shray Menon's body?" She'd asked this particular question several times as recently as a month ago. So far, she'd gotten no satisfactory answers. Today wasn't going to be any better.

"No. There's no intel on either of the men," Westerfield replied quickly, letting her know that he'd known this for a while.

"Thank you." She said it to end the conversation and because she still couldn't quite shake the manners her conservative mother had drilled into her. Before she could hang up, Westerfield spoke up.

"What about extra agents?"

Christina found it odd that he was pushing his way into the conversation without her directly asking him a question. She thought for a moment, but not about the agents. "No."

"I'll send you one anyway. Where are you?"

Fuck! The conversation was getting away from her. *That was not okay.*

"No," she said again. This time, she pushed the extent of her power behind it, effectively shutting Westerfield up.

If he sent her an agent, there would be a record of it. If she had a partner, that would mean she had someone she had to control almost twenty-four/seven to make sure he or she didn't report back to West-erfield. That was unacceptable. There was also the issue that she liked the people she worked with—maybe the first friends she'd had that she hadn't "made," and she wasn't willing to mindfuck them just for the sake of her own goals.

Everything in her plan worked better if she was on her own. A partner would be paid, and therefore tracked, and the FBI could therefore track her as well. There were so many reasons she couldn't do this. She said it again with as much force as possible. "No."

"All right. If you insist." This time Westerfield's tone was docile in a way he would never be if he were the one controlling the conversation.

"Thank you," she said again, that damn etiquette rearing its stupid head. The people she pushed were never going to remember the conversation later. Then again, maybe it was like people who suffered short-term memory loss—they didn't remember specifics, but they had a "gut feeling" about whether they should or shouldn't do something.

Christina pushed the button to hang up the phone and then dropped it onto the blacktop and ground her heel into it. She stomped it again, crushing it into little black shards. Looking around first, she bent over and scooped up as many of the fragments as she could. She would dole them out to various trash cans along the way.

Westerfield wouldn't remember their conversation. In fact, none of this would ever come up, unless someone was combing his call records. Because she called his personal cell, that would also make it more difficult to track.

Five miles down the road, she dropped the first handful of plastic into a trashcan near a roadside gas station. It did occur to her that Westerfield might very well be scouring his personal calls. The more she thought about it, the more she was confident that he would do it. She was actively missing—she knew that much—and he knew what she could do. All the other agents did too, thanks to some very well-timed tricks she'd shown them.

Son of a bitch. She'd believed she'd done everything she needed to cover the conversation. But because he knew what she could do, her boss would likely be looking for traces of contact from her. He would certainly check his phone periodically to see if he'd missed a call. Or better yet, to see if he had taken a call he didn't remember.

She turned the car engine off and sat for a moment at the side of the second gas station. Taking a deep breath, she pushed, doing the best she could to erase Westfield's desire to find his rogue agent.

4

"I don't even know how this happens!"

Noah Kimball flinched as his SAC slapped the report down onto the desk in front of him. Being called in for a review was shitty, even when you were an FBI agent. Maybe especially then.

"What you're saying," his boss continued, as though Noah hadn't replied, "is that this suspect—who had been running from officers for hours—suddenly stopped, got out of his car, and decided to surrender. He went face down on the pavement of his own accord, and laced his fingers behind his head?"

Noah sighed.

Yes, that's exactly what happened. But he didn't say it out loud. It was in the report. In fact, there had been five Miami PD officers and two other agents there who had seen it all happen exactly that way. Noah was confident their reports matched his, even if the others had no idea why it had happened.

"What did you say to him?"

His SAC demanded an answer, as though he hadn't asked this same question five times before, as though his tone conveyed some fresh irritation.

Noah had been here before. He had a knack for making his suspects comply. Sometimes they called it "good luck" or "karma." Mostly they called him "The Perp Whisperer."

"I asked him to get out of the car, get on his knees, place the keys on the ground beside him, and lace his fingers behind his head," he repeated wearily. Though others had said the same thing, it was when Noah's voice had broadcast over the bullhorn that the suspect had suddenly complied.

Every once in a while, someone up the chain of command demanded an extra explanation. Noah always told the story exactly as it happened, and he was always let off the hook. After all, he brought people in who needed to be brought in. So right now, he worked at remaining calm as he added details. "I stood behind my car door." He didn't add *as per protocol*. "My fellow agents and the Miami/Dade officers had their sidearms drawn and aimed."

The FBI and the SBI—Florida's state investigation system—had been called in when the suspect began crossing county lines. Hence the chase and the drawn weapons. Again, *per protocol*. Noah kept going in his best calm, steady voice. "He got out of the car when I asked him to, and then proceeded to set down the keys and lay face down on the ground—"

"—yeah, yeah, with his fingers behind his head. He performed each task as instructed." The SAC walked through the last steps in an exasperated tone.

Jesus, Noah thought, *what else was there to say?*

"You saw the video," the SAC snarled.

Something about those words broke Noah's calm demeanor. He'd been questioned before, but never quite like this. He felt stunned and confused.

His boss had a point. No one really knew what *had* happened—except Noah—but there was very clear video of him saying exactly those words, and the suspect who had led them on a long-winded car chase had finally been forced to pulled over. When Noah had issued the commands, the suspect had simply obeyed.

Taking a deep breath, Noah tried to put himself back together. It made sense to question him about his methods when he'd been the only one on the scene, or his partner had been looking away or chasing another suspect at that exact moment. That was reasonable. But that hadn't happened here.

Other law enforcement officers had been on the scene. Multiple body cameras supported everything in the report. Noah suppressed the urge to physically throw his hands in the air. "Look, Agent Larkin, if I could tell you why he suddenly decided to comply, I wouldn't be in this job and neither would you. We wouldn't have suspects or warrants. They'd all be in custody. We might not even have criminals!"

Larkin picked up the report, as though he were going to do something with it. But what he did was slap it back onto the surface of the desk. "I can't even suspend you."

Noah felt his head snap back. His SAC sounded as though his continued employment presented a problem.

"Why in hell would you suspend me?" Noah demanded, more confused than ever. He shouldn't have sworn—even the baby swear he'd let slip in—but he hated feeling like he was in trouble.

Their perp was suspected of robbing multiple convenience stores and committing a murder while fleeing. He'd woven in and out of traffic, endangering lives all over the Miami area. They'd had to cut off traffic to both freeways and side roads, to make his flight safe—not for him, but for the others who might be on the road and become casualties of a chase. The general public didn't understand exactly how expensive that was, but the officers all did.

Noah had likely saved them miles and miles of chase, and he'd definitely saved them from eventually giving up and deciding that the pursuit was far too dangerous to civilian lives and letting this asshole get away.

"I just don't get it," Larkin muttered, now staring him dead in the eyes. "He's hightailing it hell for leather out of the city with five cop cars and two unmarked vehicles on his tail. And then he just hops out and surrenders because you asked him to?"

"We got him pretty well boxed in, sir. Maybe it was just time," Noah offered, though he knew that wasn't the case. He knew he had had everything to do with their suspect's suddenly altered decision. It was because Noah had finally gotten close enough to see the man at the wheel, so he could use his skills. But he couldn't say that to his boss.

Larkin sighed heavily at him as though he didn't know what to do with Noah. Right now, Noah figured that was a pretty accurate assessment. His boss suddenly announced, "I'm putting you on administrative leave."

"*What?* Are you serious?" Noah almost came out of the chair he'd been fidgeting in.

The case had been textbook. He'd made sure of it. "I asked him to get out of his car and he did. We caught him. No one was harmed. Are you mad that we didn't catch him earlier?"

Noah hadn't even been involved in the car chase in the early stages. Like a well-oiled machine, the local officers had followed until they lost jurisdiction. Other districts had come in. One car would attempt to blockade the runaway car and leave other officers to drop in and out as necessary. Noah had only been part of the pursuit for the final leg—the part that had gone well.

Maybe he needed to let some of these guys slip through the cracks. Get a less-than-stellar record.

Maybe he wasn't even going to get the chance to do that.

"Here's the thing," Larkin said as he lifted a stack of folders from the chair beside him.

Noah's brain skipped out of the conversation. That was the real travesty—that somehow so much of their shit was still on paper. Even though Noah had filed most of the reports electronically, someone had had to kill some trees, print them up, and put them in a good Manila file folder for backup. And now Larkin was using it for visual weight.

"*This* is the problem. It's not the first time this has happened."

"Right?" Noah said, drawing the word out with a question mark at the end. "It's *not* the first time I've arrested someone or told someone to get on the ground on their knees. It's not the first time I've made a clean arrest." He left it hanging like a question.

"No one else has a stack of files like this, Kimball."

He could only shrug in response. It was absolutely not the appropriate response to his boss, but he was holding back his exasperation as well as he could.

"When the numbers are unusually high, they get reviewed. I haven't seen anything in here myself, but I'd be remiss if I didn't have you fully investigated."

"Are you fucking serious?" *I shouldn't have said the F word.*

"I have to do it," Larkin told him, but his voice didn't hold the regret that Noah thought it should. "You're officially on leave."

It took half an hour before Noah made it back to his own apartment. He was still shaking from the interview.

He'd done what he thought was good work. And now he'd gotten put on leave for doing his job *too well.*

What Larkin couldn't know was that Noah *did* actually have

something working in his favor. He couldn't have explained exactly what it was. He just knew it had always been there. But the investigation wouldn't find that. *Or if it did, no one would believe it.*

Noah had handed in his badge and gun, and wandered home. He'd bought a burger and fries as if the grease would fill the hole in his chest or unknot his gut. After he fell onto his couch, Mercury and Jupiter both jumped into his lap and began purring.

"Yeah," he told them. "Really shitty day."

He stayed there for nearly an hour, just feeling *rattled*. Then he tipped his head back and took his first good, deep breath. Standing up, he went to his desk, opened the side drawer, and pulled out the card.

It read, *FBI Special Agent in Charge Derek Westerfield.*

5

Christina Pines sat at another bar in another town, looking for all the world, like she was sipping at a scotch. She swirled the dark liquid in her glass and appeared to be talking to no one.

She was getting closer.

She liked bar patrons. It was easier to erase herself from their minds when they were already liquor-hazed. The day drinkers were a wealth of information. And, for the first time, someone had seen Dr. Marks less than twenty-four hours earlier.

Good, she thought.

She'd considered calling GJ Jansen and asking what she knew about her grandfather, but it seemed wrong to press GJ for information that could easily end with her beloved grandfather getting killed.

Christina had met the youngest agent often enough to know that it wouldn't be something she'd want to be part of, but she'd feel obligated to tell what she knew. Hunting her grandfather had been hard enough the first time around. Christina considered squeezing information out of GJ and then erasing the conversation from the other agent's mind, but she wasn't ready to go that far yet.

This time, Christina saw no other end for Dr. Murray Marks than death. They'd captured him once. Six months ago, he'd disappeared from prison.

Three weeks ago, Christina had disappeared, too.

Being solo was her default setting these days. Christina wasn't one much for partners in the first place, and having finally found one she trusted, it had been beyond difficult to lose Dana Brantley in the line of duty just a year ago. The two little shits that had been responsible for Dana's death had met their own end not much later. But the fact that they were both gone didn't change Christina's need for revenge.

She knew exactly what she was doing.

Heading out the back door, she aimed for the shadows at the side of the building where she'd left her car. She'd picked this spot in part for the location—it backed up to the woods and lacked security cameras.

She was getting close.

Though she'd always believed Marks was headed to the de Gottardi/Little compound, she was now certain of it. She pulled open the door to her car and was about to climb in when a movement just off to her left caught her attention.

A noise made her jump back. Using the car door as a shield between her and the stand of shifty trees, she looked around and saw nothing. *It was probably a raccoon.* But just as she had that thought, two spots of blue light caught her attention, and she recognize them for what they were: eyes.

Not a raccoon.

Moving slowly toward her with a sway that suggested a four-footed gait, the eyes slowly became clearer, as did the outline of the creature that owned them.

Oh my god, Christina thought in awe. *It's a wolf.*

6

E leri hit the button for her voicemail and listened dispassionately as Donovan's voice came through clearly.

Where all his previous messages had been calm—or at least she could hear he was attempting some serenity—this time there was no pretense.

"Eleri—" he stuttered it out. "El."

She didn't know why he needed to say her name at all—it was a voice message that was clearly only for her—let alone twice.

"I'm at my house. I just arrived... and it looks empty. But I can smell him. Bodhi was here less than five minutes ago."

That might have been the only thing he could say that would have made her sit up straight. The only thing that would have shaken her out of the funk she had been in for almost a full week.

Bodhi Banerjee? she wanted ask, but voicemail wouldn't answer her.

Donovan's brother.

Bodhi's response to meeting his older brother had been less than ideal. More than once, Bodhi had come close to killing Donovan, though neither Eleri nor Donovan had ever figured out if those were actual attempts on Donovan's life or just hardcore threats.

Donovan had been blindsided, of course. He'd had no clue he had a brother at all, while Bodhi Banerjee knew all about Donovan and had been spending his time looking for him. Bodhi Banerjee had been born to Anisha Banerjee *Heath*, whom Donovan believed died when he was seven.

Poor Donovan, Eleri thought for a moment, as she reached out to toy with the screen of the phone. Should she call him back? What could she even do in this scenario? How would she be useful?

She was hundreds of miles away.

But not that many hundred, she thought.

If she got in her car and started driving, she could be there relatively soon. That might be a good transition. Being alone in the car would still be *alone*, which was the whole reason she'd hid out at Bell Point Farm in the first place.

The only outgoing contact she'd had was to text her mother several times. A simple, *I'm fine.* Then *Mom, I need some time alone,* followed by, *Please leave me alone. I'm actually fine.*

The only part that had been true was the "alone" part. She wasn't fine, and she knew it. So how would she be any help to Donovan? Even if she sat in the car for a good number of hours, and hopefully made a transition from self isolation to seeing people, could she handle it if the "people" was Donovan?

What if she screwed up?

Because her issue was that, in the middle of all the shit that had gone down in the Caribbean, she'd killed a man.

It was one thing when she pulled her gun and squeezed the trigger. If you squeezed the trigger, you intended to kill. That was it. FBI agents were trained to aim for center mass and take out the target permanently. So if she pulled her gun, her decision was already made.

But what she'd done in the Caribbean had merely been a fight. She felt it in her blood—the heat, the anger, the desire to kill. And then she had killed him. Not with a rational decision or a gun. Not with reason and planning, but with skills she hadn't even quite realized she had.

Her anger had controlled her… rather than the other way around.

What if she showed up at Donovan's doorstep and his brother was still there? What if they fought and she got mad and killed him, too? If Bodhi attacked Donovan, would she simply end him to protect her friend?

She didn't know. She also didn't know if Donovan would ever forgive her.

It wasn't that he and Bodhi were great friends, not anything of the sort. But what if she killed his brother before he got a chance to find out what he needed to know about their mother?

Donovan now knew his mother had lived at least a decade beyond the date she'd supposedly "died." He needed answers. Bodhi was the key.

Eleri stayed put on the plush couch. She gazed out the wide windows and played the nearly frantic voice message once again. But again, she didn't respond.

7

C hristina stared at the wolf.
The wolf stared back.

She didn't know these eyes personally, not that she remembered, but she knew the intelligence behind them. This wasn't any regular woodland creature. Still, she knew that no matter what she said, it wouldn't speak English words back to her, though it definitely knew them.

For a moment, they simply sized each other up.

"What are you doing here?" she finally asked in plain English. This bar was too far from the de Gottardi/Little compound for a casual visit. Then again, she knew wolves were everywhere. Was this one a lone wolf, or maybe a member of a local family?

It wasn't Wade. It wasn't Will Little—he had much whiter fur. She could list off a few others that she knew this wolf wasn't. Its fur was dark, almost black, and she couldn't rattle any recognition from her brain.

"Are you local?" she continued, thinking a series of yes/no questions might serve her better.

Sure enough, the wolf wagged its head side to side.

"Are you with the—" She almost said "de Gottardi/Little families, north of here" but she didn't want to list names. Not all wolves were good wolves. That was a lesson they'd all learned the hard way. "Are you with a family compound?"

This time, the creature nodded yes.

She knew the de Gottardi/Little compound wasn't the only family compound around. Christina was not going to start listing known locations of wolf families and give away whatever intel she had—not to a wolf she didn't recognize. "Are you in trouble?"

No *yes* answer, but not a *no* either. The head just tilted slightly to the right as the eyes looked at her questionably.

"Do you need help?"

The tilt changed to the other side. Not the answer she was looking for.

This time, she gave the animal a little *push*. The wolf tipped his head back to the right. She pushed again.

The response once more was only a blink. Then the head turned slightly and he gave her the side eye, as if to ask, *What do you even think you're doing to me?*

It occurred to her then that she didn't know if she could push wolves or not. Did they not respond?

No, that wasn't true. She'd pushed Donovan more than once. Wade, too. As demonstration only, she told herself, because just thinking that she'd used her skills on her friends was more than her psyche could handle. But both men had seen the information she'd fed into their brains.

Suddenly she was at a loss. She'd never met a person she couldn't push. And honestly, she could push most animals relatively easily. If she wanted a dog to bring her a newspaper, she usually said the words out loud so she could later just claim she had a "way with animals."

Pressing her lips together, and knowing it looked stupid to appear as if she were grunting as she mentally pushed this wolf, she tried one more time.

But no answer came.

"Well then, I'm leaving. Have a really nice day." She said the words haltingly, because clearly this was not how she'd hoped this encounter would go. Not that she'd intended to run into a wolf behind the bar where she was chasing a wolf killer.

She was climbing back into the car as those thoughts congealed, and she asked the creature one more question. "Do you know who Dr. Murray Marks is?"

She was standing behind the car door with her arms folded across the top edge, trying to appear casual.

This time, the wolf nodded.

Suddenly, the one-sided conversation got interesting. "Do you know where he is right now?"

No, the wolf replied, softly shaking its head from side to side.

Defeated, Christina once again decided to drive off, but she realized she had too good a source to not use it.

"Do you know where he went?" was answered with a soft shake of the head. "Was he here?" was answered with a nod.

"One day ago? Two days ago?"

At *two* she got a nod. In moments, she'd ascertained that he'd gone North, confirming the information she'd gotten inside the bar.

"Is there anything else I should be asking you?"

This was a great question, one she'd learned in interrogation class, because sometimes it made people spill their guts. The wolf shook his head side to side, and Christina decided that she finally had to be done.

Thanking the creature for its time, she closed the door and pulled onto the street. She sped north toward the de Gottardi/Little compound and hoped that she got there in time.

Whatever hell might be coming their way, she wanted to be there first.

8

Noah knew it the moment he hit the Ozarks. The smell changed. It wasn't bad, but it was a little riper, a little more farmland-y and loamy than the air from the open spaces he'd driven through on the way here. It certainly did not smell like Miami. The feeling that everything was wrong, or somehow "off" only solidified as he hit the foothills and drove farther and farther away from civilization.

Special Agent Derek Westerfield had offered him a job a while ago, and Noah had turned him down flat. But this time, it had been Noah reaching out, and Westerfield hired him from that initial inquiry call. Interesting that he could join one division of the Bureau while on forced administrative leave from another branch, but he got the feeling that Westerfield's division didn't operate the same way as the others.

Still, the fact that Noah had immediately been sent out on an assignment was beyond disturbing.

There had only been a phone call and a few emails. They hadn't even met in person—ever.

But now he was now a specially deputized consultant—the only way Westerfield could give him a gun and badge without alerting the Miami branch. Noah had never heard of that, but the new boss had been far more concerned with getting Noah on the road than with getting him properly up to speed about what he was doing.

During the call, Noah had been able to hear the SAC's pen tapping on his desk. Westerfield wasn't any happier with the situation than Noah was.

"The wolves you met," Westerfield had stated when Noah had asked what he would be doing. "There's a family compound of them in the Ozarks. I have reason to believe that an agent who's gone AWOL is headed that way."

You've got to be shitting me, Noah had thought. He knew what NightShade officers could do—at least, he knew about the ones he'd met.

As he drove along the back roads of Arkansas, Noah reminded himself that he wasn't completely out of his element. He was, after all, an FBI agent with years in the field. He knew how to handle a gun. He knew the laws pertaining to when he could and couldn't arrest someone, what a warrant could and couldn't do, and much more. Still, there seemed to be very real differences between the Night-Shade division and the branches he'd worked in before.

Also Westerfield was sending Noah Kimball out merely ten minutes after being anointed. Noah wasn't sure he was willing to hunt a rogue agent. He'd used his best *per my last email* wording. "I'm not sure this is wise."

"Do you want the job or not?" Westerfield had pushed, not answering the question Noah had implied.

For a moment, he wondered what kind of powers Westerfield might possess himself, if he ran a unit like NightShade.

Noah had almost declined the job, but then again, he had nothing better to do. It was plausible he was going to lose a job that he loved, simply because he was too good at it. Even if he did get his old position back, the agency would investigate him with extra care the next time he made an arrest or—God forbid—shot someone.

At least at the NightShade division, he could use his skills. Maybe not completely openly, but he wouldn't get reprimanded for them. *Or put on leave.*

Westerfield had been talking, and Noah realized he hadn't been paying enough attention. "The family compound is in the Ozarks. It was burned to the ground by a madman, but he didn't get all of it. A good portion of it is underground. I'm sending you the coordinates."

Lovely, Noah thought. Westerfield had taken Noah's silence as a *yes*.

"I believe that's where agent Christina Pines is headed."

Noah took advantage of the brief pause to get his own question in. "If and when I find her—"

"Call me. Let me know that you saw her." There was an odd pause, and this time, Noah didn't fill it, despite the questions still bouncing around in his head. Sure enough, Westerfield jumped in. "It's possible that when you see her, she'll disappear."

"I'm sorry. Do you mean like *actually disappear?*" Noah had to ask. He'd seen Eleri Eames blink in and out of existence more than once. "Is she like Agent Eames?"

His question indicated that he knew just what some other agents could do, even though Westerfield should have already put that together.

"No, not like Eames at all."

Huh. Noah almost made the sound out loud. *Very unprofessional.*

"Pines has the mental ability to push the people around her into believing whatever she wants them to. She can make you think the walls are on fire. She can make you think you're in a different city, suddenly, and she can easily make you believe that she was never there at all."

Noah could make people feel as if they'd been tapped, or that they'd tripped, but... "She can erase my memory?"

"Faster than you can think about it. Yes. So you need to have me on speed dial. And as soon as you get a glimpse of her, you push that button. Honestly, if I answer and you say, 'I don't remember why I just called you,' I'm going to assume you just saw Pines."

Well, hell, Noah thought. This was more than he'd bargained for. He felt like he'd agreed to hear about it, but he hadn't actually said *yes.*

But Westerfield was talking again. "You'll be getting more emails. Company card information. Temporary badge, all of that."

A temporary NightShade badge? He hadn't been issued one the last time he'd worked with them. *Interesting.*

"You'll get these emails within the next hour. By the time you get the last one, I expect you to be packed and hitting the road. Any questions?"

Noah was opening his mouth as Westerfield replied to his own question with, "That's great. Check in from the road."

And he hung up.

9

C hristina pulled into the small gas station to get gas that she didn't need and a bottle of water that she did. As usual, she interrogated everyone inside. Sadly, all of it would show up on the video replay later if anyone bothered to look. Westerfield might.

He'd been calling her repeatedly, though the time between calls had gotten longer. It was as if he'd finally realized she truly was not going to call him back.

She had called him. He just didn't remember it.

Only one of the people in the gas station—an older man with a ball cap, buying a very large bag of chips and a Coke that spoke to the shape of his figure—seemed willing to talk to her. He'd raised his hand and said, "Ma'am, I think I saw the person you're talking about. Are you looking for someone alone or with someone else?"

"Either," she replied, turning her attention to him and smiling. *Flies with honey* and all that. Also, the odd question about a companion piqued her curiosity. *Had she been right?*

"I think he might actually be traveling with someone, though I'm mostly looking for him," she said sweetly.

If she was right, the man Murray Marks was traveling with was supposed to be dead. She repeated Marks' description. "Older man. White, tall, thin, salt-andpepper hair."

"A little shaggy?"

"Maybe." Hair grew, hair was cut, hair could be colored. The description was correct for Dr. Marks, and so was the build. That probably hadn't changed much, unless he'd gotten thinner in prison. She nodded and smiled to encourage the man to give her more information. "And who was he with?"

"Another guy. Also thin and lanky. Indian fella. Short hair. Pitch black. Straight nose. Seemed to be like a sidekick."

Damn, Christina thought. He'd just described Shray Menon to a tee. "I see. Well, thank you for your time."

Then she erased the whole conversation from the man's memory.

She paid for the bottle of water, of course. If the video came back and showed her not paying, that would raise more red flags than if she actually followed protocol.

She caught the cashier's eyes and erased herself from his memory, too. She could do it even if they weren't looking at her, but it worked faster and she knew it would take better if she managed to make the eye contact. There were four other people in the store to take care of.

Making a mental note to see if she could learn to keep people from seeing her on video replay, she headed back out to the car, climbed in, and aimed north again.

She was getting closer. Thirty minutes later, she recognized the name of one small town from the last time she'd been in the foothills. She also remembered the people here had known all kinds of things. In fact, there had been several murders in previous years that Christina and the other agents had figured out, even though the townspeople didn't realize the deaths weren't just a series of unfortunate accidents.

On a whim, she turned onto a side street and headed into the nearest store. A mom-and-pop place, it ranked somewhere in between a grocery and a gas station convenience store. She checked first with the woman behind the counter, but she hadn't seen Dr. Marks.

Maybe the professor was smart enough not to show his face where he might be recognized. He was most likely coming through this way, but he could have passed right through this postage stamp of a town without meeting anyone face-to-face. He might have even made a straight shot all the way to the de Gottardi/Little compound, or wherever it was that he stayed nearby. They'd never found that out during the previous investigation.

Christina wandered the aisles looking for locals and quickly found another man who looked to be about the same age as the woman at the checkout. Though she asked him several questions, he'd not seen Marks, so Christina turned away.

She crawled the aisles carefully but found nothing. Then she turned the corner and almost physically ran into a tall, good-looking blond man. He tilted his head toward the left, almost exactly as the wolf had. But his eyes were not the same color, and the wolf had not been blond.

She frowned at him and was opening her mouth to ask if maybe he'd seen Dr. Murray Marks or his sidekick—the supposedly dead Shray Menon. But he tipped his head to the other side and said, "Christina Pines, I presume."

10

Noah waited until the woman turned around. When he said her name, she confirmed her identity with the slight twitch at the side of her eye.

That was his mistake. He wanted to see her face, to be sure it was really her, so that he didn't do something stupid like call Westerfield and then later have to say something like, *Oops, sorry, my bad*. In the moment it took her to turn around to give him that positive ID, he'd already begun to move his thumb toward the button he had programmed on his phone. Westerfield's direct line had been speed dialed to number five. Dead center of the phone. Easy and accessible, just as his new boss had ordered.

Noah's thumb made it close to position, maybe only two millimeters away, before it stopped moving. Noah would have frowned at the sensation of his thumb simply refusing to comply, but facial movements weren't happening either. Suddenly, he was frozen in place.

"I see you," Christina said carefully. She knew what he was doing.

God help me. He couldn't move his thumb two more freaking millimeters. He didn't need to frown or take a step—though he wouldn't be able to do either. *I need to push the damn button on the phone.*

Westerfield had said he would know what was going on if Noah called and then didn't speak. In fact, they'd already played out this scenario except, in Westerfield's version, Noah had been faster and Christina had been slower.

His eyes flicked downward and Noah watched as his thumb moved back to the side of the phone. His arm bent and he slid the device back into his pocket.

Damn it, he thought, even as he marveled at the fact that his body was moving almost seemingly without him. He understood what was happening—he still felt the signals—but it was clear that he wasn't completely in control here. His thoughts were running circles. Maybe that's what saved him.

He didn't know exactly what Christina was doing, but he had a better idea of what *he* could do.

He tilted his head, surprised to find that part of him was still completely his own. He shouldn't tip her off, but he wanted to show her he still had control of something.

Slowly, he watched as her own face turned to astonishment. She was plenty easy to read. As he watched, she took a step forward, her right foot jerking a little. She tripped and saved herself by lowering onto her knees there in the middle of the aisle of the grocery store.

Tap. Tap. He had his own tricks, and he played them.

She looked surprised and angry as she laced her hands behind her head.

Christina Pines stared up at him, ready to be cuffed.

Good. He hadn't been an agent for years for nothing. He knew what would make her think she had lost.

He tried to step toward her again, but found his feet were stuck to the floor. He panicked suddenly, until he found he was breathing fine. She hadn't messed with that, at least. No wonder his only job had been to spot her and follow. Instead, he'd run smack into her while stocking up on snack food for a trip to a farm in the dead middle of nowhere. And now he was finding out firsthand what his new SAC had alluded to.

Noah had mistakenly overestimated his own powers. He had zip ties in his back pocket. He would have laughed now if he could; that had been stupid.

He couldn't get to her to cuff her, even though she was on the ground, waiting.

She must have realized that they were at a standoff until she could figure out what was going on. He found his mouth worked again. So he sucked in a deep breath of relief and said, "You need to turn yourself in."

He watched as her jaw clenched and he could see she was grinding her teeth in anger. It was clear the two of them didn't do the same thing, but right now, their skills were having a very similar effect. He just needed to get her to let go of whatever hold she had on him.

Noah's own talent worked much better when he could talk his way through what his targets were feeling, but he'd been convincing enough even without words, that Christina was convinced that she was getting arrested.

She must not have liked the few words he said, because he found his jaw sealed shut again and his vocal cords refusing to even make a peep. *Son of a bitch.*

He tried breaking the hold and taking a few steps forward, but the flare in her eyes told him she knew exactly what he was trying to do and she wouldn't allow it.

At that moment, the cereal on the shelves began cracking and spitting, the floor heated beneath his feet, and everything around him burst into flame.

11

Christina was fighting hard to not give in to the gun pressed into her back. Though she was tempted to lie face down on the floor and just let this new agent arrest her, she stayed on her knees.

Clearly, Westerfield had sent someone he thought could best her. Now her brain was rolling over in her skull. Was she bested? She wasn't sure.

They had her kneeling and ready to be cuffed… but she wasn't cuffed or hauled to her feet. So what was happening?

Though she was holding him back with an image of fire, she still felt the gun in the middle of her back. The agent in front of her hadn't budged, despite the flames. And if she so much as shrugged, she got a tap from the other agent who stood behind her, reminding her that she could be killed in a moment.

Should she whirl around and surprise the second agent? Could she even do it, given that she was on her knees and the other agent was on her feet? Christina didn't think so. They'd likely been trained in all the same tactics and the agent behind her was waiting for her to make a stupid move. She could too easily end up dead.

She'd come too far to just give herself up. Still, they were at an impasse until one of them did something, and the agent behind her was merely holding her in place.

Ceding a little bit of ground, she let go of her hold on the blond man and allowed him to move about freely. She saw him jolt as suddenly he realized he was in control of his body again. After all, he was still engulfed in flames.

In her plans, the illusion of fire alone would make him flee the store and try to get far away. She could then get off her damn knees and get out of here. It should have made both agents run.

But they didn't.

Christina didn't take a deep breath, because she didn't want to telegraph what she was planning. Mentally, she counted down. *Three, two, one!*

Swiping her arm out behind her, she hoped to wrap the arm holding the gun on her and gain control of the agent. But her arm passed through empty air. Momentum and fear had her following her arm and turning to look the other agent in the face, but she received a quick, firm tap to stay facing forward and the cold barrel of the gun pressed between her shoulder blades just a little harder.

She slumped forward. She was not dead for having made a pass, but no further ahead either. *Crap.*

Christina checked around without moving her eyes, searching for a back door to the little store. Then again, if Westerfield had sent these two, she could count on the fact that they had also scouted for a back door. And they'd have those little diamonds on their badges, a subtle nod to the NightShade division. That meant the agent had powers.

She couldn't flee yet, so she turned her gaze to see him looking curiously at his surroundings. Instead of screaming and running from the cereal boxes on fire, or the little flames that slid across the floor as though an accelerant had been poured everywhere, he only looked at it in curiosity.

Shit.

"I knew you could do this."

His words matched what she'd just figured out—about one illusion too late.

"In fact, SAC Westerfield warned me about this exact one."

What? Christina thought. This day was getting worse and worse. She'd been so used to being the only one playing on her field that she was using tired tricks, throwing dirty passes, and apparently phoning it in.

Well, hell. It crossed her mind now that there might be bartenders and patrons left in her path that she'd not fully erased.

Was that how the agents had found her—her own sheer stupidity and laziness?

It was too late now.

The blond man began to advance on her. She tried something different and watched as he stumbled, smacking hard into the floor.

He clearly felt it. It had to be a harsh sting to the palms of his hands and a crack to his kneecaps, because his brain had thought he was falling into a suddenly appearing pool of water. Instead, he hit cold tile at full speed and didn't break the surface.

Bet Westerfield didn't tell you about that one, she thought. Though she felt proud of the move, she was still kneeling on the floor, fingers laced behind her head, unable to move without getting pushed back into place.

When the man looked up at her, he was no longer curious at their little standoff, no longer trying to figure it out. Instead, he was angry.

Well, she thought, *it worked*.

Moving in an odd way, he twisted himself around. Once again, he did the unexpected and crawled himself into a seated position. It would be difficult for him to jump up and chase her down if she managed to break free, but it was pretty clear that wasn't going to happen. The other agent's gun still held her in place.

Christina still couldn't mentally find the second agent to give a push and make them think she was on fire or had disappeared. Did this agent have a cloaking spell? Knowing Westerfield, that would be exactly who he'd send after her: someone she couldn't even see. But she could still see the man in front of her as he calmly sat on the floor.

"It seems we are at an impasse."

She pushed again. If nothing else, she could freeze him in place. Christina watched as he tried to move the muscles he'd been controlling only moments before. His frustration made her smile a little.

She let his mouth move and he spoke between clenched teeth. "If I let you go, will you let me go?"

She didn't answer quickly, and he spoke again.

"It's the only way either of us ever gets out of this."

Christina thought long and hard about it.

12

E leri drove the older car down I-95. Though it had been well-maintained, she noticed now that it had a bit of a rattle from age. It rolled well over smooth highways and bumpy sideroads. As long as it didn't leave her stranded on the side of the road, it would be enough.

And if it did? Well, then she simply wouldn't make it. No one was expecting her, anyway.

She tried to focus on mundane things, putting off her end goal. She'd not replied to any of Donovan's voicemails or texts. In her own mind, this was because she wasn't quite ready to communicate. But when she wasn't lying to herself, she knew she'd open the door to copping out. If she arrived and found Donovan missing, she would turn around and head back home. She could say she tried without having to actually try.

Eleri wasn't ready to leave the safety of Bell Point Farm and her solitude. Not yet. She was only on the road because Donovan needed her.

When she had first holed up, she'd been recovering from her shock and what had happened in the Caribbean. It had taken several days to form any kind of plan. When she had an idea, the first thing she had to do was get a grip on what her newly emerging skills might be.

Starting with what she already knew, Eleri focused on applying her FBI training toward this wild, new aspect of her life. In the Bureau, an agent would only hold her gun if she intended to shoot someone. The very act of pulling the gun was a commitment to end a life, if necessary. Most people thought it was just the initial threat. They were wrong.

When she pulled her gun, she laid her finger alongside the trigger guard. This was standard training, and so that if the agent accidentally flinched, no one died. Though they were ready to kill, there was to be no bullet flying into someone unintentionally. Eleri now needed those same kinds of procedures in place for her own powers.

So far, she hadn't quite come up with them.

After several days of sitting on the couch and watching the fields on her property sway in the wind, she had switched to a flurry of activity. She scoured the house. She opened every dresser drawer of every guestroom and checked every item in every closet. When that was done—and turned up nothing of value—she went back into the closets and hallways and thumped on the walls, looking for trap doors and secret passages.

She climbed to the top floor and unscrewed the trap door that led her into the attic. It had been added as an afterthought, and not part of the original design. In fact, the cut piece of plywood had been painted to match the ceiling inside the closet it was hidden in, but otherwise was unpolished. The edges were rough, and the screws used to hold it utilitarian at best.

The attic access had probably been added to bring Bell Point Farm up to some long-ago code. It certainly didn't meet today's standards. When she'd finally gotten into the attic, she expected layers of insulation and exposed beams.

What she saw instead were troves of family history. Eleri had barely poked her head up and through the hole she'd opened, and she was stunned. She had stood on a shelf in the closet—right under the access, which had seemed easier than getting a ladder—but she now would have to haul herself up and through the narrow opening.

This was definitely *not* up to code.

She felt too stunned to keep going and had fallen back, landing on the shelf with a thump. It was only luck that kept her from toppling to the floor.

The second time, with a better idea what she was facing and the dusty musty air she would be breathing, Eleri made a more concerted effort and pulled herself through the attic floor.

Clearly, someone had been up here at some point in the not-too-distant past. From the way things were arranged, it appeared this spot was not the main access point. Still, her hope hadn't been to find attic access. It was to find history.

And she was standing in the middle of it.

Everything from steamer trunks to old 1940s and 50s suitcases surrounded her. Some things were in cardboard boxes. As she scanned the dark space, she saw at least three different handwritings marking what was contained.

Unsure what to do, she'd simply beelined first for the steamer trunk, wondering what treasures it might hold. She found old clothing, but it was difficult to tell if this was the clothing that her great-great-something grandmother had put up because she didn't like it or because these were her favorites.

The short stature and tiny waistlines of the dresses held Eleri's attention until her stomach grumbled, and she realized she wasn't doing what she'd intended. Making sure she emptied the trunk so she didn't miss anything, she then replaced everything without looking. Once it was back in the box, she slid the latch into place and left it relatively undisturbed, except for the fact that it was now dust-free.

She'd lowered herself back down into the main house and cleaned up enough to feel comfortable eating. After feeding herself some lunch, she'd climbed right back up.

This time, she went with a fully formed plan. She was still ignoring the voicemails that came in frequently from Donovan's phone. On her third trip up, she'd been smart enough to bring her own phone in case something happened up here, in case she needed to call somebody to come and rescue her.

But she hadn't needed anyone.

On the second day, she'd found the main access in the closet of the master bedroom. That made the whole process much easier. And on the third day, she'd discovered the large, leather-bound book. It had been a tough call. Should she keep hunting or stop and examine the stunning piece of Hale family history that she'd found?

She'd begun alternating her tasks. Hunt in the morning, work in the afternoon. Or at least, that's what she told herself.

Donovan's messages had grown increasingly uneasy. Then, with the last one, he'd said Bodhi Banerjee had been at his house.

His long lost brother. The one who was now working for Miranda Corp. The one who somehow had known all along that Donovan existed, when Donovan believed his own mother to be dead and gone years earlier. That might have been the one thing that could get Eleri to climb out of the attic and into the car.

Now, driving down the freeway, she had a suitcase in the back seat in which she'd packed her clothes, her shoes, and anything she might need. In the passenger footwell was the small bag that held her badge and gun—things she wouldn't leave home without. And on the seat beside her was the fabric-wrapped, leather-bound volume that held family secrets for generations.

13

Christina was still breathing heavily even though it had been two hours since she left the store and the agent behind. The encounter had been unnerving at best.

Once they'd mutually agreed to let each other go, she'd still had to use her control to empty his mind of their encounter. Then she'd sent him all the way back out to his car, put him in it, and watched him drive away. The other agent—the one who'd had the gun at her back —was completely missing.

When she'd questioned the blond man, he'd only said, "What other agent?"

Christina consoled herself by asking the blond man to state his own name, and he answered with, "Noah Kimball, Miami Dade Bureau." It was reassuring that her ability to push him was still working, even though he said "Miami Dade" and not "NightShade."

Christina tried again to ask about the other agent and was met only with a confused frown. Giving up, she'd sent him on his way. But who the hell was he?

Though Christina had wanted to speed away right that moment, she'd stayed in the parking lot, standing and watching the empty road for too long. It had been necessary to go back into the grocery store and erase the memory of everyone inside.

On the way out, practically racing to her car, she ran into a newcomer.

It wasn't the other agent, but some random person doing their shopping. As empty as it had been, the store was still far too busy. She had to expend more energy to clear this new person's memory. At last, she'd slid into her own driver's seat and left.

While she'd been weaving on and off the major roads and side streets, she'd tried to recall what she'd collected about Dr. Murray Marks. Sadly, it wasn't much. That stop had been nothing but bad luck.

When she finally cleared the edge of town, Christina cut a broad loop away from the streets that agent Noah Kimball would take on the way to the de Gottardi/Little farm. Finally, on the other side of the family compound, she was deep in the Ozarks, her cell signal horrendously weak. And she was still breathing heavily.

She found a side road that presumably led to a farm or a few farms, given that it was only gravel and slightly worse than the road she'd been driving. She headed about ten minutes down the road before finding a stand of trees and a pullout spot where she could adequately hide her car from anyone passing on the road behind her.

Leaving the car in Drive, she didn't dare to turn the engine off and create a scenario where it would take her several more seconds to flee. There was no telling if she was safe here, but she fought to slow her breathing.

Not only had Westerfield sent someone after her, he'd sent a new guy, ready to deal with her unique skills—though she should have expected that.

What if he sent Eleri next? That thought stopped Christina cold.

Even as she realized tears were rolling down her face, she took a cold, hard look at where she was. *What have I done?*

She'd joined the FBI and had been a damn good agent, despite the mysterious unit and the secretive and hard-to-decipher boss. She was good at what she did. But once she'd decided to track Dr. Murray Marks on her own, she'd thrown all of it away.

She was likely facing jail time now. Certainly, she would no longer be a federal agent when this was over. Westerfield, though he knew what his agents could do and even had a few skills of his own, wasn't given to being lenient.

Christina wiped at her tears with the back of her hand and forced herself to get on track. It was started. She had to see it through.

The blond guy—Noah Kimball—was new. So new that his brain

was still cataloging his workplace as Miami? But he had to be an agent, since he'd recognized her. She'd not met him before, and he'd been relatively easy to push. She knew she'd made him see the things she'd intended—but he'd also been fully aware of what she could do *before* he met her.

If he was a NightShade agent—new or not—he would have skills of his own. But what had he done?

The second agent had pushed her from behind, just a small shove but enough to get her moving. Then she'd stubbed her toe and fallen to her knees. But what could have possibly been on the smooth tile of the floor to make her trip?

When she might have stood back up, she'd felt another shove and taps to her hands. She knew the universal signals for "put your hands on your head." Christina might not have complied had she not immediately felt the gun at her back.

Ultimately, she'd stayed put, despite trying everything she could on Noah Kimball, because she knew she couldn't outrun a bullet. And no matter how much she'd pushed, the gun's muzzle had stayed squarely pressed between her shoulder blades.

When she'd tried to push on the mind of the agent behind her, it had proved futile. The guy had not moved, aside from the occasional taps to keep her in place. She'd gotten a kick to the sole of her foot and several reminders that there was a gun at her back. It was clear then that the slightest move would make him pull the trigger.

She sat in her car, wondering just what Noah Kimball could do. Because she was now understanding that there had never been a second agent at all.

14

The knock at the front door startled him. Donovan froze. It was a ridiculous rabbit defense in response to what was likely a wolf attack.

Any wolf would easily detect that he'd recently been on the front porch. Whoever was here would smell him, just as he'd smelled his brother.

The knock came again.

Donovan turned. The floorplan was both a blessing and a curse. He could not see straight through the house. And though it would have been nice to simply turn his head and get a peek at the front porch, it was also nice that no one standing out there could see into his house.

He stepped forward slowly, sniffing at the air. Once again, he pushed his face out, trying to catch every scent.

He hadn't fully changed since he'd smelled his brother. Then, he'd changed as rapidly as possible, dropped down onto all fours, and stalked through the house. Later, when he'd checked out the whole property, he'd discovered that, this time, Bodhi had gotten no farther than the front door. But now his paranoia was definitely getting the better of him.

As he got closer to the front of the house, he thought he caught a whiff of Eleri.

Two more steps, and he was certain it was her. Without any

further thought, he ran toward the front door, pushing his face back into place. His maxilla gave a final pop as it slid into place. He flexed his mouth and twitched his nose just as his hand hit the knob.

Donovan threw the door wide, his now-human face no longer scenting his friend on the other side.

If he was wrong and it wasn't Eleri, he'd be dead.

Sure enough, she stood there on his porch. For a moment, she didn't say anything, so neither did he.

He only noticed that she looked smaller than she had the last time he'd seen her. Obviously, she'd not lost stature—but somehow, she'd shrunk into herself, which was something he'd never wanted to see.

Then, with no real thought to it, he reached out and hauled her into his arms, grateful when she hugged him back. He didn't know how long they stayed that way. And he maybe didn't know until that moment how much of his childhood—and even his adult life—had been deprived of actual human comfort. He could count it back to the day his mother died when he was seven.

At least, to him, she had died. She'd certainly exited his life. As the thought flared with pain at the old memories, a new knowledge shot through him. He stepped back. His hands clasped Eleri's shoulders, as though he feared she might bolt.

"You said Bodhi was here." She got straight to business. She wasn't yet telling him what she'd been up to during her "alone time," but for now it was okay.

Donovan answered, "He didn't get past the front porch. But he came here for something and I guess he left."

"The question," Eleri said, "Isn't *did he leave?* It's *what did he leave behind?*"

15

Christina stood at the back side of the de Gottardi/Little land. The farm encompassed hundreds of acres of rolling fields nearly smack in the middle of the Ozarks. She'd slept her panic off during the night and pointed herself back on track... back to here.

Stopping for a moment, she scanned the area while taking a deep breath of pristine air. She'd walked a long distance from the gravel road that wrapped this side of the property. This was the spot where they had suspected Dr. Marks and Shray Menon and their hunters had entered, the last time they'd launched an attack on the family They'd intended to completely destroy the compound.

That had been almost a year ago now.

Christina and some of the other agents had been here for that standoff. Murray Marks had not walked away a winner. But neither had the families who lived here.

Even from this back distance, she could see that only a few of the houses were still standing. In several areas, the grass didn't sway right because what remained of a house's raised foundation blocked the wind.

As a light breeze ruffled at the tips of the wheat, she let her eyes glaze over and she stared into the distance, hoping to spot anomalies. Though she searched the area around her, she also tried to be on the lookout for anything doing the same... trying to spot *her*.

Standing on the edge of land that wasn't hers, motionless in the light wind, she had to stand out like a... *like an FBI agent on a damn werewolf farm.*

Her gun was at her hip, concealed beneath the edge of her jacket in typical FBI agent style—not that anyone would think she didn't have a gun. Just because the letters FBI were not emblazoned across the back of this jacket, it did not mean that no one would recognize who and what she was.

She wanted to believe there were wolves out here—that the family had begun to return to their home.

If they were here, they could most likely smell her. They could probably hear her, too. With her inferior human senses, she could do nothing of the sort. Her only hope was any wolves she encountered belonged to the de Gottardi or Little families and would remember her.

Aiming toward the center of the compound, she aimed toward a patch of tall grass that didn't move quite the same way as the rest. It was a longer trek than she expected, the distance deceiving in the open space. But sure enough, when she got there, she found what had once been a house. Razed and destroyed, it was now so invisible that she'd almost stubbed her toe on the corner of the foundation before she realized she had arrived. A few hardy weeds had pushed their way up through cracks in what had been the floor. What they were anchored in, she didn't know. Surveying the four corners made of cinderblock, she tried to take stock.

The house had been built in the style of all the homes in the compound, with a typical Oklahoma prairie/mountain look. But the raised cinderblock foundation told a different story. There was a basement beneath, the thick walls acting as reinforcement.

She needed to get into it.

Was the trap door still here?

Given what she remembered, the access point should be near the middle of the house. A quick scan revealed that the floor had been covered by thin layers of silt and leaves, anything not washed off in the rain or blown away by the wind.

Did she dare set foot on the floorboards of a burned-out house? Her only other option was to find the outside entry to the basement, but she had no idea where that might be; she didn't even know which direction to look first. She was only confident that it would have been expertly hidden.

The homes had been built to conceal the underground tunnels that connected them to each other—sometimes crossing almost a mile of distance.

The de Gottardi and Little families had built themselves a self-sustaining farmland and—unlike many cults or even strict religions—they'd managed to retain many of their best and brightest. Then again, many of them had very good reason to come back.

They had teachers and lawyers. Master craftsmen and psychologists. The family had several members with veterinary degrees or MDs, allowing them to treat their own at home without concern that a standard medical provider would discover their unusual anatomy. They couldn't afford to be written up in medical journals.

The tunnels were an engineering marvel given the land. Christina was confident the tunnel design was a de Gottardi / Little invention. The trap doors were another of their clever designs, which meant she'd have to get right on top of one before she found it.

For a moment, she wondered if she was going to be too heavy for the damaged boards. Would her hiking boots be sensitive enough to tell if the floor was giving way *before* it dropped her into a basement? She wasn't confident she could get out of the underground space if she fell in. "I guess I'm going to have to hope it holds…" she murmured into the wind.

Crap. The first board creaked beneath her step.

She'd known this was a possibility and, though it was very light-weight, the cord at her hip was very strong—which was exactly why she'd brought it. For a moment, she worried that the creak she'd caused was a bad sign.

Still, she looked around for something to anchor her and spotted one post on one side of the remaining front railing. A tree would be more reliable, but none grew close enough to the house for her wrap the rope around.

Trudging through the grass around the border of the house, she reached what had once been the front steps. She shoved at the post until she deemed it stable enough. Unclipping the rope, Christina wrapped one end firmly around the sturdy leather belt she'd worn for exactly this purpose and then used her best knots to anchor the other end to the post.

Step by gentle step, she tested the floor, growing more wary as she got near the middle. She'd been out here, seen the houses, and even been inside them before they looked like this. Some of the buildings were older, supported underneath with posts at regular spaces. Others were built with modern, multi-density fiberboard I-beams that spanned the length of the house. She didn't know how this house had been constructed or how well it might have held up to a fire. So she was taking her chances.

Christina stuck her foot another length out and slowly added her weight. When she didn't fall, she let out the breath she was holding and then repeated the process. Twenty minutes later, she'd paced the entire remaining floor. She hadn't crashed through—but she still had no idea where the trap door was. There was only one answer: *Start over.*

So she did.

Being up on the raised platform, she was visible from all directions. Taking a second pass would make it clear to anyone watching her that she knew what she was looking for, and the pink in her hair would make it possible for anyone looking to spot her easily. She scanned the area once more but found nothing obvious lurking in the tall grass. In fact, it seemed she was the only human soul for miles around. This time, she paced a grid.

On the third try, she found the line. She'd begun wiping her toe into the leaves and dirt as she went along, far more confident now of the structural integrity of the place. Tracing the line of ash and dirt that her toe revealed, she followed until it made a ninety-degree turn.

It had been rained on. The wind had blown leaves across. Branches had fallen and stayed, looking desolate. Christina kicked the debris out of the way, not sure if she was giving herself space to search or just feeling angry at nature for defiling what had been a warm home. As she'd suspected, the trap door was no easy find.

As her toe hit a bump, pride bloomed warm in her chest as she leaned down to push at the leaves and dirt. She had to see if she was standing on the trap door or next to it.

Slowly, she revealed the edges. And at last, she found a pull ring—a simple and old- fashioned device for something so well concealed—and dug it out of the perfectly constructed well it sat in.

Tugging hard, she stepped back as the trap door began to lift. Christina ducked her head, to see what she'd revealed, unsure what might be waiting underneath.

16

Noah had stalked slowly closer and closer to the woman who appeared to be levitating in the middle of the field. He'd recognized her instantly and pulled his phone. But his thumb only hovered over the button. After a moment of not pushing it, he made a conscious decision *not* to call his new SAC.

He considered mashing the button, just to prove he could do it. But she didn't see him and wasn't forcing him to do—or not do—anything. In fact, she didn't even seem to realize he was here. So he let his finger hover as he waited.

When she didn't seem to spot him or his indecision, he crouched down and began heading her direction. He couldn't get low enough to disappear into the grass while he moved. If he wanted to lay on his stomach and remain absolutely still, he might stay out of sight, but he needed to move closer. So all he could do was stay low and hope the blond of his hair didn't stand out too much against the gold of the wheat-like grass.

Interestingly enough, even when he was right next to her, she still didn't seem to notice him.

He'd started his day by checking out the long, winding front drive to the big house. Westerfield had told him about the property. There were no known maps. At least, that's what Westerfield had said. Noah thought there was something about his new SAC's words that hinted he might be concealing something.

But he'd been told enough to understand that if he went out the back door of the big house and walked the property, he should run into other homes—or the remains of them. According to what the FBI knew, all the homes were burned-out shells or were shuttered when the family left. According to what they believed now, some of the de Gottardi/Little clan might have returned. So Noah had his eyes open for anything dangerous he might encounter.

He was still fighting to shake his memory of the evil selkie-beings and the mind-blowing craziness he'd encountered in the Caribbean. The worst of what he'd seen were water creatures, so he knew he should feel safe from them here in landlocked Arkansas—but the memory had him checking every creature and every human face for something more. Luckily, all he'd seen here were a few vultures and a handful of coyotes in the distance.

The property itself filled him with a reverent sense of awe. What this family had endured and what they were was pretty impressive. And the architecture… while unassuming, it was solidly crafted, with hand-carved pieces and the kind of detail that didn't exist in modern works. He would have loved to have seen this place back in its better days.

As Noah got closer, he saw agent Pines seemed to have found something at her feet. He now realized that she was standing on the raised foundation of what had once been a house. Behind her, the tilted pile of brick came into view, and he recognized the remains of a chimney. It, too, must have weakened in the fire and shifted over time.

Once again, his thumb moved toward the button on his phone—and once again, he decided not to push it. Maybe he didn't because Westerfield was the kind of man who would send one agent after another. The kind who wouldn't tell his agents everything. Westerfield seemed like the kind of man who would operate solely on the need-to-know basis. Noah didn't like the feeling he got about the new boss.

After his encounter with Christina Pines, Noah was quite confident that he did *not* know all he needed to. He was growing more and more confident that his new SAC was most likely overbearing and possibly judgmental.

For a moment, he wondered if he'd even fully—*legally?*—agreed to this assignment. Probably he had, if only implicitly by accepting the ticket and the badge. Still, he didn't hit the button on the phone. Not yet.

When at last he was close enough, he switched the phone from his right hand to his left and flipped the strap on his holster, revealing the butt of his gun. He could only hope he was a quick enough draw if he needed to be.

Slowly, he stood up. When she still didn't seem to notice him from where she was crouched down to find something on the floor, he called out.

Christina Pines popped up lightning fast, the gun in her hand aimed directly at him. Though some of the immediate tension in her stance drained as she recognized him, she didn't lower the weapon.

All of this indicated what he'd suspected—that she hadn't spotted him until now. He held up the phone as though she might see the screen from the distance. She likely couldn't read it, but maybe she could see that he hadn't yet called her in.

"Why didn't you tell Westerfield you found me?" she demanded, still clutching her gun. At least she let the barrel drop a little toward his feet. Noah didn't move.

He truly couldn't answer that question. There were so many reasons why he should and so many others why he shouldn't. The pros and cons had been weighted so closely, it had been hard to tell. In the end, the pros were just a little in her favor.

He still might push the button. His thumb was ready. So he only shrugged as she finally holstered the gun and walked easily to the edge of the foundation. She stood to her full height, towering over him by a good several feet, though when they'd met face to face, she'd clearly been shorter than him. She looked for a moment as though she was making her own decisions, and he waited her out.

"I found the trap door," she said almost too casually. "You have two options. You can call agent Westerfield, tell him I'm here, and then do your best to bring me in and shut me down. Or you can help me figure out what's going on at this compound."

17

Christina hung by her fingertips from the edge of the trap door. Her feet dangled into the dark, but she trusted it. Well, she trusted the dark below her. The weathered and damaged floorboards she clung to, not so much.

At least, if the flooring gave way, she would only drop a few feet to the packed dirt floor below. The rope was still tied around her waist, only this time, Noah Kimball grasped the other end rather than the porch rail. She might have trusted the railing more on that one.

Their alliance was a bit uneasy, and she was quite confident that he had to know she still didn't fully trust him. But he let the rope out a few feet and said, "Ready when you are."

Letting go, she quickly hit the floor, not prepared for a ground she couldn't see. Sharp pain radiated up from her ankles, even though the drop hadn't been that far.

Damn, she thought, *definitely getting older*. But out loud she called up, "All good down here. You're next."

With each move she made, Christina considered how Noah Kimball could screw her over. Right now, all he had to do was cut the rope and leave her here, which was exactly why she hadn't told him everything.

"Coming down," his voice carried into the dark. She stood in the empty space with the only light coming from the open trap door above her. She had to wonder if anyone was watching from the corners.

A point in Noah's favor had been that he'd left her with the rope.

Her erstwhile partner swung down, feet-first and not tied to anything. Stepping to the side, she watched as his form blocked out most of the light as he descended through the square above her.

With a softer thunk than she had made, he landed beside her.

"Okay," he said, immediately pulling out his flashlight. "Now what?"

She put her hand over his, motioning silently for him not to turn the light on. Not yet.

They stood and waited. Christina listened hard. Noah mostly stared at Christina, seeming to wonder what the hell she wanted.

In the end, she admitted, "I don't hear anything."

She began to untie the rope.

"I thought you wanted to be attached?" She could hear the frown in his voice. "There's plenty of rope. You can move around." He made a sweeping motion with his hand, as though she could roam her way around the entire downstairs of the house.

She ignored him and sniffed at the air. Her sense of smell was not as good as Donovan's, but decent for a human. The space smelled of dirt. Not just any dirt, but a specific scent that hit her with a sense memory of the trap door opening in the main house and wolves pouring out of the underground and into the fight.

She shook the image away and tried to focus on what she could glean now. There was no hint of dust or disuse, but the smell was full of moisture with a hint of loam.

Still, the house had more than conveyed a feeling of abandonment that matched its looks. Down here? She didn't know, but it didn't seem quite as … desolate.

Following Noah's sarcastic sweeping hand, she put her light on. Slowly, she flicked it toward all four corners, knowing what she was looking for. When nothing pricked at her ears, she was willing to move forward.

She hadn't told Noah quite what they were in for and she wasn't sure she would.

"Here we go." She dragged the words out in time with her light catching on one of the corners and watched as Noah's eyes widened.

The family could have put the tunnels dead center to the four walls, and though it would have made spatial sense, they hadn't done that. Instead, they'd attached them at the corners, as if they'd known to hide the entry points in the shadows. The locations meant that a person like Noah, even standing in the middle of this room, wouldn't see the tunnel until someone shined a light directly on it.

"Holy shit..." There was a pause as he took it in. "Do you know where it goes?"

"No." She decided she was going to have to spill some of the beans. "However, given the orientation of this house, we should be facing back toward the big house right now. That tunnel aims east, not quite the right direction at first glance, but I'm going to guess it'll ultimately connect back."

If it was possible, Noah's eyes grew even wider. "That's more than a mile away."

Now it was Christina's turn to be surprised. She thought that Noah's shock was due to seeing the tunnels in person. She'd known they were here, but that hadn't been enough to prepare her for the sight of them. They were the marvels of construction she'd anticipated, carved out of earth and rock, with only the occasional wooden support. They never gave her the feeling that she was in danger from a collapse or faulty mechanics.

Managing to be almost perfectly symmetrical, the tunnels still fit relatively well into the natural underground landscape. Occasionally, the passages would curve around big boulders here and there, but mostly they kept the perfect shape. Now she realized Noah's surprise was because he'd had no clue about the tunnels at all. "Westerfield didn't tell you?"

For the barest hint of a second, Noah's eyes narrowed. She didn't need to hear the words to understand that not only had Westerfield not explained the tunnel system, but that Noah was irritated about the omission.

Good, she thought. It changed the way she was thinking. She certainly hadn't told Noah everything, and she wasn't going to. All she had to do was tell him more than Westerfield did to gain his trust. For a moment, she relaxed. But then she remembered his thumb could hit that phone button at any point and call Westerfield. The existence of the call would be enough to let their boss know that Noah had found her.

If Noah was physically close to her, and if he was fast enough, he could actually have her handcuffed in a matter of seconds. Since he seemed immune to seeing the walls set on fire, or believing the world turned to water beneath his feet, it was unlikely she could get him to uncuff her and set her free.

If he was as smart as he seemed to be, he would do the standard maneuver of twisting her wrists and pulling her hands back to back, making it impossible for her to get to her handcuff key.

Shit. She aimed the flashlight into the tunnel as she slowly slipped her hand into her front pocket and felt for the tiny, flat universal key.

"You go first," Noah said.

Double shit. That made it harder to do this without his noticing.

Flashing him a smile, she stuffed the key into her back pocket, taking a bet that he would cuff her hands behind her, rather than in front.

Then she headed into the pitch-black tunnel with only her light and an agent that she didn't quite trust.

18

The walk was long, fascinating, and slightly terrifying to Noah.

The two of them kept a slow pace, even though Christina seemed to know where she was going and the tunnels were more than tall enough for an upright man.

He wondered why the ceilings hadn't been built lower, for wolves.

At first, the two of them had moved slowly, taking cautious steps. Though Christina seemed only to be paying attention to the space up ahead, Noah was as concerned about the ground at his feet. What was he stepping on? Snakes? Mud? Traps? It fed into all his worst fears.

With all the fracking in this portion of the United States, the area had been having more frequent earthquakes. What if one hit while the two of them were down here ? Even a small tremor could bring the walls down.

What if someone came in from either end of the tunnel and trapped them? He reminded himself that he didn't recall seeing anyone on the property. That helped, as did the fact that he'd made Christina go first. Occasionally, he touched the walls to check for stability.

They were maybe about three city blocks in, when he realized he'd already answered one of his own questions. "There are no cracks in the walls."

"No," Christina replied, almost as though it was her own point of pride.

"Are there no earthquakes here?"

"They get plenty," she said again, with the same note in her voice.

"Then either these are so well engineered that the earthquakes don't affect them or else they patch them regularly." He caught himself before he said the second part. "Which would mean they're still here and still patching them."

"It's the first." Her answer was as confident as the steps she took. Her flashlight only created a ball of white light directly in front of them, just far enough to see that the tunnel kept going. It was certainly not bright enough to show them the end.

They went a little farther before either of them spoke again. And, as per what was the new usual, it was him starting the conversation. He asked what he'd been thinking earlier. "Why aren't the tunnels lower? Wolves could walk through that easily... much smaller space, less engineering..."

Christina's stopped now and turned around to look at him. Her eyebrows pulled together. "Westerfield didn't tell you?"

This was the second time she'd said it, and Noah felt his irritation rise. It was bad enough that his new SAC hadn't told him, but worse that she kept pointing it out. "No, I guess not. What else do I need to know?"

He knew his irritation was sharp—too sharp—and that it probably shouldn't be aimed at her. In fact, he'd put his phone in his pocket and stopped hovering his finger over the button quite some time ago.

"They aren't all wolves," she told him.

Noah felt his brain start to churn. It was an effort to focus as she continued.

"They have non-wolves living here. Well, their specific ... mutation isn't ... it's genetically passed?" She ended with a question in her tone.

Would that produce this many wolves? This big a family? ... the ones he'd seen in the Caribbean? "A mutation?"

"Maybe just recessive inheritance." As she spoke, he could see her dial back, her expression saying *No, that doesn't seem right.* "Maybe dominant. Because more of them have it than not. Apologies, my partner Dana was the biologist. I'm not quite sure how to explain it."

Noah didn't miss the verb tense she used for her partner. "She's not your partner anymore?"

"She died." Christina offered the statement with the rough terminology. She could have used the more peaceful term "passed." And her choice made Noah certain that the passing had not been pleasant. He waited.

"She was murdered during a case."

Good God. He hadn't dealt with that before and hoped he never did. He offered the best he had. "I'm sorry."

"Thank you. I've been solo ever since."

He nodded along. He'd thought he understood where she was coming from, but he hadn't. This chase of Dr. Murray Marks was some kind of vendetta for her. The pieces weren't hard to put together. SAC Westerfield wanted Marks in custody. So why wouldn't he just let Pines bring the man in?

There were no good answers to that question.

As they crept down the tunnel, he walked behind her in almost absolute silence until he felt and heard his phone buzz.

Christina turned and glared at him, but he held his hands up, to show he wasn't answering.

Her return glare was far harsher than he deserved, Noah thought.

In fact, so was the string of curses that came out of her mouth.

His eyes narrowed at her.

"It's. Still. On." She enunciated every word.

He frowned at her. Yes, it was still on. And given the engineering of these tunnels, he suspected there wasn't a lot of space between the ceiling of the tunnel and the earth above. He'd not detected any kind of gentle slope, other than when they first set foot inside, so he wasn't too surprised to be getting a signal here.

"Did Westerfield give you that phone?" She ground the words out as though she were spitting rocks at him.

He brushed off her irritation, since he didn't understand it. The SAC giving him a phone was protocol. "It's FBI issued, along with the badge and gun and all that shit."

But only as Christina began to speak did he feel his eyes widen in recognition of what she was pointing out. She said it anyway.

"If Westerfield gave you that phone, and it's on, then you're getting tracked."

Fuck. She was right.

19

"Fuck."

Christina heard his swear loud and clear as he continued to hold his hands up and waited for the buzzing to pass. Even if he didn't answer it, the damage was done.

Christina stepped forward, still assuming Noah had to have been located. Westerfield would know he was already on de Gottardi/Little land… probably as of this morning. She watched as her new partner pulled the phone out and hit the power button, making the screen go black.

"There." He said it on a sigh, but Christina was shaking her head, angry at both of them.

"Just because it's off doesn't mean you're not still being tracked." She turned and started walking forward, faster now. Westerfield might already have other agents in the area.

"Do you think your SAC would track his agents even with the phone off?"

"You don't know him very well, do you?" she shot back.

Noah had the decency to look contrite for a moment. "I've barely met the man. Once he offered me a job and I turned him down—"

"Really?" Christina came to a stop, surprised by that comment. Maybe knowing what was happening here was her best bet. She waved her hand around the tunnel as though to say, *yet you're here now*. For a moment, she watched as Noah appeared to have some kind of internal debate. She told herself she didn't care how it shook out. But she waited.

When he didn't say anything, she started moving forward again with a heavy sigh. But it only took a few steps before he said, "This time, I called him."

Continuing on, hoping they were past the halfway point, she tried to keep the conversation casual. "So you turned him down but then called him back and changed your mind?"

"Not really. I didn't change my mind, I just got kicked off of my old job."

"Ooh, Miami Dade..." She remembered what he'd said at the store. "Whatever for?" But before he could answer she filled it in. "For doing things like you did to me in the grocery store?"

"Well, not that bad. Very minor things in comparison. I didn't even get caught at it. My arrest rate was just too high."

"Poor Agent Kimball," Christina replied snarkily, and then wished she hadn't.

She had a low bar here. She only had to be better than Westerfield was, and she'd already slipped a bit. "When we get up, you'll need to destroy your phone. Chuck pieces out into the grass. They'll find it, they'll know you were here.... Well, they already know you're here."

Behind her, she heard him sigh and she assumed he was nodding along. She kept pushing forward, not liking the target that was on her back and not liking that she'd been slow to spot it.

His voice told her he was right behind her. *Good.* "But given the fact that I went through one of the tunnels, won't they—"

"Maybe not. They might think you walked the distance." She pointed up over their heads and picked up the pace a little more.

"At least it doesn't incriminate *you*."

She heard the underlying accusation in his voice but ignored it. He'd taken this assignment. They'd all gotten mixed up with Westerfield, and none of them was truly innocent.

Christina kept talking. "When you destroy your phone, I'll give you the spare burner I have in my pocket."

Dammit. She'd been happy to meander along down here. The air was cool, but not cold. The tunnels were monotonous, except for the occasional spots where a granite wall jutted out from one side or another tunnel connected in. But now, knowing that Noah firmly had them traced to this exact point, she felt anxious to get out.

"I don't think—"

"You can have my burner phone, or no phone at all." She wasn't budging on this. She'd bought that phone. She knew where it was and where it had been. And she liked the fact that he would no longer even have an option to turn her in.

Then again, she was mad at herself for overlooking that he had his phone turned on in the first place. She should have been smarter. It wasn't just her joints that were feeling older and slower. She used to be better than this.

She'd been in a bit of a fog since Dana had been killed, and the only time she'd felt right had been out here, taking out Dr. Marks and his band of asshole huntsmen.

Christina didn't examine it further.

At least his phone was off now. The chances that the tracking device was also off were only about fifty/fifty, she figured, knowing what she did of Westerfield.

When they'd been silent for a few moments, Noah picked up the thread. "So I only met Westerfield once, when I was getting debriefed on the Caribbean case."

Christina nodded. "You were the new agent that was there. So Westerfield certainly knows what you can do."

Noah didn't answer that outright, but added, "He had me set up on this assignment before I even agreed to it."

Christina was not surprised.

"And he struck me as the kind of man who would manipulate his employees."

"Yet you took the job." She poked at him on purpose. She expected him to say, *Well, I was out of work,* or *I didn't have anything better to do.*

Instead, he replied, "So did you."

Ouch, that was a direct hit.

Quickly, she defended herself. "I was younger when I joined. And I wasn't allowed to join the FBI in any unit other than the NightShade division. Westerfield has someone at Quantico, looking out for—" She paused. "People like us."

"I went through Quantico, but I wasn't pegged for this division."

"Sometimes, he doesn't get people right away. Eleri was in the Profiling Division for years. He seems to figure it out eventually. Also, he goes out into the community and recruits."

"Really?" Noah sounded surprised. "You would think the FBI would have enough people coming in."

"Westerfield wants what he wants. My friend Donovan used to be a medical examiner." She kept pushing forward. Talking helped her stay calm in the dark, enclosed space that had been just fine until that stupid phone had gone off. Now she was tense and afraid. And feeling stupid. She could not get caught now. "Donovan was on that Caribbean case with you."

"I'd heard Donovan had a medical background, but he had a career?" Noah asked.

Was Noah as concerned as she was? He was Westerfield's newest hire, but he still had a lot to lose.

"Yes, Westerfield plucked him out of his job and offered him exciting new adventures and a chance to be what he was, rather than hide it."

From his response, this was all news to Noah, though he'd worked with two of her fellow agents on a previous case. Christina catalogued that little bit of information.

"All right." She pointed ahead and her breathing began to come a little easier. "See the change in color in the walls ahead? We're coming to the end of the tunnel."

"It's getting a little wider, too. Are they all constructed that way?" Noah asked.

"As far as I know. I get the feeling they took the time to build these well, right from the start."

The beam of the flashlight slowly took up more space as the tunnel widened.

They slowed as Noah looked around. Christina's gaze following his as they entered a rectangular space and he checked the four darkened corners. He had to be wondering which ones held other tunnels.

But above them, no light seeped through. They had the now important job of finding and opening the trap door above them.

"All right," Christina declared, still anxious about getting out. "I'm not trying to be rude about any experience you might have as a caver, I just don't want to be dangerous. We need to mark the tunnel we came from. Everything is symmetrical down here, and we could easily get disoriented. We need to know we can get out the way we came in, in case we can't get up there." She pointed toward the ceiling, although no access point was apparent.

"Good thought," Noah said and immediately laid his dead phone and his jacket smack square in the entryway to the tunnel where they had come from. It was perfect, too hard to miss.

They next began searching for the trap door. It was difficult to push on the ceiling because it was so far over their heads. Together, they'd worked with Noah lifting her up.

This part, she thought, she hadn't planned well enough for. How would she have gotten the door open by herself? How would *anyone* from down here?

"Wait," she told him, her hands precariously on his shoulders as she stepped down, out of his laced grasp. That had been far too intimate a position anyway. "Look around. There…" She pointed toward a darkened corner.

There, fitted directly into the crook of the wall, was a pole.

"It's got to be for opening the door."

They took turns poking at the ceiling above them. It was clearly the floorboards to a house, so there had to be a door here. It still took far too long to find the spot.

"Got it!" Noah finally offered excitedly.

She both saw the light and heard the squeak of hinges as he managed to give the door a little bit of a push. Together, they grabbed the pole, using their strength to lift the too-heavy door.

Immediately, Christina saw their next problem. As the light came in, so did the leaves and dirt. This home where they'd arrived had also been burned out and was open to the elements. She couldn't catch a break today.

Together they pushed the door up until it fell open. Being over her head, the door was out of range for her to know who they might have signaled by opening it. But they still had to get out.

Once again, Noah boosted Christina up. Even as she cautiously stuck her head up and checked the surrounding area, she was thinking she could leave him there.

She pulled herself out, staying low to the floor, her face closer to dead and rotting leaves than she would like. But Noah…. he'd be stuck down in the tunnels until he could find a way to get out—

She watched as his fingertips appeared over the edge just as she was turning around to reach down to him. He slowly muscled himself up.

Nope, she thought, *he wouldn't have been stuck.* "I was going to reach down and grab you," she whispered to him.

Catching on, he kept his own voice low. "I got it."

She wasn't sure if he was just following along or if he was scared down there in some way. Maybe he was trying to prove to her that she couldn't trap him in the tunnels.

She stayed low, not quite knowing where she was. This house hadn't burned quite as badly as the first one. Two of the walls still stood, but the one beside her was fully missing, showing her the open prairie beyond.

She watched as Noah stood up to his full height.

Stupid rookie move, she thought, just as she heard the gunshot and the wall beside them exploded.

20

E leri watched as Donovan's eyes widened at the sight of the book she'd set between them.

"I found it in the attic," she said. She waited a moment for her friend to absorb everything. They sat on his couch, on opposite ends, which was about as close as she was able to get to human contact right now. That hug had been everything she needed, but then she'd stepped back again.

"You made it to the attic?"

She was nodding as he continued.

"In my mental image, you sat on that couch and stared out the large picture window at the grass waving for days on end."

Unable to help herself, Eleri threw her head back and laughed. She felt as good as she had in a long, long time. She didn't even have to say it.

Donovan smiled, too. "Shit. I nailed it, didn't I?"

"For the first several days, yes. Then I realized I'd been sitting on my ass and staring at the grass growing for too long. And I decided to try to take control of things." She sucked in a breath before making her admission. "I could either do nothing or I could figure out how to do this right."

Donovan nodded, smiling at her comment, and something about that twisted a key or opened a door inside her, but it set her free. The words came more easily than she'd expected. "I didn't mean to kill him."

"I know." Two simple words spoken in a clear, plain tone let her know that he wasn't just speaking. He understood.

She breathed easier again. "But I decided that I can't bring him back. So I have to go forward."

Donovan nodded again, and then he—as he sometimes had over the past several years—offered some very insightful thoughts. For someone as quiet and self-isolating as he often was, he must have always been watching everything around him, because he understood far more than he'd ever let on. "Would you bring him back if you could?"

It was an interesting conundrum and one she hadn't thought about. She would have to go back and change it in time... make things such that she hadn't killed a person she hadn't intended to. It took a moment of her sitting on the couch, curled into a small ball and thinking, to say, "No, he's not worth the effort. I can't promise that if I hadn't killed him then, I wouldn't have had to kill him later on."

"I'm honestly not sure you didn't have to kill him then. I get that it wasn't what you intended, but I don't doubt that it was the right thing to do. He was coming after us. He was coming hard and with skills we weren't prepared to fight. And you saved us all."

Eleri loved that Donovan didn't say it with any kind of gushy I-owe-you-my-life tone. He said it as a statement of fact. Because, somewhere along the line, with no spoken agreement, she and he had come to terms with the fact that they would save each other's lives over and over and over.

She had told herself many of these same things already, but it was impressive how hearing them from Donovan somehow loosened the knot in her chest. She could tell Donovan anything. He wouldn't always agree and he might even judge her, because he wouldn't ever let her go batshit. But he would always have her back, right or wrong.

As she pondered this, it was Donovan who cracked the silence.

"So help me out with this Bodhi issue."

"He's not here." Eleri waved her open hand as though to demonstrate the empty room around them.

"That's the problem. He came here, and I can't figure out what he did."

Eleri felt slow, but she was catching on. "So you're saying we know Bodhi well enough—not *well*, but well enough—to know that he doesn't go anywhere or do much of anything without a purpose."

"Exactly." Donovan stood up and paced, his anxious stride giving her an insight into just how much his brother's visit had bothered him. "So, there are two options, I think. One—he came here and did something to me or to my house, but I can't find it. Or—two—he was interrupted and left before he got it done."

This time, it was Eleri nodding along.

"There's another big problem," Donovan added. "He never came *inside*. At least I can't smell him in here. But I can't smell anything different in the yard, either. And we're still missing some Dauphine sisters. We know that Bodhi was in league with them. They have powers I can't detect." He left the last part hanging.

More like me, Eleri thought, but didn't say out loud. She realized he was asking her to stay.

"You were alone for a while," he continued. His words were truthful, but she wasn't ready for decisions. He offered them anyway. "Maybe the work is what you need now."

It was plausible, she thought. She sure as hell didn't know what she needed. So she changed the subject. "I've been practicing out of the book. It's been pretty good to be at Bell Point Farm and be far away from everything. Now if I blow something up, no one calls the fire department on me."

He laughed. This time it was his turn to sweep his hand in a grand, encompassing gesture, but directing her gaze out the window. "There are tens of thousands of acres of National Forest out there."

"And what if I screw up and burn it to the ground?" she asked, a laugh underpinning her words.

"Can you really not put it out?"

"Maybe not! It depends on what kind of fire it is or … if I'm out cold." She realized only after she'd said it how much she'd given away.

"Jesus, El," Donovan said. "You definitely need someone around."

She realized he was right. The time she'd awakened on the floor with a bowl of her spellwork still burning had been a turning point. Even though she'd been out for several hours, the flames had continued to burn, telling her she wasn't as skilled as she thought. She could have used another hand.

Maybe she should stay.

The idea had barely cleared her thoughts when both their phones buzzed simultaneously. And that could only mean one thing.

21

Another shot split the air over his head and Noah pressed himself closer to the floor—if that was possible. He was inching his way back toward the trapdoor. Luckily, it was still open and inviting him to drop down and out of the range of fire.

"Don't." The harsh word came from Christina. "Don't move."

Noah had already decided that the spot they'd come from—which was empty—was better and safer than the one they jumped up into.

Christina was lying still, a silent form amid the leaves and detritus on the floor of the house. Looking around and making assessments, she operated in the way he'd been trained to do, but was finding very difficult at the moment.

Clearly, she had been shot at far more often than he had.

Behind him, the wall suddenly exploded again, sending chunks of plaster raining down. Though he wanted to turn his head and assess any threats coming from that side, he didn't dare move. Another bullet would come far faster than any of his reflexes would work.

Instead of watching Christina, he scanned the area, trusting that the agent would do what was right.

He almost lost his lunch as he watched her fiddle around on her clothing and then pull out her badge. She held it up high and yelled at the top of her voice, "Agent Christina Pines."

The silence in the air following her proclamation startled Noah, who thought these people might start shooting at FBI agents on their property. Some would and some wouldn't, but these guys were clearly already five bullets into the "yes, we'll shoot" camp.

But if the FBI was already there and they were already shooting? Well this was more likely to be a Waco or a Ruby Ridge than a *Gosh sorry, my bad.*

She hollered out again. "FBI. NightShade division. Agent Christina Pines."

This time, a gruff voice replied, "I heard you."

The statement had a definite *Hold your horses* tone to it. In any other situation, Noah would have found that funny, but here he was happy for any tone as long as his head remained attached to his body and his blood wasn't pumping out of a hole in his chest.

Christina was far bolder than he, slowly rocking upward and coming to a sitting position. She should have been on her toes, he thought, even as he debated getting up himself.

If she was safe sitting up, then he would look ridiculous lying here, face down in the leaves and dirt. But if he stood, or even moved to curl himself into a small ball, he might get shot.

If he was up, he could also be ready to run. So Noah began slowly rolling to his side and pulling his feet up. He was trying to look non-threatening as he pulled his limbs into a better position to run, if he had to.

It suddenly occurred to him that he didn't know if Christina could outrun bullets. Or did they bounce off her? He'd seen a lot of strange things in his few encounters with NightShade officers. Also, he knew what she definitely *could* do—so why hadn't she made these people think things like *don't shoot at the agents in the old house?*

He was beginning to get very irritated when she offered up his name.

"This is a fellow agent, Noah Kimball," she told the voice in the distance. And now Noah did get to his feet. He was opening his mouth to tell her to shut the fuck up when she turned and, under her breath, growled, "What are you exactly? A Pinkerton?"

He hopped up, his toes now firmly planted under him, ready to run. The fact that a bullet hadn't cut the air for almost a full minute was now making him more nervous, not less. Out of breath with his tension, he ground out a one-word response. "Later."

Even he wasn't quite sure *what* he technically was on this case.

But right now, he was more concerned with her *lassaiz faire* stance, sitting cross-legged in the dirt, while shooters pointed guns at them.

Just as he was getting ready to berate her, he watched a form appear out of the distance. A man in light-colored clothing was getting close enough to no longer blend into the tall golden grasses and the trees. He walked in waist-high grass, his rifle in his hand. At least now he aimed up, not at Noah.

He didn't relax.

The man was rounder, older. Mostly bald or with thin, pale hair. He was flanked on either side by young, virile men wearing only sweat pants. There were seven of them. Noah took stock as they slowly got closer.

He didn't see any guns other than the rifle. It matched the shots he'd heard fired. Still, Noah held tightly to his own gun, which seemed to have miraculously appeared in his hand.

"Put it in your holster" Christina spat the words at him without moving her mouth. She smiled and waved at the approaching people as Noah debated.

Christina hadn't even drawn hers. He was trusting the hell out of her on this one. But he slid the firearm back into its holster.

There seemed to be an unspoken agreement that the two groups would wait to talk until the men got to the building. So Christina turned to Noah, clearly much more relaxed than he was, and more than she'd been when they were getting shot at.

"I really thought we'd run into them sooner."

Noah took a moment to wrap his mind around it. She'd said a whole family lived here—or at least most of it. They were like Donovan. And the ones in the Caribbean. Were these wolves everywhere?

"I knew they were here," Christina said softly, almost as though she was psychic. But in the next breath, she cleared it up. "Did you notice the lack of wildlife? For a place that's been abandoned for several years, there are only a few birds. Just little songbirds here and there in the trees, but no real evidence of fox burrows or deer or cougar packs, the kinds of things you'd expect—"

Noah interrupted her. "I saw coyotes in the distance yesterday."

She narrowed her eyes at him, as though he were being ridiculously dumb. And after a moment, he realized he was. It hadn't been *coyotes* he'd seen in the distance. Fuck, yeah. He'd been dumb.

Mentally, he'd known what was here. He'd seen Donovan. He'd

never seen one of them do a full change, but it had been enough to know the form the other agent could assume. Noah had seen the men in the Caribbean, and a few women, also do it. He should have been more alert.

In fact, the closer the little group got, the clearer it became. He saw one of the people was a woman. A tank top graced her narrower shoulders and she had a firm, rigid style to her gait. Her hair was a shock of white on her head.

Noah was still assessing when Christina called out, "Hey, Will!"

Suddenly, she sounded not just confident of the people approaching, but downright friendly. She stood up and dusted off her butt. "Figured I'd run into y'all down in the tunnels."

Y'all? Noah thought. Maybe she was just adopting local customs.

But as they got closer, and Noah became more convinced that his life wasn't in mortal peril, he noticed something strange. The group of the five of them walked in almost military precision. He'd catalogued it when they first popped up, but he hadn't stopped to think about why they might be doing it.

As he scanned around, he found another person far in the distance. And as he looked further, he spotted another. He noticed the grass ruffling off to the sides of the walkers. It seemed several wolves were following along.

This was the pack. It wasn't random at all. They acted in military precision on purpose. And Noah was willing to bet the scant clothing on some was because they'd gotten close as wolves and then changed in the grass right in front of him. Only he hadn't seen it.

The group was not random at all. They'd made sure they had every weapon at their disposal—guns, opposable thumbs, speech, speed, stealth, and teeth. As they'd gotten even closer, he noticed that their eyes were wary. They looked at him differently than they did Christina. They were on the lookout for something threatening. But that something was neither Noah nor Christina.

22

Christina stayed sitting where she was, fighting an overwhelming urge to stand up and run to hug Will.

Though she'd said a proper goodbye before leaving the de Gottardi/Little land last time, she hadn't been prepared for how strongly she'd feel right now.

It was good seeing him upright, hale and healthy, a gun in hand as he stalked toward her. None of those things was welcoming, but they all meant he was here, and he was protecting his family—exactly as he had always done. He hadn't always done it with a gun in his hand. Still, it seemed he spent a good amount of his time leading the young wolves through whatever training and teaching they needed to survive in a world that didn't really know they existed.

"It's good to see you again, Pines," he said as he finally got close enough to the house.

Christina knew he'd been examining her as he approached. The assessment was well deserved. She was a little surprised to realize she trusted the man in front of her—the one who'd shot at her—more than she trusted the one standing beside her. The one from her own unit. *Interesting.*

Now that Will was close enough, she moved her hand to gesture between the two men. "Noah," she offered, "this is Will Little—patriarch of the de Gottardi/Little clan. Will, this is Noah Kimball, newly minted NightShade agent."

She added on the last part even though she wasn't quite certain about the details. Something in the way Noah squirmed made her think that description wasn't completely right.

Leaning forward, hand extended respectfully, her erstwhile partner stayed low. It made sense, given that they were sitting up higher than the others already. They had a height advantage of having the raised foundation. She watched as Will grabbed his hand in a firm shake, just as Noah said, "I'm glad your aim is off."

Will did not let go for a moment and replied only, "It's not."

Christina fought her grin, despite the fact that her heart was still pounding from the bullets that had been flying very close to her head recently. "I'm glad it was you and not someone else." She hoped to diffuse the situation a bit.

Will's soldiers stood back, shouldering their rifles and letting the conversation go on. Their eyes continued roaming the area around them.

Christina hadn't missed the fact that at least four other wolves were out in the grass, patrolling and marking a border around them.

"What's got you stalking your own land and firing on the people you see?" she asked Will, keeping her tone friendly. She wanted to ask, "What's with all the military get-up?" but she thought she knew. She'd seen too much in Westerfield's files before she went off the grid and headed this way. It was that file that had made her leave.

Still, they shouldn't have reacted to her arrival with quite so much hostility …unless Marks had already been here. But Christina wanted to hear from Will.

"We slowly started coming back about six months ago," Will began. "We laid low, did what rebuilding we could, and kept our eyes on things."

"Rebuilding?" She hadn't seen evidence of that. Her brief inspection had revealed only burned-out shells of houses. But she hadn't walked the whole property, either. It was far too big.

Just then, Noah joined the conversation. Luckily, his question was the same word: "Rebuilding?"

She wanted to motion him to stay quiet and let her handle it, but any gesture would have been recognized.

"Mostly underground. We did some small, movable dwellings in other areas on the place."

Shit. They were checking the lay of the land. *Their own land,* she thought. What a crappy thing to have to do. But even as she thought it, Will surprised her.

"About five days ago, we lost three of our own."

Quickly back calculating, Christina tried to make the timeline fit. She thought she was close behind Marks. In fact, she was relatively sure of it. "How did Marks get here three days before me?"

Will clenched his jaw, and she realized his grief was still fresh. He answered as though he were reporting on troops, but she knew. These were his family members. "Don't know. Last I heard, he was in prison."

"He escaped." Christina thought for half a beat before spitting out the information Will and his family should have been the first to have. "It was about six months ago. Were you not warned?"

"We'd heard rumors."

"Rumors aren't good enough." Her blood was boiling. The Night-Shade agents had known Marks was missing. "I would have alerted you myself if I'd had any idea the Bureau wasn't telling you. I'm so sorry."

"Not your fault," came the immediate reply.

But it felt like it was.

"We have a few channels," Will said with a rough tone. They all knew the de Gottardi/Little family should not have to rely on rumors that the man leading an army to commit a genocide on their people had escaped custody. "But no, there was no official word, and we weren't confident… not, until a few days ago."

Fuck. "Did anyone see him?"

"I smelled him."

Good enough, she thought. But as the words passed through her brain, another crack sounded between them. There wasn't even a noise—just the feeling of the air splitting around her.

She had learned working this job that things didn't come the way you thought they would. People didn't always automatically recognize gunfire. And even if she did, by the time the sound reached her, it would be too late.

To Will's far right, one of his soldiers offered only a small noise as the air left his body. The fifth in their little formation, he made one sharp, gurgling sound as he twisted and fell to the ground.

23

Noah scrambled to get low to the ground. Time passed in slow motion once again. His reaction was immediate and he hit the deck before a thought pass could through his brain.

None of the de Gottardi/Little people had raised a rifle. This had come from somewhere in the distance.

Simultaneously, he thought, *That shot wasn't for me*, as he watched one of the men twist and drop at a weird angle. Noah imagined he could see a fine spray of blood, but he wasn't sure if it was real or not.

In front of him, Will quickly crouched low, his own rifle now swept upward and poised. His finger was ready to pull the trigger as he used the nose of the barrel to scan the area, ready to kill anything that moved.

Though it all happened in a split second, his actions offered multiple confirmations that the shot was from someone other than the de Gottardi/Littles.

Noah had just been shot at by two different warring factions in the last thirty minutes, and he'd had about enough. His gun, already in his hand, was aimed outward and he was on his belly, his eyes scanning the world through the notch of the site.

He saw nothing in front of him. Nothing moved in the quadrant the shot had come from—if he'd been correct in his assessment. Split-second analysis wasn't always correct, though.

From the corner of his vision, he heard a growl of rage. Several of them, in fact. He watched surreptitiously as faces contorted and jaws moved outward. The remaining three who'd stood near Will leapt into action, none so fast, or so wildly, as the white-haired woman. Her rage permeated the air around her.

Then she was gone.

Her clothes were already peeled as her body changed, the White Wolf took one giant leap before she disappeared into the depths of the tall grass, leaving only a trail of moving grass behind her.

The other two followed quickly and Noah had to force his attention away from the fantastical scene before him and focus on the task of preventing his own sudden death.

Only Will Little remained in human form.

Noah felt his blood pumping through his system. His ears pounded in the same cadence, still ringing from the gunfire. *There were two shots*, he thought as he catalogued his memory from his position pressed low into the sharp twigs and leaves and dirt.

He considered the option of rolling over and dropping back down to the trap door. He would save himself, but then what use would he be to the others?

He also might get himself trapped. In fact, he would *most likely* get trapped beneath the houses, lost and unable to find his way safely out.

As more growls reached his ears, he realized stealth was now a thing of the past. So he watched until he caught sight of ears and snouts peeking just above the grass. All the wolves ran in one direction. They clearly knew where the shooter was, and he steadied his aim that way, watching for any movement that wasn't them.

Beside him, Christina's sweeping gaze caught his and he realized that she was likely thinking all the same things he was. She didn't nod at him; the movement would have been too big and might have drawn attention to her. But some subtle shift in her muscles told him she agreed with his plan.

Together, they turned to face the other direction, weapons swinging as they softly rolled in tandem. Any good attack would come from multiple sources at once. They needed to watch the side the wolves weren't keeping an eye on.

Noah tried to steady his breathing. His lungs fought hard to drag in as much air as possible, but without sound or movement. Noah needed silence. He needed a steady hand.

The adrenaline would keep his vision clear.

Maybe too much. It seemed as if every little blade of grass rustling in the wind demanded to be shot. As he ran a quick visual sweep, he realized that the scene had stilled.

Will and the wolves were gone. The sound of their war cries still hung in the air, but they were off in the distance, chasing their quarry.

Noah and Christina, fully human, had been left where they started, on the foundation of the house, hoping for the leaves to be adequate cover.

Forcing a long, slow breath, he dragged the air softly through his nose, his chest fighting the beat of his caged heart, his eyeballs twitching side to side, as he watched.

Maybe it was luck.

Maybe random timing was the only reason he saw the very slow movement as the head of dark hair rose above the tips of the wheat.

The shape in its hand too much resembled the shape of a gun, blackened into shadow so it didn't reflect light and give away the shooter's position.

Making a small adjustment, a pull of one shoulder, a slight shift of his hips, he executed a low, soft roll, affording a mild change in his aim.

Noah breathed in through his nose. Stopped. And pulled the trigger.

24

C hristina turned at Noah's movement. He'd already fired by the time she spotted what had activated him.

She heard what she thought was a small grunt in the distance, but she thought it was probably just her imagination. Her ears were still numb to sound and ringing from the retort of live fire.

She, too, had aimed on a rustle in the grass and fired. Only after she pulled the trigger did she regret it. Her chest constricted in on her, and she felt the heat of shame rush her body. She had not properly identified her target.

She had located the person, but she had no idea if she might have just taken out one of the de Gottardi/Little clan.

Fuck. The sound rolled off her tongue, probably louder than she intended. She didn't hear it, but Noah turned his head to look. Could he hear her? He looked back at the grass before she could ask.

She'd been uttering that word so many times recently. What had she done? With no thought for the live fire going on around her, or the fact that anyone might mistake her for the enemy, she bolted to her feet like a runner at the beginning of the race. Leaping off the edge of the building platform, she sped for the spot in the grass where she'd shot her victim.

She felt more than heard Noah right behind her. He was fast, but she was faster—and fueled by regret.

Please God, don't let it be one of the wolves. Please God.

She didn't pray often. Wasn't confident she believed in much of anything. Not with the way her own life had gone. But right now, she would take help from any higher power that was listening.

Her feet pounded the earth, and it felt good to do something. Even closing the distance was an accomplishment. Her victim had been in the distance, about as far away as one could expect to hit a moving target with a nine millimeter.

When she arrived at the spot, she pulled up a few feet short. The evidence of her marksmanship was clear on the grass. Blood spatter decorated the tips of the wheat nearby and marked a clear path away from the position.

There was no path into the spot, however, indicating that whoever or whatever she had shot had been moving much more smoothly on the way here. It didn't take much of her FBI training to realize that whoever she had shot was quite injured. The grass was leaning to the side to reveal the footsteps and what looked like the occasional fall, as her quarry stumbled away.

Noah must have sidestepped her position at the last moment, so he didn't slam into her when she stopped abruptly. He'd been running directly in her slipstream, taking advantage of her laying down the tall grass in front of him. In fact, they left a path like an arrow pointing directly to where they were.

Now, she breathed heavily. She tried to survey the area, but the grass acted as cover. She was only able to see directly down the fleeing man's path a short distance until it turned. She stepped to the side so as not to mar the tracks, noticing that Noah had already gone on in front of her, examining the evidence.

"Injured leg," he said, and pointed. "Heading that way."

When she found the right angle, the path became clearer. Then it turned again, and she'd have to move up to that point to see where it headed next.

In the distance, she heard more gunfire, but she paid no attention until Noah tugged on her sleeve.

"Get low," he hissed. "Christina, don't become the next victim here."

Yes, she thought, there'd already been another one. And she was sure this victim was one of Will's people.

Why had she shot back without fully identifying her quarry?

Crouching low made their job harder, but the two of them

together followed the blood trail, which seemed to be getting lighter the further they went. It tapered quickly until she had to work to find the next smear or drop. Whoever she'd shot was working hard to stanch the flow.

That was good, if it was one of the locals. Bad if it was one of Marks' hunters.

At last, the trail disappeared into the woods.

"I can't track that," Christina sighed.

"Me either." Noah shook his head. "I'm not getting anything."

She frowned at him for only a moment. *What did he mean?*

They stared loosely into the woods for a moment, watching for any movement, but saw none. Whatever they had followed was now cloaked behind the trees, which meant it had the advantage.

"We need to go back," Noah said softly.

Her legs aching, Christina turned away carefully. She didn't want to present her back to whatever might be waiting in the woods. Now she knew that she hadn't killed it, whatever or whoever it was. Only a few specific injuries would prevent a person from aiming and shooting a weapon, taking them down as they walked away.

She suspected she'd hit her target lower in the leg, given the way the grass was laid down. Her victim could still kill her—and Noah too.

If it was one of Will's people that she'd shot and maybe fatally wounded, she couldn't fault them if they shot back.

So she turned around and headed back to the original spot where the blood spatter remained, only to run into the white-haired, female wolf. She stood there in human form, wearing a tank top and sweatpants once again. Christina must have looked at her oddly, because she curled one side of her lip, revealing a long, white canine. It was huge, even for her kind.

"Will carries them," she snarled, motioning to her clothing and enunciating each word harshly. Her tone let Christina know that she didn't like the intrusion and that it was none of her business.

Christina nodded and apologized. "I'm sorry. I'm not sure who I got." She waved a hand at the stained grass they gathered around.

The woman offered a low, but all-too-human, growl. Even as she did, the tone changed and her face pushed forward. Christina tried not to watch, fascinated—after all, she had just been slapped back for her facial expression wondering how the woman managed to get her clothes back on.

When the growling stopped, the white-haired woman bent over, put her face down near the blood, and sniffed. Immediately she replied, "Not one of ours."

The boulders that lifted off of Christina were far more than she expected. She'd already been readying her defense. *We were being shot at.* The grass had rustled very near to a location where another shot had just come from. And the one shot that killed had killed one of Will's guards.

But the new information negated the need for that defense. The loss of guilt momentarily overwhelmed her. Christina put her hands on her knees and wondered if she could pull off looking as though she was simply trying to look closer at the forensic evidence. She breathed deeply, not because she was sniffing at the scene, but to let the shift in her body roll though.

Beside her, White Hair gave her the side eye and sniffed again. "Male. Middle-aged. Not the alpha." She chuckled a little bit, and Christina had to wonder if her victim had peed when he'd been shot. Maybe that's how this woman could read all that information.

Then again, if she could smell it, Christina thought chances were good that the area was laced with lingering pheromones.

It seemed White Hair was done with her assessment. She turned and headed back to where Will and the others were meeting up, not caring if Christina and Noah followed.

What's your name? Christina wanted to ask, to try to be friendly. But she didn't dare. This woman clearly did not want friendship. So Christina and Noah silently trailed in her footsteps.

They headed to the other site, the place where Noah had shot someone. Christina was confident that a dead body lay warm and bleeding into the grass.

Better evidence here, she thought. As she arrived, Will took one look at her, then pointed down, indicating something she couldn't see.

"Check this out."

25

Noah stepped closer and tried not to breathe. The tangy smell of fresh human blood filled his nasal cavities, and he wondered what these wolves must be thinking.

Did it smell worse to them? It certainly had to smell stronger. The scents carried far more information than what he was able to glean from them. He could only distinguish "lots of blood" and "a lot like human/probably human."

The Wolf with the white hair had extracted far, far more.

Now a bevy gathered round. He knew them all to be wolves, except maybe the old man. He wasn't sure about Will. Their faces slightly protruded as they sniffed at the body. Noah stepped closer, hoping he wasn't interfering with their process.

He felt a need to see who, exactly, he had killed. It had been a long time since he'd had to kill anyone. Mostly, he talked them down. Made them trip or think they had a gun in the middle of their back, as he had with Christina. He tapped them from behind, making his quarry believe more than one person was after them. He whispered in their ear.

None of that had been possible here. He'd seen the movement, recognized the human form, the rifle, and the aim. So he'd pulled the trigger.

As he got close enough, he saw now that he'd killed a woman. Though he fought the tidal wave of guilt at taking a life, it swamped him until he pulled himself out with the reminder that there had been no other option.

Turning to the body again, with a more analytical mind, he tried to decide if it was unexpected that the shooter was a woman—but, honestly, it wasn't. Something about the glimpse he'd caught had been enough to tell his subconscious that it was time to kill. So maybe he'd already seen that his victim was female.

She wore dark clothes, slightly camouflaged with shades of gray to break up the light. The coloring was probably better suited to evening or night than open day in the middle of a wheat field.

None of that had stopped her, though. The rifle, still clenched in one hand out at her side, was military grade and she had appeared to know how to use it. This was no random hunter out for wolves or coyotes. She was not part of a backyard militia, either, the kind with more chutzpah than training.

"It's one of Marks' people," Christina declared, even as Noah was wondering about the military grade weapons and the training.

Clearly, he was the new guy. New to NightShade, and new to this whole fucking mess. So he asked, "How do you know?"

"The gear is the same as we saw before," Christina answered, waving her hand openly, indicating that all the others had seen it. They were all standing upright now, as though it didn't matter. They were no longer open targets.

Somehow, Will and his people seemed to know that whatever pop-up rebellion had occurred, it had been quelled. Noah still felt like a target, but he wasn't going to be the only one to duck like a sissy. It might mean he was the only one to get his brains blown out, but he still wasn't going to do it.

Christina continued. "This is de Gottardi/Little land. Everyone around here knows it." She pointed back to him. "Think about how you got here."

She was right. No one could just *stumble* across this place. And now that he'd met the occupants, he was convinced the land was chosen for that purpose. A person had to be coming here to get here.

"Anyone hunting on this land, at the very least, had a damn good idea what they would find."

"They probably heard you announce you were an FBI agent," Will told her, not too harshly, but a definite tinge of disapproval in his words. Noah was glad not to be on the receiving end of that. Something about the older man commanded respect.

The white-haired wolf told the others what she smelled and then allowed several of the others to confer on what they found.

"She's alpha," one of the men commented almost sideways to Noah, and he wondered if they talked about everyone in pack terms. The white-haired woman tipped her head as though to say, *Of course.*

Interesting, Noah thought, holding his tongue and not asking, *Alpha of what?*

He had a sneaking suspicion that he was going to get a full-blown lesson very soon.

Behind him he heard the sound of someone approaching. Noah didn't move quickly or aim his weapon, even though it still weighed heavy in his hand and he was ready to act should the need arise.

As he turned, he saw one of the men walking slowly through the tall wheat. In his arms, he cradled his dead friend, perhaps a brother. They resembled the biblical sculptures of Mary carrying a fallen Jesus, and Noah felt the hit, even though he didn't know the dead man. The soldier moved slowly with the draped body cradled in his arms. It was obviously cumbersome, but far more respectful than throwing his deceased friend over his shoulder so that he could move more quickly.

As they approached, Noah saw the light glint off the walking man's face. Though his expression remained stoic, tears poured down, washing clear tracks in the dirt that Noah hadn't recognized until just then. It made a point that this wasn't just a soldier who was lost here today.

Noah swallowed and offered a small respectful, half nod. It didn't mean anything other than that he understood.

When he turned back to look at the wolves still ringing his victim, they were slowly poking at the body. One of them had even reached down and grabbed at her limp hand.

Noah's immediate response was, *Don't touch it!* They would ruin the evidence. But Christina didn't comment and he deferred to her, even though it felt wrong. Then again, the dead body was on their land. He wasn't going to say anything he didn't have to until he had a much better understanding of what was going on here.

"Look!" The one holding the dead woman's hand up pushed at the backs of her fingernails as though that were interesting.

"Really?" another voice chimed in.

This time, hands went to the dead woman's face and pushed at it, too.

Jesus, Noah thought. *Stop touching her.* But, once again, he bit his tongue.

They ran a finger along her jaw and up to the TMJ where the mandible joined the skull. Someone pointed with a swirl of their finger and they all nodded. Another finger pointed, though thankfully did not touch this time, at her long, straight nose.

Christina looked back and forth among the wolves, ignoring Noah. "Are you saying...?"

It was Will who nodded. He seemed to speak for the group. And as the others stood to their full height, and looked around one more time, the old man shocked the shit out of Noah.

"She's a wolf."

26

"E ll?" Donovan asked, his voice shaky. He needed to get her attention but didn't want to interrupt her.

She waved her hand to him, palm outward, as if to say *stop* or *stand back*. Or maybe it was simply part of some spell. He didn't know.

In the middle of the backyard, she'd pointed to a spot for him on one side of the space. Then she'd propped the ancient, leather-bound volume between them. Tilted toward her, the pages began to turn in the light breeze. Slowly, one by one, they flipped.

Or maybe it wasn't the wind at all.

Donovan didn't ask. His job was to stay silent.

Eleri's eyes looked glazed. He told himself that it was okay. He'd seen this before. He'd seen Eleri work spells with Grandmere. That still didn't stop it from being creepy as all fuck. And it didn't stop him from wondering if—maybe this time—something was actually wrong. He bit his lip and worked to not intervene.

She turned and walked solemnly into the house. For a moment, he wasn't confident that her feet actually touched the ground. Maybe she'd figured out how to walk on a slight cushion of air. She made no sound as she moved barefoot through his house. His superior hearing should have picked up the noise, however slight, had her feet actually contacted the floor.

Slowly, she moved from room to room, stopping in the middle of each, checking all four walls in turn. He could only imagine it was some spellwork equivalent of night vision goggles that allowed her to see things that the rest of them couldn't.

Eleri checked every room in his house. Every closet. In the bathroom, she slowly pulled back the shower curtain. And when she was done with all of it, she stood in his open kitchen space and turned to look at him.

Blink. Blink. Blink.

Then she was Eleri again.

"He didn't come inside." She said it with her usual intonation, and offhandedness, and damn if that didn't freak him out as much as the rest of it had. But he knew he was going to have to learn to live with it. Eleri was constantly gaining new skills.

While she'd already shown Donavan how she could now light a fire in a bowl, he hadn't yet figured out what use that particular trick might have. He was glancing around the room, checking to see if she'd left any psychic traces behind that he could see, but he couldn't.

She tilted her head and closed her eyes. When she opened them, once again, they were unfocused. Turning, she headed out the front door, her feet still not quite touching the ground. Eleri walked the yard in a grid pattern, and he wondered if he was seeing the intersection of the FBI agent and the witch.

When she'd covered everything and still hadn't spoken, she headed up the stone stairs and traced every inch of the front porch.

Blink. Blink. Blink. Then she was Eleri again.

"He pulled up the driveway," she said, as though she hadn't just emerged from a bizarre trance. "Then he came to the door. He knocked, but pretty quickly figured out you weren't home." Her eyes darted around the space, as though she hadn't really seen it the first time. "He tried to look in the window, but it seems he didn't see anything."

Donovan was grateful for keeping the curtains pulled. He'd even checked for cracks in the drapes, an old practice from his father's shady dealings. But, in general, it wasn't smart for a wolf to be seen, even in his own home.

Her voice pulled him back to the present. "And then he got a call."

"What?" Donovan asked.

"A phone call. Something that took him away."

"Did he take anything?" Donovan asked.

"No," she said, and then stopped. "Wait. He didn't take anything. But he *left* something."

27

C hristina sat on the back porch, sipping a very fine whiskey. It wasn't her usual drink—at least, in everyday life—but she wasn't going to refuse. And her morals—however slim they had proven to be in the past—refused to push Will Little and his people.

The whiskey burned going down, but she sipped politely, hoping no one noticed that she wasn't a whiskey drinker. If they did, they didn't say anything.

Surveying only the land in front of her made the scene seem quite idyllic. If she ignored the rest of the house, the porch was clean, clear, and set up with padded white, wood chairs. The rest of the house was burned out though, according to Will, there were two usable bedrooms. He'd said the clan had been using them as bunk houses.

Several of the other homes also had some usable space, and a few had full rooms set up under the raised foundations. Apparently, she and Noah simply hadn't picked the right ones, because they hadn't seen anything but abandoned property.

The white wolf shot back her fourth glass of the whiskey, ignoring Will's disapproval of her treatment of his good liquor. But he poured her another when she held the glass out. She mused, "I can't imagine the kind of self-loathing that would be necessary to do that job."

Christina blinked a little bit. There was nothing wrong with the statement itself. The woman who had shot at the de Gottardi/Little family and the agents had herself been a genetic wolf. It had been relatively obvious, once those who knew what they were looking for had come by and examined the body.

Christina wondered if they could smell what she was. Will had seemed to know right away, even though he hadn't been in wolf form. Then again, he was older than the rest, and she imagined he'd seen a few things in his time. Still, she shifted the topic. "The other shooter wasn't, though."

Christina took another sip, reluctant to speak. She wondered if anyone noticed that self-loathing wasn't the thing she wanted to have a deep discussion about. She couldn't loathe the group that she belonged to, because there wasn't anyone else like her—at least not as far as she knew. What would she do if she found someone like her? Kimball was the closest she'd come in a long time, and he had over-lapping skills, but he wasn't like her.

"Why would she kill wolves if she *is* one?" Noah asked the group, bringing the conversation back to where she didn't want it. He swirled the amber liquid as though he, too, were trying to cover the fact that he wasn't really drinking it.

Christina had to wonder just how squeaky clean Noah Kimball was. He didn't seem to understand why that woman might have joined Murray Marks's little army.

"The other shooter definitely was not one of us." The words were harsh, clipped, and almost spit from the mouth of the white-haired woman.

Christina still didn't know her name. "So they have a mix?"

"Looks like some standard issue human and some wolf," Will said. He shrugged but then added, "*We* have a mix."

True, she thought. Not all the de Gottardi/Little family exhibited these strange traits.

Apparently, she wasn't the only one who could shift the conversation. Will pointed with his glass before offering the subtle command, "Tell me about agent Kimball here." He topped off his own whiskey while he waited for her to think of what to say.

Christina appreciated that he felt comfortable enough—safe enough here—to drink, and she used it as a guideline. They must believe they could see everything coming. Whether that was because they knew that Marks' little lackeys were gone or because they had their own armed guards patrolling the perimeter, she didn't know.

She shrugged and looked at Noah. "Honestly, Will, I just met him myself, but he's with NightShade."

He huffed, as though being in NightShade wasn't truly a recommendation. But Christina couldn't think of any NightShade agent who hadn't come in here willing to lay down their lives for the family.

When the conversation stopped for a moment and Will's eyes swung back to Noah, the new agent took it upon himself to answer. "I'm technically a consultant."

"Consultant to do what?" Christina asked. She hadn't heard of Westerfield allowing consultants in the division.

"Well, I already found you."

Well played, Christina thought, as Will's eyes swung rapidly back to examine her.

"Did you leave the Bureau?"

"No." She said it, even though it wasn't completely true. She took a deep breath and this time she actually drank some of the whiskey.

"I mean, if Kimball here is maybe your replacement…" Will let the phrase trail off.

"Then that would be news to me." She could play the game as well as the rest of them. She tipped her head to Noah, indicating he should continue.

"I'm an agent with the Miami branch. I got put on administrative leave."

Well, that was a little more honest than she'd expected, but he kept going.

"Apparently, I've had too many arrests that they can't fully explain. So once I got bored of staring at the walls of my home, I called up the SAC and he offered me this position."

"When?" Christina demanded. *How long had Westerfield been stalking her with agents?*

"About ten minutes after I called him."

"You're telling me Westerfield put an agent out to the de Gottardi/Little farm without briefing them about NightShade?"

Noah opened his mouth then shut it as though he couldn't decide what to say. Then he answered simply, "Yes."

From the corner of her eye, Christina could see that Will slowly rolled forward, his feet curling under his chair. He moved his weight to rest on the balls of his feet. He was now counterbalanced and ready to spring. For once, he resembled more of the wolf she knew him to be.

Christina shook her head softly at him. Though Will didn't stand down, he did stop moving forward. Together, they waited.

"I wasn't assigned to the de Gottardi/Little farm," Noah said, looking throughout the group. He couldn't have missed the outward signs that they no longer trusted him. Will wasn't the only one ready to spring.

But Noah sat calmly, knowing his position put him at a disadvantage. He wasn't that drunk... so he had to be making a point.

"I was assigned to Christina." He shrugged. "Christina came here, so I came here."

"Well, now we have ourselves one hell of a mess," Will said, and Christina felt her stomach drop.

Had she brought Noah, and all the trouble that followed, right to the ones she was trying so hard to protect?

28

"Son of a bitch," Noah muttered under his breath, as all heads except Christina's turned toward him.

He wanted to say it again. But damn, he'd forgotten for just a moment that everyone here—except himself and Pines—had a much higher-than-normal ability to hear.

He'd made several decisions under duress today, and he was beginning to regret them. He had no phone with which to call SAC Westerfield. And as of right this moment, it would seem he wasn't getting paid.

He was still drawing his regular Miami Bureau salary while they investigated him, so that was a good thing. But getting kicked out three days into the new assignment wasn't how he'd imagined it going. He was certainly never going to get assigned with the Night-Shade division now. He reminded himself that when he'd first been offered the position, he'd turned it down flat.

He now waved off the wolf clan staring at him. He'd drunk a little more than he should have and was feeling a little dash of bold to go along with his stupid. The eyes—some hazel green, some gray, some bright blue, and a few an odd amber shade of gold—no longer stared directly at him. They didn't seem to quite let go of the embedded mistrust, though.

He sighed openly, though he shouldn't have. It was the same mistrust that they didn't quite seem to hold onto for Christina Pines

—who'd smashed his phone, ruined his job, and conned him into a situation where he almost immediately was shot at.

He shot the whiskey this time.

To be fair, he'd willingly gone with her. And he'd *let* her smash the phone. He'd also wandered underground tunnels and popped up in a burned-out home on a property where he knew there was likely to be some kind of Family Feud going down. He tipped his head back and accepted his own culpability in the mess as the whiskey burned its way down his throat.

It was strange now listening to Christina—who was often reticent and very standoffish—open up and talk to these strangers. Clearly, they weren't strangers to her.

The white-haired woman suddenly seemed more than happy to answer Christina's questions. It didn't seem as though the five glasses of whiskey she'd drunk had affected her at all. "I left the family a handful of years ago. I ran with a pack in New Orleans for a while. We weren't into anything good, that was for sure." She shrugged as though the legality or morality of it didn't matter. "Once the pack dissolved, about a year or so ago, I wandered for a while. But I heard about the family coming back here. So I came to check it out."

"She stayed," Will said with pride that a lost wolf had returned to his own pack.

Noah wasn't so sure.

Several other of the wolves told similar stories, indicating that they were free to leave and live their own lives. Several of the soldiers —the ones that Noah had considered to be Will's soldiers—had attended universities. A few had stayed close to the family, but one went to MIT. Another attended Harvard. He laughed it off. "Dual masters in poetry and English Lit."

None of this was what Noah would have expected. This was not at all the Amish-centric style of family he'd expected. Though everyone seemed to have drunk just as much as he had, Noah now could feel the alcohol molecules running through his blood. He knew he shouldn't ask, but he did anyway. "Are you all...?"

He let the words trail off, his whiskey glass tipping towards them one by one and nearly sloshing over the edge. *No, he definitely shouldn't have asked for the second refill.*

"Here? Yes," said one of the men, Darren, as he indicated all those on the porch. "But no, not the whole—"

"Not every one of us has it," Will interrupted, seeming to filter what was said. Noah wasn't sure if it was for Christina *and* him or just for his ears alone. Maybe Christina already knew or maybe they would fill her in on the details when he wasn't around.

"The plain humans don't come out on patrol," the old man added. "Their senses aren't as keen. We have about three really good soldiers who each did military time. They generally lead our groups, but they weren't out today…" There was a pause full of regret. "Didn't think we'd need it."

Noah let the scotch light up the back of his throat as it went down. Somehow, they'd built a family compound in the middle of the Ozarks with doctors and lawyers, lit majors and soldiers. This was not what Westerfield had prepared him to find.

The heaping helping of the blame for how he'd wound up was on his own head. Still, Noah felt there was plenty of guilt to spread around. He wanted to ask Christina if they knew what she could do. But it didn't matter if they knew, because *he knew*, so he continued sitting on this porch, sipping whiskey.

His thoughts were skewed—an effect of the alcohol, but it was too late to stop it.

Growing up, he and his brothers had all had a few wild talents. Only as an adult had he thought to question what kind of drugs his parents might have been taking before they'd had their kids. In school, he'd been unique. During training at Quantico, he'd tried to be less unique. And in his job with Bureau in Miami, he was *so* unique that they'd finally written him up for it.

But, here? Here he was nothing special. It was an odd feeling

He polished off the whiskey, mostly for something to do. It was a bad decision, but he wasn't sharp enough not to make it. So he didn't have to hand back a full glass, he turned to Christina and said, "I need to contact Westerfield."

"Why?" Her brows pulled together and he frowned back at her before he could stop it.

"I got hired for a job. Now I've been out of contact for more than ten hours."

They were all just watching the sunset as though they hadn't lost someone today. As though they hadn't killed an enemy combatant. As though there wasn't someone out there wounded, but probably still alive enough to plot revenge.

And he was a little bit drunk.

Noah wanted to make his way back to his car, head to a hotel room, and sleep this day off. He wanted to do the things he understood how to do. Instead, he was hanging out with creatures he'd only learned a few months ago even existed. They could rip him limb from limb, and they could probably smell the decisions he was making.

Christina raised an eyebrow at him as if to say, *That's not good enough.*

"Dammit, this is a job I took. Maybe *you* went AWOL, but I'm not intending to."

She was looking at him still. The strange look on her face clearly questioning whether he intended to turn her in.

He would have answered if he could form a truly solid thought, but his ideas were being a little slippery. As he opened his mouth, all of the wolves suddenly turned.

Noah couldn't say he'd really ever seen human ears prick up before, but they did it. The white-haired one's lips curled back, her very long eyeteeth looking almost vampiric in the fading light. She issued a low growl, even as Will reached out and put a soft hand on her arm. But they were all looking the same direction.

Unable to stop himself, Noah followed their gaze, noticing that Christina already had her gun pulled from the holster and that his hand was resting on the butt of his own.

In the distance, he finally saw what they must have spotted a while earlier.

Something rustled in the grass

29

Christina watched, stunned, as all the wolves launched into action. They flowed like water over the edge of the porch and poured into the tall grass beyond.

They shed pants and shirts, the white one's tank top quickly flung up and over the railing. Christina got the feeling that Will would have gathered the clothing had he not been standing with his rifle already aimed, the butt pressed against his shoulder, his finger covering the trigger guard.

Her own breathing had shallowed out and she watched as the wolves rustled through the grass. The humans had transformed so quickly and quietly, they had somehow managed to do so relatively out of her sight. She caught only the glimpse of a white ear here, a slash of black there as the stalks parted. Otherwise, she could only see where they had been.

It was impressive. She shuddered at the thought that their power might ever be turned against her. Her gun was raised and aimed, her own finger resting against the trigger guard. She supported her grip with her left hand, just as she'd been taught.

Though the light of the day was rapidly fading, she hadn't pulled her flashlight. She didn't like this situation. Whoever was coming up on them had been spotted in the distance. Were they announcing themselves poorly? Or were they sneaking up... poorly? Christina couldn't tell.

She watched as all the points in the field slowed, circled, and turned to come back.

Will immediately lowered the tip of his rifle until it pointed at the floorboards near his feet. He sighed heavily, the air gushing out of his lungs, sounding irritated. Christina could only take it as a good sign. It appeared they had either rounded up whatever was coming or made friends with it.

Beside her, she spotted the muzzle of another Glock. Noah was still aimed. Shaking her head at him, she lowered her own weapon, then reached out and tapped on his arm.

He was wound far too tightly right now, though she could understand. She'd known something was going on when Murray Marks' tracks led her here. There were wolves everywhere. Families of wolves resided all over the US... far more of them than anyone knew. But Marks had come back to the place he'd been defeated.

Or did he see his loss at the de Gottardi/Little farm as a win? Though he'd been captured, he and his little band of wolf hunters had burned the place to the ground.

Still, his vendetta seemed to be against all wolves, everywhere. Not just here. So why had he come back?

The man was an archaeologist and an anthropologist and, at one point, he'd been quite famous in his field, raising his granddaughter to be much the same. He'd lectured and become famous and hoarded the strange bones he'd found—which worked until it was discovered that he was not only stealing archeological finds but secretly funding a vendetta against those not like himself.

Between him and his genius forensic scientist granddaughter—now *agent*, GJ Jansen—they had discovered that the wolves had been embedded in human society for millennia.

He had a set of human bones more than 20,000 years old that appeared to have the same kind of anomalies that the modern-day wolves did. Whatever skills Christina had, or whatever she could do, she was a glitch in time. The ones running out in the field were part of an ancient bloodline and a family tradition—a network the likes of which she'd never understood.

Slowly, the clan arrived back at the edge of the porch. This time, when they stood up, there were not six heads, but seven. Christina scanned them all quickly, looking for the new face.

Even as she spotted it, she realized Will was ahead of her,

chucking a pair of the standard-issue gray sweatpants to the new guy. Then, one by one, they climbed up onto the porch.

When they'd left, they'd gone up and over the railing; now they appeared to be staying low, not quite as comfortable with being obvious.

"Taylor," Will said, still standing, his gun still aimed down. He'd backed up as the returning wolves had returned to where he was.

Christina realized that, in the fading light, the wolves were now only shadows on the porch. Tapping Noah once again, she motioned for the two of them to move out of the light as well. They were nowhere near as subtle about it, but at least they'd done their job.

"We got more," Taylor reported to Will. Whatever *more* meant. But it became clearer as he spoke. "We dispatched three at the perimeter."

"Together?"

"Solo," Taylor replied.

"How confident are you about that?" Will brooked no room for error.

Taylor shrugged. "Normally, *very*. But, right now, I'm not so sure." Then he looked around the porch and frowned. "Where's Dan?"

Will lowered his eyes and shook his head. Though Taylor's gaze immediately flicked to the newcomers, he nearly growled out the words. "They got Dan?"

"Shot," Will said softly. "Clean. The only good news is that it was quick."

A string of swear words rapidly came out of Taylor's mouth, flowing like the whiskey they'd just drunk but burning hotter.

It was clear Taylor and Dan had at least been friends, maybe more. Or maybe Taylor was just angry that another of his own had lost to the people trying to pick them off.

Now was as good a time as any to step out. "I need to talk to Noah for a moment," she told Will and wasn't surprised when, with a flick of a finger, he dismissed the two of them through the doorway, indicating they could catch a little privacy in what had once been inside the house.

She headed through, closing the door behind her, though the ceiling was missing and their little conversation would be open to the sky. She didn't know if the wolves on the other side could hear them, but the safer bet was that they could.

She let the shadows stand in for walls and waited as Noah

followed her. He was willing to come along, but was clearly skeptical about what she wanted. He was also more than a little angry about how the day had gone down. Normally, he would have covered that better—or at least, she believed he would have—but the whiskey was eating at him.

"So what do I do?" he asked a little loudly before she could even open her mouth. "You went AWOL and I protected you. But I need this to not cost me my job."

"I know," she said. "I think it's time to reach out to Westerfield."

From the look on his face, that had surprised Noah. But Christina shook her head and waved him off, almost too casually. "I didn't go AWOL for the purpose of going AWOL. Westerfield didn't want me to try to find Marks on my own. He kept trying to assign me new partners, and I don't work well with anyone. Not anymore."

Noah's face didn't change expression at all and she wondered what natural reaction he was hiding. But she didn't have time to care, other than to be pleased he might be sobering up a little. "My goal was just to come out and see where Marks was."

She almost felt the slap of her own lie, and immediately changed course. "No, my goal was to bring back his corpse and lay him at Westerfield's feet. Then I could feel I had finally accomplished something. But it doesn't look like that's going to be happening right away."

She paused, but Noah didn't move. He stared at her with his arms crossed and waited.

"We need more here than just us."

His teeth clenched, but he finally spoke. "Are you calling Westerfield, or am I?"

The words had barely left Noah's mouth when she felt the weight of a hand on her shoulder.

Her breathing stopped, and her heart rate flatlined.

No one should be on this side of the wall. The wolves were on the porch. Weren't they?

She hadn't heard anything. Nothing! And that could not be good.

She whirled, her gun raised and ready to be aimed, ready to take out anyone else she needed to today. She was not losing another of the de Gottardi/Little family, and she wasn't going down without a fight.

But even as she whipped around, the hand moved and quickly

clamped on her wrist. A quick twist removed her gun from her grasp before she could react. Her arm twisted away, and a pointy thumb put pressure at the back of her hand, forcing her entire upper body to buckle under that control.

With an immediate gut reaction, Christina felt the tickle at the back of her brain as she pushed out with everything she had, making her attacker believe he was on fire.

30

W ell fuck, Noah thought. *No more social drinking.* He'd only
downed the whiskey to get in good with Will Little, but it
wasn't the right thing. Here he was, trapped and about to get killed
and it hadn't been worth it.

None of this suited him—not that Miami Dade had really been
any better. But there had been something about this assignment
that, for a moment, he'd liked. Something felt right about being
asked to employ every talent he had, rather than hide what he was.
That had seemed good and right and purposeful... for about three
days.

Somehow, in the course of one afternoon, he'd likely become
unemployed. He also seemed to have picked up a new partner—who
was also likely about to become unemployed—and managed to drink
a little bit too much. And now he had his arm wrapped up enough to
stop him from adequately defending himself.

The liquor in his system made him want to sigh and just give up.
Luckily, his training railed against that inaction. So he assessed his
attacker.

She was smart—she'd gone for the hand controlling the gun. He
was not smart—he'd made poor choices and hadn't drawn quite fast
enough.

When her grip pressed at his wrist, activating a pressure point, he
almost gave up again. If he could have, he would have just tossed the

gun to her in surrender. The pressure point method worked because it hurt.

Her short stature and slim build gave him an advantage. So he did it: He flung his fingers open and let his weapon fall dramatically, clattering to the floor.

"Fuck. Shhhh!"

The words came from over near Christina. Noah wondered what the hell was going on.

Even as he swung his arm up and around, lifting her ever-so-slightly, she countered. His move was usually effective on a larger person. He should have had the advantage, but she hadn't flipped over or let go quite as easily as he had hoped. At least he now had her in an awkward position.

She hadn't hurt him, though she'd had the opportunity. Still, Noah wasn't going to let himself be controlled like this.

He went for an elbow strike and felt his momentum send him right past the point where he should have made contact. He'd completely missed. He managed to strike her shoulder with the heel of his palm, but she spun a little and managed to put more pressure on the hand she still controlled. His own fault. *Shit.*

From the corner of his eye, he saw that Christina was getting locked up, too. That only made things worse. She was his hope for rescue. But that was now a wash. Though no help was coming from that quarter, it also felt a little good to know that he wasn't the only one getting taken out.

"Jesus, Noah. *Stop!*" Christina yelled at him as he began to spin away, trying once more to reclaim his arm as his own.

"Noah! Stop!"

Despite the fact that her arm was twisted up in her face, Christina was reaching out with her hand. Not in a punch, or in a move to strike with an elbow. Her feet were planted, but she was bringing her arm in closer as if to *hug* her attacker.

And then she said loudly to the woman in front of her, "Walter!"

Okay, Noah thought. He had definitely had too much to drink.

Even as he thought that, a whisper came at his ear. "I'm an agent. Please, stop fighting me."

So he did. His shoulder went lax and she dropped his arm and stepped back, even as she whispered, "Shhh. We're trying to not alert anyone."

She said it with a sigh, as though Noah had messed up his own abduction by not being quiet. But that might not be the worst of it.

He realized Westerfield had probably sent another agent to reclaim both him and Christina, the moment Noah's phone had stopped pinging. That, in turn, only meant that Christina was right—he'd been thoroughly tracked by Westerfield. After all, his new boss had already been very clear that if Noah dialed him and then said he didn't know why he had called, Westerfield would assume it was Christina overriding his brain. Whatever this protocol was, it had likely been enacted when his phone stopped pinging. Noah wondered if these new NightShade agents were familiar with the de Gottar-di/Little property. They'd managed to find the one burned-out house that he was at, even without his phone giving them handy-dandy coordinates. *Lovely.*

He waited to be cuffed. The tightening of his chest had nothing to do with the liquor and everything to do with the fact that he'd lost another job.

But their new visitor didn't lock up his wrists, didn't grab him and twist his forearms and press them together behind his back or shove his face into the wall.

Instead, she stepped back and allowed him his freedom. As he watched, Christina hugged the dark-haired woman who'd just attacked her.

There were two newcomers. They were dressed in shadow, almost like Marks' people had been, but their clothing was different enough to distinguish them from the army that had been sent to take out the wolves. Christina turned then to the smaller agent—*Jesus*, Noah thought, *she looks sixteen!*—and gave her a hug. "GJ!"

But when Christina let go, the words that Noah had been thinking all along fell out of her mouth. "Oh, dear God, Westerfield sent you to take us in, didn't he?"

Walter answered, "Of course he did."

31

Christina felt her heart sink. She had to accept that her run was over. She'd chosen this path, all seven ways to hell, and it was time to face Westerfield and come clean.

Still, she needed more than just to be marched away. She'd suffer whatever punishment Westerfield meted out, but she needed to know if the family was going to get any help. Would any agents now be assigned to a unit here?

Obviously, the de Gottardi/Little family was exactly in Marks's line of sight. If they were going to recapture him, it would happen here. Unfortunately, that meant it would happen in the same place as last time, and using the same bait. The farm and the people here deserved more than being left to fend for themselves.

"So, how are we doing this?" Christina asked. They hadn't cuffed her yet and no one had dialed into the Bureau.

"Oh, we're not," Walter replied, smiling.

"You just said—"

"No, I said I was sent out to bring you in. I didn't say I was going to do it."

Walter pulled her phone out of some secret pocket in her slim pants and began tapping along with her thumbs.

"Are you messaging Westerfield?" Christina had to ask.

"No. Donovan."

Interesting, Christina thought. She'd wondered about the two of them.

"You went AWOL, but…" Walter said as she tapped away. "I got sent after you. And then I stayed a while and trailed along once I got close enough behind you."

Christina felt her eyebrows rise, but Walter kept talking.

"So I need to check in with Donovan, to let him know I'm okay."

Her eyebrows must have disappeared under her hairline. Walter Reed and Donovan Heath were a thing? Upon a little examination, it made perfect sense. Still, she had to know, "How long have you been following me?"

"A week."

Westerfield had definitely wanted to bring her in.

"You were behind me for a whole week?" She'd almost spat out the words as she realized that not only had newbie not-quite-an-agent Noah Kimball gotten the drop on her, but apparently Walter had been dogging her heels for even longer.

Hell, both Walter and GJ had snuck up on them right now. She wanted answers. She wanted an explanation of how she'd fucked up so badly that she had three other agents trailing her and had only caught on to one of them.

But there was no time for an answer, as Noah spat out the words, "Does nobody listen to your SAC anymore?"

His comment gave Christina pause. Westerfield should have been considered a commanding officer. His word should have been law. But over the last several years, the agents had been making more and more of their own decisions. They had a reasonable amount of autonomy in the field. But…. it *did* seem they weren't listening to the SAC as much anymore.

Maybe it wasn't just Christina questioning where Westerfield's loyalties and his goals lay.

Walter looked to GJ before saying, "Not as much as the chain of command would indicate. Honestly, I'm not always confident of Westerfield's motives."

Curiouser and curiouser.

Christina had felt that way for some time now. Westerfield had consistently sent her out without quite giving her enough information. She was beginning to wonder if there was some underlying link between the cases, something that would come back and reveal a cause. Was Westerfield siphoning money? Running shady deals? Or was he answering to some non-FBI or non-US-government higher power?

Sure, NightShade operated under its own umbrella. The beauty of it was that they were accountable to almost no one except Westerfield.

But who did Westerfield report to?

Christina had never really found out. And as she looked from Walter's face to GJ's, she realized she was not the only one who had been having all of those complex thoughts.

Christina understood GJ questioning things. The youngest agent had had the rug ripped out from under her and was doing wonderful work, despite it. But she'd been an academic before joining the Bureau. Walter, on the other hand, had been a career soldier. The fact that the former MARSOC operative was questioning the chain of command was huge.

"They sent you after me, too?" Christina asked GJ the only appropriate question of the myriad swarming in her head.

"No," Walter answered for her partner. "Westerfield sent me after you. I figured you were after Marks, and I spent about two days getting some real evidence for Marks being in the area."

Once again, Christina's eyes flicked between the two of them. Lucy Fisher—a/k/a Walter Reed—had gone through Quantico with GJ Jansen already assigned as her partner. That was another friendship that seemed unlikely from the outside.

Now, the two were thick as thieves. "He specifically said he didn't want GJ involved. Not with her grandfather here—"

"Where is her grandfather?" Noah cut in, confused. Christina figured that was a reasonable question. She was about to answer when GJ jumped in.

"Dr. Marks," GJ said, staying calm. "The man we are hunting … is my grandfather. He basically raised me."

Noah's expression told Christina that he was shocked, concerned, and severely questioning his life choices.

Walter went on, ignoring Noah nearly choking on his own tongue. "So as soon as I knew Marks was involved, I called her." Walter's tone was almost gleeful, or at least as close to gleeful as Walter Reed ever got.

"So you directly defied his orders?" Christina asked it so that Noah didn't have to.

"Oh, yes. Hi, I'm agent Lucy Fisher, but everyone calls me Walter Reed." She stuck her hand out and Christina waited for a moment and watched as Noah realized how firm Walter's grip was. If he hadn't understood her before, he knew now. No one dicked with Lucy Fisher.

One arm and one leg were prosthetic. The accident that took those limbs had also gotten her medical leave from the Marines. The long stay in the military hospital had earned her the nickname. The military and a few pioneering prosthetics teams had made her nearly bionic.

And none of her modifications had slowed her down any or made it any easier to hear her approaching. They all bowed down to Walter's superior skills.

The smaller agent stuck out her hand next. Her smile was genuine and almost late, though even in the growing shadows, Christina could see just a little bit of sadness in her friend's eyes. It was, after all, her once-beloved grandfather they were hunting.

"Are you a wolf?" Noah asked her, and Christina couldn't help barking out her own laugh.

32

Eleri didn't like what she'd seen when she closed her eyes. It was almost like a movie replaying... a thin film overlaying the real world. She had watched as Bodhi Banerjee made his way around Donovan's house.

"He put a tracker on your car," she announced suddenly with a spite as rude as her visions made her feel. Heading over toward the side of the porch, where she'd walked earlier, she leaned up against the railing and put her hand out. Feeling around the corner of the house—exactly as she'd seen Bodhi do in her vision—she searched for evidence of what he'd done.

It took a few tries as she patted down the exterior of Donovan's home. Her arm wasn't quite as long as Bodhi's, her reach not extending quite as far. But then her fingers brushed something. She turned back to Donovan and opened her mouth.

Only as she started to speak did she realize that she might expose them both to Bodhi if she said anything. Putting a finger to her lips, she murmured in a low tone. "He placed something around the side of the house. I felt it, but I can't quite grab it."

"Why are we being quiet?" Donovan asked softly. Even as he asked, he seemed to come to the same conclusion she had. And he talked his way through it. "The tracker on my car tells him where I go. The one on my house..."

It was all logic. Not vision. Donovan hadn't seen what she had, but he'd figured out his brother's intent anyway.

Eleri had watched as Bodhi cased the house but wasn't able to see into his mind to know what he was thinking or planning. She told Donovan what she knew. "He did this after he got that call. He was in a hurry. Maybe that's why he didn't go around to the backyard. I don't know."

She continued speaking in very low tones, not whispering. Whispers actually carried farther than low voices. The hiss could be picked up easily by far-range listening devices. "The house doesn't move, so it makes sense that this would be for sound."

Donovan nodded and seemed to direct his voice only toward her. "I'm not usually around the side of the house. I'm out front, or in back."

"Exactly." She only mouthed the word this time, realizing that she could speak at subhuman levels and Donovan could hear.

He, however, needed to speak loud enough for her to hear, hopefully it wasn't high enough volume to get picked up. They traded places and she watched as he leaned out and rubbed his hand on the wall where she had.

Eleri could tell the moment that his fingertips brushed whatever it was. Within another minute, he'd plucked the small device from the wall, and now displayed it for her.

She couldn't be certain just from looking, but she'd seen enough listening devices to believe she was on track. She only nodded at Donovan as he held it up for inspection.

Once again, she lifted her finger to her lips. This time, she hoped whatever was in that device wasn't watching.

33

C hristina fought the overwhelming urge to hug both her fellow
agents. It would surprise GJ too much and Walter would...
maybe heel slam her into next Sunday? So Christina didn't do it. But
it didn't change how she felt.

The best part was, all three of them had the same idea: Get
Murray Marks returned to Westerfield. They needed to show up with
their guy bagged and tagged—which they all hoped would get them
off the hook for disobeying orders.

That might not work, but they didn't get to finish the discussion
because at that moment, Will opened the door and stuck his head in.

"Everything okay?" The words were out of his mouth before his
face registered the shock of two new agents—agents who'd success-
fully snuck past his guards. It was probably clear from the body
language, though, that Christina and Noah were not in harm's way.

As Christina turned to explain, Will grinned.

"Walter! GJ! Good to see you both again."

GJ smiled, a hint of sadness deepening at the edges of her eyes.
"Preferably, next time, it will be under different circumstances."

Will nodded. No one liked to mention that it was her grandfather
killing Will's family, but they all understood. Unfortunately, it might
have made GJ the very best at tracking him.

"We heard shots," Walter said, getting right to the action. "Earlier."

Will nodded. "They got one of ours. We got one of theirs."

"And injured another," Christina added.

"We started by checking out the area," Walter pointed into the distance as she slid into the military training the Marines had drilled into her. She stood with her feet exactly shoulder width apart, her hands at her side, her shoulders back and her chin up as she reported. "We took out one. But that was out of necessity. He was shooting at us, and we tried to only injure, but it didn't work. We captured a second, hoping to get her to talk."

Christina sensed that there was more to the story than that. She frowned, but Walter kept talking. "That combatant is now also deceased."

GJ must have seen Christina's confusion. Turning toward her, she offered a summary that sounded less like an incident report and more like a casual conversation. "We captured her, zip-tied her and left her for a short while—"

"Why would you do that?" Noah was only hopping into the conversation periodically. It seemed he understood he was the least informed here, but he must have felt the need to ask why they would do something so odd.

This time, GJ looked at him, not put out by the interruption at all. "We couldn't haul her with us as we checked out the area, and we had to be sure we were alone before we began interrogating her."

Noah nodded and Christina found she was glad he asked. And glad she hadn't had to.

GJ sighed. This next part wouldn't be good. "When we came back —we'd only been gone for a short while—she was dead."

This time, Christina had to ask. This was NightShade, and there were too many possibilities. "She just … *up and died?*"

"Oh no, she was slashed to ribbons." Walter turned and looked at Will as if to ask, *Did you do this?*

Christina would have expected a cyanide pill, a they-can't-make-me-talk kind of suicide.

"It looked clean, very clean," GJ continued as Walter nodded her agreement. "Almost like knife work."

They all trusted her to recognize methods of death and what weapons might have been employed. She'd been on her way to a PhD in forensic science when SAC Westerfield recruited her. But more than that, she'd grown up on the dig sites with her grandfather, Dr. Murray Marks. GJ knew more about forensics, anthropology, archaeology, chemistry, human biology, and neuroscience—each—than most people would ever hope to have the concept of grasping.

"It wasn't us," Will murmured, rubbing his chin in a way that would have made Christina laugh at the cartoonishness of the gesture if the situation hadn't been so serious. But that was all he had to say about it. He motioned to Walter and GJ. "Come on out with us. I've got some good bourbon. And I've got my people patrolling all around our border."

He frowned a bit at GJ and Walter when he said it, but once again didn't ask how they got past his people. The two junior agents followed Will out to the porch. Christina trailed behind them, watching their movements.

The first time they'd come here, they'd been pulled from field-work and courses at Quantico. Poor GJ hadn't been able to finish her PhD because of Westerfield, and she hadn't ever truly finished her Quantico training, either.

She qualified as a full-fledged and experienced agent, though. Coming to the de Gottardi/Little farm the first time had been a trial by fire. She and Walter had survived. At the time, the two had still been getting a feel for each other as partners

Christina could see that awkwardness was a thing of the past. For a moment, her heart ached for Dana Brantley—the only partner she'd ever found that she felt in sync with.

Pushing the ache aside, as she'd done every day since, she sat with the others. Once again, they acted as though the porch was part of a grand house instead of the surviving backside of a burned shell. They acted as though the night around them was serene country air and not hiding killers with a prejudice against their kind.

This time, when they all sat down, Christina accepted only the tiniest amount of bourbon and watched as Noah refused. Walter, of course, could throw her shots back with the best of them, and Christina didn't doubt that her senses remained fully intact. No matter what she drank, it wouldn't slow her down one bit.

Once the drinks were poured and moments after Will's butt had hit his own seat to relax, GJ piped up. "May I speak freely?"

She softly motioned to the others on the porch. Maybe she'd met them the last time she'd been here, or maybe not. Christina had only recognized a few of the family and wolf militia herself.

Will nodded once, and that was enough.

Seeming to steel herself, GJ looked to Walter, and then back to Will. She seemed to understand that he was the one who *needed* the information, and everybody else could hear it secondhand if necessary. She spoke quietly, but her words landed heavily between them.

"You've got a much bigger problem out there than you know."

34

"There are two separate cells to the north of you," Walter was saying. The small crowd gathered on the porch hung on her every word.

Noah tried not to let his surprise show.

Will, still sitting in his white wood chair, rocked slowly, almost as though the motion helped him absorb the material. It appeared this was news to all of them.

Wishing he had a whiskey glass to fidget with, Noah found himself clasping his hands together, just for something to do with them. He watched as Will seemed to mull the new information over.

Eventually, he held his hand up as though to stop Walter, but she'd already been waiting.

"How big are these cells?"

"Twelve to twenty people each," Walter estimated.

"We can take that."

"No, you can't," GJ cut in. "Those are just the cells to the north. There are two more to the west. Three along the south side of the property—"

"Near the road?"

They didn't answer but Will's muttered "Son of a bitch" made it clear.

The words were almost lovely, overlaid with the melodic quality of his Ozarks accent. Maybe Will hadn't been one of the ones who'd left for school. These wolves certainly didn't all have that sound. It made Noah wonder more about the episode that had split the family up, and what had brought them back together.

"Let me guess," Will said, rocking a little harder. "I assume there are more to the west."

"Three more cells," GJ answered.

"You're telling me there are ten separate cells around my camp?"

"Camp" was a funny term, Noah thought. Then again, they were sleeping in haphazard bunks in burned-out shells of homes... and *under* them. So maybe, maybe that was exactly the right term.

"How can we not see them?" Noah asked, wondering if anyone would answer him this time. He felt it was a necessary question, but, as the words came out of his mouth, he realized how ridiculously stupid it sounded.

Walter turned to him, as though suddenly recognizing him as part of the conversation. "They're using cameras, heat sensors, and camo tents. Some are even sleeping in the trees."

If GJ or Walter had just said, *Well, we can't see them because they're invisible*, at this point, Noah would have bought it. Though the list of supplies and the implied preparedness was concerning, he was glad the answer wasn't something more sinister.

Maybe they are like Christina? He didn't get to think about it much, because Walter was shaking her head.

"They had standard-issue military tents, and they used ghillie-type covers for them. We saw no open fires. They're definitely keeping low."

"How long would you estimate they've been there?" At this point, Noah didn't know if he was pushing his way into the conversation or simply asking the questions that no one else would.

"Minimum three or four days. Some of it looked like it had been there longer, possibly two weeks."

It was clear that Walter had a military background. She spoke as though she knew what she was talking about. Now that they were sitting and his eyes had adjusted to the dim light, he noticed that her left hand was prosthetic. There had been no attempt to make it flesh-colored.

It appeared the mechanics of the artificial limb were covered just enough to keep dirt out of the moving parts—quite the marvel of modern technology.

Though it was difficult not to, Noah made a concerted effort to not stare.

Will thankfully stole his attention by asking, "Is there a way for me to move my people out or move more people in without getting seen?"

GJ and Walter started talking tactics and Noah wanted to listen, but Christina had leaned toward him. She'd caught him staring at Walter's hand and whispered, "She's the fucking Terminator. Do not get on her bad side."

Noah wasn't sure if the warning was intended to be fierce, sincere, or joking. So he only nodded with a smile and tried again to listen to the warfare planning.

"They've got wolves," Will said. "Our own kind turning against us."

"Why would they do that?" Maybe the whiskey was still affecting him. Noah usually controlled his mouth better than this. Normally, he tried to listen more than he talked. It wasn't working tonight.

This time, it was Walter who shrugged, but GJ answered confidently. "Historically, there are always numbers of people who either betrayed their own kind or felt the only way they could survive was to do the work of the dominant force in their situation."

Were the wolves a different race? Noah wondered, but at least this time he managed to keep his mouth shut.

"It's a combination of factors," she went on. "Sometimes individuals think that betrayal can get them ahead in some way. If you add any level of sociopathy to the personality, they just don't care about the loyalty to members of their own group. There's no shared empathy. Other times, it might be based in self-loathing. For whatever reason, they hate who they are enough to try to wipe out others like them. It's ongoing through history—the caste systems in India, American history, Egyptian history ..." GJ trailed off and shrugged as though that was all that could be said about it.

Noah wondered how these two had ended up in the FBI. It seemed GJ and Walter hadn't joined with the intention of being law enforcement officers. Both had been something else in a former life, even though GJ didn't look nearly old enough to have had one life, let alone two.

Then Noah remembered what he knew about Agent GJ Jansen. "Murray Marks is your grandfather."

Why he said that out loud, he did not know.

Luckily, she only nodded, acknowledging the fact of it. Her smile twisted a little. "I was raised by him to be an archaeologist and anthropologist. My parents were often away, so I was left with my grandfather. I didn't realize it at the time, but I had my hands on wolf bones from Egypt when I was seven."

Noah felt his eyebrows rise. He hadn't really considered the history of these people he sat with, but now he had to wonder.

GJ didn't notice his hesitation and kept talking. "And it was only recently that I learned that my grandfather had stolen those bones and kept them for himself."

Walter looked proud as she added, "GJ is now the curator of that collection."

Of course she is, Noah thought. He was just a fucking standard-issue agent from Miami who hadn't even been officially indoctrinated into this strange unit. GJ was apparently also curator at a museum, and Walter apparently could kill with the snap of her remaining fingers. Christina was able to change reality and walk away from everyone without them even remembering she'd been there.

What was he doing here?

But even as he mused about that, he heard Will announce, "So we don't wait for them to come to us. We have to go to them."

"You'll be killed." Walter made this statement as though she was suggesting it would rain tomorrow. "There's no doubt about it. You're not ready."

35

"It won't work," Christina said into the dark around her. She couldn't see much of anything and had to wonder who might be down here listening in. Someone who could be silent on four feet, maybe? Someone who knew their way around the tunnels?

The four NightShade agents were lying on small, inflatable mattresses in the space under one of the burned-out houses. Over Christina's head, a thin sliver of light showed through a crack in the floorboards.

In the far corner, closest to GJ—who said she ran cold—was a small space heater. The slight orangey glow only reached a foot away. Christina couldn't even see their youngest agent, only the corner of a mattress and the edge of the blanket she'd curled up under.

When the hour had grown too late and discussion had not been resolved about what to do, the wolves had scattered. They returned home—wherever that was—surreptitiously, through the tunnels, and then came back with supplies for the four agents. She hadn't seen it happen, but Will must have dictated that they be set up here.

The beds were more comfortable than many she'd slept on and the space heater was a nice touch, though the evening itself was relatively warm and the space enclosed. They'd been left alone. Christina wasn't sure if it was a sign of trust or distrust. But here they were.

She heard Noah's voice come from the other corner of the room. "If the wolves launch an attack on the hunters... how will they do it?

These Marks-led units are hidden in the woods in various places. That's too many to simultaneously attack them all."

"I think that's the point," Walter added in from the last corner.

"If the wolves attack first, don't we then have to arrest the de Gottardi and Little family members? I mean, these others aren't even on their land …" His words trailed off.

Christina could almost feel the three women looking at each other. Noah had a point about the legality. He wasn't wrong. But it wouldn't go down that way, not unless he single-handedly tried to arrest them all himself. Though the room was almost pleasant, the conversation was anything but.

"Jesus," Walter's voice emerged from the other corner. "Westerfield didn't tell him anything, did he?"

Though she was addressing both GJ and Christina, it was clear that Noah could hear it. Christina thought that, if she had her own wolf-level hearing, she might have heard muttered expletives from under his breath. But in fact, despite her poor delivery choice, Walter was right.

"Weren't you in the Caribbean with our agents earlier this year?" Christina asked.

"Yeah."

"And you saw what? Full, legal, FBI protocol?"

He hadn't. He couldn't have. That wasn't how NightShade ran. Though they tried, it simply didn't work.

Christina tried to make some sense of their situation. "A lot of the things our agents can do don't even fit on a scale the legal system can deal with."

"But we weren't on US soil," Noah countered easily. "So none of the US laws or FBI protocol applied."

Interesting angle. Maybe he wasn't just being dense. She tried to find a better example. Then she realized maybe that *was* the best example. "But that's just it. You were there acting—I'm assuming at least *relatively*—as agents. And not on US soil. Think about what a huge issue that is in itself."

The room had gone silent.

FBI agents worked within the national territory. The CIA and other agencies were tasked with foreign affairs. So the very fact that they'd been operating in the Caribbean as an FBI-sanctioned team was already a massive violation of protocol. Maybe it was enough to make Noah see what was going on.

"So, what's our task then?" he asked. "If we aren't here to uphold the federal laws, then what?"

When nobody replied, he continued, his voice measured. "My assignment—the only one I've actually been given—was to trail Agent Christina Pines and alert SAC Westerfield when I found her. I'm already under investigation at my other job for … too many unexplainable arrests."

"They got suspicious of your abilities?" Walter's tone said she clearly had an answer in mind.

"Yes." There was a sigh behind Noah's tone, and Christina felt sorry for him. The FBI tended to hire those who thought in black and white. Follow the law, or don't. Arrest those who break it. Leave it up to the courts to decide the punishment. End of story. Noah had gone into law enforcement to uphold the law. He wasn't a power-hungry bully who'd found a new place to be an asshole.

Christina was left assuming that he believed in the job and the agency. NightShade was going to be a strange ball of wax for him.

"My assignment was the same," Walter told him. "Although my other task was to *not* alert GJ Jansen. And you can see what I did with that."

Noah was growing more and more concerned about the job with NightShade. Christina could hear it in his voice. Walter's answer hadn't helped.

As much as Christina liked Noah, she was starting to understand that Noah Kimball was a wild card.

It was understandable. He wasn't a NightShade agent—not really. He was under investigation at the job he did have, so that could go away—in disgrace—at any moment. No matter what he was capable of doing, he was a person who probably needed a job to keep a roof over his head and food on his table. Westerfield had dangled this assignment at exactly the right time.

Shit.

Noah said he'd turned Westerfield down when he'd been offered a chance at the NightShade team the first time. The Caribbean had been too crazy for him.

Their Special Agent in Charge did not like being told "no." He tolerated his agents going off the books, and even against orders, but that was highly dependent on results. With no background with Westerfield, Noah would feel he was on shaky ground.

And Christina had to wonder if that was maybe the point.

Had Westerfield initiated the investigation into Noah's arrests? The timing was suspicious...

"If they attack, do we help them?" Noah's voice cut through her increasingly restless thoughts.

"We're here to get Murray Marks," Christina answered.

"But are we?" He came at her again, always challenging. "It sounds like none of us actually has that assignment. In fact, two of us don't have any assignments here at all." He didn't say *Christina* and *GJ*, but it was obvious who he meant.

Her teeth clenched involuntarily. She was unsure about how appropriate it was to say, *You just don't understand how things work here.* Or maybe the problem was that he was right. She had already been questioning her ability to keep her job with NightShade after what she'd done for most of this trip. Even now, she couldn't say she was sure the position was still hers. So she tried to clamp down on the sharp retort that wanted to roll out of her mouth.

"We're going to call Westerfield," she said with the most user-friendly version of her thoughts that she could find. "It *will* be our assignment by morning. And if our assignment is to recapture escaped convict Murray Marks, then yes, our assignment is to go out to them—not wait for them to attack us."

After that, the room fell silent.

It stayed dark and quiet for less than twenty seconds. Then a light popped on, illuminating Walter's face with an odd blue glow. She held up the phone, creating a blind spot in Christina's vision, but her hearing was intact. She heard Walter ask cheekily, "Why wait till morning?"

As her eyes adjusted, Christina could see the other agent's face as she hit a button on her phone. Then they all heard, "Sir. ... Yes. ... I'm on the de Gottardi/Little farm... Yes.... Yes... Yes."

Well that didn't help, Christina thought, but Walter's next words did.

"We made contact with Will Little and several of his fighters. They are here on the family land. Yes, I can confirm there are many of them here. I've seen close to forty."

Forty of the de Gottardi/Little family were here? Christina hadn't seen that many. *Damn.* Walter and GJ had really done their recon.

Walter was still talking. "I'm staying with the family. They put us up overnight. Well, sir, by *us* I mean me, Agent GJ Jensen, Agent Christina Pines, and Agent Noah Kimball."

And that, Christina thought, *was that.* The decision was now completely out of her hands.

36

Noah was still feeling a little gummy from sleeping a bit late and the after-effects of a lot of whiskey, but only a little.

The NightShade team had stayed awake last night for some time with Westerfield on the phone, helping to formulate plans. Noah had felt better that the SAC was finally in the mix. He was doubly relieved that there had been no talk of him losing his position or facing any repercussions for failing at the one thing he'd been assigned to do... or for joining a rogue team of agents.

While Noah exhaled a sigh and the weight lifted off his shoulders, he listened as Christina, Walter, and GJ continued to argue with the SAC. "You can make plans until the cows come home, sir. But if Will Little doesn't agree... Well, we'll be hard pressed to execute any of them."

The only thing Noah had distinguished from the other end of the line was a gruff noise of frustration. "You're right. Let's make three plans and let Little choose. It's his land."

This showed more leniency than Noah could have predicted.

In the end, Will agreed that it made sense to use the small task force that had been formed. Just the four of them.

A quick discussion had led to Christina being elected as the leader, despite Walter's military history, which he'd since learned was Marines, special forces. *No wonder...*

Maybe Christina was put in charge simply because she was the senior-most agent in their small group. She had well over fifteen years of FBI experience under her belt. Maybe twenty. He didn't know for certain. And Walter and GJ? Less than him, but both were clearly more seasoned than he at NightShade assignments. He'd harbored no fantasies about leading the little band.

Still, he was impressed with how easily the two junior agents let Christina step up and drive the plans. While they worked out the logistics, he began to get the idea that Christina had been hunting Dr. Marks for far longer than he'd realized. Though GJ was the man's granddaughter, it was Agent Pines who would casually throw out places he might be found, known sightings since his escape, and previous patterns of movement.

He'd gleaned much of this just by keeping silent. But then, he'd woken up, and things were suddenly moving faster than he expected.

They'd been fed a hearty breakfast, *like welcome guests*. But he'd been fed that breakfast in an underground room, connected by tunnels, *like refugees or fugitives*.

They next donned military gear the de Gottardi/Little family provided for them. He was wearing all kinds of equipment: a bullet-proof vest and camouflage clothing. He had night-vision goggles and spare sidearms and ammunition. *Like a soldier*, he thought. Next, he would be out in the grass, crouching low and watching for hand signals, *like an assassin*.

None of these things were what he was. But he was beginning to get the idea that they were what he *could* be.

Though he had stayed mostly silent during the planning, he'd eventually asked his barrage of questions and felt more comfortable that he at least understood what was going on and why.

This wasn't just an escaped convict being brought back in, not just a man with a vendetta. Murray Marks was hell bent on a mass genocide. He'd been trying to wipe out the native wolf population for decades.

Noah was still uncertain why. Was it fear and loathing, or some kind of sick, twisted, academic idea that he would hold all the knowledge of the families? Noah knew no one could answer those questions.

"He's likely after the records the wolf families have kept. Births, deaths, locations," Walter informed him, making it clear that he was the only one who hadn't already known this.

"Everyone has those, aren't they public knowledge?" He'd frowned and then clarified. "They have birth certificates and medical records, right?"

"Mostly," Christina said, filling in where Walter had left off. "But here they have religious tomes with names recorded through generations and centuries, from a time long before birth certificates. Also, for Marks' group to figure out who's wolf and who's not, they'd have to research every birth associated with any family member And that would only tell them who has the possibility of being a wolf, not who actually was. The family has kept very careful track. The information is protection for them, but it also could be their demise if Marks gets his hands on it."

Walter picked up the thread. "Apparently, Marks stayed in touch with his people and was still working at acquiring the family records even while he was in jail."

Beside her, GJ had eaten her breakfast in silence. *Surely*, Noah thought, *they wouldn't have brought Marks' granddaughter here if she wasn't able to handle it.* Noah tried to absorb as much as he could.

"He's had his people out looking for them since before we even knew about it," Walter continued. "His jail time didn't slow that down. The family here had struggled to stay alive and to protect the others they know of. The records are rumored to go back to Egypt. Understandably, the wolves guard their history closely."

"So," Noah mused, turning over the new info in his head and trying to put the pieces together and double check, "—their records are basically a hit list for Murray Marks and his team."

"His *army*," Christina quietly corrected.

Noah had shuddered thinking about how easy he and his brothers had had it, growing up. All the boys had special skills, in one way or another. They'd all tried to keep those things a secret, but they'd been kids. To this day, he had no idea how much they'd failed and how much his parents had protected them. Honestly, he was now—as an adult—convinced his parents knew almost everything and had indulged the boys, even when they were putting their family at risk.

He couldn't imagine what it would be like to grow up with an army attempting a genocide on his kind.

This outing was intended to be recon, though any outing would become an assassination of Murray Marks if they were given the chance.

There had been a brief discussion of taking him alive and questioning him. But a clear consensus had been reached that, not only would that not happen, but Marks would fight to the death and wouldn't give anything up. Even GJ had concurred.

She'd left it to Walter to point out that the last time they taken him alive, he'd escaped. And here he was once again, threatening everything around him.

The harsh discussion had Noah once again questioning the wisdom of having GJ Jansen on this team.

But he didn't mention that out loud.

Well-fed and properly attired, they headed to the edge of the de Gottardi/Little property. Just covering the distance took forever and was exhausting.

It appeared the hunters had been coming on and off the land in small groups. Noah and the small team found more evidence of this than they'd expected. MREs eaten and discarded were found in the tall grass. The occasional cigarette butt could have belonged to a family member, but not according to Will. They'd even found discarded or lost night-vision goggles... again, casually left behind, as if to let the family know they were being watched.

Though the groups had clearly been on the property, Noah found nothing that was prosecutable. They did not appear to be *staying* on the family land. He found himself—just as he had in his own naivete just last night—wondering about the legality of what was happening. His fellow agents only seemed concerned with taking out the bad guy.

Noah brought up the rear of the little group. From the back, he rarely signaled the others. He just followed along and reported what he saw... even as he wondered about the mission. He'd been given scant evidence for himself.

Though he was in good shape, his legs were protesting from all the crouched-down marching. It seemed to be tiring for all of them except Walter, who was apparently in her element. He wondered if at some point she would just stand up and he would see that there were five dead bodies scattered around her.

That would be the highlight of this trip.

The hand signals flashing in front of him indicated they were getting close to other humans. They changed their paths and arced wide to get the lay of the land and see what the groups were doing. Maybe they could identify Murray Marks himself.

Walter pointed to the ground as she hit one point. Moving her finger in a sweeping motion across her feet, she indicated the land to him. This, then, was the property line. Within three more steps, he'd be off of it.

Noah was beginning to get concerned as he watched the other three stalking slowly forward in front of him. *They should have found something by now.*

Suddenly, he felt an arm close around his throat.

With his neck and head being used as leverage, he was quickly dragged backward into the grass. His adrenaline surged as his breath was cut off. It took everything to fight the immediate reaction to kick his feet up or reach up and scratch at his captor. But that wouldn't work. His hands were covered with gloves.

Twisting his head, he managed a breath which brought a moment of sheer relief, but as he attempted to cry out, the arm shifted and cut off his air again.

So he caught no one's attention as he disappeared from his own group.

37

"Dear God, El. Is your mom messaging you again?" That was the only thing Donovan could guess. The look on her face was a Mona Lisa cross between being pleased and possibly having someone stab her repeatedly.

For a moment, Eleri's eyes flicked up to him. She sat calmly on the couch while he frantically packed his things. He wasn't sure why he even noticed the facial expressions she made at the small device, but now he couldn't ignore it.

"Avery," she said almost bleakly, holding up the phone.

"I thought you guys were kind of on a break." He hated the stupid term even as it came out of his mouth. He hadn't chosen it. But it was the word Eleri had used, even though it never made sense to him. He'd always thought of "going on a break" as an "poor man's" way of breaking up, but not really committing to leaving.

He didn't think that's what Eleri was doing. But, honestly, he couldn't be sure.

She didn't answer, just offered up that half smile and half shrug again.

Donovan tried another tactic. "I thought you told him about you."

She set down the phone far more gently than she leaned her head against the back of the couch. He was grateful for the overstuffed cushions or she would have banged her skull and winced. He almost did anyway.

"I told him that I was *going to* tell him."

"What does that even mean?" Donovan asked.

"I told him there were things about me that he wouldn't under-stand. Things that were strange, things that wouldn't make any sense. And I figured he'd leave."

Donovan almost laughed. Though he didn't know Avery person-ally, he was beginning to get a sense of the man from the way Eleri spoke of him. Even Donovan could tell that tactic wouldn't make the man go away. And Donovan was not a "people-person"—not unless they were already dead. "Let me guess. He didn't leave."

"Nope!" Eleri replied, sounding almost overly chipper.

"Did you *want* him to leave?"

She didn't say *yes* or *no*, but she did mutter, "It would have been easier."

"So you told him?"

"Nope," Eleri replied in an exact duplicate for tone and volume to the first one. Far too cheerful for the situation.

"So what's going on now?"

"The fight on the Queen's Staircase is what's going on, Donovan." Her head popped up and she nearly glared at him. "How do I tell him about what happened in the Caribbean? About what I did? *I can't.*" She answered her own question before letting Donovan get a word in.

Once she was quiet for a moment, he offered, "Then break up with him."

Her reply was only a glare.

That's what he thought. "So you don't want to break up with him."

"Of course not. I wish everything could be okay, but it's not."

"Maybe everything can be okay," Donovan replied. He wasn't the kind to go sit next to her on the couch or put his arm around her, or even fetch a bowl of ice cream. And honestly, he wasn't the kind to be doling out romantic advice, either. He truly wasn't quite sure how this conversation had come to pass. "Are you even replying to him?"

Eleri shook her head. At least she had the grace to look guilty about it.

"Reply, Eleri! Tell him. Tell him everything."

Her head move forward a little bit. Her eyes widened as though even she couldn't believe Donovan' words.

When she didn't say anything, he changed course. "Then break up with him. You really have to do one or the other. And right now, you owe the man at least a reply. Tell him you'll talk to him tomorrow, or in three days. But give him something."

Donovan turned and walked away, still stunned by the fact that he was the one demanding a resolution to her romantic issues. Not that any of her issue was romantic. It felt bizarre on all levels. He understood her wariness.

But, hell, he'd told her what he was, and she was still here. Hell, maybe Avery was a warlock or some shit and he'd fit right in. Who knew?

Donovan watched as Eleri checked her phone and sighed at it deeply. She wasn't messaging anyone. He turned away, hoping to give her some privacy. Maybe she'd do it then.

They had been packing up to leave. Eleri was already mostly done. She'd brought little with her and hardly had time to unpack.

She sat on the couch for a moment while he roamed the house, pushing his face out, scenting everything he could. This was not the first time his much younger brother, Bodhi Banerjee, had violated this home.

Though Donovan smelled nothing that he could put his finger on, it still made him squirm to think of having his space invaded. The sinking sensation in his chest was an old one—one that Donovan thought he'd left far behind the day he'd left Aidan Heath and his own childhood in the dust.

The moment that Donovan and Bodhi had met, Donovan had scented something he'd never known existed. He'd simply had a gut-deep instinct that this man was family, and not just family, but close. He'd been hit by the overwhelming knowledge of *brother*, even though he hadn't known at the time that it was true.

Sadly, there had been nothing good between him and Bodhi. He'd wanted a brother for so long. And as an adult, he'd set the wish aside, thinking he had forgotten about his childish need for a real family. Unfortunately, he was realizing now, all of those things—all the wishes and fears—had been stitched into his very fiber and remained with him.

They were unshakable.

Donovan wasn't sure that he would be packing and leaving his own home had it been anyone else who'd come inside. But it wasn't a random stranger. It was *Bodhi*. And it wasn't for the first time.

The decade that had passed since his mother's actual death—an event Donovan had only recently learned of—had given Bodhi the chance to make far more connections that Donovan didn't know about. Bodhi did know their mother. Amisha Banerjee had lived fifteen years after she'd left Donovan and her husband far behind. But who else might Bodhi be connected to?

Though Donovan had believed he'd come to terms with his mother's passing, the new knowledge had been a sharp knife in the gut. Did Bodhi have other family that Donovan didn't know about? He had taken the last name Heath in recent years. Had Bodhi met their mother's family? Donovan never had.

And he couldn't help feeling that the family had been stolen from him. Hell, his mother had been stolen from him. Through no fault of Bodhi's, Amisha had been gone from fifteen years of Donovan's life.

But he couldn't help but blame his brother. Bodhi had gotten the mother that Donovan hadn't. As awful as it must have been to lose her at sixteen years old, Donovan had lost her at age seven.

The worst part was that Bodhi had *told* Donovan about her. His little brother had stolen the happy memories of the woman who had been taken from him too soon and twisted them into a woman who had abandoned him. The dissonance of the warm memories was now tangled with the gut anger of having been left alone with his father. She'd *known* what Aiden was, and her leaving Donovan had been voluntary.

Now that he knew, the good mother of his memory had been taken from him, too.

But maybe the worst part, the thing he'd never spoken to Eleri about was that if Bodhi had been here, it was possible that Aiden Heath wasn't far behind.

38

Noah gasped and tried to sit up before he even stopped to assess whether he should. As soon as he tried it, he realized he shouldn't have.

His feet were bound with zip ties, and so were his hands.

No problem, he thought. He had a way out of that. The question was, who was around him? And how many people had he just inadvertently alerted that he was awake by the stupid manner with which he'd jerked up and probably gasped. He'd definitely been knocked out. *Maybe he should just be grateful that he wasn't dead.*

Slowly, he leaned back trying to fade into the background. Maybe the hunters hadn't noticed he was alert. He couldn't tell.

Through slitted lids, he scanned the area, hoping that no one looked his way.

There were five of them sitting around a small heater that made no glow or open flame. In the dark, he searched their outlines, trying to see if any of them was Murray Marks.

Westerfield had shown him a picture of their prime suspect, but he'd also pointed out that the picture had been taken before Marks spent time in prison. Noah had seen a second photo taken during his prison stay and before his escape. However, any smart man in hiding would do his best to change his appearance. Marks was far better than smart.

Unfortunately, none of these men seemed to be the one they were looking for.

Objective one was done. None of these hunters had paid any attention to him. He had to assume they didn't realize he was up.

His next task was the zip ties. If he could move without anyone seeing, he could get rid of them in a few seconds. But he was confident that at least one of them would notice.

He was on to Plan B, the slow version.

Being propped against a tree in a small clearing didn't help him go unnoticed. Noah wondered if his team had figured out yet that he was missing.

They must have. Worst-case scenario, it had taken them a few minutes rather than a few seconds to realize he'd been kidnapped. The bigger question was, were they coming to rescue him? He wasn't actually part of their unit. He hadn't been on the property before. He didn't recognize Murray Marks.

He realized he might be their expendable piece. Though he was confident that they wouldn't just leave him, it was also possible they were using him as bait. Even so, he wanted his hands and feet free in case he had to jump up and run.

With small furtive twists of his wrists and a few slow rolls side to side—which revealed that, of course, his gun was missing from his hip holster—Noah tested how far he could move.

They must have knocked him out hard. He remembered the arm around his throat and the fading light. But had they given him something more? Or had this camp been nearby, and he'd really only been out for a few moments? Either way, they'd had time to strip off his vest, leaving him vulnerable. *But maybe not entirely screwed.*

He wiggled his foot and was happy when he felt what he was hoping for. He'd learned several years ago on the job to stuff an extra shoelace down under each insole in his shoes.

More than once, he'd pulled out a handy-dandy shoelace to jury rig something. Now he knew it could be life and death.

His next job was to carefully get to his shoe. His feet were a good twenty-plus inches from where his hands rested. Should he move slowly or quickly?

There were no good answers, so he picked a speed somewhere in the middle. Twisting his knees to one side, he pulled his feet up close. The tight constraint of the zip tie on his ankles suddenly hurt. It probably had hurt all along, but he hadn't noticed until now. He wondered again just how long he'd been left here.

As he pulled his ankles in, he slowly looked up, checking for the position of the sun.

Not too long, he decided. The chokehold blackout had likely only lasted several minutes. That was good. He wouldn't need to eat soon —a bonus in case he was on his own. These a-holes had likely stolen all the food stashed in his pockets, too. They'd pulled his gun and knife and his ammo and his other gun. At least they hadn't gotten his shoelaces.

The odds were that he was about to be rescued, but he felt he couldn't afford to wait, just in case he was wrong. What if the rest of his team had been picked off, one by one, and taken different directions? That thought was a gut punch. Maybe they were waiting for him to rescue them…

With his feet now pulled up near his hands, he slid one finger inside along the arch and under the edge of the insole. It took several tries to hook a loop and pull the shoelace out. He would need to rethink his design to make this easier next time, but at least now he had what he needed.

Shoelaces were much stronger than people gave them credit for. It's why they were taken away from prison inmates. A person could hang himself with a shoelace. And, there was one other thing they were really good at…

Still with his eyes half closed, still hoping no one saw him, he went to work.

There was, of course, every possibility one of them was watching him and laughing. It didn't matter, he had to try. Leaning back against the tree, Noah stretched his legs out in front of him again. Not so fast as to get noticed, but not so slow that should someone look over they might see he wasn't in his original position.

The whole time he'd been plotting, they'd been talking. Noah had tried to listen as he worked, but he hadn't made out much except talk of food and which awful army meal they hated most. With one slow movement of a finger, he pushed one bound end of the shoelace under the zip tie holding his wrists and slid his hands to the side.

As he began pulling the lace back and forth, he caught a few words. They began to speculate when they would move again.

"Two days, three days?"

"Today," one of them answered, though Noah didn't think there was much "today" left.

"That was a good shot yesterday!"

Were they celebrating taking out the wolf yesterday? They tossed a few phrases around that Noah didn't understand and he kept working on the zip tie.

Holding tension down on the shoelace was hard with his hands bound, but he made it work. Tugging the lace back and forth, he listened as the group in front of him took credit for another two murders.

He'd heard from Will just this morning that two more of his unit had died yesterday. Noah didn't know how he could use this information, but his heart ached for the old man.

These idiots in front of him were soldiers. Will was running a unit of his *family*.

He continued to saw away with the shoestring, feeling the give at one edge as the zip tie began to wear away.

39

"I've got eyes on him," Christina muttered into the mic at her collar as she tried not to rush out a breath of relief. The last thing they needed was for anyone to spot them.

She had seen Noah propped against a tree, seemingly still out of it. Christina squinted a bit, trying to see if that was indeed the case.

"I got him," Walter added as she held her small scope to her eye and scanned the area. She was further away, but they'd kept better tabs on each other, no longer foolishly believing they would be left alone.

"He's awake," GJ added.

How can she tell? Christina wondered. She couldn't even tell if he was alive.

The other two worked seamlessly together. Though Christina was the senior agent, she was also the third wheel. It was an odd place to be.

That scenario left her with Noah as her adopted partner—which made her more the fool for having lost her adopted partner. The mission, of course, had instantly changed. She still hoped they could get Marks, but now, they had to get Noah Kimball back first.

Westerfield had not explicitly given them the assignment to bring in—or execute—Dr. Marks. The recon mission was all the SAC would sign off on. But together, they'd decided their top priority was to end the threat of Murray Marks forever.

It was, Christina suspected, the next thing Westerfield would demand of them. And she'd rather ask forgiveness than permission on this one.

She'd thought she had it well wrapped up when they headed out this morning. Step One—find the targets, Step Two—find Marks himself. Step Three—call her SAC and explain that it was all over.

Losing the new boy had not been planned.

"How do you know he's awake?" Christina whispered.

"See the shoelace?" GJ asked.

Christina thought, *No*.

" He has a shoelace strung through the zip ties at his wrist."

Even knowing where to look, she still didn't see it. And wondered if being the senior agent meant she was starting to have more *senior* than *agent*. Even squinting, she could not see what GJ was talking about.

Could she still be a NightShade agent with high-end prescription glasses?

But as she watched Noah, she did see that his wrist twitched a little more than they could have if they were bound. *Good for him*, she thought. Slowly, he leaned down toward his feet and began working on that zip tie. She still didn't see a damn shoelace.

It was only moments before his feet came apart. The three of them sat and watched his attempt at self-freedom. While Christina was assessing the state of her erstwhile partner, Walter was making plans.

Her voice was low. Though they were close, Christina heard the sound more through the comm than through the air. "If we go in, I can take all of them out." Then she amended that. "A couple for you. Most for me."

She was speaking over her shoulder to GJ, who did not take her eye away from the scope that was now in her possession. "If we come up from the west, it's better cover. But it means when they shoot back at us, they shoot toward Kimball."

The tone used for his last name indicated that Walter already thought of him far more professionally than Christina did. Then again, Walter hadn't been put on her knees and tapped on the shoulder by an agent who didn't exist. And Walter hadn't tried to send Noah Kimball plunging into a fictional pool in the middle of a grocery store. So Christina figured she was entitled.

"That means we need to come in from another direction," GJ prompted.

"There are basically three other options. I like North best, but it makes the timing poor."

She was right, Christina thought. "I'm voting for speed. Which means we pretty much head straight in. If we stay low, they probably won't hear us."

"Christina can cover us," GJ offered smartly.

For a moment, the senior agent remembered that the two she was with were exceptionally intelligent and talented. They might be the only "normies" in the NightShade unit, but each was far from normal in her own way.

"We have to be concerned about Kimball, too." She paused and then asked, "Are you aware of his skills?"

Walter tipped her head, but GJ answered again. "He's at least a mid-grade psychokinetic."

"Come again?" Walter asked softly.

"He can move things." GJ still didn't take her eye from the scope, though she swung it subtly side to side, still surveilling the area.

"He's exceptionally talented at touching people," Christina said, realizing of course as soon as she said it, that it sounded pervy rather than cool. She explained quickly. "He can tap people on the shoulder, make them feel a gun between their shoulder blades, touch their toes and make them trip."

"Do we want cover going in?" GJ asked, interrupting Christina's list of Noah's abilities.

"Yes," Walter was quick to reply, the tip of her rifle swinging everywhere her eyes went. If this group of soldiers in front of them suddenly caught sight of their stalkers, Walter would have taken most of them out before she was spotted. Christina had no doubt.

But once again, it was GJ who lacked any military training, but who made a wider assessment. "What if there are others besides us? And what about other groups just north or west of here, protecting their flanks? The question is, who haven't we seen yet?"

"I can't do anything to them until I know they're there," Christina reminded them of her own limitations.

"So you two go in, guns blazing. And I'll keep us covered from this direction." GJ clutched her firearm, not quite aiming like Walter, but ready to take all comers.

"Okay. They won't see us coming. I can make sure of that. But I don't know what Noah will try." This time she looked to Walter. "How tough will it be to keep one of them alive?"

But before Walter could answer, a bullet cracked the air and splintered the tree just above Noah's head, causing all of them to jump.

40

Noah leaned forward, yanking his wrists apart. He'd ducked for cover with everyone else when the shooting started, but tried to pretend his wrists and ankles were still bound.

He wasn't quite as agile as he wished. He'd been sitting just a little too long, and his ankles definitely wanted to take a moment to reorient themselves to standing. But he didn't have the time. Squatting low, he began to move.

No one looked his way. They all stood, guns up and aimed, the conversation coming to a dead standstill.

The shot had been a gamble. He hadn't known if he had the power to move anything with enough explosive force to resemble a bullet strike.

Tapping people on the shoulder was easy. He wished he'd practiced blowing apart the bark of a tree in a single, seemingly spontaneous burst. But he'd never tried it before.

His captors' attention was off him at last as they turned away and began fanning out, rifles up and ready.

As Noah came fully to his feet, he took one last glance around the small encampment and slowly slid his body around the trunk of the tree he'd been resting against, using it as a shield now. He took a breath and wished he had his body armor back.

As he stood pressed behind the tree, he saw three figures darting out of the grass toward him. One held a finger to her lips, motioning for him to stay quiet. He froze for two breaths before he realized it was Christina and Walter and GJ. Good thing he hadn't pushed them backwards or tried any moves on them. They might have shouted at him out of sheer surprise.

The three were on high alert, ready to find whoever the shooter was—just as his captors had been.

Noah shook his head at them and held up one hand motioning for them to stand down. He mouthed the words "No gun," and watched as they frowned.

Trying again, he slashed hands through the air to say "No." The movement was small and controlled, since he didn't want to draw too much attention to himself. When no one shot at him, he pointed with his fingers in the shape of a gun and once again shook his head *no*.

Walter still didn't lower her gun. With one gloved hand, she motioned for him to get down as she continued to scan the area.

Noah almost rolled his eyes. He waved his hand one more time, and this time he pointed at himself.

I did it. No one is coming for you. All that they needed to do was get out of here.

It was Christina who caught on first and motioned for all of them to drop low. This time, even Noah complied, although they were still a good distance away from him. The tall grass covered them, but there was no place for him to hide if he darted away from the tree. He couldn't decide if he should make a break for it or not.

The activity was dying down. His captors couldn't locate the shooter, and they were trying to figure out what to do about it.

What they needed was another shot, another distraction. *It worked once*, he thought but he needed a moment to gather his breath.

Leaning forward, he put his hands up over his ears, hoping to gain some concentration and block everything out. He was counting on his three fellow agents to keep him safe. Taking a deep breath, he pictured the tree in his mind.

He blew out his breath. In the split second, as the air left his mouth, he heard the air split and tree bark shatter. He heard the small movements of a professionally trained group immediately shifting directions, squatting lower, and searching for yet another shooter.

Noah smiled.

Even Walter raised an eyebrow toward him and tipped her head in a small mock bow. Her next motion was an instruction, and not for him to get low, but to come forward. Noah gratefully obliged, hoping he could get away before his captors realized he was missing.

41

C hristina was both elated and frustrated.
"Glad to be back," Noah whispered, speaking in as low a tone as he could.

She saw his lips move but she couldn't hear him. Not a surprise. Once they'd spotted him, they'd tried catching his attention in his earpiece and concluded it must be missing.

Now she could see that he'd been stripped of all weapons, communication devices, and safety equipment. *They left him walking around out here like a little duck.* Christina pulled a spare earpiece out of her pocket and held it out to him. She was down to one spare now and she didn't like it, but this is what it was for.

Her outstretched hand competed for his attention with Walter's. Only Walter had offered him a spare gun and holster.

They stayed low as he awkwardly checked and holstered the new gun and then slipped the earpiece into place. "Good to be back."

She tried to file it into her memory that he was still without a vest…

It had taken too long to find him. The four of them had managed to get far enough away from the little cluster of captors before they'd begun to talk, but now they were too close to another group.

This time, seven soldiers were hunkered down in the grass and hadn't seen them. No one even twitched as she and her little group approached. Christina had worked hard to make sure that happened.

So far, she'd only managed to drop a quick message to Will, giving him locations and numbers. The sky was losing daylight and she was losing hope that they might simply run into Dr. Murray Marks out here.

Her list was getting longer.

Don't let GJ kill her own grandfather. Don't let Noah get shot, he has no vest. Don't forget to update Will on what they found.

"What do we do?" The voice in her ear belonged to GJ, but Christina had seen no movement from the junior agent. *Good for her.*

"We came out here to get one of them," she replied. But even as she said it, Walter shook her head.

"Recon." She held up one finger—*their number one priority.*

That was true. Their intent had been to learn as much as they could. They didn't yet have enough agents to leave anyone back at the compound. Their explicit instructions were to gather intel but their second highest objective, which was Cristina's favorite, was to grab one of Marks' people and see if they could make them talk. Between Noah and herself, she figured the interrogation techniques might work better.

Unfortunately, the only person getting captured so far was Noah. It wasn't his fault. Everything else he'd done had proven he was sharp and on his game. She told herself, it could have been any of them, though she wasn't quite sure she believed it.

"Are we going back?" The words traced across her ear drum, low enough that they were barely more than a sensation. Christina didn't quite have an answer to the question. Though they were prepared to be out overnight, it was a backup plan only.

She didn't like operating on backups.

Even as she was thinking it, GJ motioned around with her finger toward the ground as though it were a map. "We have more places to check. If we continue recon through the night and head back in the morning, we won't wind up sleeping out here."

"It cuts our vulnerability," Walter added, perfectly in sync with her partner.

Christina thought it through. They'd been prepared to sleep in shifts. Set up a tiny camp. However, as they moved slowly toward another set of Marks' soldiers, she began to think their camps might be relatively easy to find. If they slept, Christina could cover them—no one would see or hear them—but the mental work would have left her exhausted. Being the only one with that particular skill meant she would be up all night, while her fellow agents slept. It was not a good situation to have one agent fully expended.

GJ's plan made the weight of an overnight a little easier. She nodded. "We'll stay out, but we still want to get one."

Walter tipped her head as if to say, *Don't we all?* But Christina knew Walter was still military-rigid in her decisions. Her first objective remained recon. Capture and interrogate would become her issue *only* if it became available.

With a return nod, Christina looked at the others and made a motion.

They continued toward the north, farther from the de Gottardi/Little family property line.

She thought about that for a moment, finding it odd... The first person they'd seen had been a lone gunman, seemingly standing post. He'd been on the actual property, while everyone else was forming a ring around it.

Then that thought blended into another. People seemed to have little concern for the law out this far, but Marks' soldiers were watching the property lines like hawks. They knew when they crossed onto private land, as if they were ready for some local sheriff to come in and harass them. As if *trespassing* was their concern.

It continued to nag at the back of her brain. *Such an odd situation.* But she pushed it aside to keep her eyes forward.

As the sun slowly set, they zigzagged wide trails. At one point, they came almost face-to-face with two armed guards. Christina wanted to grab one or both and head back in. But Walter mouthed "Recon" to her with a harsh glare, and Christina ceded.

Walking slowly, they stayed low and remained undetected. She wondered if they'd passed any clusters of Dr. Marks' people—if they'd been seen and allowed to pass...

She wouldn't be surprised if someone actually knew they were out here ... and was letting them get away with it.

She was having this thought as she slowly rounded a tree. It was getting harder to stay vigilant, but it had been a while since they'd seen anyone. She was beginning to conclude that the ring around the property was only about two, maybe three clusters of guards deep—which was still a lot, but maybe not as much as Walter had originally predicted.

Moving together, they aimed for a large tree and then slowly came around. Christina's weapon was aimed at the ground in front of her. As she cleared the other side, she came up against two guards.

Her heart felt like it spiked in her chest.

Even as her body thought to suck in a breath, her brain countermanded it and fought for reason, stability, calm.

Hoping the others would stay behind and duck back when they saw what she'd encountered, she looked at guns aimed her way. It would be an advantage to appear that she was a lone idiot out in the fields.

Her gear would distinguish her from a lost hiker certainly, but maybe she could convince them—

Her relief lasted only a split second, as one gun swung, aiming at someone behind her.

Walter? GJ? Noah?

She couldn't turn her head and look. Swearing to herself, she watched as five more soldiers popped up from the grass, and she realized they were outnumbered.

42

E leri almost smiled as Donovan let out a very impressive string of swear words.

"Creative," she commented, even though she felt her muscles tense as their phones rang simultaneously. It could only be Westerfield.

She was reaching her thumb to push the button when Donovan held up a finger. "Walter's good. She just checked in."

Then he held his phone out to motion suggesting that they should pick up together. Only this time, Eleri waved her hand at him, *no*.

Maybe it was better if Westerfield didn't know they were in the same place if he hadn't already figured that out. Turning, she left the room, not watching when Donovan picked up the call. In the other room, she waited until she heard his voice, then pushed the button and held her own phone close to her face, hoping that no ambient noise would filter in. Hoping that Westerfield wouldn't figure out his two agents were only a room apart.

"Eames," she answered.

"Now I'm four agents down," her SAC offered by way of greeting.

"Four? What?" Eleri asked it a split-second before Donovan. Even though she was startled that Westerfield was rapidly losing agents. She was also congratulating herself and Donovan. They'd done a good job sounding like they weren't looking at each other while they said it.

"I sent the new guy after Pines."

"What new guy?" It wasn't that there was a new guy that confused Eleri—there was *always* a new guy—but was that Westerfield seemed to think she would know about it.

"Why would you send someone new after Pines?" Donovan volleyed. It was better that they weren't looking at each other. "That's a high-level target."

Eleri winced. She would never have referred to another Night-Shade agent as a "target."

"Kimball. The one who worked with you in Miami and down in the Caribbean."

Eleri could almost feel her ears perk. Hadn't Agent Noah Kimball turned Westerfield down? Yet somehow, he was off looking for Pines. Eleri tried to connect all the small dots. "And now *he's* missing?"

"He was. He caught Pines...or she caught him. It took a while for them to check in together."

Eleri wondered if the tone in his voice was unwarranted. As far as she knew, Christina never did anything to hurt anyone. She made people think and see things, but then she tended to leave. No one had been harmed directly by Christina. She'd just manipulated situations ... so if Westerfield thought she'd captured Noah Kimball and was holding him hostage, Eleri was certain he was way off track.

The dissonance she felt about Christina Pines being accused of such a thing was as concerning as the thought that Westerfield could be off track. It was his job to be *on* track, and Eleri was getting more and more confused about what that track was. It was clearly not the storyline she'd been fed when she joined.

"So, Pines went basically AWOL? And then you sent Kimball after her?" Donovan also was connecting the dots and seemed to have gotten sucked into the void as well.

"Not how I would have put it." Westerfield's words were short, clipped, and irritated. Eleri figured his discomfort was maybe his own doing.

But before she could even try to find the next dot, Westerfield barked, "I sent Fisher after him, too. Fisher grabbed Jansen even though she was specifically told not to."

Eleri breathed a sigh of relief, even as she fought to hide it from her boss. Donovan had been wondering where Walter was for a while now. Thank God for the text that had just come in. It was as though Walter knew Donovan needed to hear it.

"Fisher is supposed to be out on her own. But now she, Jansen, Pines and Kimball are together at the de Gottardi/Little farm." Westerfield obviously had his suspicions. "So I need you two—right now—to tell me everything you know."

Eleri fought the sudden urge to laugh hysterically. How could she tell her boss that she'd been holed up in her home, practicing spells for the last week and a half? She knew absolutely nothing that would be valuable to him.

Well, except they already knew that Walter was okay. And Kimball was apparently working with them now, too. Eleri concurred that Walter most likely had called Jansen in on the job. The two were nearly inseparable.

But why did she hold all this back from her boss?

43

Christina raised her weapon and held it steady, even though every organ inside her fought to get out of her body. Her heartbeat felt as if it was going to pound her ribs until they cracked and everything shook apart.

They had just gotten Noah back. It figured.

We should have turned around. This was entirely my fault.

She thought she recognized the man in front of her... but the soldiers' faces were distorted by shadows. The rim of their thin but sturdy helmets and plastic protective eyewear altered the shape and color of their eyes. She couldn't see their hair color. In fact, the only real markers she had were height and the shapes of their mouths.

She wanted to dart her eyes to the right and look to GJ for answers, but there was no time. GJ would know if this man was Shray Menon.

Menon had been her grandfather's assistant since she was at least very small, possibly even before she was born. Christina didn't know about the relationship between GJ and Menon, but she did know that Shray Menon was supposed to be *dead*.

His body had not been recovered from the previous encounter at the de Gottardi/Little farm. Christina had always had her suspicions, given that the body had disappeared. It was possible that Marks' people had simply stolen the corpse, to keep some pertinent information out of NightShade's hands. But without a body, Christina hadn't been fully willing to believe he was dead.

Even then, the soldiers had been organized, trained, and clean in their maneuvers. In the heat of the battle, she and the other agents had been forced to leave Menon where he fell. When they'd come back, the body was gone. She'd had her suspicions all along. That's why she'd asked after Menon when she'd been trailing Marks.

Now she was practically certain that the man in front of her was one and the same.

Christina did the only thing she could do. She barked out orders as though they weren't aiming weapons at each other's heads. "You need to stop crossing onto the de Gottardi/Little property. You need to leave."

"Leave what? The area?"

"Yes, you need to leave the state," she said. Realizing from this first volley that this was going to get tedious very fast.

"Why would I leave? This land belongs to my friend."

Friend? She wondered as she made a mental note to check up on that. Beside her, she felt Walter stiffen slightly. She could only hope that no one had grabbed Noah Kimball from behind her once more, but Christina kept talking.

"Your people have moved onto that property—" she motioned behind her, not wanting to say the name again. Had she given them information they didn't already have? She didn't think so. "—more than once. It's trespassing. We have ample evidence. We also have a dead family member."

As he opened his mouth to counter that her evidence was slim to nonexistent, Christina cut him off. "I'd hate to see you all get charged with murder. The rifling on the bullet matches a gun registered to your group."

That last bit was an utter load of bullshit. In fact, he was probably silently laughing at her right now. The likelihood that their guns were registered to anyone even mildly associated with what was going on here would be absurd.

Christina lowered her voice and gave it all the authority she had. "You need to leave, or you'll all be arrested." She pushed, even though it was only a veiled threat. It should hold up, at least as far as the people in front of her could see.

They held rifles against the NightShade agents' handguns. Seven against four—possibly more. She didn't know if any were hiding in the grass, waiting to pop out. "Why are you here?"

She pushed once more, the generic questions seeming almost random.

With a tip of his head, Menon—it *had* to be Shray Menon—replied, "We're merely camping on my friend's property."

This time Christina threw her head back and laughed. Despite the fact that her heart was pounding, the laugh itself was genuine and hearty. She'd learned to control the exterior she presented, and she could only hope that her outward calm was threatening to these people. Leaving only one hand on her gun, she waved up and down the length of him with the other. "This is not camping. This is armed warfare, malicious style. And *yes*, it is illegal."

She'd given them ample warning, as any Bureau agent was obligated to do. She was starting to feel like Noah, concerned about the laws—as though that was why they were here.

Menon merely shrugged and repeated himself. "Camping."

Christina played one last card. It was one that Will had slipped into her mental pocket late last night when they'd had a moment alone.

Will had his suspicions. And if this was Menon, then he was the one to ask.

"Tell me, Shray," she said casually, as if inquiring about a game on Friday night. Christina watched for an almost imperceptible clench of his jaw. Hard to see with the strap of his helmet directly in the way, but his eyes were harder to watch with those damn wraparound glasses. "Did you know they've got the Federal Bureau of Investigations on their side?"

She tossed that factoid out first, in case he needed a reminder of the force and might that now stood behind the de Gottardi/Little family.

His complete lack of reaction told her that he didn't care.

This was no little military operation then. Nothing that would be swayed by the FBI moving onto the property.

While the gear, the tactics, and the sheer numbers had forewarned her that this was funded and run by something higher up, Will had given her a hint.

"Tell Aegis X that the de Gottardi/Little family will never be theirs." She watched for the imperceptible tightening along his jaw again.

There it was. Not much, the movement was just strong enough to be perceived, despite the shadow of the strap under his chin.

Holy fuck. Will was right, Christina thought as none of the others reacted.

Until now, none of them had quite known what they were up against. But now Christina did. Her eyes took one sweep across the soldiers.

If that wasn't Shray Menon she was talking to, it was definitely their new leader. None of the other six had flinched at her words. None of them knew about Aegis X. Hell, she hadn't known until last night.

Now she was grateful for her time in the bars along the way here. Grateful that she'd practiced erasing herself from the minds of sometimes eight, sometimes ten, or even fifteen people at once.

She knew she could handle all seven in front of her and any new threats that popped up unexpectedly.

Christina lit them all on fire.

44

Noah had been holding his weapon, but as the soldiers in front of him began to jerk and scream, he clenched his arm muscles and moved his finger from the guard to the trigger.

He'd been prepared for a standoff and ready to shoot at a moment's notice. Was this that moment?

A voice came through his comm, though it was hard to hear over the rustling of the grass and the soldiers twisting and screaming in front of him.

"They're on fire," Christina's voice told him. Then she repeated it two more times. "They're on fire....They're on fire."

Probably she'd said it to make sure that everybody had a chance to hear it. It still took him a moment of his mouth wanting to open and say, "No, they aren't," before he realized what she meant.

Shit. She'd turned the advantage. There were only four of them against seven soldiers—but suddenly, they could have the upper hand.

Christina was smart, playing to her unique ability, she used every tool she had available. Noah knew he should do that, too.

He watched as Walter aimed her weapon downward, and though he was confused by her action, he felt the push outward from him as he sent out pops of force. He watched as it hit the soldiers, almost like rounds of rubber bullets.

Not sure if he'd hit hard enough, he realized he'd done enough to send them stumbling backwards from the force. If they already thought they were on fire, and they believed they were also getting shot, maybe they would do anything to make it stop. He could only hope.

Walter lifted her handgun, having replaced her rifle. Though why she'd downgraded when they were looking down the barrels of multiple, high end, scoped and retrofitted rifles, Noah couldn't explain.

Somehow, she managed to hold the gun in her right hand in a relatively relaxed stance, but that wasn't what shocked him. It was that she ran headlong into the fray. She ran right into flailing arms, screams about fire, and weapons swinging wildly and aiming all directions with a dangerous lack of control.

Walter reached for the barrel of the first weapon. She grabbed onto the barrel, aiming it toward the sky even as the trigger was pulled.

Noah waited for her to scream. He figured she'd at least react. Surely she would yank her hand away from the searing heat of the barrel after the bullet passed through, but no sound came. In fact, she didn't even jerk back.

In a fluid motion, she pulled the gun out of the soldier's hands, swung it around, and whacked the soldier upside the head with butt of it. Then she tossed the expensive rifle off into the distance.

She might have just thrown an enemy combatant another weapon, but she couldn't have gently set it down within reach of the close-at-hand soldiers, either.

There was no time for analysis. Noah rushed into the fray himself, his own hands pushed together in front of him. Crossing his thumbs, he reinforced his position. His response would have to be much more human than Walter's. Her metal hand had taken the brunt of the burn. He, on the literal other hand, had to protect his own skin. He would need to stay away from the barrel.

Noah aimed for one of the mid-level looking combatants, thinking to save the smallest for GJ. He barreled into the other person, shoulder to chest—his unprotected, theirs covered by gear—and he shoved the gun upward.

Like Walter, he shoved the barrel away, aiming any live rounds out of the way of him and his friends. He honestly couldn't care less if these fuckos hit each other, but he wouldn't let them take out any of his people.

The fight was a struggle. It was hard to find a spot to hit or tap to send the man tipping where Noah wanted him. The soldier flailed about, though that was mostly because the idiot thought he was on fire.

Noah had the advantage of knowing he was not engulfed in flames. As he pulled the rifle away, he decided not to follow Walter's example and swing the gun around, using the butt. But that would ultimately aim the barrel toward him and his friends. Instead, he reached up with his own gun in his hand—it would yield less force, he knew—and aimed the heavy butt for the strap of the helmet under the man's jaw.

Noah watched as his opponent sank like a rock. To his left, another went down, as a bullet cracked far too close behind him. The sound spun him around. As quickly as it all happened, Noah still managed to catch the look on the woman's face, as it turned from disbelief to shock to nothing.

He then noticed that her helmet had a hole out the front. Her hand was starting to reach up to her chest, but it never made it. As she crumbled, she revealed GJ standing behind her, Glock raised and practically smoking.

From the look on GJ's face, she'd had no issues with pulling the trigger on this one. It looked like she'd put the barrel up and under the back of the small helmet, firing the gun through the hole at the base of the skull. At that close a range, it wouldn't matter if her aim was good or bad.

Another combatant down.

"Noah!"

His name split the air. He didn't have time to absorb if it was GJ or Walter who warned him, but he twisted around, his gun coming up as he did it. Though he would have preferred to clock the woman under the chin like he did the first one, there wasn't time. Instead, he aimed the barrel and pulled the trigger, watching as half her face exploded with the shot. The force pushed her backward and out of sight as his ears rang with the noise and his stomach folded with the image he would never unsee.

Only then did he notice that Christina was running. She was chasing the man that had given her the twitch in her eye before, the one she called by name—though Noah couldn't for the life of him recall it now.

The way her quarry was running away, he did not seem to have caught on that he should think he was on fire.

Walter appeared beside him, and then GJ. They seemed to have made the same assessment that he did: the other six were down, either knocked out or dead. None so much as twitched.

"Oh shit," Walter said as she spotted Christina getting farther and farther away.

In a too-smooth move, Christina slung her rifle across her back and pulled out her handgun. Just as cleanly, she began shooting at the man's back. It was clear that her bullets hit him. But, though he went down, it was uncertain whether she'd hit anything vital or just put enough lead into him to force his momentum forward.

Even as she disappeared into the distance, Noah thought to give chase. *What if she needs backup?*

Walter turned to the other two then, taking charge of what was left of their unit. She pointed to three of the six. "These are still alive. Kill the third. We're taking two of them back."

She issued the order as though she hadn't just ordered an assassination. Then she ran off after Christina.

45

"He's supposed to be dead." Christina pushed the words out angrily through clenched teeth. She fought not to wail them.

Shray Menon had gone down. She'd hit him multiple times. Surely, he had broken ribs and it looked like some part of him was bleeding—an arm, a leg, she didn't know.

Christina had been spraying bullets all over his retreating form. He wore a vest and helmet, so many of her hits had simply failed to kill him. But she'd battered him to the point where he'd fallen, then raced to the spot where she'd seen him disappear below the tall grass, only to find …. Nothing.

Hadn't she run fast enough? She knew she had! There hadn't been enough time for him to get away—but somehow, he had.

He must have crawled away.

Following the trail—blood droplets and broken stalks of the wheat-like grass—she found a point where things changed. It appeared that someone had found him and quickly dragged him out of range. She could still see where the grass was bent, but the way the blood thinned out along the trail indicated he'd been moving fast. She wouldn't catch up. And he wasn't alone.

Even if she could track him, she shouldn't.

Fuck.

Walter looked at her a little sideways, having caught up faster than Christina expected. But that was Walter.

"He's damaged, that's for sure," Walter said as they turned away and headed back.

The others were in view sooner than expected, so she hadn't run quite as far as she'd thought. Still, her heart hadn't stopped pounding and her anger hadn't dimmed.

She was speaking to all of them, though Noah probably didn't fully understand what she meant. "The last time we were here, we were quite certain that fucker was dead."

No one else commented. And she knew it was because there was nothing more to say. She'd had Shray Menon in her sights … and he'd *gotten away.*

Giving up, she led them back to the de Gottardi/Little land. They took turns dragging the unconscious instigators behind them. It was slow going. Dead weight was hard to pull, but harder to carry. By the time they arrived and Will's people greeted them, they'd been awake more than twenty-four hours and Christina was exhausted. Only Walter looked ready to go back out.

Christina fought the urge to swear at her.

Once she was changed and showered, she met up with the others, whom Will and the family were already feeding some kind of meaty stew. Only after she was well into her bowlful did Will ask, "It means Marks is here, doesn't it?"

"I'm almost certain he is," she replied. She looked up from her food. "I can't be positive it was Menon, but…" *It had to be.* Christina looked to GJ, who nodded silently. *It was him.*

Looking to the others, she wondered if Walter or GJ had anything to add. Christina stared for a moment, knowing that the junior agent knew more than she said.

"Do you think your grandfather is here?" Will pressed GJ without softening the blow.

It turned out that what GJ knew was that she didn't know. "In the past, I would have said that was true. Shray was my father's personal assistant, and he's also a PhD archaeologist. He was always on the digs I went on with my grandfather, and only occasionally left behind when they had to split up. That would be only when someone needed my grandfather to be in two places at the same time."

She paused, but then picked up the thread again. "The last time he was here, Grandpa—" she cut the word off, no longer the right term for the man they hunted. "Dr. Marks was here. But I didn't know that

Shray was alive. And I have no idea where my grandfather's been for the last six months. His assistant's presence might mean that Murray Marks is nearby, but I can't be sure."

That wasn't entirely true, Christina thought. Dr. Marks had broken into GJ's lab at some point. The lab that had once been *his lab.* GJ and Walter had found secret passages, missing bones, and stolen documents.

GJ had grown up in the building, working at his side. She probably knew every bone and had a pet name for it. So when GJ said something was missing, Christina believed. And when GJ said the only person who could have gotten into the secured and locked lab was her grandfather, Christina believed that, too.

But GJ wasn't sharing that with the family yet.

Will ran a hand over his military-short, white hair—*as though that even did anything.* "So, we know for sure that Menon is on site."

"Well, we know he was until this morning," Christina corrected.

"We can figure it out, right? We've still got two of their people." Will rubbed his hand over his head again. "Though I'm not sure what you plan to do with them."

Christina was certain she heard a tone of censure. Will had said once before that he wasn't in favor of killing, so he probably wasn't in favor of torture, either. However, Christina also knew he was in favor of keeping his family alive and keeping the farm property in the hands of those family members.

The question was, *Which one did he believe more deeply?*

But there was also a second question: *Did she care?*

Will knew they'd killed four others in the field. Maybe he thought that murder was only justified if the other person was actively trying to kill him. She didn't know.

But Christina needed information from the two soldiers that they had tied up.

She'd already sent people to attend to their wounds. Though she wasn't offering grade-A medical care, she'd asked Will's medics to be sure they didn't die from any cuts or hits they'd received in the field.

The medics had reported back that both captives were alive and well, awake, and angry. She'd ordered them left in one of the dirt rooms under one of the burned out houses, a short walk away from where she sat now.

Guards that Will felt could handle whatever happened if the

captives got loose, sat in waiting outside the trap door. They would work in shifts until Christina decided that it was time to go back and interrogate them. But she wasn't ready yet, and she figured they could sweat for a bit.

Christina looked to her group. They were all at the end of their energy. "We need sleep."

At least they were fed. She pushed away the empty bowl from the first hot, full meal she'd had since yesterday. Even so, they couldn't do a decent interrogation when they were all half dead. They hadn't just been awake, they'd been running at high adrenaline the whole time and even dragging unwilling captives behind them.

She looked to Will and was satisfied when he nodded in agreement.

"You'll head back once you've slept?" When she nodded he added, "Let us know when you want a wake-up call."

Christina just wiggled her phone at him. It was a nice offer, but they could take care of it themselves.

Still, as she stood, she realized she had another thing to deal with. "Noah, did you leave your vest with whoever Will said?" Honestly, she didn't know who that was. She'd just asked Will to direct her new partner.

Noah had been wearing a vest they'd stolen from one of the soldiers they'd killed. Putting it on Noah to keep him safe on the trip back had been her primary thought, but now she hoped some of Will's people examine it for any kind of forensic information that could be gathered. Hell, even the manufacturer tags might be helpful, if they could be traced.

Will held out a hand and waved her on. "We got it. They're already looking at it."

With that, she turned and gathered her tiny crew of NightShade agents. They headed from the enclosed dining area into a room with huge holes in the walls, letting in the growing daylight. The four of them hopped down through the trap door and into the tunnels, to head to the other house.

Once they were back at the room that held their beds, Christina sat down, grateful she hadn't had to walk her agents through the grass. She was more convinced than ever that everyone above ground was a target. Walter was right—there were far more soldiers out beyond the property than she'd even imagined. They were fitted with excessive safety equipment and long-range rifles and scopes.

But what are they waiting for?

She hoped to find out from the soldiers they were holding in the compound, but first she told the others, "We still have to call Westerfield."

Though Noah seemed to have no reaction, GJ's and Walter's eyes immediately darted toward each other, as if drawn by magnets. Both looked back at her and replied, "Later. When we're awake."

Christina had to admit, that made sense. If they weren't in any shape to interrogate the soldiers they'd brought back, they were certainly in no shape to get interrogated by their boss.

Almost simultaneously, they all plugged in their phones to charge. They each turned to their corners, to peel clothing and climb into whatever "group appropriate" pajamas or clothes they would sleep in. Privacy was out the window on this mission, and Christina was far too tired to care.

It shouldn't have felt so damn good to crawl into her bed, but it did.

She was grateful that—despite the dawning daylight—the room down here remained nearly pitch black. She was asleep instantly.

Before she felt rested or that any time had passed, Will was shaking her awake.

Has she even slept? She blinked at him, turning her head to look to the face of her phone. Even as he spoke words she didn't comprehend, she managed to check the time and absorb his tone.

"Christina, you have to get up. We have a problem."

Four hours. She'd been out cold for four full hours.

It wasn't long enough, but it would have to do. She looked up to see Will staring at her. And the words he'd said started filtering through her cloudy brain.

"Problem... Soldiers... Dead."

46

"Holy shit." Noah wanted to say he'd never seen anything like the bodies in front of him now. But he had.

His first year as an agent, he'd come across a case like this. It had been written off as an animal attack. He was putting the pieces together now. He'd known mentally—he'd been *told*—wolves were everywhere. But he hadn't quite believed they were in Miami Dade. Apparently, he'd been wrong, because that "random animal attack" sure looked a damn lot like what he was seeing in front of him. And he knew this one had been caused by a wolf.

"GJ?" he asked, wondering if she could tell anything else about the slashed corpses of Marks' people—the ones he'd helped capture and drag back here. Damn, this made his stomach roll.

"This was not accidental," she replied.

Noah added, "It's not a full moon," thinking maybe he was funny.

But GJ turned and narrowed her eyes at him. Apparently, he was not funny.

"No." The word dripped with scorn, and he wished he could dial back what he'd said. *Too late.*

He didn't follow that thread anymore, but he'd just learned for certain that the full moon/werewolf thing was *not* a thing. Noah switched topics. "How do you know it's not accidental?"

The scorn disappeared and GJ turned fully academic, pulling a small pen from her pocket. Noah quickly realized it wasn't a pen at all, but an extendable pointer, as though she might not always be prepared for a raid or an enemy combatant capture, but she was definitely always prepared for a lecture.

"This here and here." She moved the tip of the thin baton to motion where she was indicating. "Do you see how this cut is a true cut? The whole thing looks like a shred, but it's not."

He nodded. Deep, knife-like gouges covered the body, flaying the flesh open for all to see... and smell.

"Do you see that they maintain even spacing across?" GJ looked up and, when he nodded, she continued. "Often, if the hand comes around in an uncontrolled motion—" she demonstrated with her arm extended, "—the fingers splay out wide. Then, as they rake—as they make the cut—they get closer together. But this—" She moved the tip of the pointer along the line of the cuts, "—indicates this was a controlled slash. It wasn't a fling of a hand. Whoever did it intended to slice."

Noah started to move away, look around, thinking she was done.

"Also—" the pointer moved, hovering just above the surface of the wounds again.

Yes, he thought. *As a forensic scientist, she would not touch anything.*

"—here, here, and here. Those are strategic. Look at the cut into this arm."

The bulk of the limb was hanging by threads of tendon and muscle. The bone was intact, but clearly scored. Noah fought a shudder thinking of how sharp those claws must be to cut that deep, that cleanly. He didn't let GJ see his concern or his revulsion. He just looked where she'd instructed.

"This one went for the brachial artery. And it definitely hit it." She motioned him to step back carefully and then turned, now using the pointer to motion along the ground. "You can see the arterial spray."

He added in what little he knew. "So the heart was still pumping when this slash was made?" *It might have been the first cut*, he thought.

"This was fatal and intended that way." GJ didn't mince words.

Noah nodded, catching on. He ventured again at putting in his own two cents. "The brachial artery is pretty difficult to hit if someone's defending themselves, right?"

She grinned, as though she were proud of her student, despite the fact that he had a handful of years on her. Then again, maybe she was older than she looked. "I was wondering if you'd see that. Whoever did this was someone they knew."

"Well, one of the soldiers obviously got down here. So why didn't he—or she—help them escape? Why kill them?"

This time, GJ stepped back, probably removing herself from the blood spatter and forensic evidence. Turning around, she asked, "Where would they go … when they escaped?"

"Any of the tunnels," he commented, because it seemed obvious to him. "Whoever killed them knew enough to get down here. Well, unless they dropped in through the trap door. But that was guarded by two of our people, who claim no one came through."

"True." It seemed he'd hit the end of GJ's knowledge and she, too, was no longer explaining but looking for answers. She checked the entrances to the tunnels, but the floors had been packed hard through decades of use. Footprints would be difficult to find…

"We're probably out of luck on tracks," Noah commented, then forgot he shouldn't be funny and added, " unless somebody had managed to step in mud just before leaving the room."

GJ looked up at him, startled. And they spoke at the same time.

"Or blood."

Now they pulled out phones, snapping on the flashlights and looking for tiny details.

The light that had been set up in here for GJ's inspection didn't reach every corner. And Noah looked down one tunnel as carefully as he could while GJ talked him through. Or maybe she was talking to herself.

"I don't see footprints in the blood spatter. Which is interesting. That's another thing that makes me think they knew the killer. He or she had enough time to take a very deep cut and step out of the way of the spray before coming back for the open body slash. But if they even stepped a little in it, it should create a track… Damn, I wish I had luminol."

Even as she lamented her lack of supplies, he saw it. "Holy shit! Here."

Boot tracks.

Not a full track, only the corner of one edge of a shoe. But it was definitely blood. Or at least, he was almost sure.

GJ came over from where she was inspecting one of the other corners and added her light to the faint impression of tread that

Noah had managed to spot. He would have said he was proud of himself, but he kept quiet, letting GJ do the real work.

He watched as she aimed her light forward some set amount and waved it in a nearly perfect arc. It took him a moment to realize she had calculated the distance of the stride and was looking for the next step.

"There!" But instead of illuminating what she'd found, she shined the light directly at her own feet and gingerly stepped around, determined to not ruin the scene. She was preserving even evidence she might not have yet found.

"Unless they're trying to throw us off the scent, whoever it was left this way."

"Well, *one* of them," Noah added, before realizing he should have asked.

GJ shrugged. Even with the blood highlighting a portion of the heel, the rest of the footprint was gone. The floor was simply too hard to make an impression, and there was no dust to leave a negative.

He heard the trap door open over him and watched as Will Little seemed to kneel down, his head nearly coming through the hole. "Find anything?"

"Yes!" GJ hollered back, as she was already a good distance down the tunnel.

"Can I drop down?" Will asked him, and Noah wanted to ask him if he actually *could*. The old man did not appear spry. But even as the thought passed, Noah watched the white-haired man lithely swing down, hang from his fingertips, and then drop the last few feet. The small grunt as he landed was the only thing that attested to his age or ability.

"What do you have?"

But GJ asked her own question. "Are Christina and Walter still on with Westerfield?"

Will nodded and Noah felt his heart sink. The conversation going on that long couldn't be good. But he didn't have time to dwell as Will pressed them. "Find anything?"

GJ slowly emerged from the tunnel, walking on her tiptoes, still avoiding unknown evidence. As she reached the center of the room, both she and Noah looked to Will, who was giving the bodies a once-over with a weather eye.

She looked to Noah, as if to ask if he'd come to the same conclusion she had.

He hadn't. He was not a forensic scientist. He understood what she'd said, but he hadn't figured any of that out for himself. Not fully.

"Well, that's bad news, isn't it?" Will asked.

GJ stopped a few feet away from him.

Noah felt his body freeze at her next words.

"It is. I'm fairly confident it was one of your people who did this."

47

D onovan winced as Westerfield's voice barked through the line. He and Eleri had tried again to sound like they weren't together, but it had been one thing to do it when they were in his home. She'd easily moved to another room. This time, they'd been driving on the freeway when their phones rang simultaneously.

Donovan had motioned Eleri to quickly pull to the side of the road. As soon as she'd stopped, he hopped out and shut the door, hoping to leave her in the enclosed car, and him on the side of the road—sounding as if he was in a different place. He had no idea if Westerfield had any clue what they were doing or if maybe their boss was in his office, fully aware and laughing.

Neither of them had ever quite figured out what Westerfield's powers were. Sure, he'd demonstrated moving small objects on the desk. He walked that quarter across his knuckles with a smoothness that appeared preternatural. But what other skills might he have? The ones Donovan had seen were small potatoes compared to what the agents possessed.

"There's too much going down at the de Gottardi/Little farm." Once again, Westerfield decided to forgo any polite hellos.

"But everyone's accounted for?" Donovan asked, knowing that Walter and Jansen were hooked up with Pines and new guy Kimball and that she said they'd checked in with the SAC. Donovan was glad that he was no longer getting grilled about the whereabouts of his girlfriend.

"Yes. There's not only an entire army ringing the joint, I was just informed this morning that there's a mole inside."

Donovan swallowed and felt his shoulders clench at the idea that Walter was in the thick of it. He reminded himself that she could handle it and that she probably didn't need him.

"Have they located Marks yet?" Eleri interjected. Donovan only heard her voice through the phone, though he could see her mouth move through the car window.

"No, and it's worse than we even thought. They shot Shray Menon."

Donovan wondered what the people driving by must think of him, standing on the side of the freeway with his phone to his ear. Even with his specialized hearing, he found himself covering his other ear to block the loud zing of traffic.

Westerfield hadn't yet asked about the zooming noises, and Donovan wondered if his boss would. If he even cared.

But his muscles clenched as he listened, his brain shocked and concerned by what Westerfield was telling them. He'd always been the staid medical investigator. It was his job to *not* be surprised by anything. But he could not control his eyebrows rising, his body stiffening at each passing phrase.

"I thought Menon was dead."

"We all did." The three words from Westerfield covered pretty much everything they needed to know.

Then, Westerfield did something unusual. He dialed back a bit. "We're not actually *positive* it's Menon, but all signs point to it."

"His body did disappear at the time," Eleri said. "It always made me wonder." She paused. "Who identified him?"

"Pines."

No one answered, but Donovan saw Eleri's lips purse. She trusted that answer, too. If Pines thought it was Menon, then it was almost certainly Menon.

"Well, I don't think we'll be wondering much longer. I need more people out there."

Donovan looked through the car window, his eyes making contact with Eleri's as Westerfield kept talking. "I need you to grab your bags and get ready to leave today. I've got flights for each of you—"

That still didn't indicate if he knew they were together or not.

"I'm sending in as many agents as I can. I hope this time we can end it."

Donovan had believed they'd ended it last time. But things were clearly bigger than he'd thought, and he said something for the very first time.

He nodded once at Eleri and watched as she agreed. Then, without waiting for a moment to lose his nerve, he simply replied, "No. We can't go."

"I'm sorry?" Westerfield asked, his tone as stunned as Donovan expected it to be.

"No, sir," Donovan replied, as though the "sir" might massage the answer. "Eleri and I are together. We're heading down through Georgia, possibly into Florida. We've got a lead, and we're following Bodhi Banerjee."

"Well, shit," Westerfield replied. The swear word had one syllable, but three notes. Donovan wasn't sure what that might mean. But he waited. They'd had these moments before.

He and Eleri had things in their own lives that, once in a while, were worth quitting the job that he'd come to embrace and leaving the co-workers he'd come to love. He reminded himself he could go back to being a medical examiner if he needed to. He didn't reevaluate that he would almost certainly have to move, which he didn't want to do, and he would no longer love the job. He'd only liked it at the time because he didn't know another possibility existed.

All these thoughts swirled around and were pushed away as he waited for a follow-up to the swear word.

Eleri had chased her sister's trail until they found her. Donovan had followed, risking his own position and thinking there would be nothing like that that he'd ever need to ask from her. But, suddenly, here it was.

Silence dragged from the other end of the line. And Donovan waited.

48

N oah folded his hands and sat at the table quietly. For once, the NightShade agents outnumbered the de Gottardi/Little members. Only Will and a woman he introduced as Jen represented the family.

Noah figured he'd listen rather than speak. He was definitely the low man on this totem pole. Even Jen, whom he hadn't met before, was clearly in Will's favor. Noah wasn't certain he was in anyone's favor.

Once they were all seated and introduced, GJ launched into presenting her evidence. "Whoever it was that did this, they got into the tunnels."

"How?" Will immediately volleyed back.

"You tell me."

Noah was thinking his own way through the incident, pondering how little he knew about the underground network, except that it was extensive. When the talking trailed off, he decided to screw silence. "I'm just playing devil's advocate here."

Brainstorming worked best if people kept talking. Since no one else was doing it, he did. "What if someone found a door? Some of the tunnels go to the edge of the property, right? And they open out into the fields?"

That's what he'd been told. Then again, maybe he'd been lied to.

But Will nodded first, before amending, "I don't know how they would find one… though I suppose it could happen. Also, the tunnels don't go to the edge of the property. There would be no doubt you were trespassing if you even got close to one of the doors."

So it wasn't as easy as Noah might have thought. "What if they did find a door? And made their way in to where the soldiers were kept?"

Will's brows pulled together and his features darkened. "Then they'd have to be able to find their people."

Jen hopped in, though her voice stayed relatively quiet. "The tunnels are too extensive. They don't all lead to the heart of the land… well, not directly."

Will, though not fighting too hard, was clearly holding stubbornly to the idea that his own people could not have done this. He added, "They would have to be wolves."

"Why?" Christina pressed. Now the NightShade agents were the ones frowning.

"I don't know how else they would find their own people down there. It's all mazes, like Jen said. They either already knew exactly where the soldiers were being kept, or they would have to scent them and follow that trail." He sighed, clearly not liking the answer he'd arrived at. "Honestly, that far away, through multiple tunnels that we didn't drag their friends through…? It would be too hard to tell. I don't think even the best wolf could do it."

Eyebrows darkened around the table as the idea seemed to spread like wildfire through the group. The killer couldn't have come through the tunnels blindly and found their prey.

"So," Christina asked on a deeply concerned sigh, "is it possible they already know the tunnels?"

Will's head swiveled toward her, just as Noah's did. That had not occurred to him. He was told the tunnels were private and secret, and he had simply believed it to be true.

Will looked to Jen with a question in his eyes. When she shook her head in reply to the silent communication, he added, "I suppose in the grand scheme of things, it's a possibility. But I don't think so."

There was something of a tremor in his voice and Noah could tell the old man was giving the idea his best consideration, even though he didn't like the implication.

"Could they have gotten their hands on maps or anything?" GJ tossed that idea out to the table.

"There are no maps. None that I know of." Will shook his head at her, and once again, Noah was reminded of how fiercely this family guarded their land and their secrets. How fiercely they had to.

"If there are no maps, then someone gave them the information. Someone who lives here and knows the layout. It may mean you don't have a *killer* among your people, but you definitely have a mole."

"Fuck." The word emerged low and breathy as Will again lifted his hand to rub his nearly naked skull. "If we believe that no one could have knowledge of the tunnels without living here, and no one could simply wander in and find their people—"

"—and get back out undetected—" Walter tossed in.

Will conceded that point with a nod as well. "—Then they must have had guidance."

When the table remained silent for a while, Will shared another piece of information that lent credence to the idea of a mole. "The soldiers had been down here for a while, in the same place—but even I can't sniff someone out from that far away."

Well, that answered one question for Noah: He'd wondered about Will's genetics. By his guess, Will was likely one of the superior wolves. After all, he'd wound up as the head of the family.

If Will couldn't come onto this land and just find people, Noah was willing to bet no one else could, either. They'd wander around underground until they got lost.

"There are miles and miles of tunnel," Walter commented. The words sounded almost off-hand, but Noah was confident she was leading to something.

"That's just it," Will said, his shoulders slumping. "Even if they got incredibly lucky and headed the right way by sheer, random choice, and then scented their friends…. they probably still couldn't get back out."

"How did they not run into someone else?" GJ asked next.

Will looked around the room. The day was growing darker and he seemed to check that, yes, they had drawn all the shades. Now he reached out and twisted on a flat disc at the center of the table that offered up a dim glow.

In a bit, this room is going to be flat-out creepy. But the conversation pulled Noah away from that thought.

"How far were you able to follow them?" Will shifted gears. Noah didn't even understand what he was asking. Who had followed who?

The deflection was confusing, and he wondered if the change of topic was serendipitous or strategic.

"Honestly, sir, after five steps, the blood was gone." GJ seemed to know what Will was asking, and her clear answer let Noah know they were talking about the killer's boot tracks.

"So, we know which way they initially fled."

But GJ's response was to hold her hands up as if she didn't really know. "I truly only have evidence of one person. I can't even say it's the killer. Just someone who stepped in a spot of the blood and then headed down that tunnel."

"But you think it's the killer?"

"Most likely." She sounded like crime scene techs he'd met on scenes in Miami. They were willing to say exactly what they'd found, but the best anyone could get from them about what had actually happened was speculation, and they always emphasized it was no more than a guess.

The problem was, that she also sounded like she was still holding back...

GJ had been sitting with her hands folded until this point. Pushing them flat onto the table now, almost as though she were going to stand up, she instead leaned forward. She went preternaturally still as she began explaining.

"We can speculate all day, but you all need the rest of the evidence. The blood spatter from the one on the left—the man—was from a brachial artery."

Noah knew this, they all did. But he waited her out.

"That kind of cut should send a spurting spray forward—"

Noah tried to remain scientific rather than thinking about blood.

"But there's no outline of the killer or anyone standing in front of them. We usually see when someone gets in the way of the spatter."

GJ paused, and when no one jumped in with comments or questions, she kept plowing ahead. "Both victims were leaning against the wall. So the killer wasn't behind them." She turned to Noah, next to her. "May I?"

The moment he started to nod, she grabbed his arm and held it out to his side, across the front of her chest. Reaching her hand over his arm, she made a clawing motion. "If the person had done it like this, the spray would move forward. Their hand would be very bloody, maybe to the point of dripping, depending on how fast and how clean the cut was."

The cut had been very clean, Noah thought, *so they might have gotten away without too much evidence dripping off of them.*

"That kind of position would send the arterial spray forward, like we saw." GJ motioned with her hand. "But these two had their backs against the wall, and the evidence is that they died where they sat. So someone got in front of that person and managed to cut the brachial artery, before the soldier realized he needed to defend himself."

Again, silence ringed the table.

"I mean, look where the cut is." She motioned once again to Noah's arm.

And while he understood the need for something to demonstrate on, having her repeatedly demonstrate how his brachial artery could be cut open and he could bleed out in less than two minutes was unnerving—especially now that he knew just how sharp those claws could be. He hadn't really thought about it until he'd seen the bodies and gotten a firsthand view of how straight and deep the lines went.

"But," GJ continued, "the second person was *also* killed. This time, they hit the carotids in a clean slice across the neck. And again, no evidence of the killer in the blood spray."

"Could they have stepped to the side?" Christina asked, finally getting into the issue of the scene itself. "I think it would be easy enough to step to the side and stay out of the way."

"Yes!" GJ said. "But only once. I don't know how *one* person kills one of the soldiers without getting anything on them, then steps toward the second one, who doesn't even tug too hard against his zip ties at his wrists…"

She trailed off letting the evidence speak for itself. Noah could practically hear the thoughts around the table getting deeper.

Will put voice to what GJ's evidence was suggesting.

"So I don't just have a mole," he said with a shudder. "I have a mole who's moving at least *two enemy killers* through my camp, undetected."

49

"It would explain why you seem to have always gone the wrong direction when looking for Marks and why you didn't see all the soldiers," Christina commented. She didn't like it any better than Will did. If she'd been younger, her stomach would have still been turning.

She could handle blood and she could pull the trigger, but after her own disloyalties, she saw this kind of sabotage as high treason. This time, she was certain Will and Jen did, too—even if they didn't see yet what she did. *The mole was just the start of it.*

"It explains why Walter and GJ found everything. They did a full perimeter search before they met up with you. Before they did anything directed by the people who live here." She didn't mention that she'd just cited very good evidence for the de Gottardi/Little mole to not just be a family member, but to be relatively trusted in the organization.

This wasn't just a random peon they'd managed to insert.

Somehow, two people from Marks' army got into the middle of the compound without anyone noticing. *Because it was an inside job.* She looked at Will for a moment and waited while he put all the pieces together.

"If I have a mole and the mole goes out to fetch these two murderous soldiers, and tells them we have live captives…" He trailed off.

GJ picked up, seeming to already have realized what Christina had just figured out.

"They bring back two more soldiers. These soldiers do the killing, and then this mole gets them out of the compound."

She could see that Will was thinking things over. She understood it was the more appealing scenario—though he would still have a bad guy in his midst, his people weren't killers. *Just accomplices.*

But Christina had already dismissed that possibility. She looked back to Will. "Does everybody who lives here recognize everybody else?" She truly didn't know how big the group was. Will had been working with the FBI for a little more than twenty-four hours now, but he hadn't divulged everything. *Clearly.*

"For the most part, we do." He raised his eyebrows and his shoulders. "You'd be hard pressed to pass someone you didn't know without…" His voice trailed off and he looked to Jen.

"You would ask who it was. Expect to be introduced." She said it with authority that Christina appreciated. It made sense. The compound was under attack, ringed by heavily armed forces that didn't just want the land, they wanted genocide. If a family member saw someone they didn't know, trusting them might be a matter of life and death.

"I guess it's possible I don't know everyone here." He turned to the woman Christina was beginning to understand was his new first-in-command. "Do you?"

"Yes, I do. If they are here and I don't know them, then that's a problem."

"Jen checks everyone in, assigns beds, makes sure we have food…"

That made sense, Christina thought, though she wished she'd been filled in on that fact sooner. Still, the vibes that Will was giving off indicated he was having a silent crisis while he sat at the table. There was nothing Christina could do to change that. He still hadn't figured it out. And when he did, it would only get worse.

Will seemed eager to escape from the inevitable conclusion, but Christina grabbed the thread and helped it unravel. "So they change clothes. They come in, they get escorted through the tunnels by this mole… How do they avoid running into people?"

Jen sat stiffly in her tank top and old jeans and Christina wasn't sure if this woman was one of the soldiers who'd been in the field the other day. Maybe Dan, the one who'd been killed, was a personal friend. Christina didn't remember Jen from her last visit to the farm.

More brains at the table were better, but more brains also increased the chance that they'd somehow let the mole inside their little secret meeting—or let the mole know about the meeting. Right now, Will was the only family member on this farm that Christina truly trusted. She wasn't yet confident of Jen.

But the woman answered Christina's question as succinctly as possible. "It's possible to walk the tunnels and not run into anyone, though it would be difficult. You and Noah seemed to do it the first day, but we knew you were here. When they were first built, the network went from home to home, building to building. As the family stayed and added on—"

Jen didn't look old enough to have this in her own memory. It sounded more like she'd been taught these things.

"—more tunnels were added. Sometimes it was easier to connect into another tunnel, so we have a handful of *H bars.*"

When Noah and GJ frowned at her, Jen's eyes darted between them and she kept explaining. Christina liked that about the young woman, but she refused to be taken in. They needed a damned psychic here to tell if Jen had acted in good faith or not. But Christina had only the agents she had.

"H bars are tunnels that only connect one tunnel through to another, already existing tunnel, making the crossbar of a capital H."

"Do these tunnels have names? I understand there are no written maps…" Christina added, "—but are there mental ones?"

"Not really. No names," Jen answered, seeming reluctant, maybe only because they were all looking at her.

"How do you give directions?" Christina pressed.

"We don't. If you live here, you know the tunnels, or you learn damned fast. If you visit, you get an escort so you won't get lost." She looked to Will and, though Christina didn't see it, something passed between the two of them. Once she had his permission to speak freely, she went for it.

"There aren't a ton of H bars, so you can't just wander from tunnel to tunnel. You'd be pretty hard pressed to get completely lost. But you could easily go a long way before you wound up at a house, and you might wind up at a random building instead of the one you meant to. But then you could get above ground and get your bearings."

None of this surprised Christina. Still, she pushed. There was information here, and if she didn't have it, she and her team couldn't protect the compound. They also couldn't use it against Marks.

The tunnel system was interesting, both in the assessment of how someone had possibly gotten in to kill their captives and for her own knowledge. She tucked it away for later. "So it's possible that your mole, and two soldiers—or more—could have come in from somewhere out in the field and ducked off into a side tunnel every time they heard someone coming."

"Plausible," Will said.

But as she watched, his face fell. He'd thought of something. Shaking his head angrily, he turned to Jen.

Jen stared at him for only half a beat before seemingly catching on.

"If someone had come in here and walked two unknown soldiers down the hall, one of us should have scented them." Will's breath rushed out and his shoulders slumped as he ran smack into a conclusion he clearly hated. "They can't be unknown soldiers. Any of us would have smelled two people we didn't recognize. It would have raised an alarm."

Not a physical one, Christina understood, but it would have put Will on alert.

Jen piped up. "Like Will says, we all know each other in some capacity. Many of us grew up here and are returning. Hell, most of us are closely related. We've been here, under the tunnels, gathering the family back into place. We get a handful of new people some days, but they aren't really *new* people." She paused. "We recognize them. No one comes in without going directly to find a room and get something to eat."

Which Jen coordinates, Christina thought.

"I think I do know everyone here," Jen added as she thought about it.

"That's why she's here," Will filled in. He'd brought someone he implicitly trusted, someone who could recognize things even he wouldn't.

Christina looked around the table at all of them, waiting for any more alternative theories to pop up. "But that puts us back at GJ's worst case scenario. Will, it wasn't a soldier who was brought into the compound. We've eliminated every possible way for that to happen.

Which leaves us to conclude that it was one of your own people who did this."

She paused. When he only pressed his lips together and didn't counter her, she continued. "The question is: who and how?"

He didn't have an answer. That was evident in the angry set of his jaw. Unfortunately, neither did Jen or any of the agents. And, right now, neither did Christina.

"There's one more important question, Will," Christina said, leaning forward. "You went down into the room with Noah and GJ." She was speaking before she'd fully formed the thoughts—a truly bad idea, but she didn't like her next question and had to get it out of the way.

"You saw the bodies, Will. So who did you smell who had been down there with them?"

50

"Yeah, there's a reason for that…" Will shook his head, as though he were disgusted with himself.

Noah watched as Will leaned back in the chair. The old man looked up to the ceiling and, once again, Noah took his own time to look around.

He was struck by how clean and perfect the small room was. The wall to his left separated this room from a bedroom on the other side, a bedroom that had a hole gaping out to the outside world. Bricks, muddy and dirty and covered in leaves, littered the floor, making it likely you would twist an ankle if you tried to casually walk through. But in here, Will and his team had cleaned the walls, hung blackout curtains, brought in a table and chairs, and set a small light in the middle of the table.

As the daylight fell, it felt as though they were in any random house, not a shell leftover from a war.

As he had expected, the ambience was becoming creepy as the day grew longer and the shadows started to fall. Despite the good looks, this place had no power.

"Here's why," Will said at last. "One, you might have noticed I'm just a little older than most of the others. I don't shift my face as well as I used to."

Dogs got arthritis. Noah wondered if that applied to these wolves, too. How painful shifting must be if that was the case. But

Will was still talking, and Noah pulled his wandering thoughts back on track.

"My sense of smell has been going, somewhat. It's still better than most humans, but not as good as the rest of my people." He sighed. "Second, I wasn't even thinking of identifying the people I know who had been there. So I don't remember who I smelled, just that nothing was unusual. We should get someone else down there, ASAP. It's better if they don't know about a mole. Just ask someone to list who came through. And maybe head down the tunnels, to see where our killer went."

But there was something about the way he said it that made Noah think maybe he was holding back. Noah wished there was something he could do right now—tap the old man on the shoulder? Maybe he was even strong enough to scoot a chair leg, to jostle and startle him enough to tell the truth. But none of that was really useful here.

Christina looked to Jen, almost as though she suddenly trusted Jen more than Will. "Yes, do that. Get someone down there as soon as possible. I want to know who was there."

Jen's eyes hit on every single one of them before she stood. "If it's okay, I'll go myself."

"Yes." Christina nodded to dismiss her.

As Jen headed for the door, Will put his hand over the light., Christina jolted. "Wait! Don't go there alone."

Will looked at her, puzzled.

"Will, where she's going is two houses over, and we have a killer in our midst. What if that person is down there right now, trying to cover up what they did? What if they see her?"

GJ was already standing, ready to go with her. "Three is more of a threat than two. We'll get a wolf who tracks well and doesn't know the situation. Better data."

This, Noah thought, *just got a hell of a lot more complicated.* They would turn up at least one, and probably two, moles. But would the agents be going back out to find more captives? Would they still try to interrogate somebody to know what Dr. Marks was up to

Finding the mole seemed the most pertinent way to keep themselves safe. But he wasn't in charge here. In fact, the call with Westerfield had told them that yes, they should interrogate their captives. They should figure out if Murray Marks was alive and in the area. If the man Christina had her run-in with was in fact Shray Menon...

There was still too much to sort. And Noah was growing more confident that Will knew more than he was saying.

Shit.

Though GJ had trailed Jen out the door, Noah thought their little meeting might continue right along until the two women came back with information. If Jen had a keen sense of smell and a wolf was nearby that they could take with them, they might be back in as little as twenty or thirty minutes.

But given GJ's keen sense of forensics, she also might keep them there for hours. She would add Jen's scent information to what she already knew and reconstruct the crime scene again.

Surprising him, Christina dismissed their little group. Standing, she announced, "One of my agents and your second are gone. We can continue this later."

Will seemed to have a lot on his mind. Noah was confident they weren't done.

Watching as Will turned off the little light, he noticed that the sunlight outside was almost entirely gone.

"Do you know where you're going?"

So while Will didn't trust all of his own people, he at least seemed to trust them.

"We're good. We may head to bed, and we can continue tomorrow with the new evidence," Christina replied.

Confused and dog tired—probably since he'd barely had a few hours of sleep—Noah looked at Christina oddly as she grabbed his hand. She whispered something as she started to tug him out the door and motioned for Walter to follow.

They headed out of the room but bypassed the trap door in the floor and walked carefully down the steps and out into the grass.

There was nothing subtle about their departure, but Christina needed to talk to her agents. Crouched in the grass, she motioned the other two to get down and then mouthed and motioned, "Pat yourself down for trackers."

Holy shit. Now, they didn't even trust the de Gottardi/Little family. *But how could they?*

The family was in the middle of a war, and he was seriously reconsidering his stint with the NightShade division.

He ran his hands along his pockets and seams as his irritated thoughts churned. He could be at home, watching movies and drinking beer with Mercury and Jupiter. His cats would not almost get him killed. Aside from his numbers with the Miami Bureau, that investigation was going to yield nothing. Unless somebody decided to say, "Hey, we've got a psychic here who's moving shit around"— and even then, nothing was going to happen to him. And no one was going to say that anyway. There was no precedent for a psychokinetic agent.

Noah knew it would suck to be investigated, and they might continue to do so periodically, but running down the occasional drug dealer or tracking a possible terrorist were both starting to look a lot safer than where he was. Even with his gun pulled and his adrenaline high, he was about fifteen thousand times less likely to die in Miami than in Arkansas, with the shit he'd gotten himself into now.

Christina looked at him, almost as though she could tell he was having a miniature life crisis as he patted his own ass and thighs, checking for devices that he might not have otherwise noticed.

For a moment, he wondered if he'd been fed something. If that was the case, then any device inside him was simply going to have to wait until it came out.

"Here?" Walter asked, as though to suggest it was indeed odd to be squatting and patting themselves down in the tall grass.

Christina shrugged. "It's as good a place as any. I mean, I'd rather not be inside one of the buildings."

That seemed obvious. Anyone willing to put trackers on them would be more than willing to bug a room.

"All right," Christina said. "I'm going to ask Will if I can see the family records."

Noah was nodding along but, beside him, Walter nearly gasped. He was wondering what would make Walter gasp like that, when Christina explained.

"They don't share them with anyone. No. One. Most of the family members don't get to see them. They offer genetic tracking of a handful of major families of wolves through the generations."

"And that's why the family guards them," Noah said. He'd caught on.

"As much as they'd be interesting medical records for someone like Marks, it's more likely he'd use it as a kill sheet. But," she said, "I don't know if you remember when I was out there, when we faced Shray Menon and what I asked him."

Walter nodded, and Noah thought for a moment. Christina had said some odd things, but in the heat of the battle, he wasn't sure he would remember anything specific.

She clarified. "I asked him about Aegis X."

"And?" The name meant nothing to him.

"Menon looked like he knew what it was," Walter said. She had been able to both fight and pay attention.

"Aegis X is tied to someone you might know, Kimball."

Huh, he thought, *she'd last-named him.*

Aegis X is the corporation that owns—via several other shell corporations—that wolf-based company running drugs in the Caribbean. Miranda Industries."

Holy shit.

51

"Will's at the schoolhouse."

Christina looked at Jen with her eyes wide and questioning.

"Well, you can go this way and cut left, or that way and cut right on the H bar."

Christina now headed down the long tunnel by herself. Jen had aimed her this direction to find Will. And Jen's insistence that they all knew the tunnels and didn't "give directions" had been hammered home.

She'd decided to come alone with the hopes that she would get more out of Will if it was only her asking, if it was only her eyes that saw.

Noah had reacted as expected. "Are you serious? This is related to Miranda Industries again?"

She'd nodded. She only knew about Miranda because she'd been pulling documents about corporations and following the trails of filed tax holdings. She'd run into shell companies and more, all of which had wolves on their roster, according to the files NightShade was holding on them. Though, honestly, many more places actually had wolves working for them.

Eleri had once said she didn't even know her friend and fellow NightShade agent Wade was a wolf until after she'd found out about

Donovan. Wolves guarded their secrets fiercely, and they were out in public, in schools, and in the workforce.

Some of their employers knew about them. Some specifically recruited and trained wolves, and apparently, NightShade was tracking them, the same way the rest of the FBI tracked the KKK and other radical militias. The companies often worked on agendas that depended on wolf families.

The fact that Dr. Murray Marks was somehow involved in Aegis X concerned the shit out of her.

"Will?" she called out as she turned the corner. She did not want to surprise anyone, not with moles out and about and Will probably being jumpy as hell.

Yesterday had been quiet, thankfully. She'd intended to interrogate the soldiers, but a dual murder had gotten in the way of that. Without a positive ID on the killers—Jen and the wolf she'd brought along had scented too many people near the bodies to narrow it down—Christina had slept a full night after they disbanded their little meeting.

She'd slept better after finding out that none of her agents had trackers on them and there were none in their little room, either. But it was time to tell Will what she knew. It was time to ask him to share with her what he knew. They both knew more than he was telling…

"That you, Christina?" Will flipped up the trap door and she emerged up into the schoolhouse.

Sometimes one of the tunnels had a ladder stashed to help tunnel-goers get up into the buildings but she'd found that, most of the time, she simply had to make a good leap, grab by her fingertips and haul herself up.

She'd always wondered how they'd done this with children—when the family had all lived here, before they were being attacked. Maybe they had ladders readily available then. In the main house, the last time she'd been here, there had been stairs leading right up to the door. But things had changed, and now was not the time to ask about ladders.

She let the older man help haul her up, as it was no easy task. But once she was on her feet, she got down to business. "Will, you and I need to sit down and have a frank conversation."

He looked to the two men who had been standing behind him and, with a simple nod, he dismissed them. When the room was clear,

Christina got close to him and whispered, "Are you sure they're going?"

He nodded, not worried about the two he'd just sent away.

"Are you sure no one is listening?"

Even though his lips tightened at her mere suggestion, Will gave another short nod.

She went one step further and put her face near his shoulder. "Remember, there's a mole. Let's check for five minutes, to be sure we're clean."

They searched the room from ceiling to floor, turning on their phone flashlights, even though the daylight was relatively bright already. She needed to see into the corners. They checked under the edges of the countertops and inside cabinets. The school building had stayed mostly intact, leaving the small kitchen in the corner and the restroom still fully functional. Nothing was left unchecked.

"I don't see anything," Will told her, but Christina held up a finger indicating one more place to check.

Holding up her own phone, she hit the power button as a demonstration for him and watched as his eyebrows raised in question. Pulling the protective case, she slid the battery off the back, then showed him all the empty pieces, before nodding at him clearly suggesting, *your turn.*

He shrugged. Taking a phone apart was a pain in the ass, but it was necessary if they were going to be sure they were in the clear. The last thing she wanted was to have this conversation and find out later it had not stayed between them.

"Son of a bitch!"

The words caught her off guard as he pointed to the tiny tracking device laid flat between the phone and the battery.

Fuck. She mouthed the word for him and put a finger to her lips, even as he reached to put a fingernail under the edge of the device and try to pry it loose.

Christina put her hand over his and shook her head mouthing, *leave it.* At least until they decided what to do, it wasn't wise to take it off or dismantle it. Whoever was listening would know immediately.

She motioned by circling with her hand, indicating he should speak and make something up. It took a moment for him to catch on. And then he hollered out, "What? Wait, what? Okay, okay. Now? Christina, I'm getting called away."

"Fine." She played along, impressed with his dedication to the lie. "But we'll meet up later." Then she watched as he walked out the door and onto the porch. He put his hands on the railing and looked out over the land for a moment. Her heart squeezed. *He's an open target. What if he gets shot?*

But a few minutes later, Will turned around and came back inside, having left the phone casually on the railing. Back in the room, he closed the door. "Was that what you wanted to meet with me about?"

"Sadly, no, it was just a quick check to be sure. If you've got a mole, it makes sense somebody could get in here and listen to everything. They can be sending signals, not just to themselves, but back out to Dr. Marks." *Or worse*, she thought.

"Well, it explains a lot." Will sighed, his face falling, understanding that he might have been the conduit for the death of some of his own people. "So what did you want to talk about?"

"I need to see the family records, Will."

He's shook his head, instantly denying her request, letting her know that answer was just a regular course of action and nothing he'd thought about. "No one sees them, even most of our own people."

"I know, but you and I together—" she hoped that would soften the blow, "—need to sit down and comb through them, because you have a mole. And it turns out, while Dr. Marks is out there with his well-funded soldiers and his army, he's not just here because he wants to wipe out wolves."

She paused as Will frowned at her. Her next words changed the game.

"He's working with Aegis X."

52

"Nothing," Eleri said, sitting in the passenger seat with her eyes closed. She was trying to track Bodhi Banerjee.

She and Donovan had driven down into central Georgia, based on what she'd seen. Donovan had no doubt that her visions had them on the right track.

It felt odd to be trusted implicitly. She'd operated for so long on the idea that she was simply *chasing hunches*. The impromptu trip had gotten in the way of her contacting Avery, too, but not in the way of Donovan nagging her about it.

"Have you messaged him?"

"No, *mom*. I haven't. It's not the right time."

She was pretty sure she heard him mutter, *It's never the right time,* but she ignored it.

"How much further do we go before we call off—" She'd almost said "the dogs" but that felt wildly inappropriate. "—the search?"

"You haven't picked up anything for a while? Even that we're going the right direction?"

"I would give anything for a clue or a spark of idea, because right now…" She turned and shrugged at Donovan, as if to say, *I can't get any of it.*

They could have called this a road trip if not for the fact that she'd handed the keys to Donovan some time ago and climbed into her own passenger seat. If not for the fact that she was trying to psychically trail Donovan's piece-of-shit brother. If not for the fact that the words that came out of her mouth were not in the direction Donovan probably expected.

She turned and looked at him and mused out loud. "Is he stalking you? Is he trying to get close enough to hurt you? Or is he just trying to make contact?"

Donovan frowned and looked at the side of the road, seemingly checking for exits.

They needed a break. Hell, they might even cast a spell, to see if they could find Bodhi that way. This way didn't seem to be working anymore.

"Do you mean something like, he's trying to contact me to get out of whatever group or cult he's gotten into this time?"

Yeah, that is problematic, she thought.

Bodhi had been part of a gang in New Orleans. That was where Eleri and Donovan had met him, in the middle of a nasty street fight. When Donovan had first realized the man was his brother, it had opened a can of worms.

But that gang had somewhat disbanded. The sisters who ran it had fled town, and Eleri had no luck finding them. They were better at cloaking than she was at finding.

Then she and Donovan had run into another group specifically hiring wolves and moving with a bit of a wolf agenda. And not a good one. Bodhi was in the middle of that again.

They'd disrupted the group, but there was no telling if Bodhi had found his older brother and wanted to change his ways or if he was going to get initiated into some crap wolf gang by selling out Donovan. Eleri was not about to let that happen. She'd light every bowl she could find on fire if that's what it took. Because, right now, that and murder seemed to be her main skills.

Donovan seemed to consider her ideas without speaking. Then he pointed out a sign and she nodded. It looked like as good a place as any to get off the road.

The middle of Georgia offered an exit for a state road. Probably, once they drove past the large gas stations and tchotchke shops, they would get to some empty space where they could pull over and have a real discussion.

And maybe cast that spell.

"I don't think his intentions are good."

Donovan broke into her thoughts, pulling them back from the bleak place they had strayed. "He put a listening device on my house. He knows where I live. He didn't wait for me. He didn't write me a letter."

"A letter can be traced," she pointed out, not sure why she was arguing in Bodhi's favor.

"True. Still, he got the call and he left. You said he put the tracking device on my car *before* the call came. So it wasn't because he was called away and wanted to find me."

"I don't ascribe any good intentions to that one," Eleri didn't argue. She *wondered*, but she didn't argue. Donovan had a right to be livid at both his mother and his younger brother.

If he shot Bodhi Banerjee on sight, Eleri would stand and defend him. She was just trying to throw out alternate possibilities.

They stayed silent for a while, pulled off at a state road a few miles later, and found it was exactly as they'd expected.

"If we go up that little road there, it looks like it might be empty. No one's driving that way. We should be able to find some trees...."

Donovan took the turn and Eleri was reaching into the back where she'd stashed her Book of Shadows under a towel on the floor, when the spike of sensation went through her brain.

And the vision hit her.

53

"Aegis?"

Will put his hand to his temple as if he suddenly had a throbbing headache.

Christina watched as he stilled, absorbing the name she'd thrown at him.

"How do you even know that name?"

She tipped her head to the left, as if to ask why he was being stupid. "I found it in the archives, Will. I told you I looked up all the wolf-related cases."

"And you found the name Aegis?" He seemed stunned.

"Yes, and if I can, lots of people can," she reminded him. "Why are you so surprised? Is the group supposed to be so well hidden that even *we* wouldn't know about them?"

"Well, frankly, yes," he said. "What do you know?"

Christina paused a moment. If she wanted more from Will, she was going to have to give more herself. "Well, I followed them backwards from Miranda Industries."

"Miranda, hmm." He apparently also knew who they were.

Maybe he knew more than she did. But she thought her card of knowing that Aegis X was involved here, now, was worth a whole metric ton in trade. She kept showing her cards.

"Miranda's running ops out of the southern US and the Caribbean. They hire wolves and use the full extent of their skills.

They are running a lot of drugs. The wolves can tell that the drug scent is adequately masked, getting them past guards and customs. And they seem to run crowd control, too."

She felt her lips press at the underwhelming term. Guards and inspectors at several customs centers had been found shredded...

"We had agents involved in a case with them. So that's where I started."

Again, Will looked at her skeptically. "They shut Miranda down?"

Christina almost laughed. A single case would not shut down Miranda Industries. She shook her head. "The agents got out clean. They got information. And they solved a case that had led them to Miranda. But they sure as hell did not shut down Miranda Industries."

MI was far too big for Eleri and Donovan to close down, when they'd only just discovered what they were. *That will not be happening.* Though Christina wished it would.

"And Aegis was there?" Will prodded.

"Apparently not. I think if I go back to those agents and ask, unless they've done the same kind of paperwork research that I have, they won't know the name. I don't think they connected that link."

"You start first." Will leaned forward, his hands folded, his pale blue eyes intent on her and her knowledge. "What do you know about Aegis?"

Christina knew she was handing over everything, playing all the cards she had. Will still hadn't agreed to show her the family documents. But she did understand where she stood with him. So she talked, because it was the only way she would ever get into the records.

"There are lots of links to follow through shell corporations. Ultimately, it becomes clear that Aegis X owns a large portion of Miranda industries. They're definitely in bed."

Will nodded at her to keep going. This was not news to him, although it had been to her just a month ago when she'd found it.

"Aegis X is involved all over the world. Miranda seems to be limited to Central America. And while it's expanding, it's not running full-scale worldwide ops like Aegis X." She paused. "There seems to be some lore that Aegis X was named for a person, but I don't really know the whole extent of that."

Still, Will stayed quiet. It was an excellent tactic, one she often used, but this time she let it work on her. Though she was tempted to reach into his brain and push him to begin speaking, she respected the man too much to do it. This wasn't her high school football star boyfriend or some criminal she could freely manipulate.

Ultimately, the skill was hers to use in the best manner possible. She was trying to cling to that now and be a better person than her past would suggest. "Here's what I put together. We originally thought that Marks was here in an attempt to wipe out your family."

"I still think that," Will interrupted. His tone was clean and clear, without emotional attachment to the genocide that seemed to keep coming.

"I thought they were here to wipe out *wolves*. And I thought your family was a target because they were wolves."

Another pause. When he didn't speak, she jumped in again. Still, she held back pushing on him, though she desperately wanted to. "That's why I want to see the family records, Will. Aegis X is a wolf organization. So why would they want to wipe out wolves?"

"They don't," he said, sighing once again. The grim set of his jaw showed he knew what was coming and it wasn't good.

"They don't want to take out wolves," he repeated, "They just want to wipe out *us*."

Christina nodded, comprehension dawning. "That's why the family moved out to the country."

"We had to. If it's Aegis, they don't want to remove wolves from the earth. The goal is to remove *other* wolves, any independently functioning individuals and families. To leave Aegis standing in control of all the remaining families on the planet."

"It's still genocide," Christina commented before she thought better of it.

"It is." Will seemed resigned, as though he wasn't sitting in a schoolhouse that was now fortified as a bunker on a burned-out plot of land where his family was only just beginning to come back together.

And they were still getting killed for it.

"What that means, though," Christina bumped the conversation forward again, "—is that your mole might not even be working for Dr. Marks. They might be linked directly to Aegis X."

That was it. She was out of cards to play until he gave her more information. She'd told him everything she'd figured out, and he'd already known most of it. Will was the kind of man to figure things out himself. She kept forgetting that.

Now, he started talking. His voice was almost monotone. "Aegis is credited with being the first known wolf to walk the earth. If you look at it in genetics terms, the mutation was dominant. I don't know if he was like some kind of Genghis Khan, fathering hundreds of children on many continents… And I have no idea if the rumors are true. Maybe he wasn't the first. Maybe he just pulled some Alexander the Great shit and people believed it."

He sighed. "A lot of wolves claim descendancy from Aegis though."

"You?" Christina asked. Once again, she aimed at her original purpose for coming here, even if she didn't ask outright again. Not yet. More than ever, she wanted to see the family documents to see where the split might have occurred—and why Aegis X was after the de Gottardi and Little families.

"My grandmother."

Will said them with such simplicity, the words almost startled her.

She nodded even as he laughed and waved his hand as though to brush the whole thing off. "You know how Americans like to claim that someone in their history was Native American? And now with the research and the tools that we have, they go back through their genealogy and discover it was just this story that people in their family liked to tell?"

Christina was catching on.

"Aegis is like that for wolf families. So yes, my grandmother claimed to be a descendant. But as of right now, I have no way of telling how true that is." Will tipped his head as if to tell her to erase whatever connections she thought she'd made.

"I'm thinking," Christina said, offering up a subtle shift in topic and holding tightly onto her brain cells, so that she didn't inadvertently push him. There had been a time when she manipulated thoughts so indiscriminately, that she'd often done it without intending to do so.

She hadn't known for years if she had any real friends, because she'd been pushing everyone all the time. Now sometimes when the urge for what she wanted was strong—and even more, when she believed that what she wanted was righteous and good—it was so easy to slip and push on someone. Even if she didn't mean to.

So she held on tight to her own reins and said, "Will, I'm thinking if you and I looked through the family records together, we might be able to find that link. And more importantly, right now, I might be able to identify your mole."

Will stayed still for a moment. And then slowly, he nodded.

"Come with me."

54

S *hit, shit, shit.*
Noah stalked slowly forward, the tip of his rifle raised, his body sideways to make a slimmer target. Right foot crossing over left, left foot stepping out, he slowly advanced through the field.

He wasn't off the family property yet, but he was within feet of it. Something from his sense-memory made the invisible line feel physical and his stomach clenched.

His eyes flicked away from the scope for a second. First to his left, then to his right. He still couldn't see his fellow agents.

He and Walter and GJ had spread out just enough so they couldn't all be taken at once. Instead of being one target, they'd become three. He was rethinking this plan, but it was far too late for that. It was possible—since he couldn't see or hear any of them—that either of his colleagues had already been dragged backwards into the grass and trees, just like he had last time.

There was no recon on this mission, only the attempt to catch one or two enemy combatants. It wasn't a term he liked: "enemy combatants." He'd always preferred to think of himself as a guardian, but a lot of his training had been about taking out the enemy. He still tried to function in the better capacity. But here? He didn't think there was any guardian factor to be found here. He'd been sent out to stun, disable, and take a hostage.

Still, despite the cold sweat running down his back and the

massive concern that all of his teammates had been killed, he was finding the job was growing on him.

Noah, shut up, he told himself. *Now is not the time to have a midlife crisis.*

They'd made the assumption as a group that the northern pods they'd seen before were probably on higher alert. They knew that they'd been found out and had lost several members. *Even if it was their own decision to kill those members*—or so Noah thought from what he'd gleaned.

So, the three agents had headed west.

The landscape was hillier this way. The trees came in clusters that Noah could easily maneuver around. But having lost sight of his fellow agents made him very, very nervous. Working without Christina there to make anyone they encountered think they were on fire also made him very, very nervous. As far as he knew, Walter and GJ wouldn't be able to help with any extra-curricular interventions.

He told himself that's why they'd put him in the middle. Not because he was the weakest link. Though that was entirely plausible.

His orders—should he encounter one of the soldiers they were looking for—were to head forward. Get in close enough range to use a stun gun—without getting dead. Then zip tie and drag his capture back to the compound.

No problem, he whispered to himself.

Then he heard the grass rustle in front of him in response.

He stilled for a moment, but when nothing else came, he crept slowly forward. The tip of the rifle still sweeping the landscape in front of him, looking for "enemy combatants."

The attempt to stay low was wearing on his thigh muscles. He figured even he wouldn't bet on himself being the one to capture their next prisoner. Walter—definitely. Hell, even GJ had a better shot at this than him. He could imagine her dragging some massive soldier behind her, commenting how she'd calculated the angles and estimated the mass of her opponent to use his momentum against him.

Noah, on the other hand, was sweating bullets out here.

Christina had gone to talk with Will once again, and that left the three of them to execute Westerfield's orders of getting someone they could interrogate. Though Noah was radically against torture—though he was confident that, between himself and Christina, they could avoid that—they did need information. They were surrounded, getting killed, and had only a vague idea of why.

Few grand conclusions had been drawn.

Walter, Noah, and GJ had spent some of their time reviewing the short list of those that Jen had scented near the bodies.

"Add Jen." GJ had pointed to the list.

Walter had merely raised one eyebrow at her, but she'd written the additional name down on the piece of paper. She'd pulled out a legal pad, not wanting anything hackable or traceable.

Even between the three of them, they'd not come up with much of anything. No one on the list jumped out, despite the fact that it only included ten people. Some of them might have been in the room before the soldiers had been killed. About half were referred to as *new* or *returning* flock. Very few people had stayed to guard the compound after the last big fight with Marks' people.

So most had returned after the compound was up and running. Others were like Jen, who had only the slimmest genetic relation. Once she'd figured out what she was, she'd gone looking for others of her kind. And once she found it, she'd stayed put. Aside from a short stint when they scattered, Will could account for Jennifer Crunk's whereabouts for the past eleven years. If she was the mole, she'd been here more than a decade, or she'd been radicalized during the three months the wolves were scattered. Neither seemed likely.

Jen had rapidly returned to the compound once Will had opened back up for a few who wanted to stay and help the family integrate back into their home. That move had helped her rise up in the informal ranks and become a coordinator for the family.

Noah still couldn't tell if that had been her plan or a serendipitous happenstance.

But though his brain wanted to wander back to the list, he couldn't—shouldn't—try to solve any of that now. He had to stay focused on staying safe. Taking three more steps forward, he crouched down lower for a minute. Stopping gave him the opportunity to get a better view, swing his rifle a good one-hundred-eighty degrees, and keep an eye out for his fellow agents.

If he was the only one who returned, then this was not going to go well.

To his right he heard a small pop and hiss. Then a yell, the gurgling kind that a person made when they'd been hit. For a moment, his shoulders relaxed and his lungs breathed easier.

Walter.

He'd been on the money. It sure sounded like she'd hit someone.

But it was GJ's voice that came over the comms, breaking the agreed-upon silence.

"One more," she said.

One more than we agreed to get, Noah thought testily. Then again, maybe something was wrong with this one. He didn't know.

He sniffed the air, his mere human senses detecting an odd smell. It wasn't enough to make him change course, so he took three more steps forward. He was slowly setting his foot down again, when the man appeared suddenly in front of him, naked and pushing to his feet.

Noah quickly came to the conclusion that this man had just transformed from his wolf shape. However, that didn't tell him if this was friend or foe—not with what was going on.

The man stared, his moss green gaze turning to a glare as Noah failed to obey whatever psychic command he must have thought he issued. His brown hair shone in the late afternoon sunlight in a way that was wholly inappropriate for the situation. Whatever he was upset about, it seemed aimed at Noah.

Then, in a deep and almost feral voice, the man growled out one word.

"Run."

55

Despite the rifle still aimed at him, the brown-haired, naked man walked forward. He bypassed the barrel of Noah's gun and, for whatever reason, Noah didn't pull the trigger.

Still, he was shocked when the man grabbed him by the shoulders, turned him, and once again demanded, "Run!"

That was when Noah smelled it: Death. Sulfur. Blood. He couldn't be sure, but this time he knew enough to run. And he headed straight back toward the compound, yelling into the comms in case Walter and GJ hadn't caught the strange scent or felt the hair on their necks rise.

He saw them, as they popped up and aimed back to where they'd come from, to the cluster of tiny houses where the agents were sleeping. *Thank God.*

The smell grew stronger, almost as if it were a cloud taking over the land where they ran, the man a few paces behind, his footsteps odd, but moving with Noah. Noah simultaneously wondered about the steps and thought he should see a yellow or green-gray gas in the air, given what he was inhaling each time he sucked in a breath. But the day was clear.

If not for the demand of the stranger and the smell, Noah would think he was an idiot. But he ran.

Behind him, the grass crunched and he heard only one or two odd sounds that he didn't process until Noah saw a brown-colored wolf run past on all fours.

It had to be the man. They had the same color hair all over as he saw in their human forms. Noah had learned that in the Caribbean. The man turned and looked back.

As Noah passed him, still running for the base, the man leaped closer and bumped him. It was just enough of a nudge to keep him going forward.

Behind him, noise grew to match the smell, almost overwhelming him in a deafening wave.

For a moment, Noah almost turned to look. Something about the noise told him it would be like watching a nuclear bomb go off. From a clinical lens, it might be fascinating, or stunning, or insane. But it would be, from a practical perspective, still the last thing he ever saw. So he ran.

The heavy gear weighed him down, but he pushed on, the sweat trickling down his back a non-issue now. He would have chucked the rifle and removed its weight and clumsy rhythmic whack against his side, but it was strapped to him. Off to either side, he saw Walter and GJ both bolting away from their original target.

Fighting to lengthen his stride, Noah reminded himself that he was in good shape. But he should have gone running more. He could have run faster, back when he ran.

As he was having these thoughts, something tackled him from behind.

It had hit hard against the back of his vest, but he was unable to distinguish what had struck him. Hand? Paw? Maybe even a bullet! The punch was that hard.

Noah fought to right himself. But he didn't win that battle, and he plunged face down into the grass, the heavy weight on his back holding him down.

He waited for teeth to tear into the flesh of his neck where it was just a little bit exposed despite his heavy gear. He must be seven kinds of fool for running because a stranger told him to. He was going to die a painful but deserved death because of a stupid mistake.

But even as he braced himself to die by tooth and claw, the world exploded behind him.

56

C hristina watched as Jen applied hydrogen peroxide, alcohol, or iodine to the wounds of her team. Who knew what she was wiping on? It was mostly clear with a bluish tinge. But Christina didn't want to call out someone Will trusted, and she let her teammates each decide if they wanted Jen's help.

They'd all been bloodied and bruised by the blast.

There were six of them now in the room below the burned out house. Their four inflatable beds still lingered in the corners, but now they were down here for sheltered medical care. Jen was the only one allowed, because she was the only one Christina trusted, given the direction their conversation might go.

GJ had already been cleaned up and Noah was fighting not to yelp. Christina almost yelped for him. Walter and Wade waited, helping each other with locating the worst of their injuries before Jen got to them.

Turning her head away, Christina tried not to watch. Medicine wasn't her field of choice. She had no issues with damage in the field. She could do the work when it needed to be done. But no one wanted her as their EMT right now, and she chose not to look at their exposed flesh and angry welts and bloody cuts.

She still didn't know what it was that had caused the tiny nicks and cuts in so many places. They each claimed to have been far enough away to be relatively safe, but she'd sustained cuts straight through the fabric of her pants and shirt. Walter had pulled out a shiny black shard from her forearm before Jen had stopped her.

Like the others, Walter had areas with no real damage as well as swaths of skin where she had only bruises. For Walter and GJ, it was the middle of their backs, where their vests covered them—the Kevlar wasn't just bulletproof but shrapnel-proof. For which Christina was grateful.

She sat, tilted to one side, the cuts on her own ass already washed and bandaged.

As she and Will had looked through the family records, someone had banged on the door. Will had lifted his face and sniffed the air, and then run from the room.

Shocked that he was abandoning the records he was ready to die for, she'd closed and locked the door and run after him. They arrived in the daylight and headed straight out into the grass to see what was happening, Will shocking her with his speed. He ran, leading with his face, following a scent trail she lacked the equipment to distinguish. But she'd jogged along after him, noticing that the air "felt weird."

She didn't even get a chance to say it or to ask him what was wrong. She didn't really absorb that all the wolves around her were acting strangely, many of them bolting right toward her.

"Run!" Will had yelled at her, and she'd turned around and managed three steps before others were screaming at everyone to take cover.

She'd dropped and protected her head and her chest. And left her damn ass up in the air. The back of her hands were peppered with small cuts, and so was her butt. She would have sighed and been far more irritated by that, but watching Noah get checked to see if he needed stitches was tamping down on her pissiness.

Most of them had gone straight down and huddled in the grass, like she had. Standard protection position. The backs of Walter's legs had been spared and Christina took that to indicate that she'd gone fetal, rather than ass-up like she had.

Judging from the way her wounds were spaced, apparently GJ had been smart enough to stop, turn around, and face the blast before going down. This placed her helmeted head and Kevlar vest toward the oncoming shrapnel. Even so, she had plenty of open wounds.

Only Noah had relatively large swaths of undamaged skin. Sure, the backs of his hands now sported a few taped pieces of gauze and a spot on his lower side was blooming in a spectacular bruise. He also had a cut near his temple that Jen was now inspecting. But that was about it.

She pulled back and grinned at him. "Chicks dig scars."

Christina almost scoffed. She felt like hamburger, and Jen was telling him that he was going to get a sexy scar. Hell, Noah wouldn't even care if chicks dug his scar. Jen was barking up the wrong man, but Christina didn't tell her that.

It was Wade who was sliced up the worst. From the looks of it, Wade had taken the brunt of the shrapnel that he and Noah had received.

Christina knew now that Wade must have arrived at the compound while she'd been in the archives. How he had run into Noah... well, she hadn't figured that part out yet.

Still, despite the blast and the shitty timing, she'd never been so glad to see Wade de Gottardi. She would have hugged him had it not been likely to make them both jump back and yell out from the pain.

"I cannot tell you how happy I am that you are here," Christina sighed, even as she sat on one butt cheek on her inflatable bed. With her wounds already dressed, she was clothed as best she could be, wearing a borrowed pair of basketball shorts and her own tank top. She sported tube gauze down her left arm and up her leg.

"Well, I was glad to be home, but then shit blew up," Wade offered with a shrug. He didn't make a move to hug her, either. She understood.

Jen declared Noah finished and moved on to Walter, who had gingerly removed her prosthetic arm and leg. The embarrassment on her fellow agent's face was one Christina could only attribute to Lucy Fisher certainly not hardened agent Walter Reed. She looked away. Everyone had their issues, apparently—even Walter.

At first, Walter had been pissed because the hostage she'd been dragging back had not only slowed her down but had not survived the blast, but she'd now moved on to muttering about getting cleaned up.

Jen handed her a piece of gauze and said, "Hold this," as a noise above alerted Christina.

Looking up, she watched the trap door open and Will swing agilely to the floor in the middle of the room. "I've got scouts out checking what happened. Though, honestly, there's little damage."

Christina felt her face pull to one side as she tried to frown at him. The blast had flattened the four NightShade agents at different locations. It might not have been a full-scale bomb drop, but something big had gone off out there. "How can there be little damage? *We're* all damaged!" She motioned around the room to her bruised and bloodied coworkers.

"The grass is flat," he said, "but it's not broken. It's already starting to straighten and spring back up. There's clearly an area where the blast originated, but no one is there. Not any of their people, and now just a few of ours checking it out. There's untouched earth in the center, about a four-foot radius—" he moved his hands to gesture the layout, "and then scorching for about ten feet around that—"

"Ten feet?" No way. That had been a much bigger blast than that.

She caught Noah's eye, his expression echoing her own. "How is that even possible?"

GJ looked around, still standing. She started to cross her arms but must have bumped a cut or a bruise and let her arms fall to her sides. "Where's all the shrapnel? We had some of it in our skin."

"I have no idea about that either," Will answered, but then turned and pointed a finger at Christina.

"We can't find any more damage than that one small scorched area. Yet here we all are. My people are just as cut up as you."

He motioned around the room, but for some reason his attention stayed on her. She was about to find out why.

"There's only one way I can think of that we all got hit with a bomb that wasn't really there. Was it someone like you who did this?"

57

Noah sat on the edge of his inflatable bed, and though he ached everywhere, he was the only one able to sit with even reasonable comfort.

That was because of the man who had tackled him: Wade de Gottardi.

It turned out the stranger was not only a family member, but also a NightShade agent. Noah was outranked on both counts.

When the blast hit, Wade had protected him. In his wolf form, he'd huddled as best he could over Noah. Their shapes didn't match up, and Noah still had plenty of cuts, but—unlike Christina—his ass wasn't peppered with nicks and bruises.

The thick fur had been some help protecting Wade, too. Noah didn't know if the other man had decided that Noah was some mewling baby who needed to be covered, or if it was just one of those heat-of-the-moment reactions. Noah was the stranger, and Wade was on home turf—at least that part made more sense now.

Still, the fur hadn't protected the other agent enough against the kind of shrapnel coming their way. Noah had felt the hits to his skin, even through the tactical pants, and face-down in the grass, he'd realized that Wade's instruction to run had been the correct one.

He'd felt the odd movements after the blast had finished its shock wave and figured out that the wolf on his back was sliding to one side and slowly changing. Out of respect, Noah didn't look until Wade said, "Sorry. It's probably not every day you get tackled by a naked man."

Noah had started laughing. He laughed until his bones hurt. Whether it was shock or what the still unknown man who'd saved him had said, Noah couldn't tell. Still chuckling, he'd turned his head and looked at the hazel green eyes alight with either a sense of kinship or his own hysteria. Noah played his best card in response. "I'm not against getting tackled by naked men, but I really need about three dates first. I also have to know their name."

As soon as the words left his mouth, his laughter died. He'd probably been hit in the head harder than he'd thought. Despite being saved, he still wasn't quite confident which side the brown-haired, hazel-eyed man was on. And Noah had decided to announce which team he played for. *Dumb move.*

His only saving grace was that he quickly changed the subject. Once his brain had registered what he'd said, he jumped to another topic. He choked out, "Are you okay?"

The man opened his mouth, but it turned out he wasn't okay. But they hadn't noticed because he was laughing so hard. "This hurts."

"Don't laugh. There's shrapnel in your back." He'd looked and winced immediately. There were shards, black and shiny, protruding from Wade's naked back, changing color in the afternoon light. They looked almost like glass, the pointy ends buried deep in the back of his savior's skin.

He didn't even know what it was. He reached out for a moment, trying to figure out if the shards should be left in place because they were stanching the blood flow or if they were poisoning the man and should be removed immediately. Noah decided to ask the person whose life was at stake if he knew about it. "Do you want me to pull them out?"

At least this time, his tone came across as serious and professional, despite the fact that they were still two grown men lying face-down in the tall grass. One of them naked.

The man shook his head. "The change to wolf should push them out."

Noah probably looked surprised. That this man *already knew* that changing would push out any embedded shrapnel was concerning.

His voice pulled Noah back. "Give me a minute. We need to head in. We're not going back out in that."

He'd pointed toward the west, the direction Noah had been headed when the blast hit. Then he moved a few feet further away, putting some grass between him and Noah. As close as he was, Noah should have heard the sounds of changing, but his ears were still ringing from the blast. And he realized it was entirely plausible that he and Wade had been shouting their entire conversation at each other.

Great, he thought. *Everyone heard me tell which side I'm hitting for.*

The man had changed quickly, and Noah had run his hands through the fur, checking for loose glass shards. He found a few caught in the hair, but not any still dug into the skin during these disturbingly intimate movements. He kept his thoughts professional. That was the thing about this kind of work: the foxhole mentality of war was real.

As he spent a moment checking limbs for the man, his brain had wandered back to his earlier thoughts on Will and whether wolves got arthritis, and how they might change if their joints felt like that. It might be worse with injuries everywhere, even small ones.

Eventually, he'd declared Wade okay, though they both had small cuts—some concerningly deep—in a variety of places. They'd headed back to the houses.

Though the others were grateful and glad to see Noah, everyone was thrilled to see Wade. That was his name.

Christina reached out to hug the man but backed off when she realized they were all cut up. Walter welcomed him with a smile she didn't unpack very often—at least not that Noah had seen. She immediately told Wade that she'd had a captive but had dropped him when the blast went off.

At least Noah hadn't been cavorting with the enemy, finding out that Wade was an agent had stunned him and embarrassed him even further. So he sat on the edge of the bed now, in his corner. Walter, GJ, and Christina occupied their own respective corners, and Wade somehow holding court in the middle.

He, too, had been cleaned up. He now wore loose khaki pants and a white T-shirt with a plaid button-down over that. With the glasses added, it would have been nearly impossible to recognize him as the wolf who tackled Noah and saved him.

"Are you bunking with us?" Christina had asked. She laughed and offered him an inflatable mattress in the center of the room. Wade had given her the side eye and replied, "Why, yes, I'd love to have anyone drop down on me from the trapdoor. Maybe jump directly onto my bed while I sleep. No, thank you."

Then he'd turned more serious. "Let's all stay underground until we make some decisions. I'll be back in the morning and I plan to stay with you, starting tomorrow. Tonight though, I'm bunking in with the family. I haven't been back in a while."

Noah's brain churned with too many possibilities. He tried to consider things as they pertained only to him, ignoring the family here and what was quickly escalating into a war. He'd signed up to track one person, and he'd just taken shrapnel.

He needed to talk to Westerfield privately. On the one hand, he was invested. He felt for the de Gottardi/Little family, and he wanted to win this war. On the other hand, maybe he should be called home.

It might be the better option for all of them.

Christina had said, "Come here, Wade," and patted a spot on the bed next to her. She raised up on one hip, leaned onto one elbow, and sank slightly into the air mattress.

Wade joined her, sitting with one butt cheek on the edge. But it was still enough to rock her precarious position. Everyone was having a tough time. Even GJ, who'd been smart about getting aimed the right way, had not managed to avoid being shredded in spots.

Once Wade was seated and Christina had righted herself, she addressed whole group.

"Alright, I need to catch you up." She turned first to Wade. "The big news from today is something you might not know yet. I talked with your grandfather."

Noah could only assume that would be Will. *Wonderful.* Not only was Wade de Gottardi a family member, he was the grandson of their leader.

Yep, bad choices in the field, Noah, he reprimanded himself again. He needed to keep his mouth shut next time an attractive, naked man tackled him in the line of duty.

But Christina was still talking. "The army out there... Marks may be in charge of it, but he's not the top of the chain."

GJ's head jerked back at the announcement, but she didn't say anything. Her expression morphed to suggest that wasn't right, but whether it was because the news just surprised her or if she'd thought her Grandpa was the shit, Noah couldn't tell.

"You want to take one guess who it is?" Christina looked at Wade. Wade looked around the room.

When it became clear from the looks on everyone's faces that no one else even came close to having a clue, he said, "Given that blast and the smell and the shards... I thought it was just... Honestly, that's *wolf lore*. I never thought I'd actually see it. If I hadn't heard the legends as a kid, I wouldn't have even known what to do."

Noah was stunned. *Wolf lore?* Even Christina looked surprised at Wade's words, and she already knew the answer.

"It sounds like Aegis."

And that sounded like a made-up fairy tale, Noah thought, wondering if Wade was maybe a little crazy. But he was even more stunned when Christina nodded.

"That's exactly who it is."

58

"That would be exactly who's out there," Christina spoke to the room in general, educating her agents to the best of her ability. "And, as Wade said, even Will thought Aegis X was a legend—some kind of fictional, Genghis Khan character the wolf clan is only beginning to find out the real history of this ... guy."

Was Aegis even a person? She didn't know.

Christina watched as the other three absorbed this information. Walter believed what she was told. Noah was turning over the new information and checking it from other angles. GJ calculating something that Christina didn't understand yet.

"They're not trying to wipe out wolves in general," she went on, trying to explain her theory. "Wade seemed to make all the same connections, and he agrees."

She hadn't been surprised, because she and Will had put all this together from the records. Now she added the blast from earlier as additional evidence, weighing whether it supported or undermined the theories they'd stitched together.

The problem was, the de Gottardi/Little family had come back together from all over. "As we checked the genealogy, which we spent a good portion of today doing, we found there are a few wolves here supposedly descended from Aegis."

"Is that *real?*" GJ asked.

"Have you heard of it before?" Christina realized that GJ was just joining the conversation. She'd been calculating something that kept her brain occupied for a minute. That was a long time for GJ.

"Not like this, but ..."

Christina watched as the youngest agent's eyes pulled up and to the right, clearly searching her memory. "I know the name is in the files I inherited from my grandfather. *Aegis* was a term he used for some of the bones we'd found. I figured it was an area where they'd been found or a cult that they supposedly belonged to."

It kind of is, Christina thought. It now seemed there were some wolves who had descended from the man as a matter of genealogy, and others who followed him like some cult leader.

But GJ was still talking, still untangling what she was digging out of her memory, and Christina definitely wanted to hear it.

"It didn't occur to me that it was actually a lineage."

Wade leaned forward to ask, "Do you have any bones in your lab from Aegis? Or Aegis descendants?"

GJ's grandfather had kept his own laboratory with hundreds of sets of human bones. GJ had only recently discovered that the majority were wolf bones, the skeletons of *changers* like Wade and Donovan and the de Gottardis and Littles. She'd been raised at her grandfather's knee, on his excavations and in his lab. Only now was she putting together all the hidden pieces. She seemed to be grabbing floating pieces of memory and tying them to new knowledge but that was what GJ did best. She solved puzzles.

They all waited and watched as GJ went very, very still.

"Son of a bitch," she whispered.

Christina forced herself to sit quietly and not react, knowing that she couldn't push the other agent. It was better to let her sit and figure it out, so she could deliver her answer fully formed. But, God, the wait was killing her.

GJ turned to Walter. "He broke in. He stole skeletons. He stole parts, at least! Remember?"

Walter nodded, and Christina returned to her quiet mode. She'd heard this. The lab break-in hadn't been a *bona fide* sighting of the escaped convict Dr. Marks, but it was widely considered evidence that he'd returned to his home ground just a few weeks after escaping. Who else could have gotten into the doctor's own locked and secured laboratory? Who else would have taken specific bones?

"I wasn't able to quite identify it," GJ said, beginning to explain her thoughts to the group. "Several months ago, right after he escaped, he broke into my lab… *his* old lab. He stole specimens, and I tried to figure out which ones and why, but I couldn't." Her eyes darted up and to the right. She was trying to make pieces of her memory fit.

That's right. The house and lab and everything were hers now…

"Let me add this to the conundrum," Wade interrupted. Because he was sharing the same air mattress with her, Christina could feel his tension. Wade continued, "The rumor is, you can *build* Aegis."

"I'm sorry. *What?*" Christina almost laughed, thinking about someone constructing an ancient dead guy from random bones. But maybe they weren't random… ? Unable to hide her amusement, she asked, "Is there like a skeleton army coming next?"

But Wade didn't laugh back. "No. It's rumor, or legend. Aegis is the boogeyman that we warn our kids about. Normal human children have monsters under the bed. We have Aegis. We hear he looks like the old Egyptian dogs, the ones in the paintings and sculptures from the era."

Holy shit, Christina thought. Of course, he did. How had she never put that together before?

"And the rumor is that his bones were buried when he eventually died—though his death is at best speculation and legend—and … well, you know what happens when larger-than-life people die. Later his bones were supposedly found and moved and moved again, and so on. If you have the skeleton, you have him."

He stopped a moment, seeming to consider what he'd just said. "Well, I mean, I guess if you have the bones, you're supposed to get whatever power he had. When we look back at Alexander the Great, it seems he was actually just a man. So, scientifically speaking, I guess I'd always assumed, as an adult, that the Aegis stories were rumors we told our kids to get them to eat their vegetables."

But Christina picked up his thread and kept pulling at it. *Shit.* She was getting very, very worried. "But I've seen what Eleri can do."

She'd been around Eleri enough to know that her kind of magic could be quite powerful when wielded correctly. The other agent, at least at her core, was human. She'd been born. She'd been a child— and endured a rough childhood that one. She'd grown up. But the idea of an ancient, immortal creature, who was also a wolf and who might be imbued with Eleri's kind of power? That was beyond Christina's comprehension.

She turned to Wade for this one. As the only wolf in the room, he was the only one who had been raised on this history. "Do you think Aegis is real?"

He shrugged half-heartedly. "Yesterday, I would have said no. But when you tell me that GJ's grandfather broke into the lab and stole bones? That she knows the name Aegis? Now we add in that strange sulfur and onyx bomb that went off today... and I don't know how I can say *no* any longer."

Christina stilled. She thought she'd uncovered the bigger part of this, talking with Will today. She'd thought that the big reveal was that it wasn't about wolf genocide; this was about removing a handful of other resistant wolf families. The goal was to leave Aegis and his legions as the sole owners of the wolf world.

But somehow, it was now bigger than even that.

This wasn't just an army outfitted like high-end soldiers and well-funded. Somehow, something or someone—maybe even Dr. Murray Marks himself—had unleashed an ancient evil.

By accident? On purpose? She supposed it no longer mattered, because it was becoming clear that it was here.

As she looked to the others in the room, she had to ask the question: "What is he going to do next?"

59

Noah opened his eyes to the dark of the small room under the house. The tunnels coming off four corners were just far enough out of the way so that no one would bump into the sleeping agents if they came running through in the night.

He'd been on strange assignments before—hell, he'd just gotten back from the strangest of them. But this was getting even weirder than that one.

He caught a movement in the open face of the tunnel and wondered if that was what woke him. Though he didn't automatically react with fear to someone was in the tunnel near him, he did remember there was a mole in the family who had already slaughtered two people.

Wade stepped out into the lighter portion of the room, and Noah was grateful he'd had a moment for his eyes to adjust. The other man motioned for him to follow down the tunnel. For a moment, Noah looked around the room as though he needed to find the light. Instead, he was asking himself if Wade could possibly be the mole.

"Is no one else awake yet?" he asked.

"I don't think so."

Noah wanted to frown. Didn't wolves have superior eyesight? He knew they had better hearing, then realized it didn't matter in this case. He noticed the faint amount of light that existed, glinting off of the glasses Wade was wearing. He'd seemed to struggle a bit to focus when they'd been out in the field, too. Maybe this particular wolf's eyesight wasn't superior.

Noah stood up wearing only what he'd slept in—a tank top, old sweat pants, and bare feet. He didn't quite notice until his soles hit the dirt that the floor was cool to the touch, and he followed Wade along the tunnel completely unarmed, except for the ability he had. Maybe Wade didn't know about. That depended on what Christina had told him.

Everyone had been so excited to see Wade—the family, the agents, all of them—that Noah didn't know how much the other agent and favored grandson had been told in the barely half a day he'd been here. Or what he'd known from before he arrived.

Still, there were moles in the family. Noah didn't know anyone here, which would be an advantage if he could keep his eyes open and actually listen to what he was hearing with no bias. He had no clue right now if he was walking down the tunnel to his death or just meeting another agent for a chat.

He thought for a moment of what his brothers would say if he died here, if he never came back from the farm. They would only hear of his *disappearance.* There was also the possibility that Westerfield might call his family and tell them that Noah had joined an elite unit, and that he was just gone. They would all assume he was working... instead of dead.

His brother Bennett would assume that Noah was living the high life and had decided to stay with the special unit because Noah had told Bennett about the first assignment. But as of right now, his brother still thought he was in the relatively safe position of tracking another agent—not in the middle of a war that was getting bigger and more dangerous by the hour.

He trailed Wade down the tunnel, wondering if they were getting far enough away to not wake the others when they talked. *Maybe he wants us far enough away so the other's won't hear me die.* He wouldn't see Bennett's children again, or any of his future nieces and nephews. He thought these things as he padded barefoot down the hallway. His brothers would have to explain once again to their Mormon family and community that, no, not everybody was the same, and they would have to continue doing it with the desire to both increase goodwill toward anyone different and without revealing what their own strange skills were.

Then again, Wade had thrown himself on top of Noah yesterday and taken the brunt of the shrapnel. He was a favored grandson of the leader and a NightShade agent. So he probably wasn't getting murdered. That was just a leftover layer of paranoia from being pulled from sleep.

On the other hand, Wade was in a position to be the best mole ever.

Once the other man deemed they'd move far enough away, he turned around and started to lean a shoulder against the wall, then quickly thought better of it. *He must have a cut or bruise or something that he pinged,* Noah thought.

"Are you new at NightShade?" His first question was easy.

"Yes."

Before Noah could fully respond, Wade added almost clumsily, "Christina sometimes calls you *agent,* but sometimes other titles, so that made me wonder."

"That's fair. I'm stationed at the Miami branch of the Bureau. I was tapped to work with NightShade agents on a local case that wound up in the Caribbean, and then the SAC offered me a job," Noah explained. He didn't bother to detail how he'd turned it down before winding up with an investigation on file at his regular job. "Technically, he has me on as a consultant, because my Miami SAC retained my issued badge and gun."

"That sucks," Wade commiserated, and then promptly changed the subject. "What do you know about what's going on here?"

Something in the way he tipped his head and narrowed his eyes made Noah curious. So he flat out asked, "Why are you asking me? I've never been here before. I don't know any of these people."

"And that's exactly the point," Wade replied. "You're fresh eyes. According to Christina, there's probably more than one mole in my family."

Noah felt his eyebrows rise, even as he crossed his arms on his chest. *Ugh, even that was painful.* He tried to not show it. "How do you know it's not me?"

"Christina says she found you outside, well beyond the family compound, and everything checks out. Westerfield vouches for you. And I called Eleri and Donovan."

Whoa, damn, Noah thought. He'd slept through being fully vetted, and he didn't even know it.

Wade pushed again. "So what do you think? Any ideas about who the mole is?"

It was the first Noah had outright been asked about it. No, he hadn't consciously sat down and tried to figure it out, but he had been forming ideas. They probably all had.

"It might be Jen. According to Christina, Jen has been in and out of the family for more than ten years. Will claims he knows where she went each time, but I think Will's assessment is based on the belief that Jen has been telling him the truth. There may be a weak link there."

"I know Jen," Wade said casually. "I'm the one who brought her into the family.

That was a huge strike against her being the mole... or at least, against anyone in the family *believing* it was her.

Noah didn't think she was it, but he pointed out the possibility that she could be an issue when everyone else was running on trust. Noah dropped it, but Wade didn't.

"You make a good point, though. She didn't seem very radical when I met her. She just wanted a home that matched who and what she was. But if you want to infiltrate an organization, the best option ... is to get someone who's already inside. Someone already trusted. Then you radicalize them. Jen would be a good target for that."

Interesting, Noah hadn't considered the idea that someone hadn't wormed their way into the family, but maybe they were already in before they'd been converted. He needed to look at the options through that lens, too.

But Noah wasn't so sure that was how their mole had gotten in. "Well, via that option, the mole could be you, or Will."

Wade laughed. "It's not my grandfather."

Noah didn't say anything, but the expression on his face must have given him away.

"It's not me and it's not my grandfather," Wade repeated.

Everyone knew so much more than he did, but Noah didn't know what he didn't know. Jen made sense because she was so happy in the organization and because she hadn't been born to this direct line of the family. Noah threw out what he'd been told. "Christina said a lot of wolves have come into the group over the past six months, looking for shelter. Will takes them in."

Wade nodded. "It's part of what he does. It's part of what his grandfather did before him, and why this compound is so big. It's a safe haven."

Though Noah understood—it was a moral imperative to the family to provide shelter and home to others like themselves, but that also created a path for anyone to infiltrate them.

Despite the strangeness of the cases and the danger he'd continually been put into, there was something about NightShade that fascinated Noah and made him consider the job as a more permanent option, even though the others weren't quite like him.

With this group of agents, his skills were on display and he was requested to use them rather than being investigated for being "too good" at the job. It felt welcoming in a way he'd never experienced before. And the way he was trusted by a senior agent he'd just met also felt good. Then again, he partly considered staying with the division because he just might not have a job to go back to in Miami.

"Do me a favor?" Wade asked. "Keep your eyes open? I think you see this—*us*—without the blinders and preconceived ideas the rest of us have."

"Will do," Noah agreed, wondering if Wade was wrapping up the conversation. The day had been planned to relax and heal. Other wolves who'd previously stayed close to the base were being sent out on patrol, guarding the edges of the property and making sure that nothing went down. The compound was already heavily fortified and guarded in the west where the blast had come from.

"If we go out later, I'll see if I notice anything strange."

Christina had even asked a few of the wolves to go out today and search, to see if they could find any direct evidence of Aegis. She told Will that she wanted to look for anything that might look strange, ancient, or evil.

Though Noah could attest that those instructions seemed quite vague, he didn't question them. But there was no timetable, and no specifics in the instructions, just a bit of "See what you can find."

The wolves on patrol had been given pictures of Dr. Murray Marks and asked if they could spot him. Noah didn't expect anything to come of that. He knew now that identifying an individual meant you had to get directly up into their faces, because of the helmets and gear and goggles they almost always wore.

But he agreed to Wade's suggestion to keep his eyes open. He'd do what he could.

"I trust that you have a clear eye," Wade said.

Noah almost laughed. "How can you tell?"

"I can smell it." Wade grinned which only made Noah chuckle, until he wondered if maybe it wasn't funny. Maybe there was a way to smell bias, and he simply didn't have the required or refined senses to sniff it out.

But even as he opened his mouth to ask about it, a blast shook the building.

He was knocked off his feet, unsure if he heard the rumbling sound or felt the shaking of the ground first.

As he failed to catch himself with his hands, Noah realized that he was going down and attempted to roll with the fall. But the ground was moving and he felt the side of his head smack the hard-packed dirt.

A garbled sound came from Wade's mouth, and as Noah's eyes rolled and the world went black, he felt the rumble of the earth beneath him once again, and thought, *This was no ordinary bomb.*

60

Donovan stood by the car, basically holding position as watchman. He offered a mild visual block between the freeway and his partner.

Eleri had wandered out into the grassy field, then cut behind a small clump of trees. He could still see that she was there, but he didn't have a clear shot of what she was doing. He saw enough to stop her if someone came running through the woods yelling, or if something drove by on the road, or something came up that she needed to stay hidden from.

Though he hadn't watched intently—he was more focused on watching the nearly non-existent traffic while looking bored—he'd seen her pull out her book and lay it open on the ground in front of her. She next spread out a towel that she pulled from the trunk of the car, stepped both feet onto it, and raised her hands to the sky.

Next, she'd muttered something that he didn't understand—a spell, an incantation, or a swear. He wasn't sure. But after a moment, he realized she was cussing a blue streak. Eleri lowered her hands and turned back toward the car. From her expression, it clear that she'd dicked something up.

As she got close, he heard her muttering. But he didn't interfere, just watched as she reached into the back seat and pulled out the bowl she'd brought. Holding out an angry hand she asked, "Can I have your water?"

She seemed to want the one in his hand. Rather than argue, Donovan handed it over and watched. He could get another one from the car if he was thirsty.

Heading back to her spot, Eleri plucked leaves off the trees as she went by and, this time, she added the bowl—now full of random-looking crap—to the setting at her feet and raised her hands. When she spoke, he knew the words were a spell.

It took her all of four to five seconds to catch the contents of the bowl on fire. Donovan leaned back against the car and crossed his arms. He didn't know how this was supposed to go, only that she was looking for Bodhi—to see if he'd been here or turned off the road a ways back. So Donovan stayed quiet and watched as smoke rose up from the bowl. Or maybe it was steam from the water.

He listened as her voice kept repeating the same set of sounds over and over. The sound rose with each repetition, as did the flames. He would have been impressed, but Eleri was getting good enough that even he was getting jaded.

A car drove by on the country road behind them. Slowly, he turned his head as if to see if he knew them. He wouldn't, but he looked anyway. But if the occupants of the car saw anything, they apparently didn't think it was worthy of their time.

They were over the hill out of sight, and quickly beyond his hearing.

Looking back toward the trees, he watched Eleri as the flames she conducted changed from blue to green. The smoke changed from a hazy gray to a sharp purple tone.

Donovan had no idea what any of it meant. Eleri wasn't in any position to answer questions, so as long as she seemed safe, he stayed still. The fire climbed higher, almost to her waist. Though it didn't change color again, it began an audible crackle and suddenly became noticeably brighter.

He'd frowned at the sight and was starting to move toward her when the contents of the bowl exploded, knocking her backwards.

As his lungs stopped working, his feet started. Donovan ran. The short distance was enough to raise his heart rate, though probably more from fear than activity.

Adrenaline surged through his system, a white-hot flood that scared him as much as anything else. He was halfway to her before she hit the ground. But he still wasn't fast enough, and she hit hard.

Her head knocked against what he could only hope was just dirt and not stone. His stomach turned, but he kept moving.

It seemed in slow motion that her body bounced and rolled and came to a stop. All of it happened before he could get close enough to do anything but watch.

Though he'd run at full speed, he pulled up short just as fast. Skidding into place, he made sure not to step on her or cause more problems than she already had.

Nearly sliding in like a baseball player, he leaned down to check for a pulse. His fingers were pressed to her slender neck, exposed where her head had rolled to the side.

Her eyes were open, glassy, and unseeing.

Donovan pressed his fingers harder, searching for a pulse.

61

C hristina felt the ground shift under her feet. This was a harsher, more violent movement than what she'd felt when she and Will had run headlong toward the first bomb.

But it was also the same. The feeling of it, the feeling of earth wrenching rather than rattling. The rolling of her gut told her it was coming up underneath her, not just down on top of her.

Steadying her hand on the wall to stay upright, she looked to Walter and GJ, both of whom had been asleep, curled into the dip of their inflatable mattresses.

Noah was missing, his bed clothes thrown toward the wall as though he'd rolled out before her. She'd thought nothing of it when she'd awakened all of a minute ago and stood up. But now? One of her agents was gone.

Walter—whose prosthetic leg and arm waited right beside the bed while she slept—was now already in the arm and starting to buckle the leg on.

Damn, she was fast, Christina thought. Not that that surprised her.

What she hadn't quite noticed before was that GJ also laid her clothes out at night, ready to jump into them at a moment's notice. Christina had thought it was OCD or GJ's inherent overachieving. No, she saw now, it was that GJ had slid into her own clothes and now stood beside Walter. And while Christina was still pulling on her shoes, GJ was dressed and ready, across the room, holding out

Walter's shirt in a way that allowed Walter to slip into it even before Christina had her shoes tied.

If the ground wasn't still vibrating from the shock, if she wasn't braced against the wall for another hit, she would have taken a moment to be stunned. She still remembered when these two had been new agents together. Even then, they'd worked well in tandem, but Christina hadn't quite attributed the level of teamwork they had.

Now, she realized with a twist of her heart, that she couldn't afford the time to miss what she no longer had. Still, she did miss it. *Dearly*.

"That one was much closer," GJ stated the obvious, knowing that she was merely starting the conversation with something they all understood.

"Agreed," Christina replied before they heard the shout from down the tunnel.

"Help!"

It was Wade's voice. Strong and clear, not panicked, but not okay either. "Noah's down!"

Just in case she wasn't already vibrating at a high rate, Christina felt her system crank up another notch, and she ran down the tunnel that opened next to Noah's bed. Her brain cranked possibilities. They were leaving on a mission and things went wrong. Wade was questioning Noah. Noah had wandered down the tunnel and Wade ran into him... she dismissed the last one.

She yanked her phone and popped the light on, letting it direct her to where Wade's voice had come from. They hadn't gone far.

Noah was laid out on the floor with Wade standing over him. She would have asked but Wade was on top of the situation already announcing, "He hit his head. He's breathing and his pulse is steady. I think he's just out."

But as he looked up at her, Christina thought none of them were Donovan Heath, MD. Never mind that most of the former medical examiner's patients were dead; he still had far more training than any of them. They were limited to assessing the situation with only the training than they'd received at Quantico and the occasional continuing education to help agents in the field. Like now.

They both put what skills they had to use.

"He's alive," Christina declared, more than grateful to be able to make that statement.

Wade was feeling around Noah's skull. Then he pointed to the back of Noah's head on his right. "I think he hit here."

When he pulled his hand back, Christina saw the blood on his fingers. Not his. *Son of a bitch.*

She was both horrendously worried about Noah and concerned that the last thing they needed right now was an injured agent. Together, they checked his neck and spine as best they could, stepping back when GJ moved in.

She watched as they cleared space for her. "I'm an anthropologist, not a doctor," she offered as a disclaimer. Still, she had the highest-rank understanding of what a human should be.

After a few moments assessing the newest agent, she declared, "No broken bones that I can tell without an x-ray. I think he's mostly okay. We need to move him."

Though no one commented on it, Christina's concern was that Noah had made no noise up to this point. Not a groan or a peep, nothing to indicate he was coming around.

"Did he hit his head yesterday?" GJ was smart enough to ask.

"Good point." A second hit to the head was far more dangerous than a first. She didn't want to think about it.

But Wade shook his head no. "He had his helmet on. And he was fine immediately after it went off."

Thank God for small favors, Christina thought. "Then let's move him."

It was Wade who scooped up Noah's limp form and carried him back to the inflatable mattress. As Wade gently set him down, one arm slid over the side, his fingers brushing the floor. The man she was beginning to think would wind up being her new partner was completely unresponsive.

"We've got him," GJ announced, speaking for herself and Walter. "You guys go out and figure out what the hell just happened."

Though it wasn't really GJ's place to give orders, Christina realized she was right.

Tapping Wade on the shoulder, she interrupted where he was still examining Noah. Wade was opening the younger man's eyelids, lifting and dropping his hand, and lightly slapping his cheek, as though any of these things were real medical tests.

Nothing was happening, so Christina tapped him one more time. "Come on. You and I need to go out. GJ's right."

For a moment, it appeared the words hadn't registered. But when she spoke the third time, Wade finally moved. Abandoning the unresponsive man to Walter and GJ, who were already in full action, he followed Christina.

She ran to the trap door, knowing Wade would be right behind her. In fact, she felt his hand reaching up to push at her foot, helping her launch onto the platform of the house floor above as she went through. As she turned around, his fingertips were already locking at the edge of the opening of the trap door, and he was hauling himself up. She stood carefully, wary of stray bullets or another bomb blast that might throw her backward.

The scene upstairs was chaos.

Wolves trotted through the grass, once again migrating homeward *en masse*. Some of them walked as wolves, dipping regularly to one side with an odd gait. That took only a second to translate as injuries. Others stood up, some probably nude, some in tanks and sweatpants, many holding others in their arms. Whether the limp forms were dead or just injured, she couldn't tell.

But she did know this: They were now completely outmatched.

62

N oah opened his eyes slowly, as though he were prying open an old box. Walter and GJ hovered over him like mother hens. Whatever had happened, it must have been bad to have Walter checking his pulse.

He moved his hand, waving her away and apparently startling the ever-loving crap out of her. He started to laugh, but his head throbbed with the first hint of sound. The pain washed through with a memory of the blast, or at least the part where he had been thrown to the ground. Judging from the current state of affairs, he'd probably hit hard.

Noah lifted his hand to his head, despite the soreness that still pervaded his muscles. But fingers grabbed at his wrist and pulled his hand away.

"You don't want to touch that."

Then he felt something else touch his head.

He jolted upright. "Son of a bitch! Why did *you* touch it?"

"I have to assess the wound!" GJ scolded, even as she laughed. "I'm sorry. This is going to hurt."

Walter sighed. "Well, he's still Noah."

"You're bleeding from a head wound," GJ explained.

He didn't reach for the throbbing point again, but as he pulled his hand around to look at it, he saw his fingers were tinged with the red of his own blood. *Damn.*

"Bandage me up?" he asked.

"Well, I was *trying*," she commented, attitude dripping from every word.

He would have apologized for bleeding on them, but apparently he'd been out cold. But for how long? "When did the blast hit?"

"Maybe five minutes ago," Walter told them, her tone military tight once again. She handed gauze to GJ, and GJ looked at him as though his head was a puzzle to solve.

After mumbling something to Walter, she looked back at him. But Noah watched as Walter stood up and moved across the room, fetching the bag of supplies Jen had left behind for them to use as they needed. She probably had thought they could change the dressings they already had. She couldn't have known they'd need bandages so soon for new wounds.

"We need to get going," he told them. GJ's return look seemed to say, *No shit Sherlock*, but she was not to be interrupted. She would get this bandaging done, regardless of her patient's feelings.

A few minutes later, he had several pieces of gauze placed against the wound, which had been smeared with an ointment. Probably antibiotic—he hadn't asked. He also had a stretchy gauze headband strategically holding it all in place. He was starting to look like a refugee.

The trapdoor up to the main house opened just then, letting light flow down. But no one looked in to check on them. That wasn't why it was opened.

They all three looked up at the voices overhead. Mostly, he recognized Christina's. "Bring them here, she was saying. "We'll lower them down. We have some supplies."

He watched as, one by one, people began to drop down through the open square. Each person blocked what little sunlight came through and for a moment muted the voices from overhead. The sounds they made as their feet hit the ground momentarily cut out the words he was listening for.

A third one came in, and then a fourth. He watched as Jen hit the ground near him and then almost immediately jumped up onto the shoulders of the first man down. None of them paid attention to the three agents in the corner.

Noah's eyes widened as they handed the first limp woman down, angling her through the open hole. Her head lolled to one side. Their handling was as careful as it could be, but it wasn't gentle. But she didn't wake despite the jostling and the noise.

This must have been what he had looked like just a moment ago, except she had cuts—bad cuts. Her arm was open deep enough for him to see the red of muscle that should have been hidden behind skin. Her foot dangled at an odd angle.

They moved her to the side and another body was started through the process of being handed down.

Noah looked back to the woman. By the time she was placed on the bed, all four of the people who had transported her, and the bed itself, were covered in blood.

63

"I 'm sorry about the beds."

It took Christina a moment to even process what Will was talking about. She stood upright at the edge of the foundation of the house, probably a clear target despite the fact that she was under a remaining piece of roof and holding the only section of railing still standing.

"Don't worry about it." It had taken a moment to understand that he meant the blood on the beds the agents had been sleeping in.

They would not be sleeping there tonight. The sheets were ruined beyond repair. But the beds weren't hers to give, and she would have assigned them the same way if she could. The de Gottardi/Little family members occupying them were in serious condition. If they were lucky, they were resting after being bandaged or stitched.

If the last she'd seen held true, there was at least one person in each bed waiting their turn at care or attempting to rest. She wouldn't begrudge them an air mattress. Christina was simply grateful it wasn't her own people taking up space in the newly minted medical center.

Turning slightly to get a better look at the old man, she asked, "What do you think this is, Will?"

Her hands still clenching the railing, she almost waved a hand forward, as if to say *about all this*. The walking wounded were still making their way in toward this house. From the sound of the grass rustling, there were many more staying low but moving in.

"Well, he said, I don't think we can mount a battle we can win. I suspect we've got to infiltrate whatever's over there and find out the best way to strike."

She nodded. It sounded reasonable at the basic level. But she didn't really have the means to pull it off. Not like she wanted.

Christina had wanted more agents. She'd gotten one. And she was more and more sure now that she wouldn't get the extras she'd requested—at least not in time She would have to make plans to run with the five she had. Well, maybe four—that depended on just how injured Noah was. Hopefully, he'd be back in commission soon. But she planned for four.

Will wouldn't be coming on the recon journey. Despite his prowess for his age and his skills as a wolf, he wasn't physically up to it. She didn't say this. Instead she asked, "What are the goals?"

She had her own, but she wanted to know his.

His eyes slid sideways toward her. In front of them, another two soldiers stood up to announce their arrival at the homestead. One of them was in full gear and his gait jolted with each step. The other, naked, quickly shook off her obvious exhaustion and headed over to intersect his path.

The number of incoming injured had dwindled greatly as most of those had beelined immediately back.

"I already counted ten dead, far more injured.," Will said.

She knew that while he was working on a strategy, Will's heart was breaking. "We have to take out Marks and Menon." Again, his eyes flicked to the side to glance at her.

"Can you do that?" She wasn't sure he could, not after the injuries they were seeing now.

"My fighters can." His confidence was clear, and he reassured her, as though somehow there might be Bureau dictates and federal laws in place that she had to work around. As though the Federal government had anything to do with what the protocol was when a genocide was occurring on a species that the vast majority of the public didn't even realize existed. "Can you get intel?"

"We can handle that." She nodded, still watching as the woman now supported the soldier with his arm slung over her shoulder. She aimed them toward the house in the distance.

"I want you to take some of my people with you," was Will's immediate follow up.

But Christina wasn't sure. "Who?"

Did she trust his judgment about who his mole might or might not be? She wasn't sure yet. They had ten names—Jen's was one of them. Though Christina was beginning to agree with Will that, if she was the mole, she was so deep no one would ever know.

Darren was another name on the list that she recognized—a wolf she'd met the first day. And that was it. The other eight were completely unknown to Christina. Despite Will occasionally pointing out or saying "he was here on the porch with us the first night" or "you met him when you got your gear from us for your first recon," none of those helpful hints had jogged her memory. So she had eight unknown names on her list.

She would have put Walter and GJ onto the research again today. But then the ground had shook and she was standing here now, looking out over the land.

Every plan had been shaken apart as the earth rumbled beneath them. They had to regroup and reconsider their priorities.

Christina had no idea when the next blast would come, but she knew that it would.

64

Noah tightened the strap under his chin, making sure the helmet was in place and wouldn't slide around. The fact that the helmet had been put on over gauze, rendering his head a Frankenstein-style masterpiece, didn't make him feel any better about this outing.

Beside him, Walter reached out and bare-knuckle tapped on the head of GJ's helmet, which was already in place. GJ was checking her weapons almost by rote—a better soldier than he'd given her credit for.

"Third time's the charm," Walter muttered, and Noah stopped cold.

They now had Wade gearing up beside them. All five of them were getting ready to go this time, but Noah was not willing to rely on charms.

"Weapons check?" he said to the group. He wasn't the leader of this outing. He wasn't second, third, or even fourth in command, but he also wasn't walking out without knowing what he had in his pocket and what tools they commanded, should they need them.

Walter held up her gun, her eyebrow raised and her mouth quirked. Christina tipped hers and frowned at him, as though to say the answer was obvious.

But it wasn't. Not to them. So Noah clarified. "What weapons does the other side possess?"

He didn't know how else to ask it, but he watched their faces and, of course, it was GJ who caught on first. "They have people like me and Walter. Humans—non wolves."

Noah nodded. "True." Though he wondered why she didn't list him and Christina in with them. He was definitely a non-wolf.

"There are people like him," GJ continued, pointing to Wade.

Noah nodded and wondered what the ratios were on the other side. Previously, he would have thought it would be just a few wolves. But now, it was likely half or more. It turned out the wolves were running the show, not being used by it.

Christina picked up the thread. "They have a massive unknown."

"Yes," Noah agreed, glad he'd gotten the conversation rolling. It was hard to work against unknowns, but that was the whole point of this mission: make the unknown known. "But what is known about it?"

"They have bombs," Walter threw out. "He can bomb the entire area."

"But does he?" Noah found his brain taking different paths, as even the conversations between the agents were enlightening to him. They looked at him oddly. "It's true that both blasts killed people. But the shrapnel from the first one was bizarre."

"We haven't been able to find any of it to test it." GJ's weapon was lowered, aimed at the ground, as her brain was her primary concern right now. "Some of Will's people went out to scour the grass, but it was gone."

"The cuts were real," Christina argued, as though to contradict GJ.

"True." But GJ didn't have an answer. She only shrugged.

"It seems," Noah said, "and correct me if I'm wrong, but the blast gets you. You sustain whatever damage you get as it's going off. That's yours. But afterwards, it's over. All the evidence is gone."

Christina twitched one eye as though he was being ridiculous.

But he shook his head at her. "The shrapnel is all gone. Even the piece Walter had in her arm. No one can find it."

Next to him, Walter nodded in agreement. "The trees are still standing. There's no evidence. No cracks in the earth, the soil isn't out of place. Hell, even the grass is barely bent. Two hours later and it's upright again! So far, Will has claimed to have found a ten-foot-radius scorch mark. And that's it. A backpack of C-Four does more damage than that."

Christina began nodding, finally understanding where he was going. "We don't know what else he can do, but we know about these bombs," she filled in.

Wade, who'd stayed silent and listened through most of it, tossed out the most damning piece of information. "We don't even know if there is an Aegis. We just assumed that's what it is. The bombs might be the extent of the weaponry."

"Even though Dr. Marks stole the bones? And everything lines up?" Walter asked. She seemed to sincerely wonder.

Wade shrugged. "As far as I know, it's a fairy tale. That doesn't mean they don't have it. But it also doesn't mean that they *do.*"

There was no solving that one, Noah understood. Not until they saw it with their own eyes. Maybe not until everyone walked away... if they could.

Time for the other side of the coin. "What do we have?"

It was Wade who spoke up again. "We have the normies over there." He grinned and pointed at Walter and GJ. "And we have me. We're evenly matched. Wolf against wolf, human against human. Roughly the same as what they have."

He was right, Noah thought. Their gear and weapons were similar, although honestly, Noah wasn't quite certain if anyone was like Walter Reed—or even GJ. Who knew?

"But Christina..." Wade said, pointing an almost accusing finger at her. "I don't think they have anything like Christina."

Then his finger swung back to Noah. "And I've heard about you."

Holy shit, Noah thought.

He didn't fit in. He wasn't a wolf or a psychic. Not a super soldier or a genius. And yet, somehow, he and Christina were the only weapons at NightShade's disposal that weren't matched by the other side.

"Oh!" GJ cried out, an idea clearly forming. "Oh! I've got it!"

65

Christina stayed in close to her teammates. The last time, she'd had them spread out, but this time, huddling tight made more sense. They needed to be in one place to provide backup to each other.

Though she had her rifle on her, it was her handgun that stayed up and at the ready. The smaller gun simply didn't require as much space to operate as the rifle did. So she consciously relaxed her grip and let her eyes glaze, hoping to spot anomalies.

She didn't find anything, so she pushed forward again.

They'd headed north, like the first time they'd come out. Actually, there was no evidence as to which direction the soldiers would strike from next. Maybe whoever was in charge was working their way around the compound counterclockwise, and the agents should have gone south.

But some of the troops would still be here guarding this line of the property, if only to keep the wolves in. She'd chosen this direction in part because they'd been up here before and knew the layout better than they did other areas surrounding the family compound.

In her hopes, Christina and her team would figure out what Aegis X was. Maybe it was a weapon. Maybe it was an idea or a plan. Maybe it actually was the ancient boogeyman that baby wolves were threatened with to keep them behaving.

She hoped Will's team could take out Marks and Menon. But if her team found them, they'd be just as dead. She really wanted that news to be something GJ could hear about later as a report, and not anything she had to be involved in herself.

Christina held no illusions that this time, they might capture a soldier and get them to talk. That wasn't even on the table now. Two separate, deadly blasts had made that clear.

To the west, a faction of Will's wolves had the same executable orders as her team. As wolves, they were able to move fluidly and quietly through a landscape they knew better than the soldiers did. Her team did not have that advantage.

But the wolf team lacked the two weapons that Noah had pointed out, giving her team a different advantage—and these other soldiers probably had no idea what Christina and Noah could do.

At the front of her cluster of agents, she once again made her hand signal to pause and look around. They'd crossed the property line, and though the area appeared abandoned, she didn't believe that for a second. There were simply too many troops out here. Even if they'd been trying to space themselves apart, at least one of them would be close by.

Surely, they haven't all cleared out. Christina began to believe that, with every step, she was getting farther and farther into enemy territory and that she would soon be—if not *already*—surrounded.

Still holding up her hand, she waited as five sets of eyes swept the area around them. Hand signals came back one by one.

Nothing.

Nothing.

Nothing.

With a motion at her shoulder, she told the group to press forward.

She only made it about twenty feet farther than she'd thought they would before she caught sight of a small piece of equipment apparently abandoned near a tree.

With more silent hand signals, she alerted the others. As a group, they checked it out, but it appeared the machine was only some kind of detritus left behind by a group long gone. It was one of the small, no-light heaters she'd seen when they'd tracked Noah before.

The whole area looked as though it had been simply abandoned by whatever soldiers had once held this ground. Walter leaned over and picked the thing up, shook it as though checking for fuel, then shrugged and set it back down. Her broad arm gesture swept the area to say, "This is nothing."

Exactly as they had planned.

Christina didn't hear it, but more sensed... something. Keeping her hand down at her side, she tapped each of the others, no longer making the big hand gestures that anyone that distance could probably decipher as the signals they were.

In her head, she counted down.

Three...

Two...

One...

But it took another five seconds for it to happen. It was not the sharp onslaught she was ready for, but a slow change in the landscape. She realized that suddenly, there was one face, one human form, to her right. And then another appeared in front of her. Slowly, soldiers materialized around her agents where they stood. Every one of the combatants was heavily armed with helmets, rifles, and tactical vests.

They meant business, she knew.

She also realized they probably weren't wolves. For a wolf, all the gear would be too hard to get out of when they wanted to change form.

Maybe she'd just learned something, and the armies were split—humans in one faction, wolves in another. She pocketed that away, slowly swinging her gun from one face to another.

Working on the proposition that she had to look scared, she found one soldier to focus on. For whatever reason, this one grabbed her attention. But his face seemed mildly familiar, so she turned away from him and aimed at the man next to him. His plastic goggles warped the shape and color of his eyes while they protected him.

Christina breathed easily. She aimed center mass, and pulled the trigger, starting what she hoped was a war.

66

Noah's head swiveled as Christina's opening shot ripped the air with both sound and the vision of the soldier flying backward.

By the time he yelled in anger and stood back up, his hand clutching the front of his bulletproof vest to be sure that it worked, everything had gone to hell.

Noah only hoped it was a controlled hell.

He shot at the woman in front of him, hitting her square in the middle of her vest and sending her backward, too. But his satisfaction with his shot was short-lived as he was punched forward by a bullet to the back of his own vest. Peeling himself upward off the ground, he groaned at his aching ribs and caught just enough of the action to watch Walter stumble backwards and fall ass-first into the grass.

They were outnumbered, and four of the five of them were on the ground within the first minute. One of them pointed a rifle at Christina's head.

"Call off your troops if you want them to live," he ordered.

They'd quickly been cuffed and cleared of their weapons, and now they were marching off, destination unknown.

"Keep going."

Noah heard the voice as he felt the tap at the back of his legs. Both were equally annoying. The rifle barrel was nudging at the back of his calves, encouraging him to move faster, as though that were possible with four other NightShade agents walking directly in front of him.

They trudged through the tall grass with their hands tied behind them. Moving forward, Noah kept a respectable pace, despite getting the backs of his legs repeatedly tapped.

At least this time, his captors had left him with his vest on. *But why?* He wondered. What was the difference this time?

He found out soon enough.

The discussions of their captors were relatively clear, even from just hearing the one side. "Bringing them in ... five, sir."

Though it was tempting to make a bid at escape, Noah held back.

Right now, they were merely walking, and they didn't know what waited at the other end of this line. The five of them were in a tight cluster. It wasn't the smartest move on his captors' parts, but Noah wasn't going to point that out to them.

Just a few minutes later, they came up to a group of enemy soldiers, and Noah had to fight to keep his jaw from falling open. There were so many of them *right here*. So close to where they'd been the last time the agents had done recon in the area.

"Maybe they weren't here before, maybe this was a new installment," Wade whispered, seeming to see the look on his face.

Maybe, but it would have to be very, very new.

Though their communication systems had been removed with their weapons, no one seemed to be policing them too intently. They stepped close to each other as they shuffled from foot to foot so they could whisper for a moment. As long as they didn't make any quick moves, they were only nudged back into line.

"Sit, here." The soldier motioned with the tip of his rifle, a move that always gave Noah a case of shudders. But the seat in the clearing offered a chance to gather some intel, even though he was tied.

Sitting on the ground wasn't the easiest task with their hands behind their backs, but they all managed it. Even Walter, whose one leg—though impressively bionic—didn't fold quite as well as the other was able to look relatively comfortable. Noah wondered if anyone had noticed she was part Terminator, but it seemed they'd missed the leg and, given the gloves she wore, no one had figured out that they didn't want a punch from that left hand.

They stayed sitting there for about thirty minutes. Soldiers ringed the small space, leaving no chance for escape. Apparently, decisions were being made while they sat and waited, and Noah became concerned about the plan.

He was beginning to get worried that the soldiers intended to execute them all. But it quickly became obvious that they were going in an entirely different direction.

"They're ransom," one of the men in front of them said, gesturing back toward the group and not caring if the five agents heard what he said.

"The family will trade us to get them back."

"What would they trade?" one of the women asked, as though a trade were the most horrifyingly stupid suggestion she'd ever heard. "They don't have any of our people."

She almost laughed the words, and Noah wondered if she knew his team alone had captured or killed a decent number of "her people" already.

"Are these idiots important enough that they'll give us some of their other people? They would be lower-quality stock anyway. It doesn't work because we aren't dumb enough to get caught."

Oh, joy, Noah thought. There could be nothing good about a conversation that referred to him and his friends as *stock*.

"They'll barter," the man said, as though confident of things he didn't understand.

Walter looked up then and managed to join in with the conversation. "We're not family. We're agents. They won't barter for us."

Noah almost laughed that she didn't clarify *agents of what*, but her words changed the expressions on those standing in front of her.

"Who wants you back?"

One of them leaned over and looked at the group with fresh scrutiny.

"The Federal Bureau of Investigations." Christina, on the other hand, had no trouble saying exactly who they worked for.

It didn't have quite the impact she'd hoped for. Two of the workers just shrugged to each other and were immediately distracted as another came in, smacking them on the shoulders. "It doesn't matter who barters or for what. We're not doing the bartering. Our job is to bring them in."

Noah saw Christina fight the quirk at the corner of her mouth, keeping her eyebrows drawn as though she were angry or maybe merely just cranky. At least they knew now what was going on.

The others dispersed, though a few soldiers were left forming a ring around the small dirt patch where they sat. One of them brought water, setting the five bottles in a neat ring at the center of their feet, where no one could reach them.

Then even that group disappeared until only one soldier was left, silently stalking a circle as he stood guard. His rifle tip aimed at the ground as he walked, his swagger showing he had more ammo than sense.

He made the full circle, then stopped.

Noah began to wonder if they could take him. They probably could.

But then the soldier turned his glare toward Christina.

67

Christina felt the rifle smack softly against the bottom of her shoes. The move was meant to indicate that she should pull her feet up.

She rolled her eyes and glared at the man who'd done it.

"Hey," he gruffed back. "Out of my way." He said this as he walked directly into the path where her legs stuck in front of her. He'd done it only to cause problems.

This was the part she hated, playing nice, playing victim. He tapped on her shoes again. Sarcastically, and with an additional glare, she pulled her feet back maybe six inches.

He walked around the space she'd vacated, his rifle swinging until he turned around and swung the barrel up and toward her. His eyes sighting down at her. But what Christina found odd was that the barrel was aimed all of six inches to the left of her hip. *Jesus, is he a Stormtrooper? That had to be was the worst aim she'd ever seen.*

Then he started talking, his voice harsh but low.

"Listen." He moved the rifle a bit, changing his aim as though he were pointing with it. "I just wanted to let you know that Will has people embedded on this side, too."

It took everything she had not to let her eyes pop wide and her mouth fall open as his words hit her. His tone was angry. His expression was focused and rude. Both were discordant with his words.

Is this a trap?

Surely everyone knew Will. It would be so easy to say that… This soldier might think he could get her and her people to spill secrets to use against them.

She glared at him in response, and in reply, he reiterated what he'd said. "We're taking you to someone higher up the chain. Just so you know, no one's going to hurt you for now."

The "for now" part bothered her, as he seemed to be sharing information. Maybe it was a subtle threat. Maybe it was tacked onto a not-too-subtle lie.

It seemed he realized that she wasn't quite ready to trust him or his ploy for allyship.

He knelt down, pushing up close to her face as though glaring at her. His rifle was now down at his side, and her fellow agents watched the odd conversation. Christina wondered if they were close enough to hear that his words didn't match his actions.

Reaching up with his free hand, he pulled down the goggles and let her see his eyes with no obstruction. The icy blue color was familiar. The black hair just sticking out from under the edge of his thick protective helmet also triggered a memory.

As she remembered that particular combination of coloring, he said, "We met outside a bar. At the edge of the back parking lot."

The wolf in the woods, Christina thought. The one who'd barely answered her questions and then disappeared.

Somehow, he was here, now. With the Aegis team.

He walked a circle around them again as though monitoring the space for a surprise attack. Then he reached down and grabbed for the water bottles, giving each of his captives a moment to get a drink.

Just like before, his motions indicated he was angry or irritated that he even had this job. But when he cycled back to Christina, he said, "I was out monitoring the numbers coming into the area. My job was to join up with anyone on Marks' team and relay information back to the compound."

Then he leaned down and murmured, "When you get back to see Will, let him know there's a mole in the family."

She almost threw her head back and laughed.

They *all* knew there was a mole in the compound.

She wanted to ask what he meant, to see if he understood what he was saying. Because honestly, it was a great gambit to throw out to a captive, true or not. She was about to ask him to prove his side by stating who the mole was, but the other soldiers reappeared then and made it clear that her agents were going to be taken on the move again.

Rough hands yanked her to her feet. The five of them once again line-marched through the grass and trees. She checked the angle of the sun and her own internal compass. They were headed mostly northwest. And, though they were a good distance from the property line, they weren't getting any farther away from the compound.

Interesting, she thought. The ring around the de Gottardi/Little farm was tight.

Less than fifteen minutes later, they came upon another group, even bigger than the last had been.

The first had surprised her with their size. This one was stunning. How were there this many people, and this much activity, so close to the edge of the farm property?

How had they not been found and reported?

Surely Will would have noticed if his soldiers came out here. They would have seen this and told him... or, she realized, they might have come out this direction and never returned. But Will would have figured that out. Were they concealed? Were they somehow cloaked —something along the lines of what Christina could do, but on a grander scale? She didn't know.

Her attention was drawn away as the crowds parted.

A lot of these people wore no helmets or even gear. Christina initially assumed they were wolves, but she saw some faces she knew and realized that wasn't entirely the case. They were here and they felt safe enough to be unarmed and unprotected.

She recognized Shray Menon right away.

Without the gear covering him almost head to toe, it was obvious this was the man she'd suspected. Christina could now check the box that he had survived their last encounter here at the farm.

Fuck, she thought, *no one needed that reminder.* Even as she thought it, she began to wonder if Marks wasn't far behind. It took only another few seconds before she spotted him.

Marks stood up and covered the distance from the center where he held court to where the captives had been hauled in. But Christina wasn't the only one who'd recognized him.

Beside her, GJ went rigid. Without permission from their captors or instructions from her, the junior agent began to stalk her way forward.

Though one of the soldiers put out an arm to stop her, it was Marks himself who waved the man away. He recognized his own granddaughter, despite her helmet and heavy gear.

She marched straight up to his face and greeted him, her eyes pinning him with a stark glare, her tone vicious as she snarled, "Grandfather."

68

"Untie her."

Noah heard the infamous Murray Marks give the command, even though he was a good bit away. GJ had stalked her way through the crowd of soldiers to go face-to-face and toe-to-toe with her own grandfather.

This wasn't Aegis X, but Marks was certainly part of the mission.

Noah looked to Christina.

According to the pictures he'd been shown, Shray Menon, Marks' assistant, was standing not three feet away. His fellow agents showed, by their expressions, that they'd all seen it, too.

This had been the plan: get captured and get taken to the higher ups. Christina shot him a warning look that clearly said, *Not yet.* But Noah was getting antsy.

The soldier with the rifle—the one who'd been talking to Christina before—now circled them, guarding the remaining four closely.

Wade had slowly crept closer and now leaned in and whispered, "I heard what he said to Christina. It seems he's friend, not foe."

But even as Wade whispered, Noah was bumped from behind. They'd been seen.

The harsh word came at him loudly. "Careful."

As though it were Noah's fault the bump had occurred. But as the man they'd just been gossiping about stepped away from him, Noah realized that his wrists were loose.

Though GJ was now rubbing at hers as though she had been horribly wronged by having her wrists zip-tied together, her hands were completely free. Noah's zip cuffs were still in place, but cut so he could easily pull one hand out and have free motion.

As he watched, the soldier moved over and began giving Wade grief, too.

One by one, Noah saw that his fellow agents each had their wrist ties cut, and he began to believe that maybe this man actually was an ally.

His thoughts had been distracted by his hands, but Noah began to listen carefully to the conversation between GJ and Murray Marks. And he understood why Christina had wanted to wait.

"Just say the word, GJ. There's a place for you here." The doctor swept his hand at the group as though the woods were a palace and the soldiers his servants. At least the second part seemed to be true.

GJ shook her head firmly. "I can't do this. I can't help you commit genocide."

"It's not genocide!" He sounded sincerely offended, and GJ played dumb.

Though that had not been part of the original plan, she began to rail against her grandfather, her hands gesturing much the same way his did. It tugged at Noah's heart to see that they had obviously been so close that, even in the heat of this life-altering argument, they mirrored each other. They had the same eyebrows. The same straight nose. The same glare.

She turned hers on him. "You're killing all these wolves, grandfather. How is that not genocide? You came here to wipe them out."

"I came here to give them a chance to convert."

"*Convert?*" She wielded the word like a sword. "You sound like a fucking religious zealot."

The older man ignored the swearing. "It's not about that. They're not safe out in the world, this group."

"They're wolves!" That GJ managed to pull off a stunningly surprised face was impressive. She was not only facing the man who'd basically raised her, she was *playing* him.

Noah worked to make his expression fit the scene in front of him and at the same time watch Christina, Wade, and Walter. All followed suit with varying degrees of conviction. Noah was no actor. He figured he was probably the worst of the lot. Maybe when he finally got hired into NightShade—assuming that he survived this assignment—they would teach him how to pretend he had no idea about Aegis X.

"The wolves all have to band together if they want to survive—"

"Grandfather." She cut him off. "The only thing harming this family is *you*. Leave them alone and they'll survive just fine."

It was a stupid argument. Noah wondered if Murray Marks understood just how brilliant his granddaughter was. If he did, that would have been the clue that gave them all away. But he maybe didn't want to see that she had changed sides.

GJ wasn't his acolyte anymore.

Marks continued talking, trying to reason with her. "If we don't put these groups together now—if the wolves stay separated—then everything will fall apart for them. Technology today will reveal them for what they are. They can't even go to the doctor! Their medical records show how strange they are. We've already quashed more than one attempt to get their 'bizarre physiology' written up in the medical journals."

Beside him, Noah saw Wade stand up straighter at the comment and he began to wonder if that was something every wolf went through. Was agent Donovan Heath maybe a physician simply so he could take care of himself? The thought had not occurred before.

This time, GJ altered her expression to look confused. "You sound like you're protecting them grandfather, but all I've seen you do is kill them."

"I *am* protecting them. They're a valuable species, and a key part of the ecosystem. They've been around since before many other species." He said this as though he wasn't an anthropologist, as though he were some preservation specialist. But then again, the history Noah had read said that Marks had been doing covert work relating to the wolf populations for decades. He was studying them long before anyone had realized what he was doing.

And who knew what he'd gotten up to since he'd escaped from prison?

"You broke into my lab!" GJ cleverly shifted the conversation with another attack.

"*My* lab," he corrected, his tone suddenly darkening. He had to know that it was legally hers now.

"You went to jail."

Her grandfather dropped the anger and darkness to offer up a now nonchalant shrug. "I did what I had to do. I'm trying to save a species here. The work is bigger than me."

Noah was going to get whiplash from the arguments. Was he saying he was trying to save a species by killing an entire family of them?

Marks acted as though his logic was sound. And that may have been the most surreal part—the man actually seemed to actually believe what he was saying.

It was then—smack in the middle of the conversation, when no one was paying any attention to the rest of the agents—that Christina gave the nod.

With a deep breath, Noah gathered up whatever focus he could. His move was the first. GJ had planned it all out using the weapons at hand: *them.* The weapons that Marks and his soldiers just might not know they possessed.

Noah let fly with the feeling of bullets slamming into shoulders. He hit legs, necks, arms—anywhere left unprotected. He chipped bark from the trees, making it look as though an attack was coming from all sides at once. And he did it with a skill he'd not believed he possessed until a few days ago.

Before today, he'd only tapped shoulders or made people feel like a gun was pressed to their back. The force to shatter bark like a projectile was new… *What else could he do if he didn't have to hide what he was?*

Everyone ducked, even Marks and GJ, who now had her hands free. She was only a few feet from her grandfather, and she used the element of surprise to dive forward. It was exactly as she was supposed to do, the sound of his fake bullets signaling her to go. Whoever was closest to Marks was going to execute the choke hold.

GJ had maneuvered herself to be the closest, and though he was her grandfather, she didn't falter. She was quickly behind him with her hand snaked under his neck, executing the martial arts move perfectly. That was another thing Noah had not expected of the diminutive genius.

He watched as she hit the ground, her back smacking dirt as he drew breath to flail another round of "bullets" into the crowd. Though they hit hard, she didn't let go of her grandfather. Her knees bracketed either side of his ribcage and her fingers locked into her opposite elbow, forming the requisite triangle to shut him down. She pressed her palm tightly against the back of his head. The expression on her face was one of sheer pain as she worked to make her grandfather black out.

Noah let another hail of bullets fly. It was happening so fast that it took him a moment to realize that the other agents were up and acting.

Christina nodded to him. *Signal Two.* And, as he watched, grass fires began in between all the soldiers, cutting them off from each other.

If they'd worked with Aegis X, if they'd thrown those strange bombs at the de Gottardi and Little families, then they would probably believe the fire was supernatural in origin. But did that matter?

It didn't seem to as they screamed and ducked into protective stances. Some beat at the flames, others shied away, only to find more fire at their backs. Noah took another breath.

Wade and Walter ran forward.

They moved with their weapons out and they fired real bullets, taking out soldiers as they went.

With his last mental round spent and the war sufficiently started, Noah pulled his weapon and joined them. Taking advantage of those cowering in their circles of flame felt wrong. They were already trapped. But he also knew that their crimes were bigger than this little battle he'd started. They had killed members of the de Gottardi/Little family, just yesterday. There was no good way out of this.

He pulled the trigger several times.

He took out two of the soldiers and turned to face a third when the flames suddenly snapped out of existence. Whirling around, he removed his finger from the trigger, so he wouldn't inadvertently spray bullets. But he caught sight of what he feared most: Christina standing in the center of it all, her face blank.

Her eyes rolled upward, and she looked surprised for a moment, right before she crumpled.

69

C hristina watched as the fires went out. Confused at her sudden loss of control, she tried desperately to light the flames again. But it seemed all her powers had been turned off.

Around her, the others moved in concert, just as they were supposed to. Walter looked like an action movie in slow motion—an elbow here, a fist there, a bullet over there. She spun, throwing a punch with her prosthetic arm, and Christina watched as the man reeled backward, almost flying. Clearly, he'd expected to meet bone and flesh, not metal.

Noah was staring at her, a disturbing look of alarm on his face, but she waved him away. Without her fake fire holding them down, the soldiers had begun to stand and put up a real fight. Christina knew her team was outnumbered. They needed Noah fighting, not making faces.

As she reached for her own gun, she tried again to reach inside and reignite whatever power she had.

It didn't work. But this time it might have failed because she was surprised and distracted.

Eleri Eames walked calmly through the crowd.

Where she'd come from, Christina couldn't figure out. "Eleri!" she called out, not managing to keep the surprise from her voice.

"Christina," the other agent replied with a friendly wave and a tone that didn't lend credence to the bullets flying around her. Her hair hung in waves nearly to her shoulders and her pale green eyes were bright. She smiled as though she were walking into a picnic, not a battle.

Did a bullet just fly through her friend? Christina blinked in disbelief. Eleri seemed unfazed. She didn't even jolt or look to the side.

But as she got closer, her expression changed. Sobering and with a sense of urgency, she leaned in and spoke to Christina. "Aegis isn't real. Not in the way you're thinking."

Okay. Christina wasn't sure what Eleri was saying or why in hell she was saying it now. She made a move to push her friend out of the way. Bullets were flying. They couldn't stand here and have a philosophical conversation. Maybe when they got back to the compound...

Even as she pushed Eleri away, Christina squeezed several times on the trigger, taking down a soldier coming at her. Eleri moved only one step to the side and continued speaking.

"The bones are part of a spell. If you steal the bones, they will have nothing to hold the illusion together. Then you'll have the upper hand."

"It's real enough," Christina cried, once again turning and firing off a shot at an approaching soldier.

"Oh yes," Eleri replied, "It is. And some of them believe, too." She waved at the soldiers around her. Her sweeping gesture included the other NightShade agents, who didn't even see that Eleri was here.

Still pulling the trigger, still fighting to get them out of this intact, Christina looked over and watched as Dr. Marks went limp, his granddaughter still holding on tight. GJ seemed unwilling to let him go or stand back up and fight.

Christina would need to go and put a bullet in him. She'd already decided she would not be asking GJ to do that again. She started toward the two, ready to end this, but Eleri put out a hand and stopped her.

"They believe, but that doesn't matter. All of the power comes from a spell."

"It's a pretty powerful spell!" Christina shouted, exasperated, so she wasn't surprised when she pulled the trigger it only clicked. With a sigh and a smooth motion, she traded out her magazine and aimed her gun again.

"Like all spells," Eleri continued, as though she hadn't been interrupted, "it's only as powerful as the energy put into it over the centuries."

So many centuries, Christina thought. *No wonder it seemed so strong.*

"If you get the bones," Eleri repeated firmly, "you not only break their power, but you can claim it for yourself. You can work the spell. *You* can control Aegis."

"Well, you'll have to get them," Christina said. There was no way in hell she or any of these yahoos on her NightShade team had half the wiccan skill Eleri had. Hell, if they did, they would probably blow themselves up first.

"I can't," Eleri replied.

"Sure, you can." Christina turned, pulling the trigger on a soldier who had almost lunged at her.

Why was Eleri not fighting? None of this made sense.

"How do we get the bones?" Christina asked.

But Eleri slowly began fading from existence as Christina watched, stunned, even as she noticed a tapping sensation at the side of her face.

The tap grew more frantic, turning into a slap as Noah materialized above her.

Christina found herself lying on the ground, looking up at the sky. Noah smacked at her and demanded, "Wake up, Christina! Wake up."

Eleri Eames was nowhere to be seen.

70

E leri walked back across an open field slowly and with a
lightness to her step that she'd not experienced before. She
looked up into the trees and saw the wind in the leaves. She saw it
blowing the grass.

But her feet didn't feel the grass. In fact, she didn't even feel the
earth when she took a step. As she looked down, she struggled to tell
if she was actually pressing into the dirt.

She breathed deeply next, checking for a point of reference. The
motion of her ribcage felt normal, though she didn't feel the oxygen
passing through her nose and mouth.

Strange, strange days.

As she walked farther, the tug in her belly got stronger and
stronger. It kept her moving forward at a fast clip until she saw the
light in the distance.

It was the blue fire from the bowl she had lit. The urge was strong,
and she picked up her pace, even as time passed sloppily.

Suddenly, she was there, standing over herself, lying on the
ground. Donovan hovered, checking her pulse, turning her head side
to side, leaning his ear down next to her chest—though what specifically he was listening for, she didn't know. Maybe breathing.

He seemed worried, but not frantic.

Good.

The tug in her gut became overwhelming.

The flames in the blue bowl flared, catching Donovan's attention. He turned and stared at the change. He should have seen her here in the field but, somehow, he didn't.

Eleri wondered why the flames continued to burn when she was no longer stoking them. She watched as individual spikes of fire reached out and pulled her closer and closer with an urge she couldn't fight.

Her feet remained on the towel she'd laid out. The makeshift stage for the spell from her great-great-grandmother's book was still set, even though she had apparently passed out.

Suddenly, everything around her warped, the tug in her belly taking over. The decision was no longer her own.

In a moment that felt almost as if she'd fallen asleep and jerked her head back awake, she opened her eyes. The air rushed into her lungs. When she jerked, she felt the ground materialize behind her, almost as if she'd fallen into her own body. Her eyes flew open.

"Eleri!" Donovan turned toward her, his eyes pulled from the now-dancing flames.

She smiled.

"Oh, thank God. You're back."

71

"I'm fine," Christina announced, angrily waving Noah away as she stood up.

"No, Christina, you're not. You were out cold for about three minutes."

She nodded, understanding what he meant. For what he'd seen, he was right—but he hadn't seen everything.

Feeling steady on her feet now, she searched the field, trying to parse the melee still going on around them. Something about the way she had passed out and come to had left her laser-focused.

A short distance away, she saw GJ standing with her feet planted apart, her gun pulled, and aimed at the man on the ground.

Christina's heart broke for the youngest agent. Even as she acknowledged that GJ was doing what must be done, she saw Walter flying toward her partner, her feet eating distance, her own weapon pulled. She aimed a gun she'd probably stolen from one of his soldiers and pelted bullets into the man on the ground, an assault he would not survive.

Walter hadn't changed the outcome, but Christina realized Walter had made it possible to claim her own bullets had killed Murray Marks, hopefully taking the burden from her partner, the old scientist's granddaughter.

Christina spun around at a soft noise behind her and leveled her own weapon at a soldier who thought he could take her back. The man fell quickly with the shot, though Christina wasn't certain he was dead.

The training to aim for center mass was strong, and she might have just popped him backward with a bullet to his Kevlar. But she'd take the win.

"Eleri?" she asked into the air, even though she had a pretty darn good idea now what had happened. Eleri's absence confirmed what Christina had figured out.

The number of soldiers was lower now, much lower. Many were on the ground. GJ and Walter, having completed one of the major tasks of this mission, looked until they spotted Christina.

With one finger in the air, she made a circular motion, indicating they were to wrap up and get out. Wade was the first to her side and he placed a hand on her shoulder, as if to steady her. She brushed him off, too.

If there had been time and there hadn't been bullets flying—both real ones and those invented by Noah—she would have rolled her eyes.

"I'm fine," she protested again as the three of them dropped to the ground. Looking to the blond man on her left, she asked, "You got this?"

He nodded easily. He almost seemed surprised that he did, in fact, have this.

She signaled next to Walter and GJ, who exited the area from a different direction.

As they all cleared the space taken up by the soldiers, Noah sent another round of fake bullets flying. The soldiers who were left behind wisely scattered.

It took a few minutes for the agents to reconvene as a group.

A reasonable distance from the scene and the dead bodies, Christina's group huddled together at the base of a tree, hoping they were covered by the tall grasses.

All five of them were now breathing heavily as their adrenaline began to wane.

"You got hit," Walter told her casually, pointing at her chest.

Stunned, Christina looked down to see the tear in the front of her shirt and she poked a curious finger into it. She felt the flattened piece of metal against her protective vest. It had done its job. That had once been a bullet. Did it still feel warm to the touch? Maybe it was just because she knew it should. There was no time to pry it out of the Kevlar, so she left it in place.

Despite not having felt the hit, she knew she was probably going to pay with bruises and broken ribs that she couldn't yet distinguish.

They had no time to think about tomorrow.

"Now what?" Wade asked, his head back to look up at the sky or check for soldiers in the tree above them, perhaps.

"Go back," Noah replied, but Christina shook her head.

Despite everything, they were not yet done.

"Eat." She gave the command even though it would be hard to do as they were breathing heavily. But the soldiers who had captured them had searched them only briefly and hadn't stolen their food. The agents began pulling energy bars and snacks from pockets and taking forced bites.

Looking to the small group first, Christina assessed that they were okay. No serious injury. No twisted ankles, no blood soaked sleeves. So she turned to Noah.

"I passed out, you said."

"*Yes*," he replied, with a tone that indicated she should have already figured this out.

"I saw Eleri."

"Where?" Wade now looked at her like she was nuts. But she brushed it off.

"I saw Eleri, and she said we need to get Aegis' bones. That Aegis himself isn't real. It's all spells."

The others nodded at that, at least.

" Well that explains the bombs," Wade stated, though they'd already had their musings about that.

"How do we steal the bones?" Walter jumped in, ever practical.

But Christina had heard one last phrase from Eleri, the words hanging in the air even as the woman had disappeared. Her voice lingered now. And Christina turned to GJ.

"Eleri told me that *you* would know."

72

"They haven't left," Noah told the group.

They all looked back at him as though he were crazy. Luckily, Wade caught on and picked up the thread. "He's right. Marks is dead... What about Menon?"

Walter offered a short nod to let them know that she confirmed that Marks' assistant had also been taken out.

GJ swallowed hard, as though the news wasn't going down easily. From what Noah had gathered, getting rid of those two targets was supposed to mark the end of an era. Instead, they were still up to their necks in the fight and not much better off than before.

GJ sucked in a deep breath through her nose and steeled her gaze. She could grieve later. Noah had to respect that.

"Well if those two are gone," Wade continued, looking at the group for answers, just as Noah had, "then who's in charge?"

They all looked to each other, finally understanding finally what Noah had been trying to ask.

If the leader is dead, why hasn't the group disbanded?

"Because the leader isn't dead," Christina said with the irritation of realization.

"So who is the leader now?" Noah asked the group, figuring he was the only one who didn't know.

But everybody shrugged.

"Then how do we find the bones?"

Another round of shrugs in reply.

Well this sucks, he thought. They were out here like sitting ducks partially hidden by the foliage. They were not safe. They had only the weapons they'd stolen. No water, only a little food. And no real plan.

"Are we going back?"

He'd asked this before, but he was now wondering if maybe this was the final straw. They could regroup, get backup....

But Christina shook her head *no.* "First, we need to go back to the site and steal more weapons and ammo off of the bodies. We have to be prepared."

As Noah looked at the other four faces, he saw that everyone else in the group seemed to agree. It wasn't his place to say that it was a crazy idea, or that it was equally nuts to search for missing, ancient bones in the middle of an armed insurgence. They didn't even know where the bones were! And their current course of action was only the belief that "GJ could do it."

He decided to quell at least one of his fears, even if he was asking about a vision one of his fellow agents had had. "Why did Eleri say you could do it, GJ?"

GJ smiled before she replied. "When I first met Eleri and Donovan, they were on a case. I was on the same case, but for different reasons. We were all looking for a set of bones. They got to it first. But I stole the skeleton from them."

Noah felt his gaze narrow. "So Eleri thinks you can steal bones from a well-oiled machine of heavily armed soldiers, because you've stolen them from NightShade agents in the past?"

"No," GJ said, still smiling. "She probably believes I can steal the bones, because after she and Donovan got them back from me, they put them into evidence. Then I stole them from an FBI facility."

Holy shit. Noah couldn't imagine stealing something from a secured Bureau evidence lockup. Hell, it was hard enough checking out his own evidence when he was the arresting agent. Maybe Eleri was right. Maybe GJ *could* pull this off.

"Is everybody fed?" Christina asked.

As he nodded in answer, Noah noticed that his heart had slowed from a gallop to a trot. Though he didn't like any of this, he was ready to go.

"Come along." Christina stood slowly, checking the area around her. When she deemed it clear, she motioned everyone else to their feet. Still, they all stayed low as they made their way back toward the soldiers who had died or fallen in their small battle.

None of the invaders had arrived to clean up or check on the wounded yet. Despite all the noise they'd created, the scene was empty. Only a few of the fallen moaned where they lay. A path here or there showed evidence that someone well-damaged had limped or been dragged away. But everything else—everyone else—had been left where they fell.

Someone must have been close enough to hear the *bullets* and the *screams*. How could they have missed that? Or did they just not care that their own soldiers had fallen?

In fact, Noah looked around and said, "I haven't even heard anyone come to check on this—but we can't be so far from other groups that they didn't hear the massacre…"

Christina held one finger up for him to be quiet. Then she motioned as she pulled the comm system off one of the soldiers.

Ew, he thought, but he followed suit, wiping down the earpiece and dialing the system to a frequency that Christina had chosen before he spoke again. "No one has been here. Someone had to have been close enough to know what happened…"

His implied question was overshadowed by his fellow agents pulling guns and clips from the bodies. He did the same, checking the number of rounds in each magazine, before setting the safety and sliding the gun into a pocket on his pants or into his emptied ankle holster. He took both the holster and its knife from one of the dead and strapped it to his own thigh. *This monster blade might come in useful.* He ignored the fact that he was raiding a body—one he might have killed himself.

He tried again. "You'd think with all the noise, someone would have heard, and come to check on their own people." Noah waved a hand at the at the destruction as if to say, *Clearly, this should have been checked on.*

Wade shrugged again and Noah began to very much dislike getting shrugged at as an answer. He thought he'd seen everything in the Caribbean. It turned out, all he'd done was peek behind the curtain. Still, there was something exciting about this work—something about being asked to *do* what he could do, rather than being punished for it—that made him want to stay.

Despite the shrugs, he realized he trusted these four agents. So he gathered everything he could fit into his pockets, including a still-sealed water bottle he found as they were finishing up.

Wade placed a finger to his lips then quickly motioned the others to get down.

Noah followed suit, having no idea what was going on—although at least this time, it looked like *someone* did.

Wade next motioned to his ear, and then made a second motion about walking.

Were they supposed to walk? But then he heard it: the cadence of footsteps. By the sound, a large company was marching right toward their group. In fact, a voice called out.

"This looks like it, and it doesn't look good."

Christina waved to get her agents' attention and motion them to stay low. She whispered into the comms, "Stay still. I've got you."

73

For a few heart-pounding moments, Christina watched as the soldiers made their way around them.

She breathed carefully in through her nose and out through her mouth, feeding constantly into the mental push required to hold the illusion. There were so many soldiers to push and five people to remove from their vision.

She kept her focus as pure as she could and tried to let the others observe what was happening. None of the soldiers seemed to notice that there were five spots they just didn't step in.

If they walked into one of the spots where her agents crouched, they'd feel that they hit someone, so the trick was to make them not notice that they avoided those places.

She just wished she'd had enough warning to get her team close together, because at any given time, there were several soldiers standing between her and each of her fellow agents. Christina didn't like it.

There was nothing she could do to change their positions now, so she held the illusion until well after the soldiers' footsteps had receded into the distance.

Once she motioned that it was safe to get up, she waited while everybody else slowly began to look around.

Eleri had gotten hunches. She knew things. There were other agents in NightShade who could sense things before they happened.

Christina had worked with Dana so long that she took those visions as just a matter of course. But she'd been privy to very few since Dana had died, and no one here had that ability or even anything close. It left Christina feeling horribly exposed.

Walter turned to the group, looking confident, and said, "Follow them. That's where the bones are. That's where the leader is."

The team began walking slowly along, staying low and quiet. The bent-over posture seemed to be getting to all of them and made it difficult to keep up with the soldiers.

When Noah stopped them, Christina's irritation flared. They were getting even further behind. But his eyes zeroed in on hers. "Can you make us blend in? What if we look like them? Then we can walk straight into the compound with them."

He said it so calmly, but holy shit. *Why hadn't she thought of that?*

Christina rapidly nodded and pushed the mental image of the five agents outfitted as Marks' soldiers outward to anyone within sight. They all stood up, looking at each other. It took a moment before it occurred to her that, though she was working to make everyone else see them, she hadn't made *them* see them. They had to know what people saw when they looked. So she took another deep breath, nodded, and held up one finger.

For the first time, she pushed her friends.

It felt awful—a cranking sensation twisting at her emotions and sitting like a rock in the bottom of her chest. Even though she knew it was the right thing to do, she was still breaking an oath she'd made to herself. And she'd broken it so easily.

She didn't even tell them she was doing this for the first time in years. Christina had worked so hard to avoid exactly this. But here she was.

She opened her eyes to see that Noah was perhaps the most surprised, even though it was his own idea. He looked between the other agents, assessing them each as soldiers.

Though Christina had left their faces intact, she'd outfitted them to look exactly like Marks' people. To a certain extent, though Walter tried to hide it, they all examined their new looks in awe. They ran their fingers down the arm of their clothing, or along the seam of the slick, black camo pants, probably to see if it felt the same as it looked. Their actual Kevlar was FBI issued, but now it looked like a basic, black layer version that could be purchased in any military-style outfitter. They had knee pads—the same as she'd seen some of the upper- level soldiers wearing.

Noah reached around his back, feeling for the rifle she'd visually draped there. His hand knocked it a little bit, but she shook her head at him. If he pulled it and fired the weapon, he'd give her too much work to do to maintain the illusion. The less she had to alter, the better.

He nodded, seeming to understand.

Then Walter got them back in the groove. With two fingers, she motioned to all of them to move forward. This time, they stood up straight and walked quickly, as though they were just catching up with their unit.

Christina's thighs thanked her for the newer, straighter position, and she wondered if all the younger agents had handled this any better than she had. She was in very good shape, but she was beginning to wonder if it was good enough.

Luckily, the path ahead to catch up with the other soldiers was clear. Walter appeared to have been correct about everything leading to the center, for only a little while later, yet another unit joined up.

Even as it did, there were mild acknowledgments between the soldiers. So she and her agents joined in, nodding and motioning with two fingers to their brows in salute. Walter's salute, certainly sharper than everyone else's, maybe would give her away. But Christina couldn't clean that up.

Even as the new group merged into the bigger one they followed, a smaller group—maybe six or seven of them—appeared in the distance, ready to join up.

She recognized the dark-haired, pale-eyed man—the wolf she'd met outside the restaurant. She'd known, and the others had known, not to shoot at him during the melee, but he'd quickly disappeared. Christina now breathed the sigh of relief, glad that he was okay. Unfortunately, with that relief, she watched as her friends' outfits shimmered just a little as she lost her focus.

With a shake of her head, and two hard steps to reorient her priorities, she pushed the illusion back into place. This had been so much easier in high school when she made her class elect her as prom queen.

It was almost thirty minutes before they came upon an encampment. There were so many of them now, covering the distance.

Christina knew the land well enough to know they stayed at a relatively constant distance from the perimeter of the de Gottardi/Little farm.

But she almost stopped and stared at the mobile city in front of her. In her peripheral vision, she again saw Noah's uniform shimmer as she was distracted.

How had Will's people not found this? she wondered again. Or had they and Will simply not shared the information with her?

She and her own people had gone out on recon several times, but only to a few specific locations. It was entirely possible the Night-Shade agents had missed this—but how did Will?

Was he only sending the moles out and they lied to him upon return? Could there even *be* that many moles in his family? If there were, then he was fucked. The other option was that Will was holding back information.

She didn't know. But as she followed the band of soldiers, she and her agents worked hard to remain at the rear. They followed the arriving group right into the middle of the camp.

74

The agents were trying to stay together as a group.

Noah watched as the soldiers splintered into smaller factions and was glad there were only five agents to account for. It made it a little easier to simply look as though they were their own group. So far, no one had given them a direct order to split up.

They had been sent to one corner to gather supplies and check comm systems.

It was stupid, rote work, the kind given to grunt soldiers. But that was good, too.

Noah thought it would have been better to be assigned into the biggest tent in the middle. But this work meant they could slip away easily, and no one would notice.

Slowly, as they checked the comms laid out on a folding table, the five of them worked their way toward the end of the lot. Then, one by one, they peeled off and stepped aside.

Christina was the last, and when she joined them, they all began speaking at once. But she put a finger to her lips, waited a beat, and then said, "Okay, you can talk now. They shouldn't be able to see or hear us."

"The big tent looks like where things are going down. They're definitely planning a raid tonight," Walter said and Noah blinked.

He hadn't picked that much up. Then again, he wasn't ex-military. "What makes you say that?"

"The fact that they are checking every system. The only reason they need *all* the comms and *all* the food and *all* the weapons inspected right now, is because they're getting ready to move with it. This isn't routine."

Noah nodded.

"Which means we have a very short period of time to get in there," Christina said. Her head turned to the side and Noah followed her gaze.

They all watched as a pair of soldiers, clearly taking a break, ate some kind of sports energy bar and drank bottles of water. Then they walked directly toward the tree where the NightShade agents were gathered.

Slowly, and seeming not to understand what they did, the pair veered around the group as they continued their little conversation. If they tracked their path in the grass, they would notice something was amiss, but they didn't look.

As they left, Noah began to relax. Christina had done it, but she didn't seem ready yet to pat herself on the back.

"The first thing we need to do is get into that tent. My hope is that the bones are in there."

GJ had not been paying much attention to the approaching soldiers or the conversation. Really, she seemed not to need to. She was keeping up, nodding along, and agreeing with Walter that the group was prepping for something big. But now she motioned to the group, her head not turning to check that they saw. "Look at what they're carrying in."

Noah watched, trying to figure out what she'd gleaned. He didn't understand it. Several soldiers were carrying what looked like sheets. Others carried stacks of very large bowls. Some had bottles of water, the pre-packaged plastic kind, which looked very out of place. Others carried bags stuffed with smaller items he couldn't see from here.

"That's for spell work. The bones are in there," GJ's conviction that she was correct was clear in her tone.

"So if we cover you, can you get in and get the bones and get back out?" Christina asked her.

Only then did she turn to face the group. "I can. You need to be in there with me, Noah."

Why him?

GJ seemed to read the expression on his face. "I need Wade out here concentrating. He's got better eyes and ears than the rest of us—"

"Not eyes," Wade interrupted, but GJ shrugged him off.

"Better ears, then." She gave him a lopsided grin. "We need you listening. We need Walter as our cover. And Christina has to maintain whatever… *glamour* …she put on us."

She'd seemed to search for the right word, but she was still going on. "That means you and I go in. It means you can cause a commotion inside, once you see what's going on. That will allow me time to gather the bones."

It all sounded reasonable in a purely insane way. "I'm assuming you know what you're looking for?"

"I have no clue what I'm looking for," GJ replied cleanly. "I'm hoping I'll know it when I see it, though."

Well, that sounds like a real solid plan, Noah thought sarcastically, but it was the only one they had. "When do we go?"

Looking at the group again, he waited for one of the senior agents to say something brilliant. But it was Walter who told them, "Now. We go now. The longer we wait, the more prepared they get. If they're going to cast a spell, every second gives them another chance to start it. We need to get organized. We need to get in and then get out."

It was all of five minutes later that Noah and GJ picked up some of the folded white fabric and carried it into the tent. Now that he looked at it closer, it looked like maybe it wasn't sheets, just fabric. He followed GJ and the soldiers who were carrying more bowls. Behind him, some of the others were on round two of delivery and were hauling large rocks and heavy bags of flour.

Noah wanted to make a face at all the oddity, but knew he needed to act like he belonged, like he knew what he was doing. Sure enough, when they entered, he saw the set-up.

The white fabric was cut into long strips, and the workers unrolled it and laid out the pieces, connecting the ends into most of a circle. When finished, it would encompass almost the entire floor space of the large, square tent. At regular intervals sat the huge, hammered copper bowls, which were much easier to recognize up close. Inside each bowl, a large rock or a crystal sat, each one different.

A woman stood nearby, arguing about which one went in which position.

"Put those over there," she commanded, instructing GJ and Noah to finish the circle. She didn't recognize them for the traitors they were, and they scrambled, acting like good soldiers.

As they unfolded the linen onto the floor, Noah realized they must have brought in the last four pieces. He laid out his pieces carefully, working to complete the ring. That made him nervous as hell. He didn't like helping with a ritual that was clearly designed to hurt, even if he didn't know how.

Another soldier called to the woman who appeared to be in charge. She wore a dress so red, it was almost as dark as she was. The midnight of her skin seemed to shimmer, and Noah fought not to have his attention caught by her beauty.

"Alesse, I think we have the rocks wrong."

The woman's immediate response was irritation. She looked at each one and counted around the circle before declaring, "You're right. They're wrong. Move these ..."

She pointed and moved to the center of the circle, making Noah even more nervous as he placed the last edge of the last sheet into place. No one else seemed to notice that she took a breath and straightened a little as he closed the circle, as though he had completed something.

Even as she was organizing the rocks, her hand reached back, white nails glowing in the pale light, and snapped at others. "Salt," she demanded. "Put down the salt."

One of the soldiers turned to Noah, motioning that he should hold the heavy bag. He saw then that it was not, in fact, flour. The other soldier snipped the corner off the bag and together, they poured the salt onto the white sheets, making a ring around the circle.

Salt was to ward off evil, wasn't it? Or was it to release it? Why hadn't he read up on witchcraft more? He thought he'd left sorcery in the Caribbean, far behind him. But here he was, making a salt circle and clearly setting up this woman's spell, and he wasn't even sure whether he was doing it for gods or demons.

GJ was getting farther and farther away from him, but he spotted her on the other side of the tent. She'd stepped out of the way, motioning at him to keep doing what he was doing, as though she had figured everything out. He hoped so.

He and his new soldier buddy emptied the bag, but it didn't complete the circle. Others were already pouring a stream of salt over the other parts, and they would meet up. Alesse now absently motioned the two of them to an old steamer trunk.

There was something about the trunk that made Noah want to hold back. Black and oily, the surface seemed to capture light rather than reflect it, and it made him think this wasn't a remnant from the 1800s but was probably millennia older.

The trunk had to be it. GJ was headed toward it now. They had to steal the steamer trunk. But how in hell were they going to get it out of here?

Just then, the woman in the center—Alesse—looked upward as though she could see the sky beyond the tent. With one hand, she motioned to the others. "It's getting very close to time. You must work faster."

She pointed to Noah and his buddy and she snapped at them. "Get the trunk!" She pointed, glaring at them as though they'd been too stupid to understand the first time.

He headed over as GJ ducked behind a drape. Though she was safely out of sight, his trepidation was growing. Along with the other soldier, he grabbed one of the handles and picked up his end of the trunk. It was heavy, but not as heavy as he'd expected.

"Out, now! All of you!" Alesse demanded, but Noah was still moving the trunk and soldiers were still finishing tasks at various points in the space.

Only a few of the soldiers filtered out of the tent, but she motioned to Noah and his buddy to set the trunk down and lift the lid.

75

G J stuck her head out from where she'd hidden and motioned frantically to him.

If Alesse was starting the spell now, then there was no time left.

Noah nodded back, even as he moved the trunk into place inside the circle.

As the other soldier reached down for the lock and opened it, following Alesse's orders, Noah sent his first hail of bullets into the room.

It had worked before, and he wasn't up to inventing a new trick right now.

This time, the soldiers hit the ground or scurried to get out of the tent.

Alesse only turned and glared at Noah. She knew instantly who the maelstrom of bullets had originated with.

Oh crap.

Her eyes were now black as pitch, and if he hadn't seen that before with agent Eleri Eames, he would have screamed and passed out. Instead, he stared back at Alesse and once again flung his fake bullets into her skin.

Her hands flew up in front of her, palms flat and outward, as though she was pushing on something. As though she could stop his bullets. It looked more like she was casting a spell.

In fact, she must be incredibly powerful, because as he watched, the air shimmered red in front of her. But his fake bullets still hit her skin, shocking the shit out of her.

It probably worked because his bullets weren't magic. They were some kind of science he hadn't yet explained. She was doing ancient spellwork, but what he was doing, apparently, was radically different.

She threw up her hands again, a rebel yell coming from her mouth with words in a language probably so ancient that he could never understand it. The sound seemed to fly from her crimson lips and meld with the red around her, no longer simply shimmering in the air, but forming a full globe.

Again, she seemed to think this would protect her. And again, he pushed his fake bullets into her.

She called for backup. But no one came.

Every time someone so much as ventured through the tent flaps, Noah ripped him with a fake bullet. He saw in his peripheral vision as his bullets hit hard, watched as skin split and blood began flowing. He realized that even the little practice he'd gotten had made him much better at this. He could shoot somebody now, or at least close to it, without a gun in his hands.

It was a terrifying ability, but he didn't falter. He remembered after the battle on the Queen's Staircase, how Eleri had been so shaken. At the time, he hadn't quite understood, but now he was getting the first taste of it for himself.

He noticed that, behind Alesse, GJ was opening the trunk and reaching inside. She seemed to be sorting through a variety of objects. Even though he wanted to stop—even though he desperately needed a philosophical and moral discussion with himself about what he was doing—he hit Alesse again.

But she was wising up. Though her skin tore and blood flowed from her wounds, the pain barely seemed to affect her. As he watched, her skin sealed and closed on its own, leaving the rivulets of blood down her arms looking as if they'd come from nowhere.

"I needed blood for this spell anyway," she taunted him.

But he didn't let up.

He tried not to let his eyes give away what was happening behind her, but he could see GJ pulling things from the trunk. Finally, having made her choice, she gathered a bundle of what looked like thick and relatively large human bones. She grabbed one of the sheets, shaking the heavy salt off of it, and wrapped them up. She tied it into a tight knot and tossed it to him.

"Here!" Her voice startled him through the comm that had stayed relatively silent the whole time.

He barely caught the bundle in time. The streak of white through the air caught Alesse's attention, and she turned to level her spells at GJ.

"Are we good?" he whispered back, even as he tried to get Alesse's attention away from his fellow agent. He tried for a knife slice and managed to cut the front of her dress.

Even he was shocked at the outcome. Blood poured down her side, and the witch screamed an unholy sound. Soldiers poured in through the tent flaps, aiming their guns at him.

"Do you have enough to break the spell?" It was Christina's voice now, and Noah noticed the team charging in with the other soldiers, even as he watched the guns trained on him start to swing wildly... as though they could no longer see him.

Alesse yelled at the soldiers to get them—probably meaning him and GJ—but GJ blinked out of his vision as the red around the witch shimmered and thrust outward like a shockwave.

The only thing that saved him was that he saw it coming and flattened before it could knock him over. The adrenaline in his system altered his sense of time. He noted ground scraping against his skin and the rattle of the bones in his arms.

GJ's voice came to him through the comm, and though he noticed movement in the trunk, he still couldn't see the small agent.

"With what we have, I think we can break the spell. But I'm going to get the rest." Then she told them all, "Go!"

They couldn't go without her. What special skills did she have? Would Christina's illusion hold enough for her to make it out without him throwing bullets to keep the soldiers occupied?

He stood, hugging the packet of bones to his chest, and threw another round of random bullets into the confused soldiers.

He was still afraid the precious pieces he now carried might fall out an open end and get lost, so he held it close even as he saw GJ phase back into existence.

At the other side of the room, he watched as Christina, Wade, and Walter appeared. They hadn't materialized, they'd arrived on foot—but no one had seen...

Alesse turned her rage toward GJ, now in sight, as the agent pawed through the precious bones. The other team members shot at her with actual bullets, but she flicked a wrist blindly and sent Christina and Wade flying backward, along with several of her own troops.

Joining the effort to distract her from GJ, he threw more bullets directly at Alesse, since he seemed to be the only one who could hit her. Once more, she screamed with both surprise and anger. She chucked another shockwave at him, and he ducked again, holding her spell bones up as a shield.

One of them rattled from inside the sheet, as though it was trying break free and escape of its own accord. Noah clamped down his grip as GJ pulled more bones from the trunk and tossed them onto another sheet she'd shaken the salt off.

He did the only thing he could and tried to cut Alesse again. Only this time, it didn't work. She was onto him and rapidly learning how to counter his attacks.

Wade and Walter and Christina were pushing other soldiers, shooting at them, and getting them out of the way. Though Alesse had made GJ visible again, she hadn't yet figured out that the other three were there.

But as GJ stood up and wrapped the other bones—smaller pieces, and more of them than the ones that he held—she motioned to him once again to leave.

Then GJ ducked out the tent behind Alesse and out of her sight.

At the same moment, the soldiers suddenly spotted him, all their guns aiming his way at once.

He turned and ran.

76

Christina bolted as hard and fast as her legs could carry her. Luckily, she was the very last of the group of NightShade agents, so she didn't need to turn around or slow down to check up on the others. They were all in front of her, all slightly faster than she was. Right now, she was grateful for that.

Behind her, screams tore the tent apart. Christina wasn't sure if the woman just angrily stomped through a flap that was already there or if the fabric had rent itself apart from the sound she unleashed.

Alesse.... The name tickled at the back of Christina's brain, but she didn't have time to contemplate anything that didn't keep her team alive in this moment. The woman ran after them, one hand wrapped around her middle where Noah had apparently gotten quite a clean cut. *Good for him.* But it wasn't slowing her down enough.

No one else had come out of the shadows or swooped in from somewhere beyond the tents. This woman wore no helmet or other gear and didn't carry a weapon—unless Christina counted her bare hands and clearly potent witchcraft. Alesse also didn't interact with the soldiers in a military style, as she appeared to be the one running the spells.

Was she truly in charge of the attacking legion? Christina hadn't yet figured that out.

Still, Christina ran. She worked to focus her thoughts, both on moving forward—getting them all aimed directly back toward the de

Gottardi/Little compound—and on focusing her efforts on keeping her agents hidden from the powerful witch giving chase.

She pushed herself, too. It had been a long time since she'd done that, but once Alesse had uncovered Noah, Christina realized it wasn't enough to push the illusion into place She had to see what others saw. It was the only way to know her agents were covered.

The grass was tall enough to slow them all down. For brief moments, she would peek at one of them, keeping track of their positions. But as the scream came from behind her, Christina saw Noah wink into existence once again.

Fuck! Whatever skill she had with covering him, Alesse had *un*covered.

Christina was turning her head for a quick look back. But even as she spotted the woman behind her, something told her not to linger. She hadn't seen anything of value to her—no red streak pulsing through the air beside her. But what she got was a gut feeling that Alesse's stance—her free hand aimed forward, fingers claw-like, and anger smeared like dirt across her face—was enough to telescope what was coming.

Christina had only needed the split second to see it to turn back in time to see Noah get struck in the back by whatever Alesse had sent out. He was flung forward, face-first into the grass.

Somehow, her heart pumped even harder. Her feet moved faster. Noah and GJ had been first to leave the tent, and they were still holding the bones GJ had wrapped up. Unfortunately, the bundle he carried was as important as the man himself. So Christina watched now as the other agents merged on him.

Sometimes she saw them as mere shimmers of a shape as she released her own hold on herself. But she knew they were there. She saw the package of bones handed off to Wade. She saw GJ slow, turn, and look back.

But Christina waved both GJ and Wade onward. They couldn't stay for their fallen friend. The bones had to get back to the compound. That was the mission.

Each gave her a sharp nod of understanding. Even though no one liked leaving others behind, GJ and Wade each took off like a shot. Christina worked hard to push whatever protection she could over them. However long it lasted, it would help. Anything Alesse couldn't see would be good.

Reaching Noah, Christina leaned over, watching as Walter pointed to the back of his shirt. The fabric was burned away and for a heart-stopping moment, she expected to see singed flesh. Luckily, her brain figured out quickly that the black she saw was the Kevlar vest, burned and damaged beyond repair. But it wasn't Noah's skin. *Thank God.*

A few quick shakes of their heads over Noah's still prone form, and Christina and Walter agreed that Noah wasn't horribly damaged. Though he probably had cracked ribs, they grabbed him under each arm and lifted him in tandem.

"This is going to hurt like hell" Christina muttered.

It was clear from his dirty look that she'd not delivered any news.

To his credit, Noah didn't scream out and quickly got his feet underneath him.

As they moved forward, Christina asked Walter, "How do we hold her back?"

With Noah between them, they were too slow. Alesse was still coming, and she was definitely going to catch up to them.

She seemed to move forward through the sheer force of her rage, not worried about her speed. Her expression suggested that no matter what she did, she had faith she would catch up to them. That concerned Christina the most. Alesse was clearly very powerful, and she knew exactly what to do with that power.

A sudden tug from Walter made Noah jerk and Christina felt the jolt where she held him. She barely had time to react as Walter took them all face down into the grass. She felt the rush of air pass over their heads and heard the crack as it split around them.

How had Walter known?

But there was no time to ask.

"We have to surprise attack her," Walter said, her breath soughing through the comms.

"But Noah is injured," Christina replied, listening to him breathe. She didn't need the comms to hear him. *He might even have a punctured lung.*

But Walter was right—Alesse would be here in a minute, and they needed to protect Noah, and GJ and Wade out in front of them. Christina could only hope they'd gotten far enough ahead to stay safe.

"You go!" she told Noah, wanting to smack him on the back like a horse but knowing that might be the meanest thing she could do.

He tried to refuse.

"We need to do this without worrying about you. I'll get you covered!"

"She can uncover me," he countered quickly. "I'll be the target."

With that announcement, he took off before she could reply. He was faster than she expected, his lungs still wheezing against whatever damage he'd suffered. But he didn't give up.

"Well, shit…" Christina sighed as she turned back to Walter. "Now what?"

77

Every breath felt like he was fighting to drag in enough air. With all the running and fighting and marching before he'd fled for his life from the witch, Noah had none to spare.

Still, it didn't stop him.

He turned, thinking to wave frantically at Christina. The problem was that he wasn't certain that even she could see him, and then he remembered the comms. "Christina, let her see me!"

"What? No, get back, we've got this."

"Trust me."

He felt it the moment the illusion disappeared. Though it was petrifying to know he was wide open, it was good to be trusted.

Alesse turned on him immediately. She seemed to already know exactly where he was. Then again, maybe she was just shocked at the magic she was up against.

Though Noah knew it wasn't magic, he did know it was all they had—and he played it for all he was worth.

He jumped up and moved in an exaggerated fashion. The gesture was far too painful for him, but he had to be sure he was the one who caught her attention.

Her arm came away from where it had been wrapped around her middle, and Noah had no doubt that she'd managed to heal the deep slice already. Whatever they managed to do would probably only keep her down for a little while. They needed to stop her long enough to get safe.

She'd seen him, all right.

They were close to the edge of the farm and he was praying there was some kind of inherent magic at the de Gottardi/Little property line. He could only hope.

Turning away, and giving Alesse his back again, he ran further. His chest ached with the movement, sharp pains hitting him and spreading around the entire left side of his ribs. This made no sense, as he'd been hit squarely in the back, but this wasn't the time to evaluate it. Noah was just grateful that his spinal cord appeared to be intact.

He ran flat out, ignoring the pain as his legs pumped. He kept his left arm down at his side, as he'd discovered that pumping that arm only made the pain worse.

He'd been counting down since he'd waved his arm. He knew now how long it took her to gear up and gather her power, or whatever she did. So he knew another hit was coming.

Noah dropped to the ground as fast as he could. Still, he felt the massive wave roll over him as it crushed the grass around him and flattened him into the dirt.

She would still be coming for him.

Though he was ready to pop back up and do it again, it occurred to him that maybe the best bait was staying down.

Waiting was hard. Maybe harder than running. His body was still fighting for air and his deep-seated sense of self-preservation desperately wanted him to pop up and flee. But the grass was tall enough that she couldn't see that he was still alive and relatively sound.

"I've got this" he heard Walter say through the piece in his ear.

"To the left," Christina replied, though not to him.

Noah listened as Alesse cried out in anger. *Maybe Christina and Walter figured out a way to distract the woman.*

He recognized suddenly that splitting her distraction would only help. So he popped up one more time. Jumping to his feet as quickly as the pain in his ribs would allow, he turned to check that she'd seen him.

Alesse, whose hand was out toward Christina, shifted her attention to him.

Good.

She screeched again and he imagined it echoed the sound of an ancient quetzal rising from the ashes to destroy the city. But even as he watched her turn on him, he also saw Walter appear behind her.

Christina turned to the woman as though surprised by her, though Noah was confident it was just another bait move. She yelled back, pulled her weapon, and aimed as though she were going to shoot.

For a moment, Noah wondered if that's what Alesse saw. Because she laughed as though Christina's bullets could do nothing to her. One, she was correct. And, two, Christina was smart enough not to waste bullets on an attack that wouldn't work. But as he watched, Walter slipped into place, just behind the tall woman's shoulder.

He didn't see what Walter did, but Alesse's body jerked forward, red blooming from a gaping wound on her left side. Her gleeful laugh turned quickly to stunned shock as her eyes went wide and dark.

She whirled around, ready to face Walter. It was a stunning move. She should have swayed and dropped dead in that moment, given the gap that Walter had left in her chest.

But it wasn't enough, and Alesse was still standing and now aimed at Walter, who was much too close.

78

C hristina watched in stunned horror as Alesse swiped a claw out to kill Walter.

There was no doubt in the mind of anyone watching that she intended to kill.

Walter had reacted quickly and jumped back just far enough back that Alesse's physical hand did not touch her. Still, the woman's grasp was farther than the distance of her arms.

Quickly, Christina let out a sharp, loud yell again, hoping to distract the witch from the more immediate threat. This time, it didn't work.

But Walter was still standing. And seeing what she was about to do had Christina turning her head and yelling a different name. "Noah! Down!"

Christina dove toward the earth and hoped she saw her junior agent do the same as Walter let another bullet fly into the woman.

After passing through the witch, it probably lacked the momentum to fly the distance to where she and Noah lay, but Christina wasn't taking chances. She and her agents were not going down today. And they sure as fuck were not going down by friendly fire that had just passed through whatever that woman was.

This time, Alesse went down. She stayed down.

Before Christina could jump back up and look around, Walter was already running their way. She came at top speed, not slowing down for them. Her hand motioned over her shoulder, *go forward*, her voice repeating the same. Both Walter and Christina spared a glance at Noah, but he was doing fine.

In sync with her newest agent, Christina rolled her butt off the ground, and lining her feet into a runner start, she took off with Noah right beside her. They were so close to the de Gottardi/Little property that she could taste it.

They just had to get there.

79

Noah lay in an actual bed this time, groaning as Jen administered to the wounds on his back.

"These are nasty," she said. "What caused it?"

He would have shrugged, but everything hurt now. The adrenaline of the field had kept him going after Walter had taken out Alesse. They'd run maybe three or four minutes before he'd spotted the line of soldiers and wolves coming from the de Gottardi/Little property.

He'd never been more grateful to see anything in his whole life. He'd almost dropped to his knees in worship right then.

Instead, he and Christina and Walter had run until they passed through the line and let the family take over protection. Though Walter and Christina had kept going, Noah hadn't made it very far before his willpower had been surpassed by the damage his body had taken.

He'd fallen first to his knees, and then forward on to his hands. As his left hand contacted the ground, sharp pain spiked up his arm and then radiated down his side, and he'd rolled to his right, groaning at the pain. Jen and several others who were out, not as soldiers, but following behind as aid, had rushed out to bring him to safety. They'd practically had to carry him to the burned-out compound.

The room they'd been in before was still being used as a makeshift wolf infirmary so they took him somewhere else that he didn't quite recognize. It was clearly part of the family compound, given the "Little House" style of decor, but he didn't know which house. He only knew they'd positioned him in the bottom of a bunk bed. Jen said, "It looks like at least a couple of cracked ribs."

She was pointing to bruises on his side. And Noah was looking at the shirt that she'd cut off of him before starting her assessment. While he was thinking that might have been a bit unnecessary, he was suddenly grateful that they'd considered him more important than the shirt.

Wade appeared in the doorway then, arms crossed and leaning into the frame as though he'd been there more than a moment already. Noah spotted him just as Jen repeated, "What caused this?"

"I don't know."

"You're lucky if it's only cracked ribs," Wade joined in, and Jen turned and looked at him, surprised. "Whatever she was shooting nailed him, and it was big." He'd at least given Jen something to chew on about how to treat the blooming colors on his skin. "I'm just grateful he's okay. Or he will be."

Noah was not okay right now. Although nothing was bleeding, streaks of blue and purple were sneaking fingers around the left side of his torso. Everything hurt more with each passing second.

"I think we're going to need to wrap your ribs. Tightly."

Noah figured that was what he should get, and he was glad that was all Jen was prescribing. So he nodded and waited.

The process of having his ribs bound was almost as painful as the process of getting hit in the first place. But at least when she finished, and she tied a tight knot at his side—definitely old school—he was able to take a breath. Each inhale still hurt like hell, but the stabbing pains had been quelled. The bindings wouldn't let him breathe too deeply, and maybe that's what was helping.

"Thank you," he told her, but she wasn't done.

She didn't even look him in the eye as she examined his arm, only pointed at the odd way he was holding it. "Do we need to do anything about this?"

"I think it was causing pain in my ribs when I moved it." He flexed his left arm now, and it still didn't move with quite the range that his right arm had, but he noted the pain was down. He had to assume nothing was wrong with his arm. He was lucky. *No dislocated shoulders, no big gashes, limbs intact.* And, again, he was grateful.

Wade jerked his thumb over his shoulder. "If you're ready, we're trying to figure out what to do with our spoils of war."

He must mean the bones, Noah thought as he stood up to follow along. But Wade only pointed a finger at him, motioning up and down.

"You might want a shirt."

Yes, Noah thought, sighing and wondering if Jen had given him any drugs in the water.

He just hoped no one was watching as he creeped his way through gingerly putting on a shirt Wade had tossed him. He tried not to yell out in pain. Putting his left arm through first, and then swinging the shirt around, he tried every possible maneuver he could think of. It was about as dumb and bizarre a way as he had ever put on a shirt. But he refused help from Jen, and with a few more wrenching movements, he was ready to head out.

Only as he passed through the threshold of the doorway did he realize that he had blood spattered on his shoes and down his pants. They no longer looked like the black tactical camo gear that the soldiers were wearing and had reverted back to the lighter khaki color that he and the agents had worn to blend in as best they could with the grass.

The spatters were now obvious.

Probably Alesse's blood, he thought. He'd been close enough when he cut her a few times to be in spatter range, though he hadn't been thinking about it then. But there wasn't time to change, and Wade hadn't made any comments about anything other than the lacking shirt. So Noah followed along.

Even walking made his ribs throb with every step, but he didn't want to complain. They headed down one tunnel and hooked across one of the "H bars," as Jen had called them, and then took a right.

Noah thought he felt a gentle sloping beneath his feet. And when they took another sharp turn and headed through a small door that Wade found—and Noah would have walked right by—Noah truly began to wonder.

This time, there was no question of the downward slope and the cooler air.

"Where are we going?" he asked Wade.

"To the archives."

80

"There has to be something here." Christina didn't know if she was saying it to herself or to the others. She and GJ and Walter were frantically pulling books off the shelves of the library Will had led them into.

She was not giving the records their due respect, and she knew it. On any other day, she would have. They were old, bound in leathers that she suspected weren't bovine. Some were even ancient, and she should have been afraid to touch them for fear the oils on her skin would permanently alter them. But she didn't have time for reverence. Though GJ was being careful and had snapped on a pair of blue nitrile gloves that she'd pulled from her pocket, she'd then sworn a blue streak that she didn't have any for the other agents.

"What are we looking for?" GJ asked, her blue finger tracing the spines as she passed.

Though Christina was operating under the guise of *We'll know it when we see it*, it was Will who answered. He wasn't pulling books off the shelves but flipping pages through the ones the two women had dismissively stacked on the table.

"Spells. We're looking for spells."

Christina stopped and stared at the older man. "You have *spell books* down here? You knew this?"

"This is a library." Will said it as though the idea that the wolf compound had witchcraft spells must be obvious. "I'm the protector, but not the curator. I don't know exactly what we have or where."

Christina kept glaring at him. The things he had withheld again bothered her to her core. She was about ready to say "Listen, old man," when he began talking.

"We have records going back to Aegis. If the spell we need *is* regarding Aegis, there's a very good chance that we have it."

Though Christina had quit her work to glare at him, Walter and GJ had not stopped pulling books off the shelves. They looked at each one, flipping it open and then shutting it. Christina admired GJ's restraint. On any other day, the youngest agent would have spent hours nose down in one of the tomes. But now Christina fought to keep her frustration to herself.

She was startled as GJ excitedly held up a heavy book and declared, "This one! Look!"

She flipped a few pages in and pointed with her blue finger, motioning to the symbol in the corner.

"A triskadel…" Walter murmured, recognizing a universal symbol of witches. Christina turned to Will, waiting for him to say something else. But he stayed silent.

Will just nodded, holding his hands out—no gloves on him, either —as GJ laid the book reverently in his hands and opened it to the page she'd found with the symbol on it. But even as she did, she reached up and flipped through several more.

"They're on every page. It's the whole book. How will we find what we need?"

Christina could hear the edge of panic in the agent's voice, such an unusual feature for GJ Jansen. That worried Christina more than anything.

A noise from the hallway had them all turning to see who was approaching, but it was only Wade and Noah entering the room.

"He's patched up," Wade announced. Then, noticing the frantic activity in the room, he asked only, "How do we help?"

Noah's voice came through on top of Wade's and asked, "Where are the bones?"

His tone was almost chastising, but GJ pointed to the two white bundles left alone and tied up in the corner.

"No one guards them but us," she declared.

At least as Christina watched, Noah seemed to relax. Once again, she hadn't liked his tone, but it was not the time to pick a fight. She turned back to the books.

Finally, Wade took control. "Will, clear the table. We need GJ to get set up here."

"But I don't know how to set up until we find the spell," GJ protested.

"No, but you can find the bones, lay them out, and see what we have. That way, when we do find the spell, we can start work immediately."

Understanding, GJ turned and bent into the corner and hauled the first bundle up on the table before Will had even managed to pull three books off onto one of the waiting chairs.

"Noah and Walter and I will keep looking through the books."

Christina watched as Wade's eyes flicked to the left, toward Noah, and tacked on, "Noah will take the lower shelves."

She frowned for a moment, assuming this was because of Noah's injury, but it didn't appear he was badly wounded. At first glance, he only appeared to be a little pale and otherwise hale and hearty. But he turned to the task and Christina pulled another book off the shelf. The job was first.

Will kept flipping through the spell book GJ had found to see what spells might be in it. Christina wanted to watch as GJ sliced open the tied white fabric, and she wondered if Alesse could feel that cutting motion as the bones rolled free.

One by one, the junior agent picked the pale relics up and laid them out on the table. Christina could basically figure out the long bones, but GJ didn't even look at each one. She just automatically set it into it's right place.

Christina watched as a form took shape on the table.

With the bones laid out, GJ left spaces between to account for soft tissue. But not much.

"He's almost as tall as the table!" Christina declared, still doing a shit job of focusing on what she was supposed to.

"He was huge." GJ looked up at her. "Even taller when he was alive."

Christina must have frowned at her, because she immediately added, "We're all taller than our skeletons." But her mini-instruction didn't stop her hands from moving. She pushed a variety of tiny bones into a pile, quickly sorting them out with the precision of anyone else sorting Legos by color. Christina couldn't distinguish what she was looking at. But she trusted that GJ could.

As she turned back to pulling books off the shelf, her eyes were drawn to the bones. The hands took shape. Then the small bones of a foot were laid out in a radial pattern.

"Oh, my God," Christina gasped, stopping again, stunned. Her eyes swept upward from the bones of the feet, along the legs to the pelvis, and up to the head. And, and as she saw the face and jaw, the words simply slipped out of her mouth again. "Oh, my God."

81

Noah turned at the sound of Christina's stunned words, and he could only agree with her assessment. Though GJ continued rearranging the bones as she went as if she hadn't even heard Christina the rest of them stared at the head.

Noah was pretty certain the center of the face was supposed to be part of the skull, but this one was separate. The jaw was also thicker, slightly narrower, and longer…. more like a wolf.

"Was this just a feature of how he died?" Noah asked. If they died in wolf form, did the bones stay that way? He'd had the misfortune of seeing some of the fallen wolves from the fight here. Their bodies still looked like wolves.

But this one… They all looked to GJ.

"No." GJ glanced around the room at each of them. "The bones are consistent, and they don't change. They just shift to different places. This one … is an anomaly."

Surely, Noah thought, *the people he'd walked among had thought he was a god. He would have towered over them.* He was no anthropologist, but the bones looked thick and the skeleton broad-shouldered. Given his layman's assessment, this man would have wielded a great power, just because of his stature.

"Did his face look wolven all the time?" Walter asked. *Was that even a word?*

But GJ didn't balk. "It would appear so."

Noah thought it wouldn't have mattered if the man didn't have any supernatural powers. Back then, the people would have fallen in line just because of how he looked. "Obviously, they would have worshiped him."

"And if they did, then any spells he cast were powerful," Christina added, her words spoken as though into the air and not to any of them, in particular. "Eleri said a spell is as powerful as the energy put into it. They've been putting energy into this—" She waved her hand up and down the skeleton, "—since he was alive. When was that, Will?"

"I don't know, could be Egyptian times, could be ten thousand years or more."

"He couldn't possibly have been this tall ten thousand years ago."

Will shrugged. "We've always been an anomaly."

GJ tipped her head, absorbing some of that. "Regardless of how old it is, given what we saw out in the field, the energy put into this belief is very powerful."

Noah watched as GJ turned her attention to putting the last bones into place, and Will pushed his nose back into the spell book. He and Wade resumed searching through books on the shelf.

It was a daunting job. Even though the library was tiny, there were a thousand or more books in here. References. Versions of the Bible, the Quran, several Hindu Vedas. Some of the books he pulled off were just lists of names and birthdates, written in a scrawl that he could barely decipher. The next one, he couldn't decipher at all, though his best guess would have been that it was in Aramaic. While Noah wanted to take a moment to have some reverence for the tomes he held in his hands, there wasn't time.

He closed the book, put it on the shelf, and went to the next one. He was maybe five books further down—his side aching from too much movement—when Will said, "I've got it!"

He stood up suddenly, holding the book with the triskadels. Apparently, it had been exactly what GJ thought.

"That's not English!" Christina cried. Her frustration clear.

"I can read it," Will consoled her. "It's Latin. We can do this."

Noah could read some Latin, too. Maybe not much, but it didn't matter, because Will looked around the room, unhappy at what he saw. "We need more people."

It wasn't just Christina who said *no*. Noah joined in the refusal, and so did GJ.

Christina made the argument. "You've got spies in your organization, Will. They're feeding information to the people out there. They may have even already told Alesse—or whoever—exactly where we are and what we're doing. We can't bring anyone else in."

"But we need more people for this spell."

Christina looked over at the page and shrugged in irritation.

Noah, however, had gone to a private Mormon school. He butted in. "May I?"

The school had taught him Latin for science and basic comprehension, not spellwork. He just hoped that he might be able to get some of it. Sure enough, he managed to glean a few things. "We need thirteen."

Christina shook her head hard.

"—or seven."

Now they all looked around the room. Five NightShade agents and Will.

"Will six do?" Christina asked.

"Do you want to blow *us* up?" both GJ and Will managed to shoot back simultaneously.

Noah had to agree. If they were dabbling in ancient magics, altering the recipe didn't seem wise.

"Jen," Will threw the name out, and for a moment, Christina glared. She was going to say no, but Noah was beginning to think that wouldn't be an option. They needed to find someone to be the seventh or, as GJ had snarked, risk the spell going haywire. Noah figured this project was dangerous enough, even without obvious errors in performance.

Turning to Will and holding a hand to Christina, hoping she would stay back for a moment, Noah said, "Your entire family is on the line here. Is that how much you trust Jen?"

Without faltering, Will said, "Yes."

"Get her." Christina pointed to Wade, but he was already halfway down the hall.

82

Wade and Jen came bursting through the little door, long before Christina had expected them. In fact, Wade had barely gotten out of hearing range, when suddenly he was back again.

"I found her." He wheezed the words, out of breath. "She was already on her way here."

Jen looked as frantic as Christina had ever seen her. "They're storming the edges of the property," she warned, her breath coming in harsh rasps. "They want their bones back!"

She gestured to the table with a sharp cut of her hand and then stopped, stunned, just as the rest of them had been, when she realized what she was seeing. Jen had known they'd brought the bones down here, but it was a different thing to have the full skeleton laid out on the table in the middle of the library in all its glory.

Christina got the distinct impression that they were standing in a sacred place where the vast majority of the family wasn't even allowed. But Will had no time for anyone to stop and take stock of the situation or worry about it.

"Where are they?" He grabbed Jen by the shoulders, directing her attention to him, even as he turned to GJ and Noah and barked, "You two figure out how to get these things." He gestured to a list in the book.

Walter was listening intently to Jen, gleaning intel about the invasion. She felt she was even less suited to spellwork than Christina was.

Noah dove for the book, starting work on a translation. As he and GJ mentioned bowls, white fabric, and stones, Christina looked around, confused. She had no idea where to get any of these things, but she knew Jen and Will would.

Will was nearly shaking his coordinator in an effort to gain information. "Where *exactly* are the soldiers?"

"The line that went out to meet you guys—" She turned to Walter and found a welcoming motion to go on. Jen took a breath, tears leaking out of the edge of her eyes. "It's almost decimated. There's just so many of them."

She sounded surprised, and Christina felt her eyes flick toward Will, who gave nothing away. Had he known that and kept it from her? Or was he actually shocked and just so good at hiding it?

"They're on the property now. They came in from all directions at once. They corralled us, Will! They've hit one of the outer houses. It's in flames, and probably several more are by now. I ran here as fast as I could to tell you."

Her breath heaved and she turned as though she were leaving. But Will grabbed on to her shirt and held her back. "Jen, stay here. This is how we fix it. We need you."

She looked to the bones and then to him, almost as if to say, *Oh, hell no*, but he didn't let her go.

Noah and GJ were rattling off items that they needed. But Wade was already out the door again. Christina had forgotten for a moment that he grew up here and he knew his way around as well as any of them.

"I'm getting the fabric," he announced as he disappeared down the hall.

Behind him, Jen took a deep breath and steeled herself, seeming to make a decision. "I'll get the stones. Which ones exactly do you need?"

And then they were gone.

Even Will trailed out the door, leaving Noah, Walter, and GJ sitting at the table, poring over the book, and Christina standing there wondering what the hell to do.

83

Noah unrolled the white fabric that Wade had brought.
The other agent had brought flat bedsheets, and Noah had watched as Wade bit one extremely large canine into the fabric. Making the first puncture, he then ripped each piece longways down the center.

He'd done this several times, not knowing that Noah watched in fascination. Noah laid the sheets out in a circle, as the spell book instructed. As he put the last sheet in place, he felt the hit of *deja vu*. But it didn't matter, because Christina was placing the bowls in seven spots at equal intervals around the room.

Walter was emptying every container of salt that Jen had managed to bring. It looked very much like what they had set up in the tent for Alesse though, clearly, Noah could see now, she'd had thirteen points and they only had seven. Would this make their spell less powerful? He had no idea.

"Take your places," Will commanded, motioning them around the room.

One last small vessel—a silver chalice that Will had produced from one of the upper shelves—sat between the feet of the bones of Aegis. Empty.

"We'll have to do without," Will had informed them as he glanced around the table. "Now, who reads the spell?"

"You," GJ answered without hesitation. When Will's look questioned her, she added, "I read some Latin and so does Noah, but you're more fluent, and therefore you're the one most likely to get the pronunciation and the cadence right. Also, you're the head of the family. You have the most power here."

No one had a better argument, so they'd all moved to stand at their respective spots. Noah lifted his hands into the air like the rest of them, his left side shrieking in pain and his sensibility leaving him feeling like a rank fool. What in hell was he even doing?

With the book in front of him on a chair and hands raised, Will began to read the words. In his halting voice, they sounded almost like iambic pentameter to Noah, and he managed to translate a bit of it.

"Aegis" was repeated, and it appeared they were calling on the ancient god. Noah wasn't sure if he actually wanted this to work, or not. was getting more and more nervous by the moment. His left side ached. He wasn't able to take a full breath given the bindings at his ribs. And though Will went through the spell three times, nothing happened.

"*Son of a bitch,*" he swore. If he'd held the ancient book in his hands, he looked like he would have thrown it at the ground.

Noah finally lowered his arms. He looked to one side, then the other. But GJ shook her head at all of them. "The power of the spell is in the repetition. The spell only has the energy we give it. Do it again."

Though Noah didn't believe—and from the looks around the room, it was clear that most of the others didn't, either—he lifted his hands again.

Christina was muttering something about wishing Eleri were here, and Noah found himself thinking the same thing. Even though the other agent had gone stone-cold silent and a bit wonky at the end of their trip to the Caribbean, she still would have been far superior to what they had now.

Will repeated the incantation a fourth time, and GJ nodded at him to keep going. On the fifth round, a tiny spark lit in the chalice between Aegis' feet. On the sixth, a small flame winked into existence. But even as it lit, it fluttered right back out.

The silence it left in its wake had Noah's head jerking upward. They all heard it: the pounding of feet overhead.

"Where are we?" Noah asked, as all their arms dropped to their sides and the room went silent. *Where could the footsteps be coming from?*

"We're under the main house," Will told them and Christina frowned at him.

"There are tunnels under the main house. We're not there."

Good, Noah thought. He wasn't the only one who didn't quite know where he'd wound up.

"We're under the tunnels under the main house. Just two levels down."

The thundering steps overhead were ominous. The soldiers had completely breached the property and made it to the center.

Christina's eyes went wide. Of all the agents under her wing, she looked to Noah. He was the one who saw the fear.

He read it clearly: How would they get out? There were too many soldiers. They were trapped... until the soldiers found the library. Then they'd be slaughtered and the library would be handed over. All the records Will had fought to protect would be in the hands of his worst enemy. And given the mole, it shouldn't take very long for them to find the place...

It was GJ who stepped out of her spot, still determined to run the spell. "We've got to add blood, Will. Let's use our own." She was holding a hand out over the chalice, as if to demonstrate. "We probably don't need much. Who has a knife?"

She asked it as if cutting themselves was now a forgone conclusion. Noah had one strapped to his thigh, but he wasn't quite ready to use his stolen blade to slice himself and his fellow agents. GJ seemed to have noticed his hesitation and made a motion for him to hand it over.

"Look," she said, holding her hand out, palm up. "If you cut the meat here, at the ball of your thumb, you won't cause nerve damage and you'll get a decent amount of blood. Also, it's easy to guide it into the cup."

She motioned again as she explained how to adequately collect blood for a spell as though she were discussing spices for a turkey. "None of us are witches, but all of us together will be more powerful than one of us."

She reached down toward Noah's leg, getting ready to take the knife without his permission. And that was when Noah saw it.

84

"Let's hope this works," Christina said to the group in general.

"It will," GJ replied with conviction.

She wanted to believe the youngest agent. The footsteps overhead had not faded—if anything they'd grown more ominous—so this had to succeed. It was their only chance.

Noah stripped to only his shirt and boxer briefs as Walter peeled off her shirt, revealing her bra and the straps in the setup of the wonderfully bionic prosthetic arm—a little bit of the magic of the Terminator had been revealed.

Though both half-naked agents seemed a bit embarrassed, they'd both had Alesse's blood on their clothing. Without the time or spare clothing for a change, they peeled it and motioned for everyone to just ignore that they were out of dress code.

Will and GJ ripped at the fabric, trying to keep only the blood-soaked portions and stuffing the small pieces down into the chalice. As Christina watched, she prayed to whatever gods might be listening. They didn't even know what this spell would do, only that the book said it would "activate" the bones.

Then they all raised their hands again, and Will began going through the spell another time. With as many rounds as he'd repeated earlier, his cadence was now smoother; the words flowed out almost as though he'd begun to memorize them. Even before he was halfway through, the chalice lit, full flames shooting up toward the ceiling.

Christina was shocked they didn't leave a scorch mark, but *holy shit it's working!* Though she was tempted to cheer, nothing had actually happened yet. She lifted her hands higher, wondering if she should stand up on her toes. If she was in the right position.

Will's voice suddenly got louder and lower.

She felt the rolling tension in her gut once more. *It was coming.*

They had done it.

Will's voice boomed now, certainly loud enough that those overhead could hear it.

From the center of the bones, a glow began to form, faint enough that Christina wasn't even sure she was seeing it. But the energy in the room seemed to shift and swirl, gathering first in the pit of her stomach and then along the skeleton. Then the ball of energy shot lines between each of them standing in their respective stations. Her brain tried to grasp if it was a seven-pointed star. *What gate of hell had they opened?*

What if they were wrong, and they'd just set off a nuclear bomb in the middle of the property they were trying to protect?

She contemplated diving into Will, tackling him to the ground and stopping whatever it was they had started. But the footsteps overhead and the shouts and gunfire told her that there was no other option. In a few moments, the intruders were going to murder them all.

So she didn't dive, just stayed where she was, palms lifted to the ceiling as the knot growing in her lower gut made her want to vomit.

Then she saw it. The white hot shockwave spreading outward. It seemed to roll forward in slow motion, though she knew that was just her brain playing tricks. As she watched it come forward, she didn't have time to react, and as it rolled over her, the force casually tossed her backwards.

Her feet left the floor and she watched as GJ, Noah, and Wade were lifted and thrown as well. In her peripheral vision, she saw Jen fly into the wall, her head hitting far too hard.

But then Christina's own head must have hit something, because everything went black.

85

Noah held his hand to his head, wondering why it hurt so much. He first realized he was using his left hand. So he switched to his right, which made the pain only marginally better.

Had he crashed into the bookshelves behind him? The ache in his back from earlier made it unclear if he'd been smacked into something yet again.

Another hit to his spine was the last thing he needed.

He blinked, the fuzzy world slowly coming into focus around him. Yes, the bookshelves were behind him. He was in the library.

Rolling to his side, he slowly came to his knees and stood. As he did it, and he shook the cobwebs out of his brain, it became clear he was the only one standing. Everyone else was out cold.

Dead? he wondered.

He turned first to his right, to Wade. Reaching out and placing his fingers at his friend's neck, Noah found his pulse was steady and strong. Still, the touch didn't rouse Wade at all.

One by one, Noah checked on each of them.

Only then did he realize that everything was stunningly quiet.

Had the shockwave destroyed his hearing?

He stood still for a moment and listened to his own breathing. No, he didn't hear ringing. That didn't mean his eardrums hadn't been punctured, though. Sound traveled through the skeletal system better than from the outside, he knew. But he heard nothing.

There should have been footsteps overhead, yelling, bullets. The sounds of Will's family members fighting for their lives. But all of it was missing.

In the deathly quiet, he reached to touch the dirt wall, thinking he would feel the vibration of the soldiers marching or fighting through the earth. But he felt nothing around him, either.

No one roused, and he leaned down once more, this time shaking Wade gently by the shoulder. But the other agent didn't respond at all.

Noah patted himself down, feeling relief as he found his gun in his holster before he remembered it wasn't his. His was lost, somewhere out beyond the property line. This was a stolen weapon. Even so, he quickly ejected the magazine, checked it, popped it back in, and chambered a bullet.

The noise of his motions echoed through the library, even though the paper and the leather of the books should have absorbed it readily. He froze, wondering who might have heard him and who might be on the other side of that door.

Three.

Two.

One.

Noah reached out and slowly turned the knob, hoping to not alert anyone who was waiting on the other side. He cracked it but didn't look. Waiting for several beats, he stayed behind the dirt wall for protection. But when nothing popped through the doorway, he dared to dart his head into the opening for a peek.

The hallway was empty. Bolder now, he stepped out, walking slowly, rolling his feet with each step to be as quiet as he could possibly be. He didn't quite have the wolves' stealth, but he did all right.

At the first turn, he stopped cold.

Bodies littered the ground. Soldiers lay motionless, guns still in hands. He aimed his weapon. They were down, but they might not be dead.

Kicking at the feet of one of them, he waited and got no response. It almost surprised him. It would figure if it was only him to be up and around after whatever apocalypse they'd unleashed.

He knew that all of Aegis' men might stand up and outnumber him at any moment.

But nothing happened.

He kicked the soldier in the feet again, then did the same with another, and another. They were the only ones he could reach without putting a soldier behind his back. When still nothing happened, he leaned down to check a pulse. This one had none. Noah was contemplating the ramifications when he heard the moan.

Standing upright quickly, he swung his weapon and watched as a hand came up in surrender.

"Don't shoot."

"Jesse?" he asked, hoping he got the name right.

The man nodded. Jesse Little, another of Will's grandsons.

The man stood, fully naked. He must have been down here fighting in wolf form. But even as the thought passed through Noah's mind, another sound came from behind him as someone else stirred.

He and Jesse turned simultaneously to see a wolf slowly drag itself to its feet.

86

"Yes, sir." Christina held the phone to her ear as she walked through the tall grass between the houses. It had taken a few days, but she finally felt comfortable enough to be outside in the open.

The blast they'd conjured had gone all the way out past the property line.

"It looks like it went a good three or four hundred feet past the legal land line in all directions. But that's where it gets sketchy."

Westerfield already understood what she meant by "sketchy."

"Sketchy" determined who had stood back up after the blast felled everyone.

On the de Gottardi/Little property, the wolves and family members had all lived through the blast. Everyone had been flattened, but of the others—the invading soldiers—none had stood up. At least, not at the last count Christina had been given.

Many of them had little cuts all through their clothing. Wade and Noah speculated that these were made by something like the black shards that had gotten them the first time. There were no answers, because again, there was no remaining evidence. The agents truly had no idea what they'd done, only that it had worked.

"The woman?" Westerfield asked. "The witch in red. Did you find her?"

Christina shook her head. "So far, no."

She still had her fingers crossed, but everyone was looking and no one had reported seeing her. They'd scrubbed the area where Walter had shot her. It had been easy enough to find by the blood, but she hadn't been there, or in the tents, or anywhere else they'd looked.

"And you said they called her ... Alyssa?"

"Maybe?" It shouldn't have been a question, so she tried again. "Close, but with a slightly different pronunciation. More like Ah-*less*-ah." She emphasized the softer "e" sound in the middle.

"No." Westerfield's single syllable rang through the air toward her, and Christina had a sinking feeling. He asked, "Alesse Dauphine?"

When she didn't have an answer, he continued. "Black woman? Stunningly beautiful. Dark skin."

"Yes." It was Christina's turn to draw out the word. She hadn't mentioned any of that. So she must have been dealing with someone already known to the unit. She waited, confident she wouldn't like the answer.

"Dauphine." This time he spat it out.

The name meant nothing to her, and that's what she told him.

"Son of a fucking bitch," was his only reply.

The pause between them told her that he knew something she didn't, but he wasn't sharing it. Maybe she could figure it out on her own. She filed away the name *Alesse Dauphine* for the next time she managed to get her hands on NightShade records.

When he didn't say anything else, she changed the topic. "We have the bodies of Shray Menon and Murray Marks. We need to bring in a team to move them and let GJ decide where they should be buried."

Another pause, but Christina would rip him a new one if he said *no*. This was GJ's grandfather. And she'd had to kill him herself. *Twice.*

Christina was only grateful that the bodies were here now. They'd already been hauled back onto de Gottardi/Little property. Though she had initially considered burying them here and doing the service themselves, while that might be kind to GJ, having their bodies buried on the property would be horrifying to every family member.

"Okay," Westerfield finally said, giving in, as though he had sensed her silence for the stubbornness it was.

Good, she thought. "I'll let GJ know."

"Reports on my desk in two days," he said and hung up.

That was it, Christina thought. Westerfield had declared the case closed.

In the distance, smoke still drifted up into the sky. Two of the houses had been thoroughly burned, damaged even worse than from the first fight. Will had merely waved a hand and dismissed it. "We hadn't rebuilt them yet anyway. It's hardly any change in damage."

Still, it had turned Christina's stomach.

She hit the button to hang up her phone as though she had any control at all over the fact that the call was already done. Then she headed back to the main house. But Will was already walking out in the field toward her.

It was clear from the way the wolves were working—some bandaged, but some fully upright, as they piled and cleared away the dead soldiers bodies—that they didn't want any of this lingering on their land.

"Have them pile up the bodies, but don't move them," Christina called out to Will by way of greeting. They were long past a casual Hello. "Westerfield will send a team to come and claim them. He just confirmed."

Will nodded, probably thankful that they wouldn't have rotting bodies on their property, nor would they be responsible for burying the people who had tried to kill them. If someone discovered a mass grave at some point in the future, the authorities would have to investigate.

Though Christina had no idea what Westerfield was going to tell the cleanup team, she figured he would cover it.

Tipping her head to Will, she felt the change in blood flow, her head still pounding from the blast. It had been almost forty-eight hours now, but everyone else was reporting the same sensation. So at least she wasn't odd. The strange dizziness had already begun fading, and she took that as a sign of hope.

"Will," she asked, "did all of your wolves—all of your people—stand back up?"

He knew what she was asking.

Did the mole get taken out with the soldiers? Or maybe more than one mole?

Once they'd realized the sorting system the spell had used, she and Noah had discussed the possibility that it had taken care of the problem for them. But as Will looked at her, he replied, "Yes. Every single one."

Her heart sank. But there was nothing she could do about that right now.

The camps outside the property were full of those who had died in place. Those who had survived had fled. The remaining bodies would be taken care of by the team that Westerfield was sending. Will and his family would rebuild soon.

They'd left the bones of Aegis in the library.

GJ had studied them briefly, and Christina got the impression it was heartbreaking to leave them behind. After all, they'd been stolen from GJ's own lab. But they'd all agreed the bones belonged with wolves rather than in a collection.

So GJ had lovingly sorted them into four separate, odd groupings and placed them into four distinct-looking trunks in the corner, hoping that no one who came in would even begin to see what they had.

Will and his people would guard them just as they guarded the books and the records and the other artifacts she'd seen in the hidden room.

But the de Gottardi/Little family still had a problem on their hands.

And Christina had no idea how to solve it.

"We have about six more hours," she told him, "and then we have to head out to catch red-eye flights tonight." Her team was going in five different directions. From what Westerfield said, Noah Kimball was heading back to Miami to put in for his official transfer to Night-Shade. That made her smile. She'd already put in a bid to have him assigned as her partner. It might take a little while for the paperwork to go through, but she'd not gotten her own next assignment yet.

"I've got plenty to do," Will said, "and I don't mean to be rude, but I might not see you before you go. So I'll tell you again, I cannot thank you enough for the work you and your team have done here. You made a real difference."

He reached out and Christina did the same and shook his hand. Their firm grip was more than professional, better than just friendly.

"Keep your eyes open," she told him.

87

"We're getting closer, right?" Donovan asked Eleri as he took the turn she recommended onto an even smaller and more poorly kept road.

"I think so." But the sound in her voice waffled for the first time. "I've been having this odd thought that it's not that Bodhi Banerjee is here, but something *about* Bodhi Banerjee is here."

Interesting, he thought, but he was willing to pursue it.

She'd scared the shit out of him by the side of the road. But for the past two days, she'd been doing okay. She'd even, at one point, jolted in the passenger seat and said, "They did it!"

It had taken a moment to explain what had happened at the de Gottardi/Little farm to him, but he was grateful that she remained upright with her eyes open and focused.

They turned the corner and pulled up a small residential road to a small house. One of a handful on the street, it appeared occupied. A dirty, white SUV sat in the driveway. A plastic playset for a very small child occupied one of the front corners of the well-tended yard. A dog ran behind the fence, barking at them for having merely stopped in front of his house.

"This is it," Eleri told him, though neither of them had quite figured out exactly what it was. "Now we have an address."

She sounded pleased by that as she pulled out her phone and

starting to punch in information. Donovan followed suit and did the same.

Five minutes later, the dog was still barking its head off and maintaining its back-and-forth zigzag across the fence. But Eleri held up her phone for him to see.

"Look at this! Property records."

"What am I looking at?"

"The last owner." She pointed one nail to the very small words and tried to enlarge them. "At the previous sale, the owner was listed as Amisha Patel."

Patel was as common as Smith was in the US. But what were the chances that Eleri had led him astray to a home owned by a *different* Amisha? One that had been sold two months after his own mother died?

Even as she held the phone up and he tried to read the records, he saw the screen light up with an incoming call. His own phone buzzed in his hand where he'd rested it in his lap.

Shit, he thought, *not now*.

Westerfield knew what they were doing, though maybe he was just checking in. So he and Eleri both answered simultaneously, "Sir?"

"I know what you're doing and I know it's important, but this is time-sensitive. You're going to have to take notes and pick up later," Westerfield told them, breaking Donovan's heart. He was convinced he was looking at the house his mother and little brother had lived in after he'd believed her dead.

Westerfield's voice snapped him back to the present. "I've got a serial killer on the loose in Florida, and they need you down there yesterday."

ABOUT THE AUTHOR

AJ holds an MS in Human Forensic Identification as well as another in Neuroscience/Human Physiology. AJ's works have garnered Audie nominations, options for tv and film, as well as over twenty Best Suspense/Best Fiction of the Year awards.

A.J.'s world is strange place where patterns jump out and catch the eye, little is missed, and most of it can be recalled with a deep breath. In this world, the smell of Florida takes three weeks to fully leave the senses and the air in Dallas is so thick that the planes "sink" to the runways rather than actually landing.

For A.J., reality is always a little bit off from the norm and something usually lurks right under the surface. As a storyteller, A.J. loves irony, the unexpected, and a puzzle where all the pieces fit and make sense. Originally a scientist and a teacher, the writer says research is always a key player in the stories. AJ's motto is "It could happen. It wouldn't. But it could."

A.J. has lived in Florida and Los Angeles among a handful of other places. Recent whims have brought the dark writer to Tennessee, where home is a deceptively normal-looking neighborhood just outside Nashville.

For more information:
www.ReadAJS.com
AJ@ReadAJS.com

www.ingramcontent.com/pod-product-compliance
Lightning Source LLC
Chambersburg PA
CBHW031158020726
47499CB00002B/413